To Joy and the staff at Feltrim House Montessori and Ann and her crew at Little Apples Creche and Montessori – thank you so much for the background information. Also, my eternal gratitude for your kindness to my two beautiful boys.

Chapter 1

Grace wiped her hands on her overalls and stepped back to admire her handiwork. It might be just a shade deeper than magnolia but this paint had turned the drab, antiquated kitchen into a bright, airy space. Only the woodwork remained to be painted and she could call it a day. Tomorrow, she would leave the painting to the rest of the team and concentrate on the soft furnishings.

'It looks lovely, dear,' Mrs Magee said before collapsing into another coughing fit.

'I'm glad you like it but I'd be a lot happier if you went over to the Centre for the rest of the day until the smell of the paint wears off.' They had deliberately chosen odourless paint, but that didn't seem to make much difference to the old lady's lungs.

Mrs Magee laughed. 'Don't worry about me, love, it's hard to kill a bad thing.'

'All the same,' Grace linked the woman's arm and led her towards the door, 'a cup of tea would be nice.'

'It would,' the woman agreed, 'but you must have one

too. You've been working solidly since seven this morning and it's time you had a break.'

Grace was tired but also exhilarated. This project was giving her more satisfaction than doing up any of the mansions in a fancy Dublin suburb. She had initially balked at getting involved in the renovation of the pensioners' flats; there were twenty-four of them and she knew it would mean giving up a lot of time. But it was her parish and she felt it only right to give something back now that she was doing so well. Who knew what the future held? Maybe she and Michael would end up in a place like this one day and be grateful for such charitable deeds. It seemed unlikely, of course, since apart from her own success, Michael was the sort to make sure to provide for the future. All he ever did with his money was save it.

The one serious investment they'd made, after huge pressure from Grace, was to buy their beautiful detached home in large gardens at the foot of the Dublin Mountains. Michael didn't see why they needed to move at all. Their three-bedroom semi was perfectly adequate and much closer to town. Grace had felt like screaming with frustration. What was the point of them working so hard, of making a success of two businesses if they weren't going to reap some rewards? It wasn't as if they spent all their money on holidays or hobbies. Both of them still worked long hours and rarely thought of taking a break. So at the very least, Grace told her husband, they were entitled to come home at the end of a busy day to a bit of comfort. Michael still wasn't convinced, until she pointed out that a bigger house would allow them both to work from home, thereby reducing transport costs and increasing family time. That was what finally clinched it, although it hadn't really worked out that way.

'Grace, come and have a cup of tea.' The parish priest advanced on her, smiling broadly. 'I can't begin to tell you how grateful we are for your help. You're doing a marvellous job.'

'It's a good team, Father O'Dea,' Grace said, waving a hand at the twenty or so men and women who were beavering away around the complex. 'We are lucky to have so many skilled people in the parish.'

'Indeed we are,' he agreed. 'I had thought that the flats would just be getting a lick of paint but now they've been rewired, had new bathrooms fitted and word has it that your curtains are stunning.'

Grace laughed. 'I wouldn't go that far, but with the new carpets it should make the flats comfortable and warm too.'

'And that's another thing.' The priest clapped his hands together. 'Did I tell you about Jim Michaels – you know, the man who owns the electrical shop in the village?'

Grace nodded.

'Well,' Father O'Dea went on, 'he's supplying and installing new electric fires in all of the flats – completely free of charge.'

'That's very generous. The residents must be delighted.'

'Most of them are.' He rolled his eyes. 'But a few are already complaining about how it will affect their electricity bills.'

Grace laughed. 'Yes, I have been taken aside by one lady and told that it was all very well having pretty curtains but that they needed to be well lined to keep the heat in.'

'Nora Dunne,' the priest surmised.

'That's the one.'

'She doesn't mean to be so grumpy. I think she just needs to feel involved. She used to be quite senior in the Civil Service, you know.'

Grace shook her head. 'I didn't. Maybe we should get her more involved in the whole project. She might feel a bit marginalized, what with us all marching into her home and taking over.'

'You may be right but I think you have been very sensitive in that area. I'm told that each flat will have its own colour scheme and style tailored to fit in with the resident's taste.'

Grace shrugged. 'That's my business, after all. That's the part of it I love. I'm hardly going to impose my own taste on them. They're the ones who have to live here.'

'That's not the way many people think,' the priest murmured. 'There are some who feel the residents should be grateful for whatever they get.'

'Yes, well, they're not in charge, thankfully,' Grace said, her mouth settling into a determined line.

The priest waved at someone behind Grace and called out, 'Well, if it isn't Michael Hughes! Have you come to see the wonderful work your wife is doing? Or,' he winked at Grace, 'maybe you've come to help.'

Michael looked slightly uncomfortable as he joined them. 'Sorry, Father, I have quite a lot of work on at the moment.'

'Of course, I shouldn't be greedy. One member of the family is quite enough, especially one as clever as Grace.'

'Glad it's going well, Father. I thought Grace would be finished by now and I was going to drag her off for a drink.'

'Quite right,' the priest nodded. 'It is Saturday after all.'

'I'd prefer to do a little bit more, Michael, if you don't mind. Anyway, I need a shower before I'm fit to go anywhere. You go on home and I'll see you in an hour or so. See you later, Father,' Grace said, and went back to work, aware that her husband would be on her heels as soon as he'd shaken off Father O'Dea. She was painting skirting boards when he finally caught up with her.

'I thought you were just doing the soft furnishings? Surely there are plenty here that can take care of that?' he said irritably.

'It's a big job,' Grace replied without looking up. 'And, if you remember, you were the one who said I should take part in this project.'

'Yes, but I thought you'd be making a few curtains, not giving up all your free time. You always take on more than you should. Nat and I hardly ever see you as it is.'

Grace sat back and looked up at him. 'Nat is going to be out all evening and I've told you, I'll be finished here in an hour or so. Why don't I pick up some fish and chips on the way home and we can open a bottle of wine?'

Michael sighed. 'Do I have much choice?'

Grace smiled. 'I'm not working tomorrow, promise. Hey, I'll even do a nice roast for the three of us, if you like.'

He thought for a moment. 'It won't be as nice as Rosa's, but I suppose it's better than nothing.'

'Bloody cheek!' Grace blew him a kiss. 'See you later.'

Grace thought of all the curtains that she had to make before Monday and wondered how she was going to cook a roast dinner as well. But she'd have to find a way or there would be terrible disappointment on Monday morning if she hadn't at least one pair of curtains ready to hang. She'd start with Mrs Brown's – she'd enjoy making those curtains with the pink roses on the rich creamy background. The curtains, like the woman, were heart-warming and cheerful and Grace couldn't wait to see the pensioner's face when she saw the finished job. The kitchen was a cheery primrose yellow, the curtains, yellow and white stripes, and Grace had even made an apron and some placemats to match. The lounge, hall and bedroom were all painted a rich creamy buttermilk. Grace had chosen the rose curtains and matching cushions which she was sure would look lovely against Edie Brown's dark red sofa, and in the bedroom she had made the curtains and bedspread from a heavy lilac cotton material that was both warm and inviting. Grace rarely got an opportunity to use so many different shades as her clients usually went for a more contemporary look. But Edie was an exotic, vibrant character and it seemed only right to surround her with colour.

It was a completely different story for Tom Devanney next door. An ex-Army man, Tom was a widower who had long dispensed with any of the feminine touches his wife had left behind. For him, Grace had used the same shade of buttermilk – it had been the one cheap paint that actually looked good – but teamed it with coffees and browns. The darkness was relieved by dazzling white paint on all of the woodwork and a golden-coloured carpet.

'Why don't you get off, Grace? We'll take care of the rest.' Olive Foley was standing in the doorway smiling down at her. A powerhouse of a woman, Olive was the one responsible for bullying, begging and threatening parishioners to get involved in the project. Anytime Grace needed anything, a word to Olive and somehow it materialized.

'I'll just finish the woodwork in here and then I'll go.'

'Make sure you do,' Olive instructed. 'If you don't get some rest soon you won't be able to sew in a straight line. And speaking of sewing, I've found you a couple of helpers.'

Grace's face lit up. 'Really?'

'Don't get your hopes up. I'd say their talents are limited to hems and such.'

'That's fine, it will save me an enormous amount of work. You're some woman, Olive.' On impulse, Grace stood up and hugged her.

'Oh, go on with you.' Olive blushed and pushed her away. 'Now all I need to do is find someone who can put up curtain rails. See you Monday, Grace.'

'Bye.' Grace smiled after the woman and marvelled again at the wonderful people she'd met in the last few days. So many of them had given up their free time, some had donated furniture and a lot had delved into their own pockets to help these pensioners out. Local businessmen had supplied all the materials either for free or at cost price, and one local electrician had lent them his apprentice to work fulltime until the project was finished. Grace, who spent most of her life dealing with very materialistic people, found her faith in mankind hugely bolstered.

It was dark by the time she got home and she hurried into the kitchen with their dinner, calling to Michael as she reached for the kettle.

'About bloody time,' he said, joining her. 'I'm starving.'

'Stop moaning and get out the plates. Do you want a cup of tea?'

He shook his head. 'I'll stick with beer. Have you lost your mobile again? I've spent my evening taking calls for you.'

'I must have left it in the car, sorry. Who was looking for me?'

'Miriam and Bridget.'

Grace raised an eyebrow. 'All evening taking my two calls, you poor man. Did they leave a message? Am I to call them back?'

'Miriam was going on about her bloody party. I hope you don't think I'm going to that,' he added.

Grace didn't bother answering. He always said that, but she knew he'd come in the end – he always did. 'And Bridget?' she prompted.

'You've to call her. I'm sure it's something hugely important like what shade of lipstick she should buy.'

Grace laughed. 'You're probably right. Well, they can both wait until we've eaten.' They sat down at the table and she divided out the food. 'God, I'm tired.'

'Oh.' He frowned. 'I thought we could go to the cinema later – there's a good film on.'

Grace opened her mouth to protest but stopped, realizing that she seemed to say nothing but no to her husband these days. 'Good idea. Just let me grab a shower first.'

Grace sagged at the thought of going out again, but at least she could doze off in the cinema. Undoubtedly it would be a film that she would have no interest in. Michael's tastes ran to the macabre and violent, both of which she abhorred. After she'd finished her food, she took her tea upstairs, sat down on the side of her bed and picked up the phone. First she called Miriam.

Her business partner was in the middle of arranging her annual party to celebrate the opening of her first boutique in September 1986. Everyone who was anyone attended these events. Miriam claimed they were the main source of new business, both for their design company and Miriam's chain of fashion boutiques, and though Grace acknowledged the fact, she still didn't look forward to the occasion. Yes, it was nice to be recognized as one of Ireland's best interior designers, but it was the inane and superficial conversations that she dreaded.

The phone was answered on the first ring. 'Miriam Cooper.'

'Hi, Miriam.'

'Grace, where the hell have you been?'

'I'm working on a community project. You remember I told you about it? We're renovating a complex of pensioners' flats.'

'Oh yes, very laudable – but don't forget you have your own business to run.'

Grace bristled. 'I am completely on top of my business, thank you very much.'

There was an impatient sigh at the other end of the phone. 'Oh, don't get prickly, Grace. I need help with the guest-list.'

'But you're much better at that sort of thing than I am.

I don't know anyone important other than my existing customers.'

'Don't I know it,' Miriam muttered. 'But Michael must have some rich colleagues or customers that we could invite? He's a quantity surveyor, for God's sake. He must know at least some of the key people in the property business.'

'I'm not sure,' Grace hedged. 'I don't think he'd approve of us approaching them.'

'Oh, for goodness sake, we're only inviting them to a party.'

'Why didn't you ask Michael yourself earlier?' Grace shot back.

'Because he doesn't like me,' Miriam said in her usual blunt manner, 'and as his wife I thought you must have ways of getting around him. Anyway, Grace, I don't care how you do it, just do it. I need some names, big names. I have plenty from the fashion industry, it's up to you to do your share.'

And of course she was right. They were equal partners in Graceful Living and Miriam had come up with more than half of their current client-list. 'I'll see what I can do.'

'Good.' The other woman hung up.

Grace drank half of her tea before calling Bridget. 'Hi, it's me.'

'Hi Grace. Where have you been all day?'

'Working.' Grace didn't have the energy to explain, and anyway, she knew Bridget Crosby wouldn't be interested. At thirty-six, Bridget was nearly ten years younger than Grace, had no children and was only interested in talking about fashion, gossip or herself. They had worked together in a large department store before Grace had left to start up Graceful Living, and if it wasn't for the fact that Bridget and Luke, Miriam's brother, had started dating, Grace knew they would have lost touch long ago. Though Bridget made her laugh, Grace had little in common with the younger woman and she wouldn't have thought Luke did either. When she'd introduced them nearly seven years ago, the attraction had been obvious but Grace never expected the relationship to last this long. Still, they said opposites attract, and it was obvious that Luke was still besotted with the diminutive brunette with the dark eyes and wide, sexy smile.

'I wanted to ask you about the party,' Bridget was saying.

'Yeah, what about it?'

'Well, everything. Who's going to be there? What's the theme this year? How glam is it going to be? I have this beautiful red dress but it's full length and I don't want to look overdressed.'

'Why are you asking *me*?' Grace asked.

'Because Miriam hates me and tells me nothing, and Luke is a man and knows nothing.'

Grace laughed. Like Michael, Luke had little interest in Miriam's posh parties but he always attended. It was important to Miriam that he was there; she loved to show him off, and he never let her down. Though a lowly plumber – Miriam was appalled by her baby brother's chosen career – Luke was handsome enough to be a male model and funny enough to be a wonderful addition to any gathering. Everyone loved Luke. It was a further cross for Miriam to bear that not only was Luke a tradesman but that he'd chosen Bridget for a girlfriend. Bridget was everything Miriam hated in a woman. She was unemployed, she was lazy, and Luke spent most of his time and money trying to please her. Miriam tolerated her because she was afraid of losing Luke, but when they were alone she left Bridget in no doubt of what she thought of her.

'Your red dress will be fine,' Grace told Bridget. 'Miriam's invited practically all of the fashion industry, and she wants me to rustle up some property tycoons. Alastair is organizing the catering – he's going for a Japanese theme.'

Bridget gave a little squeal of delight. 'Oh, that sounds wonderful, I can hardly wait! What are you wearing, Grace?'

'I hadn't really thought about it.'

Bridget groaned. 'Grace, you're impossible. I'll call for you during the week and we'll go shopping.'

'No, I don't have time. Don't worry, Miriam will find me something to wear.'

'She'll put you in something dowdy. You know she's jealous of you.'

'Don't be ridiculous, Bridget,' Grace chuckled. 'She's a very attractive woman.'

'No argument but she's still jealous of you. Gotta go now, darling. My face mask is starting to crack.'

Grace shook her head as she hung up. She drained her cold tea, gave her comfortable bed a look of pure longing and then went into the bathroom to shower.

Chapter 2

'How do I look?' Miriam twirled in front of the cheval mirror.

'Magnificent,' Grace said honestly. The dress of royal-blue jersey with the intricate beading on the bodice and long narrow skirt suited Miriam's trim figure and confident bearing. Sapphires and diamonds adorned her fingers, wrists and neck, and her dark blue eyes twinkled from beneath a shiny, platinum-blonde bob.

'It's a sample from a designer in Glasgow that I'm thinking of using,' Miriam said. 'Okay, let's go and park ourselves near the door. I want to point out the people you need to concentrate on tonight.'

Grace followed her partner down the impressive staircase of her Donnybrook Victorian mansion where the party was being held. 'Not too many, I hope, Miriam.'

'Enough to keep you in clover,' her partner retorted, slightly irritably. 'I organize these nights to source new business for you as much as me, Grace. I hope you realize that. Look at the number of clients you got out of last year's bash. This is the best way – the *only* way – to make sure that your name is the first one people think of when they want to give their homes a makeover, just like Miriam Cooper and the Lady M collection is the first name they think of when they want to give themselves a makeover.'

'You're right, Miriam, and I am grateful. I'm just not as good at selling myself as you are.'

'You don't have to. Just ask them about their homes and tell them how you can transform them – they'll be queuing up to give you money.' Miriam flashed a smile at her before clicking her fingers at one of the waitresses they had hired for the event. 'Two G and T's,' she ordered, ignoring the tray of champagne the girl proffered. 'Large ones.'

Grace was about to decline, but if she was going to have to schmooze with Miriam's guests she would probably need a stiff drink. While she felt slightly embarrassed at this party Miriam insisted on hosting every year, she did enjoy being introduced in her professional capacity and it was especially nice when people already knew her name. It made a welcome change from the years of being introduced as 'Michael's wife' or 'Natasha's mother'.

Grace tuned out Miriam's monologue as she thought of her daughter sitting at home, surrounded by books. She would enjoy hearing all about the party in the morning but refused point blank to attend. As she'd got older, Miriam had tried to push the issue, since the willowy twenty year old, with her shining hair and wide-set grey eyes, had the perfect looks and figure to show off some of her more unforgiving gowns, but Nat just laughed at the suggestion. 'Not a chance in hell,' she told her mother. 'I'd rather walk over hot coals.'

Grace had been more than happy to leave it at that. Like Michael, she was pleased that her daughter was more interested in her education than style. *Un*like Michael, she was equally happy to let her daughter make her own decisions.

'Concepta Mahon is definitely one you should have a word with,' Miriam was saying, as she straightened the strap of Grace's simple white cocktail dress. 'Rumour has it she's just bought a new apartment in Ibiza town. Play your cards right and you and Michael could get a free holiday out of this.'

'Michael doesn't like the sun,' Grace said as the waitress arrived back with their drinks.

'Take Natasha with you,' Miriam suggested, swallowing half her drink. 'She'll love it there.'

'Not with me around to cramp her style.'

'Well, take Bridget, then,' Miriam said, bored with the subject. 'My God, girl, some people would kill for the perks that come with your job. Now why does Bridget come to mind again?'

Grace chuckled. 'Leave Bridget alone, Miriam. She just likes to have fun.'

'She's a lazy cow who's bleeding my little brother dry. You know, sometimes I wonder if he's really related to me at all. How can he be so stupid?'

'She's not that bad and I'm sure she loves him.'

'What's not to love? Has she told you she's taking on Rosa?'

'Pardon?' Grace stared. Rosa Di Paola was the house-keeper that Grace and Miriam shared. She worked two days a week for each of them.

'Bridget's hired Rosa to come in on Wednesdays. She can't cope with all that housework on her own, poor darling. Honestly, how or why Luke puts up with her I'll never know.'

Grace sipped silently on her drink as she absorbed this piece of information. It was a typical stunt for Bridget to pull and it was probably less about her needing a housekeeper and more about wanting to keep up with the Joneses. How Luke managed to finance it was a mystery. He was employed by a Dublin firm specializing in commercial business, and though he worked long hours Grace suspected it wasn't easy to support Bridget's lifestyle. She wondered how he felt about Bridget acquiring a housekeeper.

'Showtime,' Miriam murmured as one of her most important clients walked through the door. 'Hilary, darling! Don't you look fabulous?'

Grace followed her partner down into the large hall and smiled as Miriam introduced her to the very large woman who was squeezed into a Chanel suit at least two sizes too small.

'You're the designer?' the woman asked.

'Hilary, she's the *only* desiner,' Miriam laughed. 'Let me get you some champagne.'

'God no, can't stand the stuff,' Hilary snorted. 'I'll have a Jack Daniel's, straight.'

Miriam nodded at the waitress and then turned towards the door as more guests arrived. 'Hilary, why don't you and Grace grab a seat inside before the mob arrives,' she said. 'I'll join you after I've done my hostess bit.'

'Hate these do's,' Hilary confided in Grace as they moved into the drawing room, 'but Miriam always puts on a good spread.'

'I think we have Alastair to thank for that,' Grace told her.

Hilary's eyes lit up as she saw the buffet table. 'He's a bit effeminate for my liking but he knows his food.'

Grace bit back a retort; she was taking a real dislike to this woman. 'Miriam tells me you have a beautiful home,' she said politely.

'I have three of them,' Hilary responded, lowering herself into an armchair. 'Where the hell is that girl with my drink?'

'I'll go and check.' Grace pounced on the opportunity to escape and made her way to the kitchen.

Miriam's husband Alastair looked up and smiled as she approached. 'I'm under strict instructions to throw you out if you try hiding in here.'

'I'm just getting a cranky old bat – sorry, a valued customer – a drink.' Grace rummaged among the bottles for the Jack Daniel's and poured a generous measure into a tumbler.

'Steady on,' Alastair said, raising his eyebrows. 'It's not good commerce to kill the customers.'

'I suppose not. Anything I can do to help?'

Alastair shook his head. 'The caterers have it all under control, but I'll stay out here for a while just to keep an eye on things.'

'Huh!' Grace shot him a look of disbelief as she headed for the door. 'It's well for some.'

He held up his hands and smiled. 'Hey, I'm not the one who's after their money.'

Grace took the drink back to Hilary and was delighted to see her engrossed in conversation with the manager of Miriam's boutique in Galway.

'Oh hello, Grace.' Jean started to get up. 'Am I in your seat?'

Grace wave her back into her chair, put the whiskey into Hilary's hand and grabbed her own drink. 'Not at all, stay where you are. Hilary and I can chat later.' And she made her getaway.

'Grace? Over here.'

Grace whirled around and saw Bridget. 'Hey you, nice dress.'

'Nice? Excuse me, it's gorgeous.' Bridget looked down lovingly at the vivid red satin that clung to her every curve.

'Is it one of Miriam's?'

'God, no, I wouldn't buy anything off that bitch.'

'What was that?' Luke murmured as he appeared back with two champagne flûtes. 'Hi, Grace.' He bent to kiss her cheek.

'Hi. You two look like you've just stepped out of a fashion magazine.' Her eyes roved appreciatively over his black suit and grey shirt.

Bridget beamed at her. 'Well, you have to make an effort, don't you? Where's Michael?'

'He had a meeting but he'll be along later.'

'Why didn't I think of that?' Luke said into his glass.

'Honestly, you're just impossible,' Bridget hissed. 'This room is full of very important people. Haven't you any ambition? Do you want to work to line somebody else's pockets for all of your life?'

He shrugged. 'I'm not that bothered. Anyway, one entrepreneur in the family is enough.'

Miriam appeared at their side and put a hand on his arm. 'Speaking of business, Luke, could you have a look at the loo in our en-suite?'

Bridget shot her a murderous look. 'Luke doesn't do that sort of work.'

Luke ignored her. 'No problem, sis, I'll just get my stuff out of the van.'

'Oh, not now, come by tomorrow.'

Bridget scowled. 'He's very busy, you know.'

'Never too busy for family, are you, little brother?' Miriam turned her steely gaze on Bridget. 'You must be pretty busy yourself, Bridget. Rosa was telling me about your arrangement.'

'What's this?' Luke asked.

'Oh, nothing important, I'm just getting some help with the housework.'

Luke blinked. 'You're hiring Rosa?'

'It's no big deal,' Bridget murmured, looking away from Miriam's victorious smirk. 'It's only one day a week.'

Grace stepped in, feeling sorry for Bridget. Miriam could be such a bitch sometimes and she was always trying to stir it between Bridget and Luke. 'She's great, Luke and she's a wonderful cook.'

'She's going to cook for us?'

'Luke, stop going on about it, you're always complaining that we eat out too often.'

'Grace, quick, there's Concepta.' Miriam grabbed her partner's hand and dragged her away.

'See you later,' Grace called with an apologetic smile.

'Let's get another drink.' Bridget smiled nervously and turned away.

'Not so fast.' Luke turned her back to face him, his expression grim. 'Exactly how much is Rosa going to cost me?'

Bridget took a deep breath. 'Fifteen Euro an hour.'

'What! '

'But she's only going to be there for seven hours and she'll clean, iron all your shirts and leave dinner ready for us.'

Luke's eyes were like flint. 'I don't wear shirts, there's little or no cleaning to be done and, at over a hundred Euro, I could order in from The Four Seasons.'

Bridget's face settled into a sullen pout. 'Why do you have to be so mean? It's not as if we're poor.'

'We're not exactly rich either.'

'We would be if you got off your backside and went out on your own. You'd easily get Miriam to invest in your business – she'd do anything for you.'

'Don't start,' Luke said through gritted teeth. 'I'm warning you.'

Realizing she'd overstepped the mark, Bridget reached up on tiptoe to kiss him on the corner of his mouth. 'Please don't fight with me, darling,' she murmured, looking into his eyes. 'I hate it when you're angry with me.'

Luke shook his head and turned away. 'I'll get us those drinks.'

Grace excused herself to go to the loo, confident that she had answered both Concepta and Hilary's questions satisfactorily and could expect calls from both women within a few days. Maybe now she could relax and enjoy a drink.

As she went upstairs to use Miriam's main bathroom, she gazed down into the crowd wondering if Michael had arrived yet. She knew that he definitely had a meeting, but she also knew that he wouldn't be in any rush to join her. It was probably just as well. He hated making small talk and would stand around looking awkward and feeling uncomfortable. That's if she was lucky. If she wasn't, he'd have had a couple of drinks and would be his blunt, plainspoken self and insult at least one of the other guests. As for when he and Miriam locked horns over politics or religion . . . well, Grace just felt like running for cover. Why couldn't he be more like Luke or dear Alastair? She knew Luke hated these parties as much as Michael but he went through the motions and kept a smile on his face for Miriam's sake. As for Alastair, he was a positive asset on nights like this. Although he didn't particularly like or understand the kind of circles Miriam moved in, it was her business and he was happy to help her in any way he could. After all, it was her ambition and her drive that had attracted him in the first place.

That was nearly twelve years ago now and friends and family on both sides had been amazed at the match; Alastair, a confirmed bachelor, teacher of history and art, lover of country walks and opera; and Miriam, divorcée, businesswoman extraordinaire and social animal. They made an incongruous pair but somehow it had worked and they seemed very happy.

Grace finished repairing her make-up and stared at her reflection in the mirror. Would anyone ever describe her and Michael as very happy? Would *she*? She started as a tap sounded on the door. 'Coming,' she called, quickly combing her long hair and straightening her dress. When she opened the door, Bridget was standing there.

'Oh, thank God it's you, I was wondering where you were.' Bridget pushed Grace back inside and closed the door. 'You don't have a cigarette, do you?'

'I don't smoke, remember?'

Bridget pushed her dark fringe out of her eyes. 'Damn.'

'What's up?'

'Miriam is stirring it up again,' Bridget grumbled. 'She's always trying to make trouble.'

'Well, you don't help matters. Why on earth didn't you tell Luke about Rosa?'

'I thought I'd just let her start and as soon as he saw how much better our lives were, he'd realize that it was a good investment.'

'Oh, Bridget.'

'Why do you always say "Oh Bridget" like I'm some kind of stupid little girl?'

Grace laughed. 'If the cap fits . . .'

'Shut up! You're getting as bad as that cow you work for.'

'Work *with*,' Grace corrected, feeling irritated.

'Whatever.' Bridget set about reapplying her lipstick. 'But we all know who's in control.'

Grace picked up her bag and went to the door and Bridget whirled to face her. 'Oh Grace, I'm sorry. Forgve me?'

Grace stared into the huge brown eyes in the perfect heart-shaped face. No wonder Luke couldn't refuse her anything. 'Yes, but behave yourself. I haven't done anything to deserve your smart comments.'

'Of course you haven't.' Bridget hugged her before turning back to the mirror. 'It's just that old bat.'

'If you don't like her, you don't have to come to her parties.'

Bridget's eyes widened as she stared at her friend in the mirror. 'And miss the social occasion of the year? Are you nuts?'

Grace sighed and sat down on the loo. 'So what are you going to do about Luke? You know Rosa won't mind if you don't take her on.'

'Of course I'm going to take her on. Luke will be fine about it. He just likes to blow off steam now and again. It makes him feel all macho and in control but he'll agree in the end, he always does.' Bridget finished applying mascara and turned to smile at her friend. 'Now, let's go and people-watch. You know, I've seen two TV3 newsreaders and that pretty blonde off *Fair City*. How on earth does Miriam do it?'

Grace led the way back downstairs. 'She invites the press along and everyone knows that celebrities will go anywhere if they think they might get their mugs in the paper.'

'Oh, maybe we'll get our photo in the paper too.' Bridget paused on the staircase to scan the crowd below for a photographer. 'I don't see anyone. Oh, there's Michael. Coo-ee, Michael, up here!'

Michael looked up and raised his hand when he saw his wife and her friend. Grace went down to meet him. 'You got here then,' she said.

'Yeah, sorry, the meeting went on a bit longer than I anticipated. Hello Bridget, you look lovely.'

Bridget smiled broadly as he kissed her. 'Hello, darling, how are you?'

'Thrilled to be here,' he muttered and then flashed his wife a cheesy smile. 'Just kidding, darling, you know that. How's it going so far?'

Grace ignored his sarcasm and took his question at face value. 'Fine. It looks like I've got at least two new clients. One of them has bought an apartment in Ibiza town.'

Bridget gasped. 'Concepta Mahon is going to be your client?'

'How did you know?'

Bridget rolled her eyes. 'Oh Grace, everyone knows that. Don't you ever read the gossip columns?'

Grace and Michael exchanged a genuine smile. 'I try not to,' she replied.

'Is Luke here?' Michael asked.

Bridget waved her arm around vaguely. 'He's around somewhere.'

'Probably having a smoke outside,' Grace said. 'Why don't you two go and find him and I'll procure a bottle of half-decent red from Alastair and follow you out.'

'Now you're talking,' Michael said, grimacing as he finished the champagne. 'I can't stand this stuff. It gives me wind.'

'Too much information, dear,' Grace murmured before moving away.

'Ah, Grace, should you be here? Have you done your duty?'

Grace sank down on the stool beside him. 'Yes, sir, all done.'

'Then let me pour you a drink.' Alastair Summers went over to the wine-rack and selected a bottle of South African Shiraz.

'I promised the others I'd meet them on the patio with a bottle.'

'We both shall, but let's have a drink together first, shall we? I haven't seen you in ages.'

'Oh, go on then. Where's Miriam?'

Alastair shrugged as he opened the wine. 'Talking someone into parting with cash, no doubt. You know Miriam, she's never off-duty.' He looked up and smiled. 'I don't know what a woman like that sees in a boring old fart like me.'

'You're not boring.'

He laughed. 'So just an old fart then.'

'Not that old.'

'Sixty-two next birthday.' He sighed. 'I can't believe how fast the years fly by.'

'You look ten years younger,' Grace told him honestly. Alastair had a healthy, outdoor glow to his skin, his eyes always twinkled with good humour and the shock of white hair against his tanned skin had a dramatic, youthful effect. He was a very attractive man.

'It's all down to Miriam. It seems as if I merely existed before she came along. Since we've been together, the pace of my life has increased tenfold.'

'That's so sweet. There aren't many people who can say that.'

Alastair noted the wistful tone in her voice. 'Is everything okay, Grace?'

Grace patted his hand and stood up. 'Everything is fine – but it won't be if I don't bring this bottle out to my beloved.'

Chapter 3

'Where's Mum?' Natasha asked, coming into the kitchen and making herself some coffee.

Michael looked up from his newspaper and frowned disapprovingly. It was almost two o'clock and Natasha was still in pyjamas. 'At work. What time did you get in last night?'

She shrugged as she put bread into the toaster. 'About one.'

He snorted. 'It was a lot later than that.'

'If you knew that, why did you ask me?' she retorted in a bored tone as she rummaged in the fridge for some butter.

Michael's grip on the paper tightened. 'Do you always have to be so sarcastic?'

'Do you always have to interrogate me?' she shot back.

'God, I can't even ask a simple question now.'

Nat said nothing, just leaned against the worktop munching her toast and reading the TV supplement.

'Oh, *Shakespeare in Love* is on tonight – will you record it for me?'

'Why, where are you going? Oh no,' he held up a hand. 'Forget I asked. I don't want you to think I'm interrogating you.'

Nat smirked. 'I'm going to a gig, Dad, okay?'

'I'll tape it for you,' he said gruffly.

'Cheers.' Natasha scraped her crusts into the bin and headed for the door with her coffee.

'Where are you off to?'

'Just meeting a few friends.'

Michael sighed. 'Couldn't you at least wait and have some lunch with us? Your mum will be home in an hour.'

'No. I've had this now, I couldn't eat lunch too.'

'I'll tell her to keep you some for later.'

'Whatever,' Natasha called over her shoulder and disappeared.

Tutting, Michael went back to his paper.

'It's not natural,' he grumbled to Grace over lunch. 'It's important for a family to sit down and eat together. When else do we get the chance to talk?'

'She's twenty, Michael, and we can't chain her to the table. Pity, though, this shepherd's pie is lovely.'

Michael looked dubiously at their lunch, courtesy of Rosa. 'I'd prefer a roast.'

Grace bit her lip. 'I'll ask Rosa to prepare one for some night during the week when Natasha is in.'

'You'd better make an appointment,' Michael retorted,

'and don't let her catch you calling her Natasha.'

Grace sighed. 'I always thought it was such a pretty name. Nat is so—'

'Short?'

Grace laughed. 'Do you remember when she was three she refused to call me Mummy?'

'Gace, she called you.' Michael's smile was sad.

'She was such a little chatterbox, so full of her own importance.'

'At least she talked to us then.'

'She still talks to us.'

'No, she passes the time of day, makes idle chit-chat, but she doesn't really talk to us.'

'You should ask her about her course or the school.' Grace kept her tone light.

'What's there to say about wiping kids' noses and teaching them "Incy-Wincy Spider"?' Michael sneered.

Grace stood up and started to clear the table, her expression closed. 'And you wonder why she doesn't talk to you.'

As she finished cleaning up, Grace brooded on the conflict between her husband and daughter. Regardless of their differences over the years, Michael had never had problems with Natasha's academic ability. She was smart, she loved to learn and she sailed through exams. Michael's most enjoyable pastime had been hypothesizing whether Natasha would become a doctor, a scientist or a lawyer. The girl excelled in science and maths but she was a good student in all her subjects, had a great sense of humour and was popular with teachers and students alike. When she'd announced an interest in teaching Michael had been a little disappointed, but not overly concerned – until she informed them that she had decided to become a Montessori teacher. He went ballistic.

'You want to throw away your life teaching nursery rhymes to babies?'

'You're showing your ignorance, Dad,' had been Natasha's cutting response. 'Montessori is an alternative to the national school curriculum and goes up to the age of twelve.'

'Really? And how many schools are there in Dublin that go to that level? Cop on, Natasha. Montessori school is a place where busy mothers send their kids until they're ready for "big" school.'

'Who said I was staying in Dublin?' Natasha murmured.

'What?' Grace stared at her.

But Michael wasn't listening. 'Be a teacher if you want, Nat – hell, even be a primary-school teacher if you must, but forget about this Montessori business. I won't let you throw away a good education like this.'

'You don't get a choice,' Natasha had said and from then on she'd refused, point blank, to discuss the matter. Michael had been at his wits' end begging Grace to talk sense into their daughter, even suggesting she get Nat's teachers involved, but his wife refused

She had given the matter a lot of thought and listened to both her husband's and daughter's arguments. She could come to only one conclusion. 'If there's one thing we've always known, it's that Natasha is very sensible. We have to trust that she knows what she's doing and support her.'

And since then, things had cooled between the couple. On the face of it, life was going on as normal but Grace knew that Michael hadn't forgiven her and she also knew that he was deeply hurt by Nat's stubbornness. Up until the first day of college, he had been sure she'd change her mind but Natasha had stood firm. Grace had tried to talk to him about Montessori – she had read all the pamphlets Natasha had brought home – but Michael would have none of it. She'd tried to explain to her daughter her father's rather old-fashioned view on education, but Natasha didn't care. As far as she was concerned, her father's opinion on the subject was immaterial. It was *her* life. Grace had tried to find out if Natasha was really planning to leave Dublin but her replies were vague and Grace had to be content with the fact that she'd applied to a college in the city.

Grace threw down the tea-towel, poured herself a glass of wine and took it up to her office so she could check her email. As she climbed the two sets of stairs that took her to her office in the eaves, she marvelled yet again at this huge house that was their home. It bore little resemblance to the tiny two-bedroomed terrace house where they had started married life, with Grace's ancient sewing machine and bulky PC taking up half of the small dining room. They had come a long way since then, their combined salaries allowing them to take out a substantial mortgage and buy this impressive, five-bedroom house in a small development at the foot of the Dublin Mountains. As the Graceful Living premises was based in Blackrock, it wasn't too long a commute for Grace, and Michael's job took him all over the county, so his location was immaterial.

Michael Hughes, a quantity surveyor, worked from home and his contact with the outside world was limited mainly to phone calls and property surveys. He hardly ever even saw the girl who did his typing, dropping off his bulky, scrawl-filled pads at her house in the morning and picking up the typed reports the same night.

His only hobbies were watching soccer on the TV – going to a match never occurred to him – and fishing. Occasionally he went on trips with a couple of other enthusiasts, but though they spent long days on the river, Grace doubted that their conversation extended further than rods, bait and the weather.

Whenever she tried to talk to Michael about his solitary existence he just said that she and Natasha were enough for him, an answer that frankly irritated Grace. Of course she loved her family, but she needed her own space too.

The launch of Graceful Living had heralded a whole new social life for her, and while Miriam did most of the schmoozing, Grace did attend some of the more important trade shows and launches. She loved her work and felt that her job satisfaction enhanced her family life. If only it were the same for Michael.

He had never been a party animal, but as he got older he seemed to become more anti-social, preferring occasional visits to the cinema or local Italian restaurant with Grace to meeting up with other couples. Grace missed the friends they used to see, the fun they used to have – but if that's what Michael wanted, there was little she could do about it. As long as he didn't expect her to do the same.

Up in her office, Grace flopped into her chair and looked around. She had thought long and hard when deciding the colour scheme of this room as it needed to feel like a proper office but at the same time be a place that would inspire her when she was coming up with her designs. She had finally settled on dusky rose for the walls and deep cream for the door, skirting boards, shelving and ceiling. Apart from the fluorescent light, she also had a small lamp that provided a more relaxing, tranquil glow in the evenings when she just wanted to sit and think.

The colours had created exactly the right atmosphere – yet she never felt completely comfortable here. In fact, she got through more work in the confines of her office in Graceful Living. The small premises in Blackrock consisted of a stock room, a sewing room that doubled up as Grace's office, and Miriam's office. There was a tiny reception area with two chairs for the rare occasions that suppliers or clients visited. Grace wasn't sure if it was the proximity of the materials, the musty smell of fabric or just the fact that it was her business that inspired her, but when she was there, she worked as if she was on speed. The ideas came so fast and furious at times that her fingers could hardly keep up as she sketched out ideas and tapped notes into her laptop.

After replying to a lengthy email from an anxious client, Grace closed down her machine and went downstairs to her en-suite to have a bath. Michael had thought she was crazy putting the oversized bath in an en-suite but on the few occasions that he'd joined her there, he'd admitted that it had its attractions. Though they rarely had visitors, Grace liked the total privacy of bathing in here, and it had proved an excellent decision, given the amount of time her daughter now spent in the other bathroom.

She heard the phone ring in the bedroom and groaned, knowing that it was probably Bridget. Her suspicions were confirmed when moments later, Michael appeared, the phone in his hand. 'It's Bridget. Shall I tell her you'll call her back?'

'No, it's okay, I'll take it.' Grace sat up in the bath and reached for the phone, gratified to see Michael's appreciative glance on her breasts. Maybe there was hope for them, after all.

'Hi, Bridget, how's the head?'

'Killing me,' her friend responded, her voice like gravel. 'Did I smoke last night, Grace?'

'You did everything last night.'

'Oh God.'

'How's Luke?'

'Not talking to me. Any idea why?'

'Er, well, let's say, you got rather friendly with a weatherman off the telly. '

'Oh, is that all? We were just having a bit of fun. It was a party.'

'If you say so.' But Grace was remembering the look on Luke's face as he watched his girlfriend flirting outrageously.

'He drives a Jag, you know, and he owns one of those apartments in that new building on the Liffey.'

'Really?'

'Yeah, *and* he's just broken up with his wife.'

Grace could hear the excitement in her friend's voice. 'So?'

'I'm just saying he's a good catch, that's all.'

'You've already got a good catch. Luke is far better-looking.'

'Yeah. Pity he's broke.'

Grace smiled. 'He might win the Lotto.'

'And I might win Miss Ireland.'

'Don't mess him around, Bridget,' Grace begged. 'He doesn't deserve it.'

'Oh for God's sake, if it bothered Luke so much, why didn't he do something about it? I mean, if anyone was coming on to you, Michael would take a pop at him, wouldn't he?'

Grace frownd. 'I'm not sure. We've never really been in that situation.'

'Oh rub it in, why don't you? You can be so superior sometimes, you know that?'

Grace closed her eyes. 'I've got to go.'

'But—'

'Bye bye, Bridget,' Grace said and hung up. 'Michael!' she called. 'Why don't you come and scrub my back?'

Chapter 4

'Alastair, open a bottle of wine, would you?' Miriam called to her husband as she turned on the lamp and settled back on the sofa to scan the Sunday papers.

Alastair appeared moments later with a bottle of champagne and two glasses. 'I thought you might fancy something fizzy.'

'Excellent idea.'

'Fancy a snack to go with it?'

Miriam shook her head. 'No, I ate far too much last night.'

'It seemed to go well,' Alastair said as he eased the cork gently out of the bottle and poured the champagne.

'Very well. Grace is going to be a busy woman next year. Pity about the floor show.'

'Ah, yes, Bridget. She was a bit of an embarrassment.'

'I don't know what my brother sees in her, I really don't. She's a parasite and he deserves much better.'

'Don't tell him that,' Alastair warned. 'You'll only drive him further into her arms.'

'Luke may be in love but he doesn't like to be made a

fool of. Did you see his face when she started dancing with that man? I wouldn't trust the woman an inch. If she hurts him, Alastair, I won't be responsible for my actions.'

Alastair smiled tenderly. 'He's a big boy, darling. You have to let him get on with making his own mistakes.'

'I'm not so sure about that.' Miriam gazed out of the window, a determined look in her eye.

Alastair sipped his drink and said no more on the subject. Miriam would do what she wanted, whatever he said. He was used to his wife riding roughshod over everyone, it had made her the success she was, but he thought she underestimated her brother. Luke might not have any of her ambition but he had all of his sister's stubbornness.

'Remember, darling, I'm off to London in the morning,' Miriam was saying.

'Right. Will you be home for dinner?'

Miriam made a face. 'No. In fact, I think I might stay the night. There's a do on that I should attend. It will be a total bore, of course, but a gal's got to do what a gal's got to do.'

'Well, if it's going to be a late night, you're better off staying over,' Alastair agreed easily. 'Why don't I drop you to the airport and collect you, save you having to worry about parking?'

'That would be great.'

'And then I might take myself off to the garden centre and have a ramble around.'

'Oh?' Miriam said absently, her gaze drifting back down to the newspaper.

'I was thinking of buying some fruit trees – not full-size, of course, the garden isn't big enough – but they do some wonderful dwarf varieties. Can't you just imagine the colour and scent?'

'Imagine.'

'I might drop in on Grace and see what she thinks,' Alastair said, warming to his theme.

'Don't go taking up too much of her time,' Miriam warned.

'I'll treat her to lunch,' he decided. 'You don't begrudge the woman a lunch-break, I hope?'

'As long as it's not an extended one.' Miriam threw down her paper and stood up. 'Now I think I'll have an early night. I've a busy day tomorrow and I want to be on top form.'

'You're never anything else,' her husband assured her.

'Are you going to keep this up all night?' Bridget exploded, glaring at Luke. She'd been sitting in front of the TV, though not really watching, too conscious of his cold, distant presence on the other side of the room. The weird thing was that she felt very attracted to him when he was like this. Cold, remote, those dark, sexy eyes like flints of ice that she longed to melt. She wanted to turn him from immovable stone to a quivering heap, so the sooner they had this row, the sooner they could kiss and make up. She shivered in anticipation.

Luke looked up from his book. 'Keep what up?'

'The silent treatment. It's really childish, Luke. If you've something on your mind I don't know why you can't just say it.'

Luke thought about this for a second and then nodded. 'You're right, it is childish. It would be much better to have it all out in the open.'

Bridget smiled in encouragement. They'd be in bed within the hour. 'Well, yes, I think it would.'

Luke nodded again.

'Go on then,' she prompted. 'Spit it out.'

Luke closed his book and looked her straight in the eye. 'I think you're a selfish, cold, insensitive woman and I've decided to call it a day.'

Bridget gasped. If he'd slapped her it wouldn't have had half the effect. 'Don't you think you're overreacting just a little bit?' She forced a laugh but even she could hear the slightly shrill note in it. 'I had one drink too many and made a show of myself. I'm sorry, okay? It won't happen again.'

He shook his head, his face sad and remote. 'It's not about last night – well, not specifically. You don't need me and you certainly don't love me.'

Bridget fiddled nervously with her bracelets. 'What are you saying? Of course I do.'

'You don't, you just love what I can give you.'

'Oh please!' She gestured around her. 'It's hardly a palace.'

His smile was grim. 'True, and it's become very clear

to me that as far as you're concerned it's only temporary accommodation.'

Bridget started to shake as she realized that he was deadly serious. 'What on earth does that mean?'

'I mean that this,' he waved a hand around, 'isn't good enough for you. It's no coincidence that every man you chat up happens to be loaded.'

'How dare you?'

'It's true and you know it. Unless I win the Lotto or rob a bank I figure it's only a matter of time before you leave me, so I've decided to leave you first.' He stood up, taking his book. 'I'll go and pack a bag. I'll pick up the rest of my stuff when I find a place to stay.'

'Luke, this is ridiculous!' Bridget followed him out into the hall but he was already halfway up the stairs. 'You can't just leave,' she said, hurrying after him.

Luke didn't bother to answer, throwing some jeans and shirts into his sports bag and going into the bathroom to collect his shaving gear and toothbrush.

'What's really going on here?' Bridget leaned against the doorjamb for support and watched him through narrowed eyes. 'There's someone else, isn't there, and you're trying to blame all of this on me.'

Luke shot her a pitying look before zipping up the bag and putting it over his shoulder. 'I'll be in touch.' He walked past her and went downstairs.

Bridget followed, her face red and her eyes bright with angry tears. 'Fuck you, you bastard, I'm better off without you. You're a loser, a nobody and you know something? You'll always be a nobody.'

Luke paused in the doorway and looked at her, his expression unreadable. 'Then you're better off without me so. Goodbye, Bridget.'

'Oh God, who's that?' Michael groaned, as the phone shrilled into life. It was only eleven o'clock, but after sharing a bath with Grace, they'd gone to bed, made love and fallen into a deep sleep, still entwined in each other's arms.

'Probably Natasha wanting us to collect her from some pub or other,' Grace mumbled into the pillow. 'I'll make you Sunday roasts for a month if you go.'

Michael stretched out a hand and groped for the phone. 'Hello? What? Who is this? Oh, okay, hang on.' He held the phone out to Grace. 'It's Bridget.'

'What?' Grace raised her head and peered at him. 'What on earth does she want at this hour?'

'No idea,' he said, snuggling back down under the duvet, 'but do me a favour and take it outside.'

'Grace climbed out of bed, tucking the phone under her chin as she reached for her dressing-gown. 'Bridget? Is everything all right?'

'He's left me, Grace, can you fucking believe it? The bastard's left me.'

Grace stopped on the landing and rubbed her eyes. 'Luke?'

'Who else?'

'Sorry, Bridget, you need to give me a minute to wake up.'

'Oh, is it late? I didn't realize. I've just been wandering around the house like an idiot. I don't know what to do, I don't know what to think.'

'Do you want me to come over?' Grace offered.

'Yes. No. Oh, I don't know. What do I do, Grace? I mean, what do you think it means? I never saw this coming.'

'What did he say?' Grace went downstairs to the kitchen and plugged in the kettle.

Bridget gulped at the other end of the phone. 'Well, he was freezing me out most of the day and then I just confronted him and told him to say what he had to say. You know what I'm like, Grace. I'd prefer a good fight any day to the silent treatment.'

'So what happened?'

'He told me that I was selfish,' another gulp, 'and cold and insensitive and that I didn't love him, only the life I had with him – and then he said he was leaving.'

'Wow,' Grace breathed, popping a herbal teabag in a mug and adding boiling water.

'And that was it. He went upstairs, packed a few things and left.'

'I'm sure he'll be back when he cools down.'

'But that's just it, Grace, he wasn't really angry. He didn't shout or anything. He just seemed detached. Oh God, what am I going to do?'

Grace heard the clinking of glass in the background. 'Drinking won't help.'

'Give me a fucking break, will you?'

'Sorry.'

'Oh Grace, it's not true – I *do* love him.'

'I know that, Bridget, and I'm sure he does too. He's probably just a bit confused at the moment. Is he having any problems at work? Any money worries or anything?'

'I don't think so.'

Grace sighed. 'Did he say anything about last night?'

'Not a word. He just sat reading his sodding book all day, until I thought I was going to scream. He always does that when he's annoyed with me. He knows silence drives me crazy.'

'So he was annoyed,' Grace pointed out. 'I'm sure he's just feeling a bit hurt, Bridget. He'll come back. Maybe you should write him a note, apologizing—'

'No fucking way. He can go to hell.'

Grace yawned. 'Look, you have to make a decision. Do you want him back, or not?' If you want him back, grovelling may well be the way to go.'

'Whose side are you on?' Bridget railed.

'Yours,' Grace retorted, 'although God knows why. I'm trying to help but if you don't want me to . . .'

'Sorry, sorry. I didn't mean it, it's just been such a shock. I never thought for a moment that Luke would do something like this. If anyone was going to leave it was going to be me.'

Grace digested this for a moment. 'So you were having problems?'

'Not really. I suppose I'm just very bored.'

'Then that's good, isn't it? He's gone, you can do what you want; no more boredom.' Grace's tone was slightly sharper than she intended but really, Bridget could be so annoying at times.

'You're right.'

'I am?'

'Absolutely. I don't need him. This is the start of a whole new life for me. Sorry, Grace, got to go. I need to make a list.'

'Forget your bloody list, Bridget, this is serious. You've messed Luke around once too often.'

There was silence on the other end of the phone and then more sobs.

'Hey, come on,' Grace relented.

'I'm sure it will work out. All you need to do is to tell him how sorry you are, tell him that it won't happen again, tell him that you love him. Bridget?'

The line went dead and Grace stared at the phone in her hand. 'Oh God.' Putting it down, she poured her tea down the sink and went back to bed.

Chapter 5

Natasha turned her head on the pillow so that she could see the clock. It was nearly midnight: she'd better get home or her dad would give her grief tomorrow. She nudged Ken. 'I have to go.'

He pulled her towards him without opening his eyes. 'Stay.'

'I can't, Dad will go spare.'

'You're not a kid any more. What the hell can he do about it?'

'Nothing,' Natasha kissed him and slipped out of his arms, 'but I'm still going home.' Climbing out of bed she dressed and moved quietly to the door. 'I'll talk to you tomorrow.'

Ken grunted in reply but still didn't move.

With an unhappy sigh, Natasha let herself out of the flat, ran down the stairs and began the thirty-minute walk home. She didn't mind having to walk, it was a well-lit route and a good neighbourhood so she was safe enough, but it still needled her that Ken would let her do it. Sometimes she didn't think he gave a shit about her.

The only time he paid her compliments was when they were in bed or when he was trying to get her into bed. When they were out with his friends, he largely ignored her, playing to his wider audience.

Ken Jackson was a guitarist and lead singer with Cutting It, a rock band that was being heralded as the new U2. Privately, Natasha disagreed, although she did think that Ken – his stage name was just Jackson – had an amazing voice and an imposing presence on stage. It was the material that she couldn't get her head around. It was very negative and rebellious, almost punk in style, and it just seemed a bit dated to her. The ballads he used to write and sing before he joined Cutting It had been far superior, although she had learned that it was better to keep that opinion to herself. Ken didn't welcome criticism, constructive or otherwise.

Natasha lowered her face into the neck of her jacket as she saw two guys approaching her, one of them rather unsteadily.

'Hey, love, wish me mate luck. He's getting married tomorrow,' one called to her.

Natasha looked up and smiled. 'Good luck.'

'I don't need it,' the groom assured her. 'My Lisa is gorgeous, she is. I'm the luckiest man in Dublin – no, in Ireland. Ah, fuck it, I'm the luckiest man in the world.'

Natasha laughed and continued on her way, feeling bad that she'd assumed the worst about the two lads. Dublin had its fair share of thugs, but for the most part, it was a great place to be, even if she still had to live at home with her narrow-minded father. While she was in college she couldn't afford to do otherwise – unless, of course, Ken asked her to move in with him, and that didn't appear to be on the cards. They'd been together for nearly a year now but Ken still seemed to keep her at a distance. Sure, he talked to her about his ambitions and sometimes – after a few drinks – his fears, but she'd never met any of his family and he hardly ever mentioned them. When Natasha asked, he'd usually fob her off with some smart comment and change the subject. She got the feeling that there had been a row. Maybe his dad didn't approve of his career choice either.

Though she never let him see it, it still hurt that her dad thought she was wasting her talents training to be a Montessori teacher. He hadn't even tried to understand or asked her why it was so important to her. He didn't care that working with the children, she was happier than she had ever been before in her life. Watching them play and learn, Natasha was astounded and charmed at the way these infants soaked up knowledge like little sponges.

Michael had argued that if she wanted to teach, why not teach science or maths to teenagers? That, at least, would be a more fitting use of her talents. But that didn't appeal to Natasha at all. Teenagers spent most of their time resenting their teachers, a depressing prospect, whereas three-year-olds were innocent and eager and loved their teachers. Also, when Natasha finished this course, she planned to go on and train to teach older children, her ultimate ambition being to help children with special needs and maybe even set up her own school one day.

Natasha smiled as she turned into her road. Sometimes when her dad was ranting on at her, she'd doubted herself and wondered if he was right and she'd made the wrong career choice. But when she stood in the classroom and looked at all those open, expectant little faces staring up at her, all of her doubts were allayed. This was the job for her.

Natasha had wondered, did others feel this wonderful sense of job satisfaction or was she just inordinately lucky? One night when Michael was out and Grace was sitting in front of the TV sewing a cushion cover, Natasha asked her mother about interior design. 'Did you love it as soon as you started?' she asked, kicking her trainers off and curling up on the sofa beside her.

'Not so much at the beginning,' came the reply. 'It was very hard work and it was years before I got to do the really fun stuff.'

'Telling people how to decorate their houses?'

'Advising them,' Grace corrected. 'At the end of the day, the customer is always right, remember.'

'Even when their taste is crap?'

'It's more of a challenge then, but I quite like that. It's wonderful when I'm able to bring them around to my way of thinking and there's a great sense of achievement if they're thrilled with the final results.'

Natasha sighed happily, 'And that's what I want, Mum.

I know Dad thinks I should be more interested in how much money I can make, but I'm not like that.'

'Probably because you're still living at home,' Grace remarked wryly.

'Oh Mum, that's not fair! You know I'll pay my way as soon as I can.'

Grace patted her daughter's knee. 'I know, darling. I'm not having a go at you but your priorities will change as you get older and think about buying a place of your own, settling down, having children . . .'

'I won't do that for years,' Natasha assured her. 'I'm only twenty.'

'I'm glad to hear it,' said Grace with a smile.

Natasha walked up the front drive now and quietly put her key in the door. That conversation with her mother had only taken place a couple of months ago and here she was, moping because Ken hadn't asked her to move in. How pathetic was that? She wasn't even sure if she loved him. Sometimes it felt as if they really clicked and he was tender and loving, but then when they were surrounded by the band and all the various groupies and hangers-on, Natasha felt she was completely surplus to requirements.

Having said that, even before Ken joined Cutting It, there were times when he was remote and cool. Natasha put it down to the creative bent. Her mother went all vague when she was working on a new design job, staring into the distance, talking to herself and spooning coffee into the teapot. Natasha would just have to accept it was part of being with an artistic person.

Her dad had told her regularly over the years that when Grace was working, Natasha was wasting her time trying to talk to her. 'She might look as if she's listening,' he said, 'but believe me, it's all going in one ear and out the other.' And of course he'd been right. So it was probably just the same for Ken and she shouldn't take any notice when he ignored her or was rude.

Climbing the stairs to bed, Natasha wished she'd fallen for an accountant or a butcher. Life would be a lot simpler and at least you'd know where you stood.

Chapter 6

By the time Alastair went to meet Grace, his head was buzzing with ideas for his garden and he was dying to get her opinion. He'd called her after dropping Miriam at the airport and she'd agreed immediately to lunch.

'Although I can't write off the afternoon, Alastair,' she'd warned.

'Perish the thought!' he'd laughed.

They'd agreed to meet at a pub a short walk from Graceful Living that did good, plain food and had a pretty little beer garden at the back. Though it was late September, it was a balmy, sunny day and Alastair was looking forward to a relaxing meal in excellent company.

Grace was already settled at a table in the garden when he arrived. 'I'm so sorry – have I kept you waiting?' he asked, bending to kiss her cheek.

'Not at all. I finished up early and it's just such a nice day.'

'Isn't it, though?' he agreed eagerly. 'I've spent all morning at the garden centre and I've got the most wonderful plan.'

'Oh?' Immediately Grace leaned forward to listen, resting her chin on one hand. 'Tell me more.'

He shook his head. 'No, let me get you a drink first and some menus. I don't know about you, but I'm starving.'

After they'd ordered and Grace was sipping her mineral water while Alastair enjoyed a glass of chilled Chardonnay, he told her of his plans for the garden. 'I was thinking of just bunging a few dwarf fruit trees in, but I got talking to this man and he suggested a *secret garden*.'

'Sounds wonderful,' Grace replied, 'but what exactly does it mean?'

'Well, from the house it would look as if there was simply a line of trees at the bottom of the garden but, in fact, there would be a little path that would wind its way through a variety of trees and lead to a small clearing, with possibly a hammock or a love seat, maybe even a water feature.'

Grace sighed. 'Oh Alastair, that sounds so romantic.'

'It does, doesn't it?' he said, pleased with himself. 'Sure I can't tempt you?' He took the wine bottle from the cooler and held it up.

'Oh, go on then.' Grace grinned. 'You are such a bad influence, Alastair Summers. You only ordered a bottle because you knew I'd weaken.'

'As if I'd do such a thing!' he said, but his mouth was turned up in a satisfied smile. ' Still, not a bad way to spend a Monday afternoon, is it?'

Grace took a sip of her wine and closed her eyes. 'It's

a positively decadent way to spend a Monday afternoon, but I don't feel in the slightest bit guilty. I finished a job this morning that I hadn't expected to get done before the weekend.'

'I didn't think you even did any hands-on work these days,' he teased. 'I thought designers just gave the orders and let the minions do the work.'

'Hah! If only it were that glamorous. Most jobs you'll find me scraping off wallpaper or up a ladder painting a ceiling. When someone on the team pulls a sickie, Muggins here has to step in or we don't finish the job on time and that's not good. Most of my business comes through word-of-mouth, and if I get a reputation for delivering late, it could be curtains.'

'Curtains! Ha! Very funny!'

Grace laughed. 'It must be the wine.'

'You really enjoy your work, don't you?' Alastair studied her affectionately.

'I do. I feel sorry for people who have to do a job they hate.'

'That's probably the majority of the population.'

'You enjoyed teaching, didn't you, Alastair?'

He considered the question. 'Yes and no. Watching students discover their talent, experiment with different styles and materials, uncover amazing abilities – that was a joy and an honour.' He paused. 'For the most part, however, my job consisted of force-feeding information into the heads of sulky teenagers, which was a bit depressing.'

Instinctively, Grace reached out and squeezed his hand. 'I'm sure you made an impression on lots of your students. I still have such fond memories of my English teacher. We shared a deep love for Patrick Kavanagh, and if I wanted to get a good grade in an exam, all I had to do was throw in a quote and I was home and dry.'

Alastair laughed. 'How devious. Oh great, our food.' A waiter set a chicken salad in front of Grace and a selection of seafood and brown bread in front of him.

'Delicious,' Grace pronounced as she tasted some chicken. 'I wish I could produce food like this, Michael would love it. The only decent food he gets these days are the meals Rosa cooks, and even then he complains that she doesn't do enough plain cooking.'

'I find it really strange that someone as creative as you can't cook.' Alastair shook his head sorrowfully.

'It's just not my thing. I feel that time spent in the kitchen is time wasted. All that work slogging over a hot stove and then it's gone in minutes.'

Alastair looked horrified. 'No, no, no, that's sacrilege. Food is a reason to sit, to talk, to relax, to connect.'

Grace smiled. 'I can't see Miriam relaxing. I'll bet while you're dishing up, she's got her phone to her ear and is checking her email on her laptop at the same time.'

Alastair chuckled. 'It is hard to pin her down,' he admitted, 'but at the weekends I ban all electronic equipment from the dining room while we eat. I even put the answering machine on.'

Grace stared at him, her expression a mixture of

incredulity and admiration. 'That must drive her mad.'

'I lower the volume on the phone so she can't hear it if it rings,' he confided. 'It's important that she takes some time out from her work, and you should too. I'm sure Michael would enjoy it.'

Grace nodded. 'He'd love it. He's always complaining that we never sit and eat together.'

'How old is Michael?' Alastair asked.

'Forty-eight in February.'

'And slightly overweight. Does he do any exercise?'

'Not really.'

'And is there any family history of heart disease?' Alastair persisted.

'Well, yes, but—'

'But nothing. He should take steps now to get healthy. Some good fresh food, plenty of fish, a few brisk walks and less of the lager.'

'Is that your secret?' Grace teased, her eyes roaming over his trim physique.

'It's no secret, it's just commonsense. If only I could make Miriam see that.'

'But Miriam isn't overweight!'

'No, but she starves herself when she wants to lose weight. She eats rubbish when she's away from home, she smokes at least twenty a day and she drinks far too much gin. It's not exactly a healthy regime.'

'Well, I may not be good with the food, but I do exercise, I don't drink much – unless I'm in bad company – and I'm not overweight.'

It was Alastair's turn to eye her appreciatively. In the cream, sleeveless linen dress she looked slim, healthy and beautiful. 'You're perfect,' he told her, 'but you need to sort out your husband.'

'Why is it up to me?' Grace said crossly. 'I'm not his mother.'

Alastair shrugged. 'No, you're not, but you don't want to be a young widow, do you?'

Grace shivered. 'Oh Alastair, what a thing to say.'

'I'm sorry, my dear, just ignore me. Sometimes I get on my soapbox and bore everyone silly. It's part of getting older, I believe. Let me get you a disgustingly unhealthy dessert to make up for my insensitive behaviour.'

Grace shook her head. 'I'm stuffed, that was a delicious salad.'

'Some coffee then?'

'Tea would be nice.'

Alastair called the waiter and ordered tea for her and an espresso for himself. 'I do worry about Miriam,' he told her when they were alone once more. 'She lives completely on her nerves, hardly ever relaxes.'

'It's the way she is – I don't think she'll ever change. And if she did, she wouldn't be the woman you fell in love with.'

'Are you trying to tell me I should stop nagging everyone and accept them for what they are?'

Grace smiled. 'That's about the size of it.'

'Okay, we'll change the subject. Tell me how that beautiful daughter of yours is getting on in college.'

'Loving every moment, apparently. You know, I never even knew she liked children. It's not as if she ever did any babysitting and there are no small children in the family.'

'Maybe that was the attraction.'

Maybe. Michael still doesn't approve, of course. He's hoping she'll come to her senses and drop out.'

'And even if Natasha did have doubts she'd probably stick with it just to spite him,' Alastair surmised.

'She is as stubborn as he is,' Grace agreed, 'but I do think she's serious about teaching as a career. I must say, it makes me feel quite proud. I never thought of her as a caregiver. I thought she'd be signing up for a career with the biggest salary.'

'She certainly won't get that in teaching,' Alastair assured her, 'but she will get job satisfaction.'

Grace's eyes widened. 'That's not what you were saying earlier.'

'That's because I'm old and cranky and miserable, but when I was young and enthusiastic and motivated, I was a very happy man.'

'You're really a very lucky man,' Grace remarked. 'You had your career, then you met the love of your life and now you're moving into a new phase where your day is your own and you can do what you like.'

'Including having a long, lazy lunch with a beautiful woman,' he added. 'Seriously, though, it's the next phase I'm looking forward to.'

'What's that?'

'Miriam's retirement.'

Grace almost choked on her tea. 'Pardon?'

'Oh, don't worry, it' s probably years away – although I hope not. I'd love to take her all over the world and for us to really enjoy life before I die.'

'Alastair, don't talk like that.'

'Why not? I'm just being realistic. If Miriam decides to work until sixty-five, that's another thirteen years and, if I'm still around, I'll be seventy-five. I could be riddled with arthritis by then or gone ga-ga.'

'Not you,' Grace said.

'But we don't know, do we? That's why I want to make the most of our time together now. Miriam does-n't need the money; she doesn't have to work, and if she wanted she could still retain ownership of the bou-tiques but just take a back seat. I mean, all these trips abroad, all the time we spend apart, it can't really be necessary.'

Grace looked away. 'She doesn't trust anyone else to do the purchasing.'

'I know that, but it's ridiculous. She has three compe-tent, level-headed managers who are more than capable of doing the job.'

'You're right, but Alastair, that's not the point. She's doing it because she enjoys it, because it's important to her.'

'More important than me?' He stared moodily into his coffee.

Grace stared at him. It was as if he'd suddenly metamorphosed into her husband. 'Alastair, this isn't a choice between you and her job. This is what she does, who she is. This is why you fell for her, for God' s sake! How can you forget that? It's only ten years ago.'

'You're right, of course,' Alastair said with a weak smile, 'but that's part of the problem. We've only had ten years together and I want so much more than that. I'm afraid of running out of time. I want to squeeze every ounce out of my life and make the most of it, and there's no point if she's not there to share it.'

Grace's eyes filled up. 'Oh Alastair, you're a wonderful man.'

'No, I'm selfish,' he corrected. 'I want her all for myself but you're right, it wouldn't make her happy. She needs more.'

Grace thought of the dalliances that she knew her partner indulged in when she was abroad and her heart went out to this man. Miriam truly didn't deserve him, but for all her bad behaviour, Grace knew she loved him. 'Have you told her how you feel?'

'Yes, of course. I'm always telling her she should take it easier.'

'But have you talked to her the way you've just talked to me?'

'Probably not.' Alastair laughed softly. 'I don't want to remind her of what a geriatric she married.'

'She married an attractive, vibrant, wonderful man and you're still all of those things. She's very lucky, Alastair, and don't you forget it.'

Alastair leaned across to kiss her cheek. 'You're so sweet, Grace, what would I do without you?'

Grace laughed. 'Find someone else to enjoy long lunches with.'

Chapter 7

Bridget banged down the phone and reached for the wine bottle. Where the hell was Grace? There was no answer at the office or on the mobile, and it was four o'clock on a Monday afternoon. Where on earth could she be? Bridget felt an irrational annoyance with her friend. She should know that Bridget needed her. If you couldn't rely on your friends at a time like this, then when could you? She'd been trying to reach Luke too but she was having no luck there either. She'd found herself going through a whole range of emotions since last night, one moment feeling that she would be fine without him, the next, confusion as to what had gone wrong, the next, anger at his horrible words and finally, a cold, pervading fear at the thought of being alone.

She paced her kitchen agitatedly, pausing every now and then to take a slug of wine. Deciding that she needed a cigarette, she started to pull open drawers and go through pockets but with no luck. Going upstairs, she went to Luke's bedside table and opened the drawer, letting out a sigh of relief when she saw the packet of

Marlboro. She quickly took one with shaking hands and then rummaged in the drawer for a match. Instead she found a lighter that she'd bought Luke for their first Christmas together. Lighting the cigarette, Bridget sank on to the bed and stared at the lighter. It had been a wonderful Christmas. Luke had bought her a leather jacket and perfume, and after exchanging gifts they'd gone to a five-star hotel for lunch, the final surprise being that Luke had booked them a room.

Silent tears rolled down Bridget's cheek. What was she going to do? She wasn't good at being alone, she was used to Luke taking care of her. He cleaned her car, mowed the lawn, fixed creaking floorboards and, most importantly, paid the bills. Bridget felt suddenly nauseous. If Luke didn't come back she might have to get a job, and it would have to be some job if she wanted to keep her car and pay for her clothes, hair, nails and monthly spa therapies. Wiping her eyes with the back of her hand, she dragged deeply on her cigarette. He couldn't leave her, just like that. She'd look like a spare part at dinner-parties on her own; she'd become an object of pity, a sad, middle-aged spinster. The thought made her shiver and she closed her eyes tight and forced herself to take deep breaths. She'd have to talk to him, make him see that it was all a huge mistake. She'd tell him she'd change her ways; maybe she'd even agree to get engaged. Whatever it took, she'd do it, she'd get him to come back. Or she would if he ever accepted her calls.

And that's where Grace came in. Luke liked her,

respected her and would listen if she were to talk to him. Bridget picked up the phone extension by the bed and dialled Grace's number again, willing her friend to pick up.

'Graceful Living, Grace Mulcahy speaking.'

'Oh Grace, thank God. Where have you been? I've been trying to get you for hours.'

'Sorry, I had to go out and I forgot my mobile phone.'

'That's not very businesslike.'

'No. So what did you want me for?'

'I need you to talk to Luke.'

'I don't think that would be a good idea.'

'You have to, Grace. Luke likes you, he'll listen to you.'

'I don't think he will really appreciate you involving someone else, Bridget. Why don't *you* talk to him?'

'Because he won't take my bloody calls, that's why,' Bridget fumed. 'No, you'll have to do it, Grace. You have to make him come back. I can't do this on my own.'

'But last night you said it was probably for the best.'

Bridget snorted. 'Last night I forgot that someone has to pay the bills. How arn I supposed to manage, Grace, tell me that!'

'You have the flat,' Grace pointed out.

'But that's not enough. I have a life – at least I had until he snatched it away. He can't do that to me, it's not fair. We've been together five years – I gave up everything for him.'

'Everything' consisted of a job in the same department

store where Grace used to work and Bridget had hated it. From the moment she met Luke, life had changed with him agreeing to her every whim.

'You should have married him when he asked you,' Grace said tiredly. 'You'd have had some rights then.'

'Are you deliberately trying to wind me up?' Bridget demanded.

'Sorry. Look, talk to him, Bridget. Calmly. I'm sure you two will be able to sort it out.'

'I've already told you he's not taking my calls, so what chance do I have to sort anything out? Oh please, Grace, just talk to him.'

Grace sighed. 'One call, Bridget, after that, it's between the two of you.'

'Oh thank you, Grace, thank you. Oh, and tell him I got the car-tax renewal in the post this morning – he'll have to take care of that.'

'I don't think we should bring that up right now, do you? He might think that you only want him back for his money.' Grace tried, but it was hard to keep her feelings out of her voice.

Bridget didn't notice. 'Oh, I suppose it can wait. Call me as soon as you've talked to him, okay?'

'Okay.'

'And you'll call him now, as soon as you hang up, right?'

'Right.'

Bridget hung up without saying goodbye. Grace pulled out her diary and looked up Luke's number, rubbing the back of her neck as she felt the tension build. She could imagine Michael's reaction when she told him the position Bridget had put her in, but what could she do? The girl hadn't anyone else to turn to. Grace picked up the phone and dialled.

Luke answered on the second ring. 'Hi, Grace.'

'Oh Luke, hi.'

'I've been expecting your call.'

'You have?'

'Yeah. I knew when Bridget wasn't able to get hold of me she'd drag you into it.'

'Sorry, Luke. I don't want to interfere but even if you're serious about leaving . . .'

'Oh, I'm serious.'

'Well, you still have a lot of things to sort out.'

'Like what?'

'Well, like what happens to the flat, who pays for what, and – well, other formalities.'

'I think that about sums it up: who pays. Yes, it sums up our whole relationship, when you think about it.'

'Luke, I understand you're angry—'

'Do you, Grace? You know, I doubt that, but then Bridget didn't either, so why should you?'

His voice broke and Grace's heart went out to him. 'Why don't you come over, Luke? It sounds like you could do with someone to talk to.'

'Is that allowed? You are Bridget's friend, after all.'

'I'm your friend too,' Grace said firmly, trying not to think about what Bridget would have to say about that.

There was a short silence on the end of the phone and then Luke replied, 'I have a few things to do here first. Would six be too late?'

'Six is fine.'

'Okay, see you then.'

'Bye.' Grace hung up and then dialled Michael's mobile number. 'Hi, darling. Listen, I'm going to be late home so you go ahead and eat without me. Rosa said she was leaving a fish pie so you can heat it up in the microwave and it will be ready in a flash.'

'Where are you off to?' Michael asked, his tone brusque.

'Bridget asked me to talk to Luke.'

'Oh Grace, don't get involved.'

'I'm not going to,' she promised him. 'I told her I'd have one conversation with him and that would be it.'

'Do you think he'll go back to her?'

'I really don't know.'

'And what exactly does she expect *you* to do?'

'He's not taking her calls so she just wants me to persuade him to talk to her. That's all I'm going to do, Michael, I can assure you. I won't be late.'

'Okay, then, see you later.'

'Bye.' Grace put the phone down and closed her eyes. Her relaxing lunch seemed an awful long time ago, all of a sudden. She was about to go and put on the kettle when the phone rang again.

'Hello, Graceful Living, Grace Mulcahy speaking.'

'Hi, Grace, it's me.'

'Miriam, how's London?'

'Hot and sticky but I have good news for you.'

'Oh, yes?' Grace stifled a yawn. Miriam was in London on boutique business so news probably meant a salacious piece of gossip that she was just dying to share.

'I have a new client for you.'

'Really?'

'Yes. He's a pilot and he's just accepted a job with Aer Lingus and is relocating to Dublin. He bought a large apartment in Portmarnock but he's divorced and hasn't a clue about décor so I gave him your card.'

'Great.'

'How are things there?'

Grace hesitated. It didn't look as if Miriam had heard about Luke and Bridget's break-up but she wasn't going to be the one to tell her. 'Fine. You?'

'Couldn't be better. I have an appointment for a wax with the hotel beautician in half an hour and a date with a delicious man at seven.'

'Oh Miriam, why?' Grace groaned.

There was a raucous laugh at the end of the line. 'That's a stupid question.'

Grace frowned in annoyance. 'I had lunch with Alastair today.'

'Oh yes, he mentioned he was going to ask you. I hope he didn't bore you to tears droning on about his bloody garden.'

'We had a lovely time, actually. He was great company.'

'That's nice. Listen, I know I said I'd be back in the

office by eleven but Nigel wants me to stay for a few hours longer.'

'What are you going to tell Alastair?'

'Oh, that the flight was delayed. God knows, it happens often enough. Right then, must go or I'll miss my appointment. See you tomorrow.'

Grace muttered obscenities at the phone as she put it down. She had such mixed feelings about Miriam it could be quite distracting and frustrating. On the one hand, Miriam had proven herself to be an excellent business partner in that she took care of all the administrative needs of Graceful Living and put a lot of business Grace's way. On the other hand, she could be an insensitive bully of a boss to the staff of her boutiques and had no respect for the things that were important to Grace, among them marriage.

Grace truly believed that Miriam did love Alastair, she just seemed incapable of monogamy. Occasionally, after a couple of glasses of wine, Grace had confronted Miriam on the issue but got nowhere. Miriam didn't see a problem with the way she lived. She had been a single woman until the age of forty-one and she was used to a certain independent lifestyle. Alastair understood that.

'Are you saying that he knows you sleep with other men?' Grace had been incredulous.

Miriam had shrugged. 'Subconsciously, perhaps he does. He knows me better than anyone else, and his sex-drive has never equalled mine.' Miriam had laughed then at Grace's red face. 'It's a fact, darling, we both know it and Alastair is a highly intelligent man. I'm sure he can put two and two together.'

But that didn't make it any easier for Grace to stomach. She adored Alastair and hated to think of Miriam treating him like this. How she could even want another man when she had someone as wonderful as him, was beyond Grace. Although, she figured as she finally got to make her cup of tea, it was all a game to Miriam, just like business. Her partner thrived on winning customers, driving the best deal, dressing Ireland's jet-set, being the best at everything she did. It was no surprise that she was the same in her personal life. She had bagged an attractive, intelligent, personable man but she continued to test her sexual prowess at every opportunity. She should have been a man, Grace mused, carrying her mug back to her desk.

Looking at her watch, she realized that Luke would be here soon and there was just time to respond to her emails. She was closing down her computer when there was a rap on the door.

Hurrying down the narrow hall she opened the door and smiled nervously at Luke Cooper. 'Hi.'

'Hi.'

Grace stood back to let him in, thinking he looked terrible – well, as terrible as Luke could ever look. There was stubble around his mouth and dark bags under his eyes and he had his shirt on inside out. 'Coffee?' she offered.

'No, thanks all the same. I need a real drink.'

'Let's go to that place down the road.'

Twice in one day with two different men – what would the staff think? Grace smiled at him. 'Sure, but let's put your shirt on properly first.'

Luke looked down at himself. 'I just threw it on when I was coming down here.' He dragged it off to reveal a stained T-shirt. 'Sorry, I didn't have time to change.'

'And I was expecting a tuxedo,' Grace teased as she fixed the shirt and held it out to him.

They strolled down to the pub in silence, Grace aware of the tension in the man walking at her side.

When they were seated on two stools at a quiet end of the bar and the barman had welcomed Grace like an old friend, she turned to look at Luke. 'How are you doing?'

Before answering, he lowered half of his pint. 'Marvellous.'

'Bridget is very upset.'

'Really?'

'Really.'

'She's probably worried about the gravy train drying up,' he said, his tone bitter. He drained his glass and signalled the barman for a refill.

'Don't say that,' Grace protested. 'She wants you to come home.'

'She'd be just as happy if I sent her my wallet and credit cards.'

'How can you say that? You two have been together for more than five years.'

Luke laughed. 'It feels like ten.'

'She hasn't been unfaithful, Luke, if that's what you think.'

'Maybe not, but it's only a matter of time.'

'That's ridiculous.' Grace shook her head in bemusement. 'You're going to throw away your relationship because of something that you think *might* happen.'

Luke turned his head to look at her. 'You have no idea what you're talking about, Grace.'

'Then tell me.' She put a hand on his arm to stop him raising his glass to his lips.

Luke carefully removed her hand and finished his second drink. 'Another,' he called and, 'Is there any food going?'

The barman looked at the clock. 'Tracey should be out with cocktail sausages in a minute.'

'Excellent. Now, Grace, why don't you have a real drink and help me celebrate?'

'White wine, please.'

The barman nodded. 'Dry, isn't it?'

Grace winced as Luke raised a questioning eyebrow. 'Please.'

'Have I uncovered something here, Grace? Do you spend your days down here boozing when you're supposed to be sweating over your sketchpad?'

'I just had lunch here today.'

'Ah, with Miriam.'

'No, actually, with Alastair.'

Luke swivelled on his stool to study her. 'Well, well,

well, I'd never have believed it. Are you carrying on with my sister's husband?'

Grace laughed. 'Nothing so exciting, it was just lunch and Miriam knew all about it.'

Luke nodded but his smile had disappeared. 'I suppose she also knows all about me and Bridget?'

'I haven't told her.'

'Thanks. I'm not looking forward to the "I told you so's". God, can you just imagine it? The champagne corks will be popping for days.'

He was right, of course, Grace knew. Miriam would be thrilled to hear that the couple had broken up. But maybe she wouldn't have to hear. Maybe there was still hope. 'Forget about Miriam. We're here to talk about you and Bridget.'

'You might be, but I'm here to drink. Ah, the lovely Tracey, I presume.' He directed a slow, sexy smile at the waitress who'd emerged from the kitchen with a tray of sausages. 'You've saved my life.'

The girl blushed, and pulling a basket from under the counter, she tipped a generous number of sausages into it and set it in front of Luke. 'There you go.'

'You are as kind as you are lovely,' he said, blowing her a kiss.

'Is this the future for you, then? Grace asked tartly. 'Sitting in pubs getting pissed and chatting up barmaids?'

Luke chewed on a sausage and considered the question. 'That doesn't sound like a bad life.'

'You can't just throw away five years. You love Bridget and she loves you. Yes, you have your ups and downs – hell, we all do.'

'Do you?' he asked curiously. 'I thought life was perfect in the Hughes household.'

Grace took a sip of her drink. 'Life isn't perfect in any household.'

'Is it Michael? Is he getting too old and grumpy and boring for you?' He inched closer. 'How about some extra-marital activity, Grace?'

She stared at him. 'For God's sake!'

He threw back his head and laughed. 'You should see your face.'

Grace felt herself redden. She should have known he was kidding. As if a gorgeous younger man like Luke would fancy her. 'I'm trying to help here, and all you can do is make stupid jokes,' she complained.

Luke leaned over to kiss her cheek. 'Sorry, darling, you know I wouldn't hurt you for the world.'

'Is there really no hope? Won't you at least talk to her?'

Luke stared into his pint. 'I don't see the point. She'll probably say all the right things but it doesn't mean anything. *I* don't mean anything. The only person that Bridget loves is Bridget.'

'That's not true.'

Luke turned to look at her. 'You know it is. If a richer man came along she would be gone like a shot.'

Grace looked away. 'I'm sure you're wrong.'

'No, you're not.'

Grace sat in silence for a moment. She realized that this was hopeless. Luke had made up his mind. 'What am I going to tell her?'

Luke's smile was grim. 'Tell her she has a choice. She can find another mug to finance her lifestyle or she can get off her arse and go out and find a job.'

'A job!' Bridget screeched.

Grace held the phone away from her ear.

'The bastard! How dare he? Who the hell does he think he is? What did you say to that, Grace? I hope you told him he was way out of line.'

Grace was feeling really tired now and quite fed up. 'Bridget, please stop shouting at me.'

'Sorry.'

'That's okay. Look, I'm sorry, I tried, but he seems to have made up his mind.'

'But what will I do?' Bridget wailed.

'Get a job – or you could always sell the flat and buy a smaller place or rent.'

'Rent?' Bridget screeched again.

'Or you could move back in with your parents.'

'Are you mad?'

'You're yelling again.'

'You'd yell too if someone had just turned your world upside down,' Bridget wailed.

'I know, darling, and I'm sorry I don't have better news for you.'

Bridget sobbed noisily at the other end of the phone. 'What am I going to do? I can't go on on my own, Grace, I just can't.'

Grace looked at the clock; it was nearly nine o'clock and she felt exhausted. 'Would you like me to come over?'

'Would you?'

'Why don't you just join the Samaritans and have done with it?' was Michael's response when she called.

'Michael, give me a break.'

'Your daughter hasn't come home either, if you're interested.'

'She went to a concert in The Point Depot – she won't be home until after midnight.'

'Oh well, thanks for telling me.'

'Look, I only found out myself this morning when she sent me a text.'

'That says it all. She sends you a text and doesn't bother telling me, the only one who really cares about her.'

'That's not fair.'

'You're telling me,' he retorted and hung up.

As Grace got out of her car she prayed that Bridget wasn't drunk. Hysterical and pissed would be just too much to handle. As she walked up the drive, the door opened a crack and a red- eyed, dishevelled Bridget fell into her arms.

'It's going to be okay,' Grace murmured into her hair. 'Come on, I could murder some tea.'

'Tea?'

'Definitely tea.' She watched as Bridget stood in the middle of the kitchen with a blank look on her face. 'I'll make it, you sit down.'

Bridget slid into a chair and clasped her hands in front of her. 'How was he?'

'A bit of a mess, to be honest.' Grace filled the kettle and found two clean mugs.

'Really?'

Grace looked away when she saw the flicker of hope in her friend's eyes. 'He's very upset.'

'*He's* upset? He's the one who left.'

Grace carried the two mugs to the table and sat down. 'He says you don't care about him.'

'Oh, for God's sake.'

Grace sipped her tea and said nothing.

'I don't know what is going on with that man, he used to be such fun,' Bridget grumbled.

'Relationshis aren't always about fun. Sometimes it's about sharing your problems, the rough times and just being there for each other.'

Bridget wrinkled her perfect brow. 'We've never really had to do any of that.'

'What about his dad?' Grace asked. Luke's dad was in a nursing home and she knew that Luke spent a lot of time with him, much more than Miriam. They seemed very close and Grace thought his long illness must be very hard for Luke to bear.

Bridget shrugged. 'He's okay, Luke visits him every week.'

'Don't you go?'

'I'm not good with old people. Anyway, they don't want me around.' She rolled her eyes. 'They just spend all their time talking about the old days.'

Grace studied her in silence. Maybe Luke had a point. Why was she wasting her time trying to talk to this selfish woman? She downed her tea and stood up. 'I've got to go.'

Bridget stared. 'But you've only just got here. I thought maybe you could stay the night.'

'Sorry, I can't.'

Bridget walked her to the door and clung on tightly when Grace brushed her cheek against hers. 'Thanks, Grace.'

'No problem.'

When she got home, the house was silent and dark. Kicking off her shoes, she went upstairs and opened the bedroom door as gently as she could. As soon as she saw Michael's rigid back turned firmly away from her, she knew he was just pretending to be asleep. Well, that suited her just fine. The last thing she needed tonight was a row. Quickly slipping out of her clothes, she went into the bathroom, took off her make-up and brushed her teeth. When she climbed into bed and turned off the lamp, Michael didn't move. Closing her eyes, Grace tried to relax and decided the best way to do it was to forget about Luke, Bridget and Michael and instead imagine herself in Alastair's fragrant orchard. Within minutes she was asleep.

Chapter 8

Rosa shut the hall door, went through to the kitchen and set the oven dish carefully down on the table. There was no note from Grace so she'd just do a general tidy around and then clean the fridge and cooker.

'Hey, Rosa.'

Rosa whirled around and smiled. 'Grace! What are you doing here?'

'I have an appointment on the north side of the city at ten-thirty so it wasn't worth going into the office. How are you?'

'Fine, fine.'

Grace leaned against the counter-top and studied the attractive Italian brunette. 'Any gossip?'

Rosa made a face. 'Where would I get gossip?'

'Oh, I don't know, I thought you might have met a wonderful Irishman who'd swept you off your feet.'

'Huh! No chance! Your men, they are too pale and they moan too much. Oh, I don't mean Michael, of course.'

Grace grinned. 'Oh, I don't know, he's pale and he moans. What about Alastair?'

Rosa's eyes twinkled. 'Now he is a very attractive man, even if he *is* Irish!'

Grace laughed. 'Better not let Miriam catch you talking about her husband like that.'

Rosa shrugged. 'It's a compliment. Now, Grace, is there anything particular you wanted me to do?'

'Not really.' Grace lifted the lid on the oven dish and sniffed. 'What's this?'

'Chicken cacciatora and no, there's no celery in it.'

'You know Michael well.'

'I know his stomach,' Rosa replied. 'Now, you just need to warm this in a low oven or the microwave.'

'Thanks, Rosa, we'd live on cheese on toast if it wasn't for you. Hey, I'd be divorced if it wasn't for you!' She took the dish and put it in the fridge.

Rosa started to empty the dishwasher. 'Cooking, it's not so hard.'

'It is if you don't know how,' Grace assured her.

'You are good at what you do.'

'Yes I'm a lot better mixing paint than mixing batter, unfortunately for my husband.'

Rosa frowned. 'He is proud of you.'

Grace looked surprised. 'You think so?'

'Sure. He's just not so good at showing his feelings.'

'You can say that again. Right, I'd better go. See you Thursday.'

'Goodbye, Grace, you drive carefully.'

Miriam woke up and took a moment to get her bearings.

The hand lying across her stomach brought it all back and she smiled a slow, satisfied smile before carefully removing the arm and sliding out of bed. It had just turned six and with luck she'd be back in her own room on the fourth floor before the hotel woke up.

'Miriam?' The man in the bed stirred as she pulled her dress over her head.

'Go back to sleep, it's early.'

'Come back here then and let me wake you up properly.'

'Sorry, darling, I have a massage booked for seven and I need to shower first.'

'I could give you a massage,' he drawled.

'If you did, I would definitely miss my plane. See you at breakfast?'

'Sure you want to eat?' he countered.

'Are you kidding? After last night, I'm famished.'

'Oh, well then, if you insist. Nine-thirty?'

'Perfect.' She blew him a kiss and left.

Miriam let herself back into her room, lit a cigarette and took a bottle of water out of the mini-bar. The massage appointment was fictitious; what she did have organized was a facial and a blow-dry. Looking good took a lot more effort as the years passed. It was why she made it a policy to always go to the man's room and disappear in the early hours. Even though she was in reasonable shape, Miriam never let a man see her body in daylight – well, except for dear old Alastair, of course. When she was naked she knew there was no hiding the ageing process, but with expertly applied make-up, a sharp haircut and stylish clothing she could hold her own against much younger women. When she walked into the dining room later that morning, she knew Nigel Prince would want to take her straight back to bed – and that's exactly the way she liked to leave him.

Nigel was the buyer for a large chain of boutiques based in London and she'd first met him at a fashion show in Dublin that was showcasing new Irish talent. That was almost six months ago now and they met up each time she was in London for dinner and a night of very enjoyable sex. Nigel was the perfect lover in that he was happy to give as much as he got; Miriam never gave anything away for free.

Apart from the fact that he was married, had three kids and lived in Gravesend, Miriam knew very little about Nigel, and that suited her fine. He did ask her about her life occasionally but she usually managed to steer the conversation in a different direction. The only successful way to manage extra-marital relations was with a great deal of discretion. Miriam refused point-blank to meet up with Nigel when he was in Dublin – it was a small town and she was too well-known – and she never spent more than a night at a time with him, although Nigel had tried to persuade her to go away for a weekend once. Miriam had fixed him with a steady gaze and informed him that it was never going to happen and if he brought it up again, their relationship would be at an end. Nigel hadn't mentioned it again.

Stubbing out her cigarette, Miriam drained her bottle of water and headed for the shower. Catching sight of her reflection in the mirror over the bath, she grimaced. Growing old was a pain in the arse, she didn't care what anyone said. Next year she would go to the States and have a face-lift, but for now make-up would have to do. Time to begin the transformation.

Miriam boarded the British Midland flight to Dublin, settled into the window seat in the front row and pulled out her Palm Pilot. She was pleased with the new contacts she'd made and the particularly hard bargain she'd driven with a supplier of the most wonderful belts and handbags. She frowned as she came across the name of the new client for Grace. God, that woman was just so ungrateful sometimes. There wouldn't *be* any clients if it wasn't for her. Grace was a wonderful designer, there was no denying that, but when it came to business she was hopeless. And what was with all that girly, modest shit? She was forty-six, about bloody time she grew up. Still, Miriam acknowledged with a small, satisfied smile, Grace's naiveté had its uses.

'Can I get you a drink?' A young, peach-skinned stewardess was smiling down at her.

'A large gin and tonic,' Miriam said immediately.

The girl quickly made her a drink and then offered her the lunch menu. Miriam waved a dismissive hand. 'When you actually serve real food you can offer me the menu.' She wasn't hungry anyway, having indulged in smoked salmon and scrambled eggs washed down with champagne. Nigel knew how to treat a woman, that was for sure, but she would need to starve for a couple of days to make up for the excesses of last night and this morning. Still, at least she'd got plenty of exercise.

Miriam took a sip of her drink and licked her lips. Sex and business was such a wonderful combination, especially, in both cases, when she was on top. She closed her eyes and smiled, remembering Nigel's long, toned body under hers. She loved the fact that there wasn't a spare inch of fat on him – not something many men in their forties could boast. Miriam couldn't abide fat and was disgusted by people who let themselves go – namely 80 per cent of her clientèle. It sickened her, seeing overweight women struggling into her beautiful clothes – what could possibly look good on them? But her love for money triumphed over her disgust every time. Of course she had the good sense to keep her feelings to herself, although she thought everyone was too bloody politically correct these days – and her husband more than most.

Alastair was still a teacher at heart, Miriam thought, not without affection. He wanted to change the world. No war, no poverty, no ozone layer and equal rights for all. Miriam was amused and at the same time turned on when he ranted about the various causes he championed. The old darling was such an idealist. An attractive one at that or, of course, Miriam wouldn't have looked twice at him. He was in very good shape for his years but she kept a close eye on him and quickly stepped in if he started to put on the pounds. It was a slippery slope, she knew, and she couldn't possibly live with a fat man. Apart from anything else, there was her image to think of.

At least she couldn't complain about Grace on that front. The woman still had the figure of a young girl with unbelievably long legs, excellent bone structure and a wonderful mane of wavy, golden-brown hair. Miriam wished she was a bit more adventurous with her wardrobe but it was hard to get Grace out of her long skirts and sloppy tops. They did suit her, Miriam acknowledged, the way she held herself and walked ensured that, but official functions demanded a more formal ensemble and Grace should realize that without being bullied into it.

The plane banked hard and the captain announced the descent into Dublin Airport. Miriam drained her glass and fidgeted in her handbag, her fingers pausing longingly over the packet of Marlboro. Alas, with the new ridiculous law she'd have to wait until she was standing at the taxi rank before she could have a smoke. It was always a difficult choice for her; fight her way out of the airport to be first in line for a taxi or hang back and have a smoke first. Rooting around, she found some chewing gum that would have to do for the moment.

Miriam, who was fearless in so many aspects of her life, was terrified of landing. She wasn't sure what it was about watching the ground come up to meet her, but she was convinced each time that, she wouldn't make it. No one, naturally, knew of this fear although if Alastair was accompanying her, he always put his hand over hers when the plane began its descent. Perhaps he knew her better than she realized. Perhaps he could read her mind.

Miriam shuddered at the thought, closed her eyes and chewed furiously.

Chapter 9

Natasha was sitting in the living room of Ken's flat watching *The Paul O'Grady Show* when her boyfriend finally surfaced. 'Hey you, I thought you were never going to wake up.'

'It was a late night or should I say an early morning,' he replied, flopping into the chair beside her with a wide yawn. 'What are you doing watching that crap?'

'You won't be saying that if you get invited on the show. Anyway, it's not crap and he's very funny.'

'Right.'

'I'll switch over to *Richard and Judy*, if you like?' she offered.

'Be still, my beating heart,' he muttered. 'Make us a coffee, will ya?'

'Sure, seeing as you asked so nicely.' Natasha stood up, dropped a kiss on his head and went into the tiny kitchen. 'Did the scout turn up then?' she called back. Ken had been all excited about the gig in Whelan's last night because apparently there was an English talent scout in town and Whelan's had a reputation for show-casing new talent.

'No idea. I hope not.'

'Why?' she asked, pouring hot water into a chipped mug.

'Because if he did, he didn't make himself known, which means he didn't rate us.'

'Oh well, I'm sure it will happen some day.' Natasha carried the coffee and packet of Hobnobs back in and set them on the rickety coffee-table. 'Maybe you should concentrate on your songwriting for a while.'

Ken shot her a sidelong glance. 'Is that your way of telling me I'm a crap singer?'

'No, of course not. You know I love your voice.' It was just the rest of the band she had problems with. She couldn't see Ken ever being discovered, as long as he was with them. Still, she was an avid viewer of *The X Factor*, and Simon Cowell was always pulling out one member of a band and sending the others home. Crikey, that was the answer! She turned to Ken, touching his dark hair affectionately. 'Maybe you should audition up for one of the TV talent contests.'

'You want me to enter a pop competition?' Ken said, his eyes wide with horror.

'Hear me out. You want to be famous, yes? You want to sing your own songs, yes? Well, getting on a pro-gramme like that would mean publicity, and though it's not your kind of thing, it's not exactly Sharon Osbourne's sort of thing either, is it? It would just be a means to an end. Think of that guy, what's his name, Tabby? He didn't win but Sharon Osboume is now his agent.'

Ken digested this in silence, his eyes alert, his fingers drumming on the table in a distracted fashion. 'How would I go about it?' he said at last.

'I have absolutely no idea but I'll check it all out if you like.'

'I like,' Ken said, pulling her on to his lap.

Natasha smiled down into his handsome face. 'But you have to promise when you do go on *The Paul O'Grady Show* to behave.'

'You can come with me and make sure I do.'

Natasha's heart skipped a beat. Ken never wanted to talk about where their relationship was going and this was the nearest he'd come to suggesting they had a future together. 'It's a date,' she murmured, before lowering her head to kiss him.

Natasha still had a smile on her face when she turned up at the Happy Days Montessori School the next morning. She had gone on to have a wonderful evening with Ken and had felt closer to him than ever before. They'd walked down to the pizza place on the corner and brought their dinner back to the flat, stopping off at the supermarket on the way to pick up wine, Pringles and chocolate. Stretched out on the floor of the living room listening to Macy Gray and Coldplay, they talked for hours about their past, their hopes and their dreams. Natasha was particularly touched when Ken finally talked about his family. It turned out that, like her, he was an only child but in his case, both of his parents were very possessive and controlling and were horrified that he wanted to go into the music industry where he would be preyed upon and exposed to the lowest of the low.

'So what did they want you to do?' Natasha had asked.

Ken laughed. 'They didn't care what career I chose as long as it was reputable, lucrative and they'd be able to brag to the relatives and neighbours about me.'

'My dad didn't want me to go into Montessori teaching,' Natasha told him, rolling onto her back and staring up at the stained ceiling.

'Why not? I would have thought every parent would be proud to have a teacher in the family.'

'Montessori isn't proper teaching as far as he's concerned.' Natasha made quote marks in the air.

'What bullshit!' Ken snuggled down next to her and kissed her on the lips. 'You take my advice, Nat, and ignore the old man. What the hell does he know?'

Natasha was in the kitchen making a coffee and reliving every wonderful moment of the previous night when Jan Prior, the owner, walked in.

'Hey, Natasha, how are you this morning?'

Natasha smiled. 'Great, how are you?'

Jan rolled her eyes. 'Tearing my hair out. Mary just called in sick, I don't know how we're going to manage.'

Mary was the glrl who ran the baby crèche along with

a trainee called Jill. 'I'd be glad to help if you like,' Natasha immediately offered.

Jan frowned. 'Well, you're supposed to be here for Montessori training . . .'

'I'm supposd to be here to learn about children,' Natasha pointed out. 'I'm sure babies have plenty to teach me too.'

'You've never said a truer word.' Jan was nodding enthusiastically. 'With babies you learn to read body language and listen for the different types of crying.'

'There you go, then. Why don't I go straight in and Jill can show me the ropes before all the babies get here. How many have we got this morning?'

'Only six, thankfully. This is very good of you, Natasha. You know, a lot of students would turn their noses up at giving bottles and changing nappies.'

'Not me, I love babies. I was very annoyed that I never had a little sister to mind so I'm going to really enjoy this.'

Jan smiled broadly. 'You do that.'

Natasha hurried through to the baby room and smiled at the sight of Jill and three babies sitting on a pretty patterned blanket, singing nursery rhymes – well, Jill was singing – and playing with plastic blocks. 'I'm your help for today,' she said, sinking down beside Jill and leaning across to tickle the nearest baby's toes.

'Oh Natasha, that's great. Your timing is perfect,' Jill said, 'because if I'm not mistaken, someone's nappy needs changing.'

Natasha sniffed the nearest baby and nodded. 'It's this one. I'll do it.' She lifted the baby girl into her arms and kissed the top of her silky head. 'Come on, little cherub, let's make you nice and clean.'

Jill stared at her. 'Are you sure?'

'Sure,' Natasha said firmly and carried the child out to the changing room, crooning softly in her ear as she went. 'You're a beautiful little girl, aren't you?'

The baby smiled a gummy smile and waved her little hands in the air. 'Arroo!'

'Yes, you are, you're beautiful.' Deftly, Natasha slipped on the disposable gloves, changed the nappy and put the dirty one in the bin. Then, holding her in one arm, she quickly disinfected the changing mat before returning to the baby room. ' So, what would you like me to do?'

'Bobby is due a feed, would you like to do that?'

'Sure.'

'His bottle is in the fridge, his name is on it and you'll need to warm it first in a jug of hot water.'

Natasha went into the little kitchen, put on a kettle to boil and went to get the bottle. 'Would you like me to make you a coffee while I'm at it?' she called.

'No, no hot drinks in here while the babies are up.' Jill's tone was sharp.

'Oh sorry, that was silly of me.'

Jill shook her head. 'No, it was a kind thought but even though these little ones don't move around much, accidents can happen very easily. Jan is happy for us to have a cuppa when they're in their cots or in the high-chairs, but I prefer to wait until it's break-time and have it in the staff room. It's safer and I'm able to enjoy it more. There's a filtered water tap on the sink if you ever need a drink, though.'

'Great, thanks.' Natasha took the bottle out of the jug of water and checked the temperature of the milk on her wrist. Carrying it back in, she settled herself on the floor with her back against a squishy sofa and took the baby up in her arms. 'Hello, Bobby, are you ready for your bottle?' Bobby opened his mouth and made a swipe at the bottle. Natasha laughed. 'I'll take that as a yes!'

'You're a natural,' Jill remarked as she settled the other two babies in their chairs for breakfast. 'Could I tempt you away from Montessori?'

Natasha shook her head. 'No, I love teaching, I don't ever want to do anything else. But any time you need a hand I'd be happy to help.'

That was their last chance for a chat for over an hour. Within minutes three other babies had arrived and Natasha was caught up in a whirlwind of feeding, burping and changing. 'Wow, I never realized how much work babies were,' she marvelled after she'd tucked one little girl into her cot and crept out of the nursery.

Jill was flopped on a bean bag, winding a sleepy baby whose long lashes were drooping on her pink cheeks. 'It's quiet today,' Jill told her. 'On Fridays we have eight babies and the other two are ten months and eleven months and have started to walk. I tell you, they keep

you on your toes! Okay, little one, time for bed.' She
stood up and carried the baby into the nursery. 'You can
take your break now if you like, Natasha,' she said when
she came out again.

'If it's okay with you, I'll keep an eye on them and do
some studying.'

Jill beamed. 'Hey, I never say no to an extra dose of
caffeine. I'll be back in fifteen minutes.'

When she was alone, Natasha went into the nursery and
gazed down at the little children, their arms flung out
and their faces peaceful and innocent. She smiled and
then went back into the baby room, fetched a textbook
from her bag and settled down to read. Within seconds
she was lost in the world of child psychology, her brow
wrinkled in concentration, her fingers absently plucking
at the cuff of her jumper.

'All quiet?' Jan had put her head around the door.

Natasha nodded. 'They're all wonderful.'

'I wonder will you still be saying that at six o'clock?'
Jan laughed and left her to it.

Chapter 10

Grace slammed down the phone and threw her pencil across the room. 'Shit, shit, shit.' She was not having a good day, and the latest conversation with an irate fabric supplier hadn't helped matters.

Grace had arrived in the office to be told by Lily, her best seamstress, that Miriam had left for Milan first thing and wouldn't be back until Friday. Normally that wouldn't have bothered Grace, but today it seemed that Miriam had left an unholy mess in her wake and there was no one but Grace to clean it up. She really didn't need this, she thought, sitting back in her chair and staring at a crack in the yellowed ceiling. Things were fraught in the Hughes household and Grace had been happy to escape the cool atmosphere this morning. She was working more and more from the office, and she didn't like to dwell on the reason why. Matters weren't helped by the fact that Bridget was always on the doorstep or on the phone.

For the most part, Michael didn't comment although he made his feelings clear with a look or a curl of the lip.

Grace didn't know what he expected her to do. Was she to turn her back on her friend in her hour of need? What kind of person would she be if she did such a thing? And it wasn't as if she was having a fun time. Bridget happy was good company, but Bridget miserable was another story. Grace felt the only time she had any real peace was when she was working, and now Miriam had screwed that up. She was going to have to abandon her design of a romantic bedroom in order to search her partner's untidy office for the missing invoice, or cheque or some evidence that Miriam had paid the supplier's bill. Sighing heavily, she went into the work room to talk to Lily. 'I'm going to have to try and sort this out, Lily. Can I divert the phone out here?'

Sure.' Lily looked up from her machine.

'But if Miriam phones, put her straight through.' Miriam wasn't answering her phone or the frantic text messages that Grace had sent her. That usually meant only one thing; there was a man on the scene. Grace put her partner and her seedy little affairs out of her mind and went into Miriam's untidy office. The pile of papers on her desk and overflowing from the filing cabinet were enough to make Grace turn on her heel, but the sooner she got stuck in, the sooner she could get back to her own work. Seating herself in Miriam's chair, she pulled the in-basket towards her. Knowing her partner's penchant for not paying suppliers until the last day of credit, it seemed like a good place to start.

But the Foley Fabrics invoice was not in the in-tray,

nor was there a cheque in the out-tray. With a heavy heart, Grace turned to the filing cabinet hoping that, against all odds, Miriam would have some sort of filing system that would quickly become apparent. She hadn't. Grace ended up sitting on the floor sorting through the mess. As she worked, she placed the documents into different bundles, promising herself that she would bully Miriam into hiring a secretary on her return. It was ridiculous, given the size of their business, that they didn't have one. Sometimes Miriam's parsimonious ways were very annoying and in this case, a downright liability. Grace pulled her hair back from her face and picked up a chequebook stub. As she scanned the names and amounts – at least Miriam had filled them in – she wondered at the number of names that meant nothing to her. Given some of the large sums, this seemed ridiculous. Perhaps Michael was right and she should take more notice of the administration of her own company. Still, these names could relate to boutique business which was none of her concern. She decided to speed up the process a little and called the manager of Miriam's Dublin branch.

'Annabel, sorry to trouble you, I wonder could you help me? It's just that Miriam's not here today and I could do with some help trying to track down a supplier. Can I call out some names and see if you recognize them?'

By the time Grace hung up five minutes later there was a strange unease in the pit of her stomach and beads of sweat on her forehead. Returning to Miriam's desk she re-examined the out-tray and then leafed through Miriam's address book. There was just one last thing to do now. Going back to her own desk in the work room, she signed on to the internet.

'Any luck?' Lily asked.

'Not yet.' Grace kept her head down in an attempt to discourage conversation. Lily took the hint and went back to her sewing. Bringing up an Irish search engine, Grace typed in the first company name that neither she, nor Annabel, had ever heard of. She let out a relieved sigh when an entry appeared, but her relief was short-lived when, on entering the site, she discovered it was an electronics firm. Doggedly, she entered each of the names, sometimes finding no sites and other times finding company names that had nothing to do with either interior design or clothing.

Shutting the lid of her laptop, Grace stood up and went back into Miriam's office. It was only when she was safely inside, with the door closed, that she allowed her legs to give way and she sank on to the floor, the evidence of Miriam's corruption scattered all around her. There were payments of varying amounts to totally fictitious companies, and Grace could only assume that at some stage they fed back to Miriam's account. How long this had been going on, Grace had no idea, but possibly from day one. Grace couldn't understand it. The Lady M's boutiques were doing well and Graceful Living was doing well, so why would Miriam cheat her?

Realizing that she would need a lot more information before confronting her partner, Grace decided to spend the remainder of the week going through the accounts with a fine tooth-comb. She would also set up a meeting with the bank and the accountant, although it occurred to her now that the accountant could be in on it too. Resting her head in her hands she closed her eyes as a wave of nausea swept over her. She sat staring into space for what seemed like ages but was in fact only a few minutes before her sadness and confusion was replaced by fury and indignation. How dare Miriam treat her like this? She would regret it, Grace vowed, standing up and going back to sit at the desk. Grace would document every bit of evidence and then she would go to the police. Miriam would pay dearly for her crime and by the time Grace finished with her, she would have no friends, no business associates and no business.

'Wow, look at this place!' Lily stood in the doorway, a mug of tea in her hand. 'I'm just going but I thought you could probably use a cuppa.'

Grace smiled. 'Thanks.' It was almost three o'clock and she'd been working steadily since eleven.

'You know, Miriam won't be able to find a thing when she gets back. She seems to thrive on being surrounded by chaos.'

'That's tough,' Grace retorted. 'Thanks for the tea, Lily. Put on the answering machine on your way out, would you?'

Lily's eyes widened. Grace had never spoken to her like that before. 'Sure,' she said, retreating and closing the door none too gently behind her.

Grace was about to follow the other woman and apologize but decided against it. She had enough on her plate at the moment and Lily would make allowances for her when she heard exactly what Miriam had been up to. Going to the filing cabinet she pulled out the last drawer and carried the contents to the desk. 'Now, Miriam, what other little secrets have you got tucked away in here?' she muttered, her face grim.

Her investigation so far had revealed eight fictitious companies that received amounts as little as 200 Euros and as much as 1,200 Euros over a steady period. Miriam had been clever and never gotten too greedy. A large amount would have created a blip on the monthly statements that she copied to Grace. Her other trick, Grace realized, was embellishing orders. Miriam often bought stock for Grace through her boutique account and then invoiced Grace, and occasionally where Grace had ordered two bales, Miriam was charging her for four. All small stuff, but it added up. Grace cursed her stupidity for not taking more interest in her own accounts; Miriam had played her for a fool. Reaching into her pocket she took out her mobile phone and switched it off. She no longer wanted to talk to Miriam Cooper, not until she was ready.

Michael wouldn't be at all surprised when he found out about Miriam's duplicity. He had never liked or trusted the woman, and he'd been incredulous that Grace had taken so little control of her own finances. She cringed as she thought of the times he'd almost begged her to let his accountant check the books, but she'd refused point blank, saying it would be wrong to show so little faith in her partner.

'Stupid, stupid, stupid,' she said now, 'but those days are over.' She didn't think she'd ever trust anyone again. For the first time she felt some empathy with Luke and how he must feel about Bridget's obsession with his money.

With an energy born out of anger, Grace worked steadily through the day. When she had enough information to go on, she called Bob Robinson and asked him to come straight over. Bob had run the accounts department in the store she and Bridget used to work in and they had always been good friends. He was retired now but Grace knew she could trust him implicitly and he would be able to confirm her fears or tell her she was making a mountain out of a molehill.

Two hours later, Bob gave her his verdict.

'I'm so sorry, Grace,' he said finally, taking off his glasses.

Grace buried her face in her hands and shook her head. 'I just can't believe it. How could I have been so stupid?'

'You had no reason to suspect her. She is your partner, after all. She's been very clever.' Bob put his glasses back on. 'And as she's the main buyer for both companies and does all the travelling, it was easy for her to invent fictitious companies in other countries. But all the same, I'm surprised your auditors didn't pick up on something.'

Grace groaned. 'The auditors always worked with Miriam's accountant and then she would sign off their report.'

Bob sighed. 'It seems as if she had every angle covered. Don't feel bad, Grace, not many people would have picked up on this. What does Michael make of it?'

Grace didn't meet his eyes. 'I haven't told him yet. I wanted to be sure of my facts before I worried him – you know what he's like.'

Bob nodded. 'Well, I'm afraid your instincts were right. She has defrauded you to the tune of several hundred thousand – that we know about, that is.'

'So what do I do next?'

'Contact your lawyer and he'll get in touch with the Garda Bureau of Fraud Investigation. They'll advise you of where to go from here, but basically you should be ensuring that Miriam can't access any of the business bank accounts, cancel her credit cards, change the computer passwords, that sort of thing. It's damage limitation. We don't want her getting her hands on any more of your money, but it's also necessary to protect the evidence.'

'But surely once I have all this, it's proof enough?' Grace waved her hand at the documents in front of them.

'It might be proof but it won't necessarily mean you get your money back. You're opening a can of worms here, Grace. You may not be the only one she's hood-winked. Look, why dont you give your lawyer a call right now. I'll have a word with him for you, if you like.'

Grace shook her head wearily. 'It's nearly six, Bob, he'll be long gone. I'll call him first thing. You go on home, and thank you so much for your help. I don't know what I'd have done without you.'

Bob hugged her. 'I wish I'd been able to give you better news.'

'I'm going to need someone to look after my accounts. I don't suppose you'd consider coming out of retirement?'

He threw back his head and laughed. 'Sorry, not a chance – not even for you, Grace!'

She smiled. 'Oh well, it was just an idea.'

'Leave it with me, I might know someone who could help.'

When she was alone again, Grace made a list of what she needed to do the next day and then picked up the phone and dialled home. Her husband answered, and he was clearly livid.

'Where the hell are you?' he barked.

'The office – why, what's wrong? Is it Natasha?'

'What's wrong is you invited Bridget over for dinner, apparently, and we've been sitting here like idiots look-ing at each other for the last two hours.'

'Oh shit, I completely forgot.'

'I gathered that.'

'I'm on my way,' she promised. 'I'll pick up some Chinese, shall I?'

'Don't bother, I defrosted one of Rosa's casseroles.'

'Great, right, be there in ten minutes,' she said, hung up and grabbed her bag and jacket.

Looking around, she wondered what to do with all the incriminating evidence. If she were to take it with her, it would delay her even further and Michael would be furious. There was no need really, as no one else would be here all week. However, if Miriam did decide to return as abruptly as she'd left, Grace didn't want her to be able to hide any of the evidence she'd uncovered. Grace decided to lock the office door instead and pocketed the key before going out to her car.

All the way home she debated what to tell Michael. She wouldn't be able to say anything while Bridget was there – the girl was a friend, but Grace had no intention of telling her what had happened. Maybe it was just as well. Grace didn't feel up to listening to Michael saying, 'I told you so.' She felt exhausted and still slightly sick, and her heart was thumping in her chest. She was looking forward to a large glass of wine and a sleeping tablet, otherwise a long and restless night lay ahead of her.

'Sorry,' she murmured to Michael when he met her at the door. 'How is she?'

'Weepy.'

Grace hurried past him into the living room. 'Bridget, I'm so sorry. I completely forgot you were coming over.'

Bridget returned her hug. 'That's okay, Michael has been taking care of me.'

He smiled. 'My pleasure. Now, I'll leave you to it, there's a match starting.'

'We can go out to the kitchen if you want,' Grace offered.

'That's okay, I'll watch it in the bedroom. There's some dinner in the oven for you.'

'Thanks.' Grace smiled gratefully but she couldn't face the thought of food and instead poured herself a glass of wine, topped up Bridget's and sat down. 'So, how are things?' Bridget had already obviously had a lot to drink and was slouched in her seat, her head lolling to one side and her eyes half-closed.

'I'm fine, just fine.' Bridget waved her glass around precariously. 'Luke has cancelled all of my credit cards and says he's only going to pay one more electricity and phone bill and then I'm on my own.'

Grace sighed. None of this was news. Luke had given Bridget notice before cancelling her cards and promised to pay the household bills for another two months. Really, he was being quite reasonable. 'Have you thought any more about selling up?' she asked.

'I certainly have not. I have no intention of leaving my home. Luke just has to come back, I want everything back the way it was.'

'I know,' Grace said gently.

'Talk to him again for me,' Bridget begged, tears rolling down her cheeks.

'Oh no, Bridget—'

'Please, Grace, you have to! You have to make him understand.'

'Understand what?'

Bridget wiped her eyes on her sleeve and looked at Grace. 'I can't be on my own.'

Grace looked in dismay at the slightly wild look in her friend's eyes. 'I'll try,' she heard herself promise.

Bridget's face lit up. 'Oh, thank you, Grace. I knew you wouldn't let me down.'

'I said I'd talk to him but it doesn't mean it will do any good,' Grace warned. 'He was very resolute the last time we talked.'

'Oh, he just wanted to teach me a lesson. When he comes back, I'll cut down on my spending, not go out as much for a few weeks and I'll have him eating out of my hand again in no time.'

Grace's sympathy dissipated. 'For God's sake, Bridget, he's not a dog. It's that attitude that made him leave in the first place.'

Bridget lit up a cigarette without asking permission and took a long drag, her eyes narrowing. 'What would you know about it?'

Grace drew back at her cutting tone. 'I don't want a row, Bridget.'

'He told you something, didn't he? What aren't you telling me, Grace?'

'Nothing, absolutely nothing. Look, Bridget, it's late.'

'I'm not going anywhere until you tell me what you and Luke talked about.'

Grace looked her straight in the eye. 'I told you everything but if you don't trust me, I certainly won't go and talk to him again.'

Immediately, Bridget's expression changed and she became an insecure, weepy mess again. She changed moods so quickly, Grace was beginning to wonder if it was all just an act.

'I'm sorry, Grace, don't mind me. I just don't know whether I'm coming or going.' She drained her glass and looked expectantly at the bottle on the table.

Grace stood up. 'I'm going to call a taxi for you, it's late.'

'When will you go and see him – tomorrow?'

Grace thought of the state she'd left Miriam's office in. 'No, I have a lot on tomorrow.'

'Then when?'

Grace felt a wave of annoyance at her friend's pressure, as if she didn't have responsibilities and problems of her own. Ha, that was a laugh! 'I don't know when.' She picked up the phone and dialled the nearest taxi rank. After she was promised that a car would be with her in five minutes, Grace sat down beside Bridget and took her hand. 'In the next couple of days, okay?'

Bridget nodded and smiled. 'Yeah, thanks. Sorry for being so pushy, it's just my nerves, they're in shreds.'

You're not the only one, Grace thought. 'It's okay, I understand – but just remember I'm your friend.'

'My only friend,' Bridget sobbed and pulled Grace into a fierce hug.

Grace patted her shoulder, relieved to see a taxi pulling up outside. 'Your car's here. Go home and get a good night's sleep, I'll call you as soon as I've talked to Luke.'

'I know yo're busy, Grace, but—'

'I'll contact him as soon as I can.' Grace led her towards the door.

'Okay, then. Night.'

Grace watched her friend wobble slightly as she made her way out to the car. 'Goodnight, Bridget.'

'She's gone then.' Grace was sitting having a cup of tea at the kitchen table when Michael appeared in the door-way.

'Yes.'

He sat down across from her. 'You look very tired.'

'Yeah, well, it's been an incredibly long, incredibly horrible day.'

'Why – what happened?' Michael's face creased in concern.

Grace hesitated. He would have to know about Miriam's duplicity sooner or later, but if his reaction was of the 'I told you so' variety, Grace thought she might well hit him. 'Oh, it's nothing really, just one of those days when anything that could go wrong, did. A good night's sleep and I'll be right as rain.'

Chapter 11

Bridget spent all of her time in bed or wandering around the house in her silk dressing-gown, only dragging on some clothes when she was forced to go out for wine or cigarettes. She had put on the answering machine and switched off her mobile, but any time she checked for messages there were none. No one gave a damn, she decided, wallowing in self-pity.

Now it was Saturday, a day she normally spent in the hair-salon, followed by lunch in town and an afternoon of shopping. She'd come home laden with bags and then spend a couple of hours beautifying herself before going out with Luke.

She lit her eighth cigarette of the day – it was only midday – and inhaled deeply. Catching sight of herself in the bedroom mirror, she frowned. She looked bloody awful, and as she moved closer to the glass, she noticed some fine lines around her eyes and mouth that definitely hadn't been there before. She stubbed out the cigarette and grabbed a jar of expensive cream. As she patted it gently on her skin, she wondered how she was going to be able to afford to keep up her skincare regime. Tears welled up and she sobbed quietly as she tried to massage away the lines. It wasn't fair. How on earth was she supposed to survive? The thought of getting a job appalled her and she couldn't even figure out what she might do. Going back to work in a department store was out of the question. She cringed as she imagined friends coming in to shop and whispering and laughing at her. There was no way she'd stand the humiliation. A new man was the only answer – and he'd have to be rich, a lot richer than Luke bloody Cooper.

Going to her wardrobe she flung it open and looked at the clothes she owned. They were jammed in, in no particular order; some garments were half off the hanger while some had ended up in a pile on the floor. She was going to have to take more care of her stuff, she realized. It would be a while before she could buy anything new. It would be an investment though, to send some of her better clothes to the dry cleaners, and some of her boots and shoes could do with new heels too. Bridget felt a bit better now that she'd made a decision, even if it was a very minor one.

Opening Luke's wardrobe, she started to pull everything out and pile it in the corner. It didn't take long. Luke had been annoyingly neat and only ever bought clothes after she'd nagged him to death or thrown out some old ones. Usually he lived in jeans and T-shirts, adding a thick workshirt in the winter and replacing his trainers with heavy boots. Of course, with his looks it didn't matter what he wore, but Bridget liked the idea of finding a man who wore suits. She'd had it with trades-men, even good-looking ones. Luke should have had his own business by now, and he would have if he'd accepted Miriam's offer. She'd wanted to set him up in business, but naturally he was too proud to take her money.

Bloody fool, she fumed, kicking a denim jacket on to the pile and then turning back to her own wardrobe. She would move all of her summer stuff and her shoes to Luke's wardrobe, and that would give her a lot more room. Her winter wardrobe badly needed updating and the colours this season were gorgeous, but Bridget knew she'd have to manage with what she'd got. Her face fell into a moody pout. She didn't like having to deny herself things and the concept of thriftiness had always been an alien one. Looking down at her chipped nail varnish, she realized that she was going to have to start doing her own manicures and it wouldn't end there. She wouldn't be able to afford to go to the beauty salon and get her legs waxed, her eyebrows shaped, her fake tan applied. 'Fuck you, Luke Cooper!' she screamed, hurling a heavy workboot across the room. 'You've ruined everything.'

She ran down to the kitchen for some black sacks and took them back upstairs. She jammed Luke's belongings into them and when she'd finished that job she took another sack into the bathroom and dumped any rem-nants of the man into it. Next, she went down to the living room and rummaged through their large collection of CDs. Most of them were Luke's but Bridget kept what she liked and threw the rest in the sack on top of his shower gel and dental floss.

She was definitely better off without him, she fumed, though it still infuriated her that he'd been the one to end it. She scanned the room for more of his possessions, her expression softening as she appreciated the white leather sofas, honey-coloured walls and deep golden carpet. She loved this flat, especially this room, and though they'd bought it together it had always been more hers than Luke's. Any time she'd shown him colour charts or catalogues, he'd smile, kiss her and tell her to pick whatever she wanted and not to worry about money – and that's exactly what she'd done.

'Can you afford this?' had been Miriam's first question when she'd come to visit and Bridget had seen the disapproving look in her eye. She hadn't said much but Bridget knew that Miriam didn't approve of her beloved little brother's girlfriend. It got worse when Bridget gave up work. Miriam was apoplectic. 'How will you manage?' she'd asked Luke, but her eyes had been on the designer leather skirt Bridget was wearing. Luke had been his usual relaxed self. He said Bridget was miserable in her job and life was too short for that. Miriam had muttered something about most people hating their jobs but they just got on with it.

'Don't mind Miriam,' Luke had said later when they were alone. 'She's a workaholic and she can't understand why anyone would want to be idle.'

'That's easy to say when you're the boss,' Bridget had snapped but Luke had immediately jumped to his sister's defence.

'Miriam has worked her butt off since she was sixteen,' he told her, 'and she practically raised me.'

Bridget had quickly learned that she'd have to keep her opinion of Miriam to herself. She was eleven years older than Luke and as he'd lost his mother when he was very young, Miriam had become more like a mother than a sister. Though he accepted that his sister and girlfriend would never be close, Luke made it clear that he expected Bridget to at least show his sister the respect she deserved.

Bridget could just about manage that and, it had to be said, Miriam had her uses. Thanks to her, Bridget alwys got free tickets to all the fashion extravaganzas and was included in Miriam's celebrated dinners.

But those days were over. Miriam had probably been popping champagne corks since Luke told her they'd broken up. She'd have a bevy of beautiful, successful women lined up to introduce to her beloved baby brother and would do whatever it took to make sure he didn't come back to her.

Bridget sank on to a sofa, her eyes clenched tight in pain. No more fashion shows, no more premières, no more dinners. She opened her eyes. Unless she found a rich, successful man who moved in the same circles ... My God, she could just imagine Miriam's face when she turned up at an event on another man's arm. She licked her lips, anticipating the pleasure Miriam's fury would give her. All she had to do now was figure out who the most suitable candidate was and how to get close enough to him to put her plan into action.

Feeling distinctly better, Bridget moved all the black sacks into the hall and went to have a shower. It seemed to have completely slipped her mind that only last night she'd begged Grace to talk to Luke and ask him to come home.

Natasha sat in her bedroom hunched over her laptop wishing she had never promised Ken she'd research talent contests for him. He had dragged her along to a gig last night promising to have her home by twelve, but he hadn't figured on the band's clapped-out van breaking down. Natasha hadn't got to bed until just after two. She yawned widely and pulled her thin cardigan tighter around her. She was due in school in two hours and instead of mucking about on the internet, she should be studying. But Ken was all excited now at the idea of being discovered and he was on to her day and night to see if she'd made any progress. That had been the best part, of course. Usually Nat was the one to do all the phoning and texting. She hated it because it made her feel needy and pathetic, but she couldn't help herself. There was something about Ken that she just couldn't resist.

A sharp rap on the door made her jump. She turned her head to see her dad standing there.

'Oh, you're up,' he said brusquely.

'Yeah.'

'Shouldn't you be going?'

'I'm not due in until ten.'

'Oh, okay. Why don't you come down and have some breakfast?'

'Nah, I'm not hungry.'

Michael sighed impatiently. 'You can't do a day's work without some food inside you.'

Nat didn't take her eyes off the screen. 'I'll get something in there.'

'You got in late last night.'

Nat said nothing.

'What time was it?'

'About two.'

'That's madness during the week. I'm not sure you should be minding kids when you're half-asleep.'

Nat swallowed hard. As if he cared. 'Dad, I'm trying to study.'

'It looks like you're just messing about to me,' he muttered and left, closing the door with an angry click.

Nat resumed her search although she knew she was wasting her time. Though there were plenty of websites with gossip about the *Pop Idol* and *X Factor* competitions, none of them gave any details about how to audition for the competition. Nat hadn't even established when the next contest – if there was one – was going to be. She went into a different search engine and typed POP IDOL and sighed at the flood of sites, most of them irrelevant. She typed in POP IDOL AUDITIONS instead. Again she got plenty of results but none gave any information on the next compettion. 'Dammit,' she muttered, and then noticed the sponsored website at the top of the page. www.starnow.co.uk. She clicked on the site and brightened as she read through the page. There were hundreds of advertisements for models, actors, singers and musicians, not only for the UK but all over the world. 'Wow,' Nat breathed, and then groaned again when she saw there were 629 entries under 'musicians'. It would take hours to go through all this. She added the website to her favourites list and closed down the machine. She would have a proper look at it when she got home from work this evening.

Going to the mirror, she pulled a comb through her short crop of golden-brown hair, tucked it behind her ears, dabbed on some lip gloss and she was ready. Grabbing her rucksack, she slung her denim jacket over her shoulder and ran downstairs, whistling softly. 'Bye, Dad!' she yelled, let herself out of the house and walked quickly down the drive. He was due to head out himself about now and the last thing she wanted was a lift.

Being cooped up in a car stuck in morning traffic with her dad was her idea of a nightmare, it was always when they had the worst of their rows. Michael would start to drum impatiently on the wheel, weave between lanes and shout abuse at other drivers. It drove Nat round the twist and scared her too. How could her usually quiet if grumpy father turn into such a monster when he got behind the wheel? He had been offering to teach her to drive for years now, but she always turned him down for this reason. She would much prefer lessons from her mother, but Grace was always too busy. Thankfully, college and school were both on a bus route so she didn't need a car to commute. Still, the independence would be nice and it would be especially nice to go out with Ken in a decent car rather than in a manky van surrounded by his equally manky friends.

She got into school early and headed immediately to her classroom to set out the chairs and the materials they would be using that morning. It was a big enough job as they had about eight to ten activities in one morning; the children couldn't really concentrate on one thing for more than fifteen minutes at a time. She was making playdough with flour, oil and water when her boss walked in.

'Oh great, Nat, you're in!' Jan said, looking a bit flustered. 'I got caught in some terrible traffic – I thought I was going to be there all day.'

'There's something to be said for quality bus corridors, so. I got here in thirty minutes.'

'Maybe I should try it. Why don't I make us a coffee? We have a good ten minutes before the troops arrive.'

'I'd love one.' Nat put the bowl of dough to one side and went to clean her hands. 'Jan do you watch *Pop Idol* and *The X Factor*?'

Jan nodded enthusiastically as she spooned coffee into

two mugs. 'I love them, they're a great laugh. I can't believe some of the people who go in for them, they're so crap.'

'I'm sure that's a set-up,' Nat said. 'It just makes good TV.'

'Ah yes, we love to watch people make fools of themselves, don't we?'

'Why is that?'

Jan shrugged. 'Because we're glad it's not us.'

Nat leaned against the counter and took the mug Jan offered. 'My boyfriend is thinking of entering. I'm checking out websites at the moment trying to find out how he goes about it.'

'You just turn up on the day.'

Nat made a face. 'Well, yes, but which day?'

'I doubt if there will be any auditions before the New Year. *The X Factor* is on at the moment, after all.'

'That's true.'

'So what does your boyfriend do?'

'He has his own band. They're called Cutting It.'

Jan shook her head. 'Sorry, can't say I've heard of them. Are they a boy band?'

Nat laughed. 'God, no! They're kind of a cross between punk and garage.'

Jan looked blank. 'Oh.'

'They're not much good,' Nat confided, 'but Ken is great. He can sing and write. I thought that if he got some exposure someone might pick up on his talent.'

'Yeah, look at Darius and that Irish guy.'

'Tabby.'

'That's him. He's doing okay, isn't he?'

'I'm not sure, I think so.'

'So how does Ken feel about going in for a competition like this?'

'Initially he was completely against it, but now I think he's quite excited by the idea. He's been gigging around the country for three years now and he isn't getting anywhere fast.'

'So will he go in on his own or with the group?'

'If I've anything to do with it he'll be alone, but he's very loyal to his group.'

'There's no room in showbusiness for sentiment,' Jan stated. 'If he really wants to make the big time, he's going to have to look after number one.'

Nat was about to reply when the doorbell went.

'Ah, looks like the troops are arriving. Let them in, will you, Nat?'

Chapter 12

Grace fiddled nervously with her chain. Miriam would arrive at any minute and it was time to confront her. Bob would say she was completely mad, of course, but it was something she had to do. She had contacted the bank, but apart from that she had just collated all of the evidence, made copies and there was now one set locked in her office at home and one in the car that she would take to the lawyer tomorrow. She had planned to follow Bob's advice but it turned out that he was on holiday and wouldn't be back until tonight. Grace had an appointment first thing tomorrow, but Miriam had flown home last night and Grace decided she just had to face the woman and ask her why.

Grace was fully prepared for the meeting and had played it out over and over in her head. Now she sat at Miriam's desk with half a dozen files on the desk in front of her. The rest of the office was immaculate. Though she had rehearsed what she would say, she knew that there was little chance of her sticking to her speech; she was too emotional. She swung from anger to disappointment but the overriding feeling was one of betrayal. She knew that Miriam was a hard-nosed businesswoman who tricked and threatened her way throuh life but naively, Grace had thought she was exempt. She was Miriam's partner; they were on the same side – or so she had thought. Now, she didn't know what to think. She'd been in a turmoil the last few days, especially when it occurred to her that maybe Luke – or worse, Alastair – knew all about Miriam's deception. It was hard to cope with what Miriam had done, but it would be unbearable if they had known about it too.

Grace jumped as she heard Miriam try to open the door. She smiled. The one thing she had gone ahead with was changing the locks. She went out to the door and let Miriam in. Her partner pushed past her, laden down with briefcase, handbag and shopping. 'What's going on, Grace? Have,you changed the locks?'

Grace followed her through to the office. 'Yes, I have.' Her throat was dry and she was conscious of a tremble in her voice.

Miriam didn't seem to hear her. She had dropped her bags and was staring in horror around her? 'What the fuck is going on? What have you done to my office? You know I like it the way it was.'

'Yes – and now I know why.'

Miriam looked at her and then back at the clutter-free filing cabinets and desk, but not before Grace saw the nervous look in her eye. 'What's got into you, Grace? If you fancy a springclean, take it out on your own home and leave me to my mess.'

'I would have done, only Tom Fox was on looking for a cheque and as you weren't around I was the only one to sort it. You know, it's funny, I've been nagging you to get a secretary for ages—'

'I will—'

'And if you'd listened to me,' Grace carried on as if she hadn't spoken, 'I'd never have found out.'

Miriam slipped into the chair opposite, her eyes on her partner. 'Found out what?'

Grace laughed humourlessly. 'I know, Miriam. I know everything.'

'What do you mean?'

'You'd make a great poker-player, you know? You don't give anything away. But the bad news is that I know what's in your hand.' Grace opened the top file and took out a single A4 sheet. Keeping her eyes on the other woman, she slid it across the table. On it was printed the list of fictitious companies and the total amounts they'd been paid.

'What is this?' Miriam's expression was blank.

'You know damn well what it is!' Grace exploded. 'Don't dare try bluffing your way out of this one. I have all the evidence right here.' She indicated the other files but slapped her hand down on them when Miriam went to grab them. 'Oh no, you're not getting your hands on any of this – and even if you did, do you really think that there's only one copy?'

'How am I supposed to defend myself if I don't even know what I'm supposed to have done?'

'The list in your hand tells you everything you need to know. Those companies don't exist. You have been robbing me blind, almost since the day Graceful Living opened for business.'

Miriam smirked. 'Oh come on, you're exaggerating.'

'Am I? Look at the figure at the bottom of the page. That's more than a year's salary for me.'

'I'm entitled to my cut. I do it this way so the taxman doesn't get his grubby little hands on it. It's really nothing for you to worry about, Grace. It's just paperwork. You wanted me to look after the administration and I have. Okay, so I have my own way of doing things, but you've done okay too.'

Grace stared at her in astonishment. 'Do you think that's it? Do you think I'm just going to accept that and go back to my sewing-machine?'

'Well, that's what you're good at, darling, and this is what I'm good at. That's why we make such an excellent team.'

'I have been stupid and blind,' Grace admitted, 'but no more.'

Miriam sighed, looking bored. 'There really is no need for all this fuss.'

'Well, you'd better get used to the fuss,' Grace retorted, standing up and tucking the files under her arm, 'because there will be a lot more of it after I talk to my lawyer and the police.'

Miriams eyes widened. 'You can't be serious.'

'I'm deadly serious,' Grace said, walking out the door.

'Okay, okay, you've made your point.' Miriam hurried after her, her high heels clicking noisily on the tiled floor. 'I'll write you a cheque for half of that amount, although I'm sure I don't actually owe it to you.'

'You're not getting out of this, Miriam.' Grace went into the workshop and sat down at her desk.

'Oh come on, Grace, don't get this all out of proportion.'

Grace looked at her. 'I've nothing more to say, Miriam.'

'Okay, okay, I'll give you a full refund of that amount and we'll say no more about it. '

'Do you honestly believe I'm going to continue working with you after this?' Grace asked her incredulously.

'Of course you are, don't be ridiculous.'

'It's over, Miriam. Now, please, get the hell out of my office.'

'But Grace—'

'Get out!' Grace screamed.

Shocked, Miriam backed out, stood looking in at her for a moment and then turned quickly on her heel and went back to her office.

Grace listened to her click down the corridor and the noise of her door close. Seconds later there was the sound of her voice and a one-sided conversation. She was probably on the phone to her solicitor or her accountant, trying to figure out a way to weasel out of this, Grace thought. But she wouldn't. At a loss as to what to do next, Grace sat staring into space, trying to get her breathing under control. It had all been so quick, so easy and such an anti-climax. She couldn't believe that Miriam actually thought she could laugh this off. She hadn't even looked remotely repentant. If Grace had any doubts about going to the police before, she had none now. This woman needed to get the message and Bob was right: what Miriam had done to Grace was probably only the tip of the iceberg.

Grace felt weak and sick and decided to go home and have a lie-down. When she told Michael what had happened she'd probably have to spend the rest of the day listening to him tell her that he'd never trusted Miriam Cooper from the beginning and she'd been a fool to leave all the administration to her. That thought alone kept her sitting in her chair. Maybe she could have a preliminary chat with the Garda Bureau of Fraud Investigation and find out how they would proceed. She picked up her pad and flicked through it until she found the number Bob had given her. Her hand was reaching for the phone when Miriam appeared in the doorway. 'Please don't call the police,' she said softly. 'If you do, I'm finished.'

'You should have thought of that before you decided to steal from me.'

'It wasn't like that.'

'Don't start that again,' Grace snapped, her eyes angry 'I may have been naive in leaving you to look after the finances but I'm not a complete idiot. You betrayed me, you stole from me and you're not going to get away with it.'

'That's fair enough, Grace, but if you call the police it won't be just me who will get hurt. Think of how it will affect Luke. Think of how Alastair will react. He'll hate me for this. If you make this public, my marriage is over.'

Grace looked at her. Miriam was very pale and there was a desperate look in her eye. 'Alastair doesn't know?'

'Of course not.' Miriam flopped into the chair across from her and put her head in her hands. 'You know how honourable he is and you know how highly he thinks of you.'

Grace sighed. 'Why, Miriam? Can you just tell me that? Why did you do it? You were a rich woman before we even started Graceful Living. Why risk it all for a few hundred thousand?'

Miriam looked at her and shrugged. 'It's what I do, it's what I had to do to make it.'

'Maybe in the past, but not now.'

The other woman smiled sadly. 'I suppose you can't teach an old dog new tricks.'

Grace looked at her in silence.

'I wasn't trying to do anything to you,' Miriam went on. 'You've done well out of this business and you know I've been the one to bring in many of your customers.'

'Oh please, don't try and excuse your behaviour.'

'I'm not,' Miriam said hurriedly, 'I'm just pointing out that it was never personal. Please don't go to the police.

We can sort this out between us. I'll do whatever it takes to make it up to you.'

'It's too late for that,' Grace muttered, turning away from the pleading look on her partner's face. She found this Miriam a lot harder to deal with than the bolshie one she was used to.

'Its not, Grace. It's not too late. If you won't do it for me, do it for Alastair.'

Grace shook her head. 'I can't work with you any more. I can't pretend that nothing's happened. I could never trust you after this.'

'I'll keep right out of your way,' Miriam promised. 'I'll use the office in the shop and you can have this place all to yourself. I'll hire a secretary to handle all the admin work from now on. I'll have no more to do with it. I'll sign something if you want.'

Grace looked down at the files on the desk. She knew there was probably enough in them to send Miriam to prison for a few months at least. While the thought gave her some pleasure she knew that Miriam was right and it would destroy Alastair. It would also mean she'd lose his friendship. And then there was Luke. He was devoted to his big sister but she knew he wouldn't condone her behaviour and possibly might not want anything else to do with her when he found out. As for their father, frail and old, he would be shocked if he ever heard about his daughter's behaviour. It said it all, Grace thought, that Miriam hadn't even thought of his feelings in all this. She was worried about her little brother's opinion but she had written her father off a long time ago. Luke was the one who visited him in the nursing home and took him for walks on Dun Laoire pier or to Sunday lunch. Miriam just sent him cards and gifts and phoned him occasionally when Luke nagged her about her negligence. Miriam couldn't have cared less about him in all of this. She would be deeply hurt if she lost Luke – but if she lost Alastair, Grace realized, Miriam would be devastated.

'Grace?' Miriam was looking at her. 'Can't we find some way out of this?'

Grace shook her head, confused. 'I need time to think.'

'Take as much time as you want,' Miriam agreed immediately, backing out of the office again. 'And look – I *am* sorry.'

Grace stood up, put her jacket on, took her bag and went to the door. She felt exhausted, drained and very sad. What she needed was a large drink. She was about to walk out the door when she realized she'd left the incriminating files on her desk. God, she was really losing it.

'Grace, hi.'

'Jesus!' She jumped. 'Luke, what the hell are you doing creeping up on me like that?'

'Er, the door was open. Sorry if I startled you.'

'I didn't hear you come in.'

'Sorry. Hey, are you okay?'

'Fine. Look, I've got to go. What did you want?' Grace

knew she sounded short but she felt too raw to talk to Luke now.

'I was looking for Miriam.'

'In her office. See you,' she said, came out, locked the door and brushed past him.

'Bye.' Puzzled by her manner, Luke watched her hurry away. He trod softly down to his sister's office and looked in. Miriam was sitting at her desk, her head in her hands. 'What's up?' he asked.

Miriam's head jerked up and she stared at him in surprise. 'Luke!'

'Is something wrong?' he asked, crossing the room and taking the seat opposite her. In all the years he'd been coming here he'd never seen her office so tidy.

'No, nothing's wrong,' she replied, bending her head over the file in front of her. 'What did you want? I'm really very busy.'

'It looks that way.'

His sister's eyes darted from him, to her Spartan surroundings. 'Yeah. We decided it was time to clean the place out.'

'Miriam, cut the crap and tell me what's going on. First Grace acts all weird with me, and now you look as if you've seen a ghost. You know you can tell me anything and it won't go any further.'

Miriam watched him speculatively. 'Do you mean that?'

'Of course I do.'

'You won't like it,' she warned.

'Go on.'

And so Miriam broke the habit of a lifetime and confided in her brother. Of course she didn't tell him everything; if she'd done that, he'd have handed her over to the police himself. But she told him enough to gain some sympathy and understanding, because she knew that if all of this did come out, she could lose him for ever.

She was careful to make it sound a lot more clinical than it was, making out that Grace had overreacted to a little creative accounting, but Luke wasn't taken in.

'How could you?' he asked, when she finally fell silent under his accusing gaze.

'Hey, it's the way I do business, you know me,' she joked.

Luke stared at her. 'Quite apart from the fact that she's your friend, don't you realize you could end up in jail over this?'

'It won't come to that,' his sister said immediately. 'She won't go to the police.'

'How can you be so sure?'

Miriam's expression was unreadable. 'Because I know Grace.'

When Luke left, Miriam sat in the dark and waited. She didn't know how long it was before she heard the door open and then Grace was standing in front of her.

'I want you out of Graceful Living.'

'You want to buy me out?'

Grace's laugh was humourless. 'I think I've already done that – very generously, I would say.'

Miriam opened her mouth to protest.

'It's that or I go to the police. Take it or leave it,' Grace said with a nonchalance she wasn't feeling.

'I didn't know you had it in you,' Miriam said with grudging admiration.

'You took me for a fool and maybe I deserved that, but you won't ever do it again. So, what's it to be?'

Miriam considered the question for a moment and then nodded. 'You've got a deal, but—'

'You're hardly in a position to bargain.'

'Hear me out,' Miriam retorted irritably and then forced herself to continue in a more controlled voice. 'There's no point in me doing this if everyone knows about it. We'll have to keep it just between us. If I'm suddenly out of the business, Alastair is going to want to know why. How could I possibly explain it?'

Grace shrugged. 'Tell him you want to invest the money in another shop.'

Miriam rolled her eyes. 'Yeah, that's very clever, except I won't have any money, will I?'

'How can you not have the money?'

'It's complicated.'

Grace shrugged. 'Not my problem.'

Miriam's lips twitched. 'But how would you explain it to Michael? Wouldn't he wonder where you'd got the money to buy me out?'

Grace was momentarily thrown. She hadn't

considered this and she knew, as Miriam did, that Michael would be very suspicious. 'It doesn't matter whether I pretend to buy you out now or in six months' time – either way I won't be able to explain where I got the money from.'

'Tell him the bank gave you a loan,' Miriam suggested. 'This is a successful business and you have a good track record. They'd definitely give it to you.'

Grace said nothing. The thought of all the lies involved in this crazy scheme made her head spin.

'It would work, Grace, trust me.'

Grace shot her an incredulous look.

Miriam sighed. 'Look, give me a break here, Grace, I'm trying to help. If we wait a few months and go on as normal, I'll be out of your hair and you'll be the sole owner of a very successful business. But if we split now, everyone will want to know why and I'll fight you every inch of the way before I give you a cent.'

'It will never work,' Grace disagreed. 'I won't be able to keep up the pretence. It's only a matter of time before Michael or Alastair notice something's wrong.'

'Not if they don't see us together.' Miriam was back in her stride now, back in control. 'I'll spend more time out of the country and I'll work in the shops—'

'Look, we normally see each other a couple of times a week. We go to functions together, give dinners together.'

'Please, Grace, please do this. Not for me, for Alastair. I'm begging you.'

Grace stared at her, looking for a hint of insincerity, a hint of manipulation, but all she could see was a desperate woman who suddenly looked older than her fifty-two years. 'Okay,' she whispered.

'Thank you, Grace, thank you so much. I'll phone my solicitor and get him to draw up the papers immediately.' She hurried out of the room without a backward glance.

Grace stared after her, wondering what the hell she'd agreed to. Despite Miriam's apologies, she couldn't help feeling that her partner's only real regret was getting caught.

Chapter 13

Grace was selecting handles for a client's kitchen doors when her mobile rang. She fished it out of her bag and answered it. 'Luke?'

'Yeah. How are you?'

'Fine – you?'

'Yeah, okay. I was wondering if we could meet up.'

'I'm on a job at the moment in Ballsbridge.'

'Can I buy you a drink in Searson's?'

Grace didn't really want to see him; she wasn't sure she could trust her own acting. After what Miriam had done, how could she behave normally with the woman's brother? Still, she had promised Bridget she would talk to him one more time, so here was her chance. 'Okay then. About six?'

'Great. See you then.'

Grace chose three handles and returned to the three-storey terraced Victorian house in Ballsbridge to show them to her client.

'I don't know, Grace,' Vera Sanders dithered. 'I think I'd better wait and show them to Will.'

Grace knew Will wouldn't give a shit what the handles looked like but she plastered on a professional smile and stood to leave. 'You do that and I'll call you tomorrow.'

'And I'm having second thoughts about installing a double oven.'

'Oh?' Grace struggled to keep her smile in place.

'Yes, my friend Marjorie was saying that it was positively sinful not to have an Aga.'

'Was she?' Grace had suggested keeping the more traditional style of kitchen with a contemporary twist right at the start of the project, but Vera had dismissed the idea, saying she wanted a state-of-the-art stainless-steel kitchen.

'Yes, and she said I should have a breakfast bar.'

'I think you need some more time to think this through, Vera. I'll cancel the fitter and you call me when you and Will have had a chance to talk.'

Grace walked out of the house, pausing in the porch to wind her scarf tight around her neck. Going out to the car, she dumped her file of samples into the boot, climbed behind the wheel and drove off at speed.

'The stupid cow is driving me mad,' she fumed when she was sitting in the pub with Luke, sipping a hot whisky. 'She refused to listen to any of my ideas at the beginning, me the professional, but when her cronies say it, she listens. Why the fuck did she hire me in the first place? I've wasted hours designing that kitchen, I had the marble and the appliances ordered and it's been a complete waste of time.'

Luke finished his drink and called for another round. 'It's their mistake. You just have to make it clear that they're going to have to pay up anyway.'

'You know if there's one thing I've learned about rich people, it's that they never want to pay for anything,' Grace said grumpily, then 'Anyway, I'm sure you didn't ask me to meet you to discuss kitchens.'

'No. I wanted to thank you.'

Grace frowned. 'For what?'

'For not shopping my sister.'

Grace stared at him.

'She told me everything. I know what she did, I can't believe that you are being so good about it.'

'I think I need my head examined, to be honest. She stole from me, Luke. She's a crook, she's a criminal and she deserves to be locked up for it.'

He nodded. 'You'll get no argument from me. So why did you let her off?'

Grace slumped in her seat and stared into her drink. 'I really don't know.'

'Have you told Michael?'

'Of course not, he'd be straight down to the police station.'

'But you can't keep all this to yourself. The stress of keeping a secret this huge is going to tear you apart.'

Grace's eyes narrowed suspiciously. 'So you're offering me a sympathetic ear? Relax, Luke, I've agreed not to go to the police and I won't go back on my word.'

He stared at her, his gorgeous blue eyes angry. 'Is that what you think? I'm here as your friend, Grace. I wanted to check you were okay and to apologize for Miriam. Yes, she's my sister, but please don't tar me with the same brush.'

Grace reached out to take his hand. 'I'm sorry, that wasn't fair. It's just I'm so angry with her, but more than that, I feel so hurt. Also, I feel very stupid.'

'You weren't stupid, you were trusting.'

'Not exactly a way to run a business though, is it? Michael's right, I should probably stay at home and make curtains in between cooking dinners and hoovering.'

'He doesn't say that, does he?'

Grace laughed. 'Not in so many words, but it's what he'd like.'

'Dear God, I'd be delighted to have a successful, rich wife. Mind you, after Bridget I'd settle for anyone.'

Grace looked at him and noted the sadness that had crept into his voice. 'You don't mean that.'

'I certainly do. My only regret is that I've wasted so many years on her. She's just been using me, and if anyone more eligible had come along, she'd have dumped me.'

'That's Miriam talking. I suppose she was thrilled to hear that you had left Bridget.'

'I haven't told her, and the way I feel at the moment, I don't care if I never set eyes on *her* again either.'

'Oh, come on. You're exaggerating.'

'I'm not, but I won't turn my back on her, Grace – how can I? She's my sister and she practically reared me.'

'What about your dad?'

'They've never been close.'

Luke's expression was closed and for the first time he really reminded Grace of his sister. 'It's okay, I don't expect you to denounce her,' she sighed. 'The whole point of this charade is that we all carry on as normal.'

'I can't see it working, can you?'

'No but Miriam says it will and you know what she's like when she makes up her mind. She intends to do more travelling and when she's here she'll use the office over the Dublin boutique.'

'Alastair is bound to notice.'

Grace smiled. 'Oh, I don't know. He has some very exciting plans for his garden he was telling me about. That should prove a good distraction.'

Luke shot her a speculative look. 'You two are quite close, aren't you?'

Grace shrugged. 'We have a lot in common.'

'It's going to be hard for you to hide your feelings about Miriam from him.'

'Then I'll just have to stay away from him, won't I?' Grace was surprised at how depressed she felt at the thought.

'But we can still meet,' Luke said. 'At least you'll have one person you can talk to, someone who knows the whole story.'

'Yes, but it's a bit weird that you're her brother.'

He put a finger under her chin and tilted her head so that he could look into her eyes. 'You do believe me when I say I knew nothing about what she was up to, don't you?'

Grace nodded. 'Yes, I do.'

'So if there's anything I can do, just ask. I think my family owes you quite a lot and I'm not just talking about money.'

Grace shook her head. 'No, this is between me and Miriam. Let's keep it that way.'

'Dad would be devastated if he ever found out. He's very much of the old school. Your good name is your most important possession, he always taught us.'

'How is he?' Grace asked.

'Up and down. Sometimes I go in and he's in great form and we have a good old chat about my mother and stuff about the family that I never knew. Other days though, he's very down and he barely says a word. It makes me feel really guilty because all I want to do then is get away.'

'You've nothing to feel guilty about,' Grace assured him. 'You've been a wonderful son. Miriam has left it all to you. You should have it out with her and make her do her bit.'

Luke shrugged. 'She wouldn't be any good to him, Grace. Miriam needs to be in control and if there's one thing I've learned about illness it's that there is no control. She couldn't handle it and it would only upset him, having her there. She's doing the one thing she can do;

she's paying the bills. I'd never have been able to afford to put him in a fancy place like that.'

'Somehow I think you'd have found a way,' Grace said gently. Luke was a good, kind man.

He laughed. 'Hey, you're forgetting this is the family waster you're talking to, the man with no ambition and no future.'

'Don't put yourself down like that.'

'No, I'll leave that to Bridget.'

'What made you decide to become a plumber? Grace asked curiously. 'According to Miriam, you were the brains of the family.'

Luke snorted. 'And what else has she told you?'

'Oh, nothing. Sorry, I didn't mean to pry.'

'It's okay, it's just Miriam drives me mad the way she goes on. The truth is, if you really want to know, I didn't go to university purely to get up her nose. She was always on my case to study, telling me how important it was that I got into the right college, the right course. She'd even decided that I should go for engineering – never even asked how *I* felt about it.'

'That's such a shame. Her manipulations have affected your whole life.'

'No, it's all turned out for the best, actually. I enjoy what I do and unlike Miriam, I've no real interest in being the boss.'

'Are you just saying that? Grace asked.

'No, really, I'd hate to spend my life making sure other people did their jobs properly or worrying about balance-sheets. I like working with my hands and I prefer fixing things to people any day. People are way too complicated and much more trouble.'

'I have to agree with you there,' Grace said, thinking of the number of difficult, indecisive or downright weird clients she had.

'Another drink?' he offered.

Grace looked at her watch. 'Lord, no, I'd better go home.'

'Are you going to be okay?'

'Yeah, I'll survive.'

'If you want to talk, call me any time.'

She looked into his handsome face and the genuine concern in his eyes and marvelled again at how different he was to his sister. 'It feels a bit odd, to be honest, Luke. What with the way I feel about Miriam and also, there's Bridget to think of.'

'Hey, what's'our friendship got to do with either of them?'

She hugged him briefly. 'Nothing, I suppose. See you, Luke. Thanks for the drinks and the support. I hadn't expected it but I certainly appreciate it.'

'It's the very least I can do,' he said gravely.

Chapter 14

'Where were you?' Michael barked when she arrived home.

'Difficult job and a very difficult customer.'

'You could have called. I was worried.'

Grace sighed. 'If you were worried, why didn't *you* call *me*? I had my mobile. Has Nat been home?'

'Nat? Nat? Who's that? I vaguely remember the name.'

Grace laughed. 'She does seem to lead a busy life these days, but then she is twenty.'

'We have no idea where she goes, who she sees, what she gets up to.'

'She's sensible, she's intelligent and she's an adult. We have to just trust her and hope for the best.'

'And that's going to help me sleep at night?'

'You know in your heart, Michael, that our daughter is a very good person. She's chosen to work with children – what more could we ask for?'

'Don't start me on that,' he muttered.

'You know she will always do the right thing,' Grace persisted.

Michael nodded reluctantly. 'She was never in trouble at school, I suppose.'

'The teachers were always telling us what an exemplary student she was.'

'But the other kids liked her too.'

Grace smiled tenderly. 'What's not to like?'

'Her moodiness,' Michael complained.

'I wonder where she gets that from?' Grace teased. 'She's just a very private person, that's all.'

'There's privacy and then there's secrecy. She tells us nothing. At least, she tells *me* nothing. I'm sure she's seeing someone. Has she said anything to you?'

'No, but I think you're right.' Grace had noticed the faraway look in her daughter's eye. The way she pounced on her mobile when it rang and the way she wore more make-up when she went out in the evening. She and Nat did have the occasional heart-to-heart but things had been so hectic lately Grace hadn't had a chance to ask her daughter about her lovelife.

'Wouldn't you imagine that she'd at least bring him home and introduce him to us?'

'She hasn't exactly had the time, what with work and all the studying she's doing for her exams.'

'I don't understand why you have to do exams in order to be a glorified nanny and teach snotty-nosed kids to sing "Twinkle Twinkle".'

Grace felt a stab of annoyance but forced herself to remain calm. 'Don't be so silly, the care and development of children is one of the most important jobs there is. If I had my way, parents would have to take a course in childcare before they were allowed to even get pregnant.' She paused for a moment and then continued more gently, 'Do you realize that Nat is working with a child with special needs? That she's managed to get him to say a few words when no one else could'

'It just goes to prove that she's clever and could have done something much more—'

'What, high-profile? Is that all that matters to you, Michael? You want to be able to boast about your daughter the barrister or your daughter the doctor?'

'No, I want to see her in a profession where she has a future and can make a reasonable amount of money. Everyone knows that teachers' pay is crap.'

'All the more reason to be proud of her,' Grace retorted. 'Natasha is more interested in making a difference than she is in making money.'

'Sentimental clap-trap. Anyway, it's easy to be principled when you have parents to fall back on.'

'Michael!'

'It's true, she's a silly romantic – I wonder where she gets *that* from!'

Grace stood up and glared down at him. 'Despite my silly romantic ideas I'm running my own very successful business.'

Michael didn't bat an eyelid. 'No, you're in partnership with a very clever woman who works hard to bring in the business.'

'Are you saying that Graceful Living's success is all down to Miriam?'

'You know your way around a sewing-machine, Grace, no argument there, but let's face it, you're no businesswoman.'

'Thanks for sharing that with me, Michael. It's nice to know you believe in me.' Grace hurried out of the room, tears blinding her so much she crashed into the banister, bruising her arm. 'Fuck.' She wiped her eyes on her sleeve and climbed the stairs, pausing at the door of her bedroom before going on up to her office. Closing the door, she turned the key in the lock and sank into her chair. She couldn't believe what Michael had said, and the matter-of-fact way in which he had said it. The words had not been chosen to hurt her, rather he had just called it how he saw it. He had never liked Miriam Cooper, but he obviously respected her.

Grace found a crumpled tissue in her pocket and dabbed at her eyes. What would he think of her now, she wondered, and what would he make of the fact that Grace would now be going it alone? For the first time, the enormity of the situation hit her. She was going to be the outright owner of Graceful Living and all the decisions would be hers, all the responsibility too. How on earth was she going to cope? She was already working around the clock. She was going to have to find someone to look after the accounts, someone reliable and honest. She hoped Bob would find someone for her; she didn't trust herself to hire someone trustworthy. Miriam had completely taken her in. Maybe Michael was right. Maybe she *wasn't* up to the job. It might be wiser to sell the business and go back to supplying soft furnishings. She could work from home, she could slow down, she could have more time for herself. She could curl up and die.

After a few minutes, she heard voices downstairs and then her daughter's light tread on the stairs. A tap sounded on the door. Grace wiped her eyes and went to open it.

'What's wrong, Mum? Why was the door locked?'

'No idea,' Grace lied. 'Didn't even realize I'd done it.'

Nat didn't look entirely convinced as she sat down in the only other chair. 'You look tired.'

'I feel it; I've had a very long day. How about you?'

'Great.' Nat's face lit up as it always did when she started to talk about her children. 'Arran didn't have one tantrum and I even got him to eat some fruit.'

'That's the child who was brain-damaged at birth?'

Nat nodded. 'Yes. The doctors said he would never talk or walk but I know he'll prove them wrong.'

'You seem to have formed quite a bond with this child. Maybe you should go into nursing?'

Nat shook her head. 'No, then I'd only see the kids when they were sick. With the Montessori I get to know the children over a long period of time and I can observe their development. Up until a month ago, Arran only stayed in the school for an hour while his mum sat in the car park. Now he stays for two. The trick was to find a spot in the classroom that was just his. We have a big soft cushion there, a fluffy blanket and his favourite toy. When he starts to feel panicky or upset, we just bring him over to his corner and keep the other children away. Fran, that's the special care assistant, sometimes sings to him too and that usually calms him down.' Nat giggled. 'His favourite song at the moment is "Sex Bomb".'

'His mother must love that.'

'His mother is delighted with his progress. She tried five other schools but we were the only ones that worked out.'

'Poor little mite, what on earth does the future hold for him?'

'A lot more than it did,' Nat assured her.

Grace smiled. 'I'm so proud of you, darling. Compared to what I do, you are making such a difference to people's lives.'

'Tell Dad that.'

'Don't mind your dad, you follow your heart.'

'Have you two had a row?'

'We never row, darling. Your dad makes smart comments, I get defensive and then we don't talk for a couple of days.' Grace gave her daughter a shaky smile. 'Just an average exchange for a couple who have been married for a hundred years.'

Nat looked at her, her eyes sad.

'Oh, don't mind me, darling. Like I said, it's been a pig of a day and I'm feeling a bit sensitive.'

Nat reached down to hug her. 'Why don't you go to bed and I'll bring you up a mug of hot milk?'

Grace clung to her daughter and closed her eyes. 'You are such an angel. Thank you.'

When Grace climbed into bed she reached into her bedside locker for her bottle of sleeping tablets. Natasha walked in as she was opening them.

'I hate you taking them, Mum.'

'I don't take them often but I've got such a busy day tomorrow, I need a good night's sleep.'

Nat handed her the mug and sat on the side of the bed, her face anxious. 'Are you sure you're okay? You look terrible.'

'Thanks a bunch.'

'You know what I mean. Maybe you need a tonic or something'

Grace nodded. 'You're right,' she said tiredly. 'I'll pick something up tomorrow.'

'Okay, then, goodnight, Mum.'

'Goodnight, darling, and thanks again.'

Miriam was feeling equally drained and finding her husband's concern intensely irritating.

'Alastair, read your book and leave me be, would you? I just have a few things on my mind.'

'Normal couples discuss their problems,' he pointed out.

Miriam smirked. 'Since when have we been a normal couple?'

'Good point. Right, I'm going to take my book and go to bed. Don't sit down here brooding all night, will you?'

'I won't.'

'Oh, by the way, is Grace in the office tomorrow?'

Miriam's head whipped around. 'Why?'

'She just mentioned she was interested in incorporating more modern art in her latest job and she was looking for ideas. I've found some books that might help.'

'Well, I can pass them on to her.'

'No, I need to explain a few things.' Alastair smiled. 'You're not jealous, are you, darling?'

Miriam shot him a withering look. 'Grace is working on-site for the next few days. Anyway, I thought you were going up to that garden centre in north Dublin tomorrow?'

'Yes, I have heard quite a lot about it.'

'And you know, of course, it's near Skerries.'

'So?'

'So that's one of the best places for fish. Apparently you can buy it straight off the boat.'

'No!' Alastair's eyes lit up.

'Yes. That famous restaurant up there gets all its fresh fish from the local fishermen.'

'The Red Bank?'

'That's the one.'

'Oh well, I'll set off first thing. Maybe I could pick up a lobster for dinner.'

'I will look forward to it,' Miriam told him, bending her head over the papers she was pretending to study.

'Okay, okay, I'm going,' Alastair laughed, heading upstairs with his book under his arm.

When she was alone, Miriam dropped the papers and massaged the bridge of her nose. She had spent the morning with her solicitor and the afternoon with her accountant trying to sort out the fall-out from handing over her share of Graceful Living. She had told them both the minimum amount of information and they knew her well enough not to ask any questions. But they were both concerned as to how she would manage her fashion business over the next few months. Though it was hugely successful, the merchandise was expensive and consumed her now-reduced cashflow.

The accountant had suggested she stock some cheaper lines that would sell quicker, but Miriam had refused to even consider the matter.

'Lady M's has a reputation for high standards and quality and that is our biggest asset.'

'But how on earth will you finance another shop within the year?'

'I'll figure something out,' Miriam had assured her with more confidence than she felt. She was usually good at pulling ideas out of a hat but she was finding it hard to think straight, mainly because of Luke. She still hadn't got over the look of total disgust in his eyes and she couldn't believe he hadn't been in touch since she'd confided in him. She should have stuck to her usual practice and lied through her teeth. She'd tried to phone him and had left messages, but to no avail. She would have to go and see him, because if she couldn't get him back on side, this would all be for nothing. Alastair was used to Luke being around. He was in and out of the house on a weekly basis and then on the phone in between visits. Luke could screw this all up and then Miriam would lose everything.

Picking up the papers again, she started to scrutinize the figures carefully. She had been in worse scrapes and if she put her mind to it she would get out of this one. She had to.

Chapter 15

Natasha hurried into the pub and pushed her way through the crowd towards the room at the back. There was no sound of music and she groaned inwardly, realizing she'd probably missed the gig. Ken had been very keen for her to be here but she'd had a late class and then she'd had to get two buses across town to get here. The fact that it was raining and she had a heavy bag of books to lug around hadn't helped. Now not only was she arriving too late but her hair hung in wet rats' tails around her face and she could feel a pimple emerging strong and painful at the side of her mouth. Not exactly the right image for an up-and-coming rock star's girlfriend.

Taking a deep breath, she walked into the dimly lit room with the small stage at the top and tables gathered around it. She easily spotted Ken standing at the bar, head and shoulders above his friends, a pint in his hand. She made her way to his side and put a hand on his arm.

He turned to look down at her and smiled. 'Hey, doll, where've you been?'

Surprised that he seemed in such good form, Nat reached up to kiss him. 'Sorry I got delayed and the traffic is shit. Did I miss the gig?'

'Yeah, 'fraid so, but don't worry about it.'

Nat smiled in relief. 'Let me get you another pint.'

'Great – and get one for my new friend, Leila Malone.'

A stunning redhead nearly as tall as Ken turned and flashed a brilliant smile at Nat.

'This is Nat. Nat, Leila is an agent and she wants to represent Cutting It. Isn't that great?'

'Great,' Nat said weakly as Leila put a proprietorial hand on Ken's arm. Why hadn't he said 'This is Nat, my girlfriend'?

'Jackson has such an amazing voice,' Leila purred. 'I know I can really do things with him.'

'And the band,' Ken added.

'Yeah, sure.'

'That's great,' Nat said again. 'What can I get you, Leila?'

'Tequila, straight.'

Nat gulped as she looked at the loose change in her purse. 'Tequila, pint of lager and er . . .' she did a quick calculation, 'a Coke, please.'

Nat stood sipping her Coke and listened as Leila told Ken of the wonderful future he had. It was clear that Leila had no interest in Cutting It, although apparently not to Ken. He drank in all of her praise and stood mesmerized as she tossed out names of big producers and record companies that she could introduce him to.

'Do you represent any acts that we would know?' Nat asked.

Leila waved a hand. 'I've represented so many.'

'How many at the moment?' Nat persisted, ignoring Ken's glare.

'Only three,' Leila replied. 'I believe in a very intense and personal service. Many agents take on lots of acts and spread themselves too thin. My aim is to concentrate on five or six acts at a time and that way I can give them my complete attention. You're lucky, Jackson, that I'm in a position to take you on.'

Nat rolled her eyes and put her glass down. She couldn't take any more of this. 'Excuse me for a minute, would you?' She made her way out to the porch at the back of the pub to have a smoke. It had stopped raining and the air was clean and fresh but very cold. Pulling out her cigarettes, she tipped one out and then started to grope around her cavernous bag for her lighter.

'Here you go.'

A lighter flashed in front of her and she bent over it. 'Thanks.'

'You're welcome, Natasha.'

She looked up quickly and then smiled in recognition. 'Hi.'

'I didn't know you indulged.' The man lit his own cigarette and smiled down at her.

Nat grimaced. 'I try not to, but sometimes—'

'Yeah, I know.'

'I really am going to give up though,' she said, leaning back against the wall and blowing smoke up into the air. 'Don't you feel like a total idiot having to come and stand outside in the cold and wet just to poison yourself?'

'When you put it like that, it doesn't make a lot of sense,' he chuckled. 'It's been a long time. You're looking great.'

Nat pulled self-consciously at her lank, damp hair. 'Do you need glasses or is it just because it's so dark out here?'

'Ah, I see that tongue of yours is as sharp as ever.'

'Sorry, but I've just been standing next to a stunning-looking woman and I'm very conscious of how crap I look at the moment. I haven't seen you here before.'

'No – well, you might have heard, I've moved recently. I've got a place just round the corner.'

Nat shot him an apologetic look. 'Oh yes, sorry, I forgot.'

'That's okay. Is this a regular haunt for you?'

'My boyfriend is in a band. He plays here a lot. I came to see him, only I was too late.'

'Oh. Are you in trouble?'

Nat shook her head. 'Not this time. He's in there being schmoozed by a woman who claims she's an agent, and he's hanging on her every word. He wouldn't notice if I danced naked on the table.'

He laughed. 'I find that hard to believe. This is the stunning-looking woman, I take it.'

Nat nodded miserably.

'And you don't believe she's an agent?'

'Who knows? She just seems to be spouting an awful lot of crap and is a dab hand at avoiding direct questions.'

He laughed. 'Sounds like an agent to me.'

She smiled. 'Of course, he thinks she's interested in the whole band but it's clear that she's not. Not that I blame her for that.'

'Aren't they any good?'

'No.' Nat sneaked a look around at the other smokers to check there were no Cutting It members or fans nearby. 'They're crap. But Ken – his stage-name is Jackson, that's his surname – he's great.'

His eyes twinkled in amusement. 'Are you slightly biased?'

'No, honestly, he's really good and he's a great song-writer.'

'Then maybe this agent will be good for him.'

'If she really *is* an agent.'

'Well, if she is, it's good, right? And if she isn't, your boyfriend will soon find out and dump her.'

'I suppose.' Nat stubbed out her cigarette and reached up to kiss his cheek. 'Thanks.'

'Sure. Take care of yourself, Natasha.'

She laughed. 'It's Nat. Only my folks call me Natasha and that's usually when they're arguing with me.'

'Well, I'm sorry, but you'll always be Natasha to me. It's too beautiful a name to shorten.'

Nat blushed as she opened the door to go back inside.

'Bye then, Luke. I'll probably see you around.'

'Probably.'

Bridget Crosby was beginning to panic. She sat in her living room, a bottle of white wine and glass on the table in front of her and her diary in her lap. She had tried out her charms with three men so far with no luck. The first had turned out to be stingy to the point of trying to talk her out of having a starter and then ordering a bottle of house wine. The man was positively loaded, but he obviously didn't like to spend it. Given that he was also the wrong side of fifty and suffered from a bad case of halitosis, Bridget struck him off her list.

The second contender was wonderful in every way. She sighed as she remembered the wonderful dinner they'd had and the fabulous hotel suite he'd whisked her off to afterwards. He had been an excellent lover too and a gentleman, insisting on escorting her home and sending her two dozen white roses the following morning. There was just one tiny fly in the ointment; he was married with three young children, and he had made it clear that he was quite happy with that arrangement. The most she would ever be was his mistress, and while that idea didn't particularly bother Bridget, it would mean she would still be without an escort and forced to keep her relationship a secret. That, added to the fact that it would be his wife who was on his arm when he went to all the best parties in Dublin, was enough to knock him off the list.

The third – she groaned as she remembered the evening – had lost his wife to cancer two years ago. Ample time, you would think, for him to have recovered and be ready to get back up on the horse again, as it were, but the man droned on all night about his bloody wife and then looked at Bridget in horror when she'd attempted to kiss him goodnight.

So Bridget thought, it was time to get Luke back on board, at least until she found a suitable replacement. Picking up the phone she called Grace. Surprisingly, her friend answered on the first ring.

'Hi, Bridget, how are you doing?'

'Not good, Grace.' Bridget kept her voice soft and allowed herself a small sniff.

'Oh, do you want me to come over?'

'No, it's okay,' Bridget said bravely. 'I was just wondering if you'd seen him?'

'Luke?'

'Yes, of course Luke!' Bridget snapped. 'Sorry, Grace, it's just I miss him so much.'

'I know.'

'So, did you talk to him?'

Grace sighed. 'I did try, Bridget, but he wouldn't listen.'

'I think maybe it's time I paid him a visit.'

'Well, I suppose—'

'He needs reminding of how good we were together. If I can persuade him to spend an evening with me, Grace, I know it would do the trick.'

'It's certainly worth a try.'

'So I'll need your help.'

'Oh?'

'Yes, I need his address.'

'I don't have it.'

'But you can find out.'

'Oh Bridget—'

'I have complete faith in you, Grace. Good night!'

Grace hung up on Bridget and immediately dialled Luke's number.

'Hello?'

'Hello, Luke? Luke, is that you?'

'Yeah.'

'Sorry, but I can hardly hear you.'

'I'm in a pub. Hang on, I'll go outside.'

Grace waited for a moment and then heard his voice again, this time a lot clearer. 'Is that better?'

'Fine. Listen, sorry if I'm interrupting anything.'

'You're not.'

'It's just that Bridget was on a minute ago. She wants to come and visit you. She asked me for your address.'

'No.'

Grace sighed. 'Okay then. Have you been talking to Miriam?'

'No, why? Has she been giving you trouble?'

'No, no, it's all quiet,' Grace murmured, conscious of Michael in the next room. 'I was just wondering, that's all.'

'How are you coping?'

'I'm beginning to realize just how much your sister did around here. I'm going to have to hire someone to deal with the accounts and administration or I'll never cope.'

'You'll cope,' Luke assured her. 'Just hang on in there.'

When Grace ended the call she sat staring at the phone for several minutes. Bridget didn't stand a chance of getting Luke back and she was going to have to tell her that. She needed to forget about him and concentrate on making a new life for herself. Getting a job was where she should start. Grace smiled slowly as the idea came to her. She couldn't believe she hadn't thought of it before. It was the perfect solution in so many ways, and it would give her a great deal of pleasure putting her plan into action. Without giving herself time to think about it any further, she picked up the phone and called Miriam.

'Grace?' Miriam sounded surprised and guarded.

'I won't keep you long, I just wanted to tell you there's an extra clause to our deal.'

'You can't do that—'

'Oh, I think I can.'

There was silence for a moment. 'What is it?' Miriam said finally, her voice tight with anger.

'I want you to hire Bridget to work in your Dublin shop.'

'Are you mad? I don't even need any staff at the moment, and if I did she'd be the last person I'd hire.'

'That may be, but Bridget wants a job and your

brother might feel a little happier with you if you were to help out his girlfriend.'

Again there was a silence. And then: 'Why the hell does she want to work, all of a sudden?'

Grace crossed her fingers. 'She just fancies a change. Look on the bright side, she'll probably get bored within a few weeks and resign.'

'I'll be amazed if she lasts a few days.'

'So have we a deal?'

'Okay.'

'Fine.' Grace hung up on Miriam and phoned Bridget. 'I have some news.'

'You got the address?'

Grace sighed. 'No, sorry, it's not that.'

'So what is it?'

'I've got you a job.'

'I don't want a job.'

'You need an income, Bridget.'

'Not if Luke comes back, I don't.'

Grace suppressed a wave of irritation. 'It doesn't look like that's going to happen any time soon.'

'Well, thanks for that, Grace. Nice of you to call to cheer me up.'

'Will you shut up for a moment and listen,' Grace snapped.

'Okay, okay, what is it?'

'You're going to work for Miriam.'

'Are you mad?'

'Funny, that's what Miriam said. Look, it's not such a

bad idea if you just think about it for a moment. The pay won't be mind-blowing but you will be able to buy clothes at cost and you'll get to see Luke or at least hear what's happening with him.'

Bridget perked up at the mention of cheap clothes. 'Would I get to go to fashion shows?'

Grace sighed impatiently. 'I don't know, probably.'

'Okay, I'll do it.'

'Miriam will call you. It might be best for the moment not to mention the fact that you and Luke have split up.'

'She doesn't know?'

'Not yet, no.'

'Grace, you crafty old thing!'

'Less of the old please.'

'She'll freak when she finds out.'

Grace could hear the smile in Bridget's voice. 'We'll worry about that when the time comes.'

'Okay, then. Night, Grace.'

Grace listened to the dial tone. 'You're welcome, Bridget.'

Chapter 16

Rosa picked up the note on the table and smiled.

> *Dear Rosa,*
>
> *You don't have to cook dinner for us this evening I'm bringing home some fresh fish – I hope!*
>
> *Alastair*

She unpacked the shopping, putting the ingredients for her Italian meatloaf, her mother's recipe, on the table. Alastair loved it and it was a great standby to keep in the freezer. She would make two and leave one in the fridge for Miriam and Alastair to reheat tomorrow night, and she would freeze the other.

Rosa turned on the radio and sang along as she chopped, grated and stirred. It was a simple but tasty meal and soon she was putting the two dishes in the oven and cleaning up the kitchen. Once it was sparkling, Rosa went to change the sheets. Miriam was very fussy about her sheets and Rosa changed them twice a week.

She didn't like silk sheets herself, cotton was so much cooler and more comfortable, but then maybe when you were sharing your bed with a man, silk was sexier. Rosa sighed, thinking it was unlikely she'd ever find out. At thirty-five it was almost impossible to find a man who wasn't either married or weird. As far as she was concerned, if a man made it to forty without marrying, there had to be something wrong with him. There was a Hallowe'en party on this weekend at the nearby Rugby Club and Rosa had thought about going along with some of her girlfriends, but what was the point?

Catching sight of her image in the mirrored wardrobe, Rosa eyed herself critically. Her skin was still good and there were no lines to speak of, but she was a little curvier than she would like. With an impatient sigh, she turned away from the mirror. She should start exercising more, but on these cold winter days, the idea of a long walk or swim was not very enticing. When the weather got warmer she'd start a new regime, she promised herself. In the meantime, she thought as she carried the sheets dwn to the washing-machine, she'd put a bit more effort into the housework. That surely would eat up some of those horrible calories.

When Alastair arrived home he was greeted with the sight of Rosa on her hands and knees, washing the porcelain tiles in the hall, her bottom wagging back and forth in time to Robbie Williams.

'Rosa? *Rosa*?' When she still didn't hear him, Alastair went over to the CD-player and turned down the volume.

Rosa turned around. 'Oh Alastair, I didn't hear you!'

'I'm not surprised,' he laughed.

Rosa brushed her hair back from her flushed face. 'I get more work done with the music, you know?' she explained.

'Me too,' Alastair said, moving gingerly across the wet floor. 'Fancy a coffee?'

'I'll make it,' she offered immediately. 'I'm just finished here.' She quickly dried off the floor and followed him into the kitchen. 'Did you get the fish?'

'I certainly did.' He opened the bag and stood back so that Rosa could inspect his purchase.

She cast a professional eye over the fish. 'Very fresh, very good quality.'

'That's what I thought. I was hoping to get some lobster but I picked the wrong time of day, apparently. I thought I'd cook the scallops tonight and make a fish stew with the rest tomorrow.'

'I made meatloaf for your dinner tomorrow night, should I freeze it?'

'No, that will be lovely. I'll freeze the stew and keep it for one of Miriam's impromptu dinners.'

Rosa went to make the coffee while Alastair rummaged on the bookshelf in the kitchen and pulled out his favourite Jamie Oliver cookbook. He flicked through it until he found the recipe he was looking for. 'Ah, here it is, seared scallops with bacon.'

'Sounds good.'

'It's a very simple dish but quite tasty and I bought a fresh baguette to mop up the juices.'

'It's the best way to eat fish,' Rosa agreed. 'These rich sauces kill the whole flavour and texture of fish.' She shook her head. ' Such a waste.'

'So are you all finished here?' Alastair asked as she handed him a mug of coffee.

'I just want to clean the bathroom and I'm done.'

'Tell me, Rosa, do you like living in the city?'

She shrugged. 'It's okay.'

'But in Italy you lived in a small town, didn't you. Don't you miss it?'

'Sometimes.' She rolled her eyes. 'But everyone knew my business – I don't miss that!'

He laughed. 'Still, it must be nice to feel a part of a tight-knit community.'

'There was always someone to turn to if you were in trouble,' Rosa agreed. 'I do miss that. Where I live now it's all flats, and people are out working all day so I hardly know any of my neighbours. It's a pity,' she mused, thinking it was no wonder she didn't meet eligible men.

'I was up in this most lovely little seaside town today. It's only about an hour from Dublin but it may as well be in the middle of nowhere.'

'I like to be close to the sea, that's what I like about Dublin. You can be in the middle of the city and yet never very far from the sea either.'

'I suppose.'

She smiled at him. 'I must go and clean the bathroom.'

'Of course, sorry for delaying you.'

'I needed the break,' she confided, 'and there's only so much Robbie Williams a girl can take!'

Chuckling, Alastair drained his cup and then set about cleaning and filleting the fish. He put the heads and tails in a pot full of water with an onion, carrot and some parsley to make a stock for the stew, and then carried his cookbook into the lounge. But he couldn't concentrate on the recipe; his mind kept drifting back over his day

Despite the fact that it was the end of October, the sky had been clear blue, and though the air was cool he had found the whole experience invigorating. Unwilling to rush back, he'd come home the scenic route along the coast, stopping off in a picturesque little village called Banford. He had bumped down a narrow road through the village, eventually emerging at a small harbour with a tiny beach alongside. Here he had parked, hopped out and, turning his collar up around his ears, he had marched down the beach, marvelling at the view and the complete absence of people. The houses surrounding the harbour were a mishmash of old and new, palatial and modest, and yet somehow, it worked.

As he got to the end of the beach, he noticed a rather dilapidated cottage tucked away behind a thick hedge. A For Sale sign swung on a pole in the gateway and he went over to take a closer look. Though the property looked sad and neglected, Alastair suspected that most of its problems were superficial. It looked as if it had been empty for some time, with two broken windows at the side and a large overgrown garden. It would take a lot of hard work and some imagination to transform it into a home, Alastair had realized, but for a view like that it would be worth it.

He had walked back up the beach enjoying the sound of the waves lapping the shore, the taste of salt on his lips and the sight of the seagulls circling lazily over the boats moored in the harbour. It was with reluctance that he had climbed back into his car to drive home to the city.

It had been a relaxing and enjoyable day, and as he hit the suburbs of Dublin and joined the traffic that lurched slowly through the busy streets, he'd felt his mood get lower and lower. Of course a good meal and a nice glass of wine would sort that out, he assured himself. It was the thought of the short days and long dark nights stretching ahead that got him down. He was, unlike his wife, an outdoor person and absolutely hated to be stuck indoors. Still, according to the man at the garden centre, this was the perfect time of year for planting trees – and so what if he got a bit wet? He would be able to enjoy the fruits of his labour, literally, in the spring.

Alastair had confessed to the gardener that he was a novice but eager to learn, and after an hour of conferring and sketching, they had come up with a plan for his garden. He couldn't wait to get started. The plants he'd ordered would take a couple of weeks to come in but a lot of preparation work had to be done first.

'Bye, Alastair,' Rosa called from the hall. 'See you on Wednesday.'

'Bye, Rosa.' Alastair looked at the clock and wondered what time Miriam would get home. She had been working very long hours recently but had promised faithfully to be home at six tonight. Used to her tardiness, however, Alastair had no intention of starting dinner until she walked through the door.

It was almost seven-thirty when she finally made an appearance. 'You look tired.' Alastair dropped a kiss on her cheek and led the way out to the kitchen.

'I am,' Miriam said, reaching into the drinks cabinet for a bottle of gin.

'There's some wine in the fridge.'

'I think I'll have this first.' Miriam poured a large measure into a tumbler, added ice, a splash of tonic and sat down at the island to watch him work.

Alastair sliced a lemon and reached across to drop a piece in her drink. 'Want to talk about it?' he asked.

She shook her head. 'Too boring and best forgotten. Tell me about your day instead.'

So, as Alastair fried bacon and garlic, he told her about his visit to the garden centre, the fisherman he'd bought their dinner from and finally, his visit to Banford. 'It's amazing to find somewhere so pretty and rural so close to the city,' he said, looking up to find her staring off into space, obviously not listening to a word he was saying. 'So I thought I'd buy a house there. What do you think?'

'Sounds good.'

Alastair sighed. 'Miriam, you haven't heard a word I've said.'

'I'm sorry, darling, I'm a bit distracted.'

'That's obvious,' he murmured, feeling a bit annoyed. She hadn't even apologized for being late. She'd made a drink for herself but hadn't offered him one. Sometimes he felt invisible. 'I was saying I saw a cottage today. I thought we could buy it.'

'That's ridiculous!' Miriam snapped, thinking of the state of her finances.

'Why?'

'What on earth would we do with a house by the sea?'

He looked bemused. 'Enjoy it?'

'I could understand it if you wanted to buy a place in another country, somewhere warm or in another city, Paris or London.'

Alastair shuddered. 'The idea would be to have somewhere to escape to, just the two of us.'

'But what would we *do* there?' Miriam looked genuinely confused.

Alastair turned away. 'Very little. Don't worry, darling, I wasn't serious.'

'Thank God for that.'

'Still, it was a worthwhile visit. I got this wonderful fish, and my trees and plants are ordered. I must show

Grace my plan – she might have some ideas about it from a colour perspective.'

'I've told you Grace is busy,' Miriam said irritably.

'Oh, don't worry, I'll call her at home. Honestly, Miriam, sometimes you treat that poor girl like an employee instead of your business partner.'

Miriam said nothing, drained her glass and went to the fridge for the wine.

'We could invite her and Michael over for dinner later in the week. I have the makings of a wonderful fish stew.'

Miriam shook her head. 'I have too much on this week.'

'Oh – what?'

'For God's sake, Alastair, why all the questions? It's just work.'

Alastair raised an eyebrow. 'You are seriously stressed out tonight, my love. What you need is a break. I'll take you up to Banford some day. It may only be a few miles up the road but the air is completely different and the views are glorious. It would do you the world of good.'

Miriam looked dubious as she splashed wine into two glasses.

'You are such a city girl,' he laughed.

'It's a long time since I've been a girl.'

He smiled at her. 'You'll always be a girl to me. Now, get the salad and dressing out of the fridge, I'm ready to serve up. I thought we could eat in the conservatory.'

Miriam frowned. 'Oh, would you mind if we have it

on trays in the lounge? There's a documentary on that I wanted to see.'

Alastair's mouth tightened as he looked from his beautifully presented food to his wife's preoccupied face. 'You go ahead, I think I'll have mine here.'

Chapter 17

Bridget put the money in the till and handed over the distinctive glossy green bag and receipt.

'I hope you have a lovely time at the ball,' she said with a wide smile.

'Thank you, I will,' the woman said.

Bridget's smile disappeared once the door closed on the customer. 'What a waste of a beautiful dress.'

Annabel glowered at her. 'That's not very nice, Bridget.'

'No, but it's true. Nothing would look good on that woman.'

'Keep your opinions to yourself,' Annabel hissed, 'there are other customers in the shop. Now go and tidy the stock room.'

'But I did that yesterday,' Bridget protested.

'And you'll do it again today.'

Bridget stormed off, her cheeks flushed an angry red.

The door opened and Annabel looked up to see her boss walk in. 'Hello, Miriam.'

'Annabel. How are things?'

'Fine.'

Miriam noted the sour face on her manager. 'How's Bridget getting on?'

'Okay.'

'Just okay?'

Annabel frowned. 'It's her attitude, Miriam. She's just so, so . . .'

'Bitchy.'

Annabel smiled in relief. 'Yes!'

'She hasn't insulted any customers, has she?'

'No, she's careful enough, it's just the way she talks about them behind their backs that drives me mad. And she's a bit over-familiar with some of our more well-known customers. Can I just ask, Miriam, why on earth have we hired her?'

'She wanted to work here and she's my brother's girl-friend – what can I say?'

'She doesn't act like a woman who wants a job,' Annabel said. 'She's always complaining. The only thing she's interested in is getting cut-price clothes.'

'I'll talk to her, Miriam said, her face grim. 'Where is she?'

'In the stock room.'

Miriam made her way down to the room at the back of the shop and opened the door quietly. She wasn't sur-prised to see Bridget sitting on a stool reading a magazine. 'Working hard, I see,' she drawled.

Bridget jumped. 'Hey, Miriam, you shouldn't creep up on people like that.'

'You are supposed to be working.'

'I'm on a break.'

'Does Annabel know that?'

'She's probably forgotten. If you ask me, that woman isn't fit for the job at all and she's really quite rude to the customers.'

Miriam knew bullshit when she heard it and yet again wondered, out of all the women in the world, why her brother had to get involved with this little cow. 'The two of you should get along just fine, so,' she said.

Bridget grimaced. 'You're so funny.'

'Is Luke picking you up after work?'

'Not today.'

'Well, could you ask him to phone me? It's important.' Miriam went to leave and then turned back. 'And, Bridget? Don't think that being Luke's girlfriend is a passport to idleness. If you give Annabel any problems you're out, is that understood?'

'Sure, boss.' Bridget sniggered quietly as the woman left, slamming the door after her.

After Miriam had gone upstairs to her office, Bridget came back out to join her boss. 'Annabel, I just wanted to apologize for the way I've been behaving.'

The manager inclined her head. 'I appreciate the apology, Bridget, and I can promise you that as long as you pull your weight, we'll get along just fine.'

Bridget made a face. 'Not if Miriam has anything to do with it. She hates me and has only given me this job because of Luke. I don't know what I ever did to upset her but she's always had it in for me.'

'Miriam's protective of her brother,' Annabel agreed. 'I suppose it's natural; she's more like a mother to him than a sister.'

'I'll just have to learn to be more tolerant.' Bridget gave a brave smile. 'Now I must get back to that stock room, it won't tidy itself.' Bridget's smile broadened as she walked away. That should sweeten the old biddy and make her think twice before listening to everything Miriam said. Bridget knew for a fact that there was already friction between the two women now that Miriam was using the office upstairs. Annabel didn't like having her boss around all the time and was obviously worried that Miriam had moved in specifically to keep an eye on her. It wouldn't take much to stir things up between them and get Annabel firmly on her side. Then there was some chance of Bridget hanging on to her job until she'd got Luke back or someone better had come along.

There was something strange going on in the Cooper family, Bridget thought as she folded jumpers, and it would definitely be in her interests to find out exactly what. Why weren't Luke and Miriam talking, for a start? They had words from time to time but Bridget couldn't remember any tiff lasting more than a couple of days. But it was a month now since Luke had left her and Miriam still didn't know anything about it. And then there was Miriam moving in here. The only reason Bridget could think of for that, was that she had fallen out with Grace over something, but Grace had laughed when she'd suggested that and said it was purely a logistics problem. They'd hired this new accounts guy, John Crowe, and he needed an office, apparently – but as he was part-time, Bridget didn't swallow that. There was definitely something amiss and she needed to find out what. She'd have to organize a night out with Grace and pour some wine down her throat. It was the only way to loosen her up.

It had been ages since they'd gone out. Grace pleaded a heavy workload but that didn't normally stop her; she was usually on for a night out at least once a fortnight. Bridget figured it was the only way she stayed sane, married to that boring old fart. God, what Grace had ever seen in Michael, Bridget couldn't imagine. He wasn't even that rich. It was amazing that between them they'd produced a stunner like Nat, although she was a bit quiet. Still, that was when she was around her parents; she was probably wild when she went out on the town. Bridget giggled. Maybe if she couldn't talk Grace into going out she'd take her daughter instead. They'd have a lot more fun.

While Bridget was plotting in the stock room, Miriam was sitting in the office upstairs holding on for Luke. Finally the receptionist came back. 'Sorry, I thought he was here but he's gone out on a job.'

'Thanks for nothing,' Miriam said and slammed down her phone. Picking up her mobile, she tapped in a text. LUKE CALL ME ITS IMPORTANT

She stared at it and watched as a receipt came back, as

it always did. Luke was receiving her mails all right; he just wasn't answering. Miriam couldn't stand it much longer. She was almost at the point of calling around to the flat, but she didn't want to give Bridet the satisfaction. Her one consolation in all this was that Luke obviously hadn't told his horrible girlfriend about their argument and she certainly wasn't going to spill the beans. Bridget could not be trusted, and if she knew about Miriam's creative accounting she would use it as a bargaining tool at every opportunity.

Miriam groaned at the thought. Bridget Crosby was a lot scarier than Grace Mulcahy any day, and she'd be very nervous if the girl ever found out what had happened at Graceful Living. Miriam dragged a weary hand across her eyes and looked longingly at her cigarettes. This smoking ban was bloody ridiculous. Here she was, sitting in her own office, in her own premises, and she wasn't allowed to have a measly cigarette. She had been smoking a lot in recent weeks, the stress of trying to keep so many balls in the air taking its toll. She had temporarily sorted her cashflow problem by reducing her purchasing for this season, but Bridget's salary had been a further strain and it was also hard to explain to Annabel why she had reduced their range of stock. Miriam had finally fobbed her off by saying that she'd heard one of their suppliers was going to the wall and it would be too risky to do business with them until they knew exactly what the situation was. Miriam figured she should be writing books with the amount of stories she'd managed to fabricate over the last few weeks. She wondered how Grace was doing, nervous that her partner's innate honesty would lead her to confide in her boorish husband. While Luke didn't approve of what she did, Miriam knew she could rely on him to keep quiet, but if Michael Hughes ever discovered the truth, her goose was well and truly cooked.

Her phone beeped as a text message came through and Miriam immediately picked it up, hoping that it was from Luke. It wasn't, but it still made her smile.

IN DUB NXT WK. MEET ME

No matter how many times she told Nigel she wouldn't meet up with him in Ireland, he still tried to change her mind. It was nice to know after nearly two years he was still so keen.

NO BUT I'LL B IN LONDON THE WEEK AFTR. C U DEN. After she pressed send Miriam picked up the office phone and dialed home.

'Alastair Summers.'

'Hi, darling, it's me.'

'Please don't tell me you're working late.'

Miriam laughed. 'Actually, I was thinking of coming home early.'

'Don't tell me, you're out of business?'

Miriam winced. 'Very funny.'

'I tell you what, don't come home, I'll pick you up and we'll have dinner in town and then maybe go to the cinema. What do you think?'

'Sounds good,' Miriam agreed immediately. At least

in the cinema she wouldn't have to talk and come up with yet more lies. 'But I've to do a couple of errands first so I'll meet you at the restaurant.'

'Okay, how about La Stampa at six-thirty?'

'See you there,' Miriam said and hung up. She didn't want Alastair coming here and getting a grilling from Bridget. Keeping him away from the shop and Graceful Living was becoming a full-time job in itself and she wouldn't be able to do it for ever. But if she could just keep him away from Grace until the woman had calmed down a bit, then she might just pull this off.

She knew that Grace was reeling from her new responsibilities, and Miriam got a certain pleasure out of that, but now that she had that drab little man Crowe to help her she'd soon settle down. Then she might start to appreciate the fact that she was now 100 per cent shareholder of Graceful Living and hopefully, that fact would allow her anger and bitterness to fade.

At the moment, Alastair would only have to look into that wide-eyed, injured gaze and know that there was something up. It was a mistake to mix business with pleasure, any fool knew that, but Miriam also believed in staying close to colleagues, so she could keep a finger on the pulse of her busineses at all times. It had worked up to now, but that was only because of the enormous amount Alastair and Grace had in common. Miriam might have felt jealous of their relationship, except she knew that Alastair was too much of a gentleman to ever consider chatting up a married woman, and Grace was too straight to even think of being unfaithful.

Picking up her mobile, Miriam checked for texts but there were none. Her brother was obviously still very angry. Dropping her cigarettes and phone into her bag, Miriam collected her jacket and went downstairs.

'I'm off now, Annabel, see you tomorrow.'

'Have a lovely evening,' Bridget called cheerily.

'And you,' Miriam said through gritted teeth and walked out. How was she ever going to stand having that woman around?

Chapter 18

Nat cuddled up close to Ken on the pub benchseat and smiled at him. 'This is nice.'

'Yeah.'

'It's not often I get you all to myself.'

'That's not just my fault, you're always studying.'

'I wasn't having a go,' Nat protested. 'We're both pretty busy at the moment, I know that.'

Ken grunted.

'It will be better once I finish my exams and the Christmas holidays start. We could go somewhere.'

'Nat—'

'Not somewhere expensive, I'm as broke as you are but there are always cheap deals going if you leave it to the last minute.' She closed her eyes and smiled. 'We could go to Tenerife and soak up some sun or catch a cheap flight to New York and see in the New Year in Times Square.'

'Look, Nat—'

'Hi, you two, sorry I'm late.' Leila stood over them, smiling widely.

Nat stared at her, gobsmacked, as Ken pulled away from her and stood up.

'Hey, Leila, how's it going?'

'Very well, Jackson, very well indeed. I have lots of news but first I'm absolutely dying for a drink.'

'Are you kidding me?' Nat glared at her boyfriend. 'It was supposed to be just the two of us tonight.'

'Yeah, well, Leila said she had some news so I knew you wouldn't mind.'

'Well, you knew wrong,' Nat said, snatching up her cigarettes. 'I'm going for a smoke.'

We'll have to stop meeting like this.'

Nat blinked angry tears away and saw that Luke was already on the porch, leaning against the wall, a cigarette between his lips. 'Oh, hi.'

'Are you all right?'

'Yeah, just a bit pissed off, you know?'

'I know.' He held out his lighter and she bent her head over his hand, pulled back and inhaled deeply.

'Oh, you needed that.'

'I did.' She sighed. 'I'm not always like this, you know.'

'Like what?'

'Bitchy and moany. I have exams coming up so I'm a bit stressed.'

'You're doing a degree in Montessori, right?'

Nat nodded. 'Yeah, that's right.'

'Are you working too?'

She nodded.

'That can't be easy.'

'It's tiring but great.' She smiled. 'Being around the kids reminds me what all the hard graft is for.'

'I went out with a girl once who worked with kids. I was only an apprentice at the time and I used to be very jealous of her.'

'Why's that?'

'She had bad days like everyone else but she always seemed to come home with at least one happy story.'

'It's true, it's hard to have a completely bad day,' Nat told him. 'There's a little boy with special needs in my class, and if he smiles at me when he's going home, it makes my day. It's hard to explain but it's very reward-ing when you see a child like that take a step forward, even a tiny one.'

'Oh, believe me, I can understand that but it must take enormous patience. I admire you, I really do.'

Nat blushed. 'I'm not a teacher yet and the way things are going, I may never be.'

He watched her steadily. 'You'll get there.'

'Yes, I will,' she agreed, surprising herself. 'Sorry, I must be boring you rigid. Ken says I never shut up about my work. I can see his eyes start to glaze over when I get started.'

Luke frowned. 'He's not much of a boyfriend, is he?'

'Well, he's a bit preoccupied at the moment.' Nat felt rather disloyal for making Ken sound bad. 'This Leila character has his head filled with nonsense.'

'So she hasn't come up with a major deal for him yet?'

'Of course not, she's just all talk but he loves every minute of it.'

'I'm afraid that's the sad male ego for you,' he smiled. 'We love being told how wonderful we are.'

Nat laughed and stubbed out her cigarette. 'I'd better get back so and save him from himself. See you, Luke.'

He raised his hand in salute. 'Same time, same place.'

'Nat, Leila's got me a deal!' Ken jumped up as she walked back in, his eyes shining with excitement.

'Now, that's not exactly what I said,' Leila protested.

Ken ignored the interruption. 'There's a producer coming to see us play next week.'

'Don't get your hopes up,' Nat cautioned, 'you've been told that before.' She flashed a disapproving frown at Leila.

'It's Tom Durrane and he will be there,' Leila assured her.

Nat' s mouth fell open. 'Tom Durrane?'

'I know, Nat – can you believe it? I have to have a hard think about what numbers to do.'

'Some of your own,' Nat said quickly. 'Some of the old stuff.'

'I agree,' Leila said.

Ken frowned. 'I'm not sure what the guys will say about that.'

Leila exchanged a look with Nat. 'I have to be honest

with you, Jackson. Tom is coming to see you, not Cutting It.'

Ken's face fell. 'But I thought you were interested in all of us, Leila.'

'Hey, I was, I am,' Leila soothed, 'but I played your CD for Tom and it's you he wanted to come and see.'

'I don't know.'

'Look, Ken,' Nat took his hand. 'Tom will see you and the guys – it's their chance as much as yours. If Tom likes you and not the band – well, that's not your fault, is it?'

'I suppose not, but we should be performing Cutting It songs.'

'If you do, Tom will walk straight out again,' Leila told him baldly. 'This is your big chance, don't blow it.'

'Ken?' Nat felt a surge of tenderness at the conflicting emotions crossing his face.

After a moment he nodded. 'Okay, I'll do it.'

Grace was up a ladder, pressing bubbles out of the wall-paper in the pilot's library when her mobile rang. 'Shit.' She wobbled precariously as she dragged it out of her jeans pocket and clung on to the ladder with her other hand. 'Hi, Michael.'

'Where in God's name are you?'

She sighed. 'On a job in Portmarnock. Remember, I told you about it? The divorced pilot that Miriam met in London who's moved here to take up a job with Aer Lingus?'

'But it's after six and the film starts at seven-thirty.'

'Oh no, I'm so sorry, I completely forgot. Is there a later show?'

'There's one at nine forty-five.'

Grace groaned inwardly. 'Great, we can go to that. I'll be home by eight. Have you eaten?'

'Yes, Rosa left a curry.'

'Wonderful, I'm starving. See you soon.' Climbing down from her perch, she wiped her hands on her jeans and looked around, pleased with her handiwork.

This was the kind of job she loved. Captain Andy Hamill had pretty much left her to her own devices and she'd designed a soothing, contemporary home for the single man. The fact that he had been away on long-haul flights for most of the time she'd been working here, meant she'd been able to enjoy her surroundings, throw herself into the job and not dwell on her other worries. Here her biggest concern was if the kitchen worktop would arrive on time and if the red tiles in the en-suite bathroom would scare her client.

Andy was due back in the early hours of the morning and she'd see him tomorrow to agree on a final colour for the bedroom carpet. He'd told her to pick one but she'd wanted him to see the room painted before she went ahead. She was reasonably confident that he would like the maroon colour she favoured, but the carpet was too expensive to take the risk. Grace was delighted with the way the apartment had come together, and she hoped he would be too.

When she'd cleaned up, she set the alarm, locked up

and hurried out to her car. As she drove, she wished she was going home to a hot bath and an early night, but for the sake of her marriage she would go to the cinema and pray for a row-free evening. At least for the duration of the film there would be some peace.

The last few weeks had been particularly difficult, and she had found the easiest way to cope was to retreat into herself and avoid too much contact with the outside world. Nat was busy studying so she hadn't noticed her mother's change of mood but Michael was a different story. He took her silence personally, and this trip to the cinema was an effort on her part to reintroduce some normality to their relationship.

She was happy that Nat was too preoccupied to be conscious of the strain between her parents, but at the same time she was worried about her daughter and the incredible pressure she was under. The rate yoghurts were disappearing from the fridge and the sweet wrappers and Diet Coke cans were piling up in the bedroom were testament to Nat's late-night cramming sessions. Grace felt a good night's sleep would be more beneficial but she knew her daughter had her own system and, she had to admit, so far it had worked. It upset Grace to see father and daughter drift further and further apart, and she wished there was something she could do to fix things. Perhaps it would just happen naturally when Nat was qualified and in full-time work. Maybe then Michael would accept his daughter's choice of career.

It was actually nearly two hours before Grace got

home, and as soon as she walked in the door she could sense her husband was in a mood. She decided to ignore it. 'Hello, darling,' she called, going straight through to the kitchen. He was sitting at the table reading the paper, the remains of his dinner beside him. 'How was the curry?'

Nice. Yours is in the oven and there's enough for Nat too, but there's no sign of her – as usual.'

'I think she was planning to go to the library on her way home. She's working so hard, Michael, I don't know how she does it.'

'She wasn't working last night. The smell of drink off her when she got in nearly knocked me over.'

'Really?' Grace didn't believe it. Nat wasn't a heavy drinker. She poured herself a large glass of wine and took a gulp before going to the oven to fetch her dinner.

'And she's smoking,' he continued.

Grace knew that was true – she'd smelled it from Nat's clothes. 'It's probably just the stress of the exams coming up. Let's face it, she can't exactly afford to smoke that much on her salary.'

'She might be able to, with the hand-outs she gets from Mummy,' Michael retorted.

'I don't give her money,' Grace argued, ladling curry on to her plate. 'I top up her phonecard or I buy her monthly bus-ticket – what's wrong with that?'

'She has to learn to stand on her own two feet. If she didn't have us to fall back on she might realize the importance of getting a decent job.'

Grace added rice to her plate and then put the two

Pyrex dishes back into the oven, banging the door slightly harder than was strictly necessary. 'Oh, give it a rest, Michael. I'm sick of listening to this crap.'

'Excuse me?' He stared at her.

'She's going to be a teacher, live with it. If you don't, you're going to lose her.'

He snorted. 'I'm not going to lose her as long as she needs a roof over her head.'

'There you go again. Why can't you just let her get on with her life?'

'Because she's making a mistake and I'll do everything I can to stop that happening.'

Grace looked at him in frustration. His colour was high, there was a pulse throbbing in his neck and he looked furious. 'Calm down, for God's sake, or you'll give yourself a coronary.'

Michael walked out of the kitchen and Grace sat down to eat her dinner, but the curry had lost its appeal. Sitting back in her chair she sipped her wine and decided he could go to the bloody cinema on his own. She was tired, overwrought and had a busy day tomorrow. She would have that bath, go to bed and get over to Portmarnock before the rush-hour traffic in the morning. The fact that Michael would probably still be asleep was a bonus.

Chapter 19

Miriam had gone to lunch with Annabel and there were no customers in the shop. It was too good an opportunity to miss. Bridget hurried upstairs and went into the office. The place was an absolute pigsty and Bridget knew it was driving the anally tidy Annabel mad.

'I really don't know why she has to work from here at all,' she'd complained to Bridget. 'Apart from the Graceful Living premises there's that mansion of hers in Donnybrook with God knows how many rooms.'

It had taken Bridget less than a week to become Annabel's confidante and best friend, and she now knew exactly how strained things were between Miriam and her manager as a result of the shared office. Annabel had finally confronted Miriam and demanded an explanation. She was concerned that Miriam no longer trusted her or worse, was thinking of letting her go and running the shop herself. Hence this lunch, which would probably be both long and boozy.

'Without me she'd be out of business inside a month,' the manager assured Bridget. 'With her sharp tongue and shrewish manner she'd soon lose her customers.'

'There's no way she'd let *you* go,' Bridget gushed. 'You're the best manager she's got.'

'I think I do a good job,' Annabel had preened, 'but she's been making cuts all over the place. I reckon she has money worries and that's not good news for any of us.'

Bridget's ears had pricked up immediately and she decided to do some detective work at the first opportunity.

And this was it. Looking in despair at the papers scattered everywhere, Bridget wondered where on earth to start. If a customer came in, she'd have to abandon her search so time was of the essence. She decided the desk drawers were the best place to start: Annabel had made a song and dance about having to clear her stuff out of there, so anything she'd find would be Miriam's. After twenty minutes of going through invoices, statements, and orders, Bridget was ready to throw in the towel. None of it meant a lot to her and she couldn't tell from either the orders or invoices if business was good or bad as she didn't know what the norm was

She was about to go back downstairs when she heard the beep of a phone. Searching through the papers on the desk, she discovered Miriam's mobile with a new text message on it. Bridget stared at the phone, wondering what to do. If she looked at the message, Miriam would know. Unless of course she deleted it as soon as she'd read it, then no one need know. Messages were lost all the time, everyone knew that, and if it was something important that needed a response, well then, the person would send another message or phone or something.

As Bridget dithered, another message came through and curiosity got the better of her. She read the first one.

IN DUB 2MORO. CAN I C U?

It wasn't signed but it was unlikely to be from Alastair as he was already in Dublin and it wouldn't be Luke either. It could of course be a girlfriend, but, Bridget grinned, that was unlikely. She opened the second text.

I'LL B IN THE CLARENCE FROM 6 IF YOU WANT ME.

Definitely a man, Bridget decided with a whoop of delight. Well, this was a better result than she could possibly have hoped for; Miriam was obviously having an affair. Who'd have thought any man would fancy the old bitch? Bridget shuddered at the thought of her in a passionate clinch. What an explosive piece of information to have on her beloved boss. What would Luke think? And as for poor old Alastair, he'd be devastated.

She smiled, slowly realizing that these two little messages could be a lot more lucrative than any pension. God, she could probably even get Annabel's job if she played her cards right. But how would she work this? Her word wouldn't be good enough – Miriam would laugh at her and no one would believe her. She needed proof. She thought, for a moment, of taking the phone. Miriam would assume she'd lost it or it had been stolen, easy. On the other hand, if she ever had to produce the evidence, that could get her into hot water. Her frown cleared as a very simple answer came to her. She forwarded the two mails to her own phone and then deleted them from Miriam's. Now she had the messages, along with the number they had been sent from.

Going back downstairs, Bridget decided that it might not be a bad idea to check out the bar in the Clarence tomorrow night either. It would be interesting to see what Miriam's lover looked like. He shouldn't be hard to spot, he'd probably have a guide dog with him. She was still smirking to herself when Annabel arrived back, fumes of brandy preceding her.

'Hello Bridget, everything okay?'

'Fine. Where's Miriam?'

'Oh, she's lost her mobile so she went back to the restaurant to see if it's there.'

'How was lunch?'

Annabel smiled. 'Very well. I gave it to her straight, Bridget, I did. I told her that I'm in this job too long to be messed around.'

'Damn right.'

'And she apologized.'

'No!' Bridget gaped.

Annabel nodded. 'Yes, she did. Said she knew it hadn't been easy on me, her moving in like that, but that it wouldn't be for much longer.'

'Oh, so is she moving back to Graceful Living?'

'No, she said that she'd make other arrangements.'

'Strange.'

'What?' Annabel asked.

'Oh, just I don't understand why she doesn't go back

to her old office. There's plenty of room there. That accountant guy only comes in for a few hours a week.'

Even though there was no one else in the shop, Annabel still looked behind her before leaning closer to Bridget. 'I think her and Grace had a falling-out.'

'Oh?' Bridget said. 'Grace didn't say anything to me.'

'She doesn't seem to be saying anything to anyone, that's the point. She hasn't been near here in weeks, hasn't even called.'

'You know – you're right, I hadn't noticed. I wonder, is she going to the fashion show next week?'

Annabel shrugged. 'No idea.'

'Speaking of which, Annabel, can I go?'

'Don't you always?'

'Yes, well, I mean in my own right.'

'You've lost me.'

'Luke and I have broken up.' Bridget bit her lip and wiped an imaginary tear from her eye.

'Oh, love, I didn't know. I'm sorry.'

'Thanks,' Bridget sniffed. 'Look, Miriam doesn't know and I want to keep it that way for the moment. She never liked me and Luke and I will have no chance of getting back together if she sticks her oar in.'

'Of course I won't say a word. You poor thing, this must be very hard for you.'

Bridget looked sad. 'I'm hoping that some time apart will do the trick. It has to – we belong together, Annabel, I just know it.'

'I'm sure it will all work out, love, and I promise I

won't tell a soul. But surely Luke will tell Miriam? They're very close.'

'No, he won't. He knows that Miriam might want to fire me if we weren't together so he said he'd say nothing. He's such a sweetheart.'

'He is.' Annabel squeezed her hand. 'It will all be fine, Bridget, and in the meantime, you come to the show with me next week. It will cheer you up.'

'Thanks, Annabel, you're a star.'

The door banged open – Miriam was the only one Bridget knew who could open a door with a bang – and she stormed in with a face like thunder. 'It wasn't bloody there, it must have been nicked. I thought that couple beside us looked a bit dodgy.'

'Can you remember the last time you used it?' Bridget asked.

Miriam frowned. 'Not since before lunch.'

'Then maybe it's here.'

Miriam shot her a dubious look. 'You two have a look down here, I'll check the office.'

'Needle in a haystack,' Bridget murmured and Annabel giggled.

Moments later,' Miriam called down to them 'I found it'

'Thank God,' Annabel said. 'She'd have been in an evil mood all afternoon if she hadn't. Now, Bridget, why don't you head off?'

Bridget checked her watch. 'But it's only three-thirty.'

'And you held the fort while Miriam and I went out

for a very long lunch and I'm grateful. Now go on home before she comes back.'

Bridget ran to get her bag and coat. 'Thanks, Annabel. See you tomorrow.'

As Bridget made the short walk to her car, she decided she would drive out to Blackrock to see Grace. Annabel was right, something was going on with Miriam, and Bridget was determined to find out what. Traffic was a disaster and she tapped impatiently on the wheel as she stop-started all the way down the Blackrock Road. At this rate Grace would have gone home for the day by the time she got there. There was no guarantee she'd even be there, of course; she could be out on a job. Bridget was thinking about doing a U-turn and abandoning the whole idea when the traffic speeded up and she decided to carry on. With a bit of luck, Grace would be there and Bridget would drag her out to the pub. If she wasn't, she could wander around the beautiful stores that unfortunately she could no longer afford to shop in.

She thought of her modest salary and how it had changed her life. When she was with Luke she'd just had to write a cheque or flash a credit card and she'd never really thought about how much money she actually spent. Luke had lost his temper occasionally but for the most part he'd been happy enough to let her spend. Unlike his sister, he had a very casual attitude to money. God, Bridget missed that. This morning when she'd gone to the cash machine she'd been shocked to see her balance was 63 Euros. That was all she had until she got paid on Thursday, two whole days away. If they did go for a drink, it would have to be Grace's treat.

Bridget finally turned into Blackrock's main street and crawled along on the lookout for a parking space. A van started to pull out of a spot across the road and she swerved over to nab it, waving two fingers at the driver of a Jaguar who'd had to jam on the brakes to avoid her. 'Keep your knickers on, mate,' she muttered, reversing quickly into the spot and hopping out on to the pavement. She rooted in her bag for money and was crossing to the ticket-machine when she saw Luke's van parked almost directly outside Graceful Living. What a bonus! Hurriedly getting her ticket, she raced back to put it on her dashboard. Then, she got back into the car and quickly touched up her lipstick and fluffed her hair. She was glad she was wearing a short skirt and high heels – Luke had always said she had great legs.

She was about to go over to the premises, then hesitated. Maybe it would be better to call Grace first and see how the land lay. This would be the first time she'd seen Luke face-to-face since he had left, and she didn't want to screw it up. Quickly, she pulled out her mobile and dialled the Graceful Living number. The answering machine cut in and she hung up. Then she tried Grace's mobile and this time, Grace answered. 'Hi, it's me, Bridget said. 'I was just coming to see you—'

'Bridget? Can you hang on a sec?'

The young woman waited impatiently and was about to hang up when Grace came back on.

'Sorry about that. Look, I'm out on a job and I won't be back for ages. I'll call you later, okay?'

Bridget looked across at the van and wondered where Luke was, if not in with Grace. Maybe he was in one of the shops or even the pub. In his line of work, he could be anywhere.

'Bridget, are you there?'

'Oh, yeah. Sorry, Grace, that's fine – I'll talk to you later.' Bridget hurried off up the street, peering into shops and wandering through pubs and cafés, but there was no sign of Luke. She'd done the whole street and was just on her way back to her car when she saw them standing beside the van. She quickly stepped into a doorway but they were too engrossed in conversation to notice her. She watched, mesmerized, as Luke bent his head and kissed Grace's cheek before climbing into his van and driving away. When Grace had gone back inside, Bridget walked back to her car, feeling dazed and confused as she tried to comprehend what she had just seen. It was probably all very innocent, of course, but why had Grace lied?

Grace sat down at her desk with a heavy sigh. She was fed up of being caught between Luke and Bridget, and she felt awful for lying to her friend. As soon as Luke had realized it was Bridget on the phone he'd put a finger across his throat and shaken his head. It was a ridiculous situation and Grace was beginning to lose patience with him.

'If you met her and talked to her, then you could put an end to all this,' she'd told him.

'I don't want to,' he'd said.

'And what about Miriam?'

'What about her?' His face was expressionless. 'And why do you care?'

'Look, Luke, it hasn't been easy for me keeping all of this to myself, but I did it. If you carry on like this though, it will have all been for nothing. When was the last time you saw Alastair?'

'It's been a couple of weeks.'

Grace sighed. 'And I've been avoiding him too. It's a mess.'

'Maybe we should just tell him and get it over with.'

'I can't. I've signed a contract that says the business is only mine if I keep my mouth shut.'

'That would never stand up in any court of law,' Luke told her. 'I don't know why you ever agreed to it in the first place.'

'We've been through all this,' Grace had said wearily.

'Yes, and we're protecting my sister in order to protect Alastair – but I'm not sure we're doing him any favours. He'd be better off without her.'

'I can't believe you're saying this. She's your sister.'

'I don't care – I've had enough of it. She's always been ducking and diving, fiddling the taxman and doing deals under the counter, but what she did to you, Grace, it's just not on.'

'She'd never let you down,' Grace assured him. 'She adores you and you know it.'

He tutted, then grinned. 'I can't believe you're defending her!'

Grace laughed too. 'Me neither, but I know it' s true. Miriam has a funny way of looking at the world. She sees nothing wrong with conning strangers but she'd do whatever it took to protect her own. My mistake was thinking that I was one of the people she cared for.' Grace was surprised at the catch in her voice.

'I'm sorry,' Luke said gently. 'I'm not much help, am I?'

'Just do me one favour and talk to Bridget.'

Luke looked at her for a moment and then nodded. 'Okay, but I don't think it will have the effect you seem to think. Bridget is like a limpet, and as long as she thinks there's a chance of hopping back on the gravy train, she'll hang on. But I'll talk to her if it will make you feel any better. And,' he sighed, 'I'll go and see Miriam too.'

She looked up at him, surprised.

He held up his hands. 'What can I say? You're right, we need to keep a lid on things for the moment if we're to carry this off.'

'I wish I was a better actress,' Grace grumbled. 'There's a fashion show next week and I'm really not looking forward to it. Everyone will be there, including Alastair.'

'And I'll be there too,' he told her.

'Oh, will you, Luke?'

'I haven't got much choice, have I? When was the last time I missed one of Miriam's shows?'

Grace thought. 'The year before last, when you had the flu and laryngitis.'

'There you go then.'

'Now, you know Bridget will probably be there?'

He looked confused. 'Why would *she* be there?'

Grace bit her lip. 'Because she's working in Miriam's shop.'

'*What?*'

'It was my idea,' Grace said hurriedly, 'Bridget needed a job and Miriam owed it to me and you.'

'I'm amazed she agreed – she's always hated Bridget.'

'Well, she thought if she was nice to Bridget, you might forgive her.'

Understanding dawned on Luke. 'Of course, she doesn't know we've split up.'

'No, and I suggested to Bridget it was in her interests to keep it that way.'

Luke laughed. 'My God, Grace, that was devious! You've obviously spent too much time with my sister.'

'Not funny.'

'But Bridget must be wondering what the hell is going on.'

'Exactly.'

'Well, we'll go to the fashion show next week and put on the performance of a lifetime.'

'Let's hope we can convince Alastair that everything's okay,' Grace said, wondering how she would be able to look in his eyes and deceive him.

Chapter 20

Nat left the house early, deciding she could do some revision in the library beside the exam centre. It was impossible to concentrate at home, what with Dad creeping up on her all the time to see what she was doing – although that was infinitely preferable to listening to her parents bickering all the time. She wasn't sure what it was about this time, but she had heard her father complaining about Grace being secretive and never being at home. Nat grinned; maybe she was more like her mother than she realized.

On a good day, she felt sorry for her dad as he was his own worst enemy. On a bad day, however, he was just a thorn in her side and she wished she could afford to move out. She felt very hurt that he hadn't wished her luck in her exams. Even if he didn't agree with her studying Montessori, surely he wanted her to do well? The only concern he ever really showed her these days was if it was raining; then he would immediately offer to drop her to school or to college. Once, on a good day, when he'd pulled up outside the school, Nat had asked him

would he like to come in and look around but he had
said he didn't have time and she hadn't asked again.

Her mother had come into the school one day soon
after Nat started and had been charmed by the children,
and hugely impressed at the hard work involved and the
obvious dedication of Jan and her staff.

'You must get so frustrated sometimes, especially with
the special needs children,' she'd observed later at home.

'I do,' Nat had agreed, 'but Jan doesn't – she's amazing. She says it will get easier with experience, and I
know she's right. Anyway, most days the reward out-
weighs the frustration.'

Grace had hugged her and said she was proud of her,
and Nat had felt ten feet tall. It had been a while since
they'd had one of their chats and Nat missed them, but
her mother did seem to be very busy. She was usually
asleep when Nat got home and gone again in the morning before she woke but there were notes shoved under
her door in the mornings, an extra supply of her
favourite yoghurts in the fridge and on cold nights, a
hot-water bottle in her bed. Mum was the best when it
came to pampering without smothering. This morning
she'd left a tiny pink teddy bear and a Good Luck card
outside her bedroom door and Nat had the cuddly toy
tucked in her bag for luck.

Since she'd started work and had an opportunity to
view other mothers in action, Nat had realized exactly
how lucky she was to have Grace. Equally, when she saw
fathers with their children she became aware of how

distant and formal her father had always been with her. He had never been the rough and tumble sort of dad, nor had he joined in when she and Grace had played Monopoly or Scrabble or just gone for a walk. Dad had helped with homework and introduced her to computers – in fact, all of their interaction, Nat now saw, had revolved around education and preparing for the future. There was nothing necessarily wrong with that, but it might have been a closer relationship if they'd occasionally had some fun together too.

He had taken her to the park and the playground when she was small, and there had been family outings to the cinema and the Christmas pantomime, but that all seemed to grind to a halt when she went into secondary school. A lot of that was her doing: she had been a typical teenager who wanted her own space and didn't particularly wish to hang out with her parents. But it hadn't impacted on her parents' relationship – they'd seemed to go on as usual. The bickering and snide remarks had only seemed to start in the last couple of years, and while her dad got grumpier and more distant, her mother spent more time at work.

Things had worsened over the last couple of months though, and there seemed to be an underlying resentment between them. A general feeling of unease hung over the household. Nat had to agree with her dad that her mum was behaving strangely. She didn't seem well, had lost weight and was quite distracted, and though she had always looked younger than her age, lately she looked all of her forty-six years. Nat had asked her if anything was wrong and she had just laughed it off, saying that as usual she was working too hard. Nat wasn't convinced but she liked her own privacy and so was willing to respect her mother's.

As she climbed the steps to the library, Nat decided to leave her family outside. She had an hour before her exam and she was going to make the best use of it.

It didn't go well. Nat was reading back through the paper at the end and realized she had left out Section C of the third question, worth 25 per cent. It hadn't even been that difficult, but she'd blown it. Quickly, she scribbled in some bullet points, but soon the invigilator was calling on them to down pens and she handed in her paper with a sinking heart. Though it was only an end-of-term exam, Nat knew it would be taken into account in her overall performance for the year, and she was furious with herself that she might lose points over such a silly mistake.

She had intended to drop by the school afterwards, but now she couldn't face it. She just wanted to crawl under her duvet and sleep, but if she went home, her dad would be there ready to give her the third degree. She decided instead to go and see Ken. She knew he'd be at home because tonight was the night that Tom Durrane was coming to see the show. He was probably a nervous wreck and could do with some company, and it would take her mind off her disastrous morning.

*

When she buzzed to be let in, she was thrown to hear Leila's voice telling her to come on up. Feeling slightly sick, Nat climbed the stairs and forced a smile as the agent threw open the door.

'Hey, Nat, how's it going?'

'Okay.'

'Jackson's just getting changed, he'll be out in a minute.'

Nat stared, wondering whether to hit her or run. Before she'd decided, Ken walked out, buttoning up a denim shirt. He smiled nervously at her. 'Hey, Nat, I wasn't expecting you. I thought you had an exam today.'

'I did.'

'Oh right, how did it go?'

'Jackson, we need to make a decision,' Leila cut in.

He offered Nat an apologetic smile. 'We're trying to decide what I should wear tonight.'

'Oh, right.' Nat dropped her rucksack in the hall and followed him into his bedroom.

'Leila thinks I need a sharper look.'

Nat shrugged. She hated to agree with the dreaded Leila but Ken's stage uniform of black T-shirt and jeans had always irritated her. 'I suppose.'

'The denim doesn't work,' Leila pronounced. 'Have you any formal shirts?'

Ken frowned. 'My interview shirt?'

'Let's see it.'

Ken rummaged in his wardrobe and pulled out a crisp white cotton shirt.

'Perfect.' Leila beamed.

'You're kidding, right?' Ken looked from Nat to Leila.

'With the jeans and your black jacket, it should look perfect. Try it on.'

Ken stripped off the denim shirt and Nat grimaced as she saw Leila appraising his toned chest. He put on the shirt and the simple black jacket, and Nat had to admit he looked good.

'Now the hair.' Leila moved forward and ran a hand through it, tousling it so the front stood up. 'A little gel, I think.'

'His hair is fine the way it is,' Nat said, uncomfortable with this girl standing so close to her boyfriend.

'It's fine,' Leila agreed, 'but it doesn't say rock star.'

Ken studied his reflection in the mirror, smiling slowly. 'Yeah, that works. What about sunglasses?'

'God, no, you only hide behind glasses if you're ugly or old, and you are neither.'

Nat groaned inwardly as she watched Ken lap up this flattery. No wonder celebrities ended up screwed up, if this was the kind of shit they were fed all the time. 'I thought Tom Derrane was coming to listen to him, not look at him.'

Leila stared at her as if she were stupid. 'He's come to see the act and Jackson's look is a part of that. He's an amazing songwriter and he has a fabulous voice, but the audience see him before they hear him and will have half made up their mind about him before he even opens his mouth.'

'That's mad.' Ken shook his head, shocked.

'But true, so it's worth making the effort.'

'What about the lads?' Ken, to his credit, still felt uncomfortable about being singled out.

'When the front man looks good, that's all that matters,' Leila assured him. 'Are you having a rehearsal before tonight?'

Ken looked at his watch. 'Yes, I'd better get over there now. Thanks for everything, Leila. You'll be there tonight, won't you?'

'Of course.'

'What time do you think Durrane will come?'

'No idea, he suits himself. Just forget about him and play your heart out. Now, I must be going. See you tonight.' She kissed him and then dabbed at his cheek where her ruby-red lipstick had left its mark. 'Bye, Nat.'

'Bye.'

'She's great, isn't she?' Ken said as he carefully hung up the white shirt and pulled on a sweatshirt.

'Yeah.'

'I'm so nervous about tonight, Nat, you wouldn't believe it.'

'Hey, nerves are good and you're good. Tom Durrane would be lucky to sign you.'

Ken gave her a brief hug. 'Cheers. You'll be there, right?'

'Wild horses wouldn't keep me away.'

He grinned. 'Cool.'

*

They left the flat minutes later, Ken to go to his rehearsal and Nat, at a loose end, to go home. As she walked she tried not to feel hurt that he'd entirely forgotten about her exam. It was a red-letter day for him after all, and they'd have plenty of time to talk after the gig.

She decided to have a long soak in the bath when she got home; even her dad wouldn't seek her out there. For once she was glad that he took no interest in her degree and she wouldn't have to admit to her pathetic performance this morning. She was just going to forget about it for now and concentrate on enjoying the night ahead.

She had to forgive Ken's preoccupation; this was his big chance and his excitement was contagious. She was happy that after all the years of devotion to his music it might finally come to something. Leila seemed to think so, and despite Nat's initial suspicion she had to admit that the girl spoke with authority and seemed to know what she was talking about. If Tom Durrane didn't make an appearance, however, Nat would throttle her.

Nat perched on a stool towards the back of the room – she wanted to be in a position where she could see the door – and tapped her foot nervously, checking the faces of the rest of the audience. She was pretty sure he wasn't here yet, but just in case . . .

'Is this seat taken?'

She jumped at the voice in her ear and then smiled

when she saw its owner. 'Luke! Hi. What are you doing in here?'

'I heard the band was pretty good – well, the singer anyway.'

'You heard right,' she laughed as he sat down next to her.

'Is tonight the night that big producer is coming?'

'Tom Durrane. Yes, Ken's a nervous wreck.'

'Nerves are good.'

'Yeah, that's what I told him.'

'What time do they start?'

Nat glanced anxiously at her watch. 'Any minute.'

'Why don't I get us a couple more drinks before they start? What's that?'

'Lager, but I really shouldn't, I have another exam in the morning.'

'Just the one. You could probably do with relaxing.'

'I could, but I don't think I'm going to. I'm as nervous as Ken.'

'We'll have to sneak out for a smoke, so.'

'Not tonight. I'm not going to budge until it's all over.' She grinned. 'That's another good reason not to drink too much.'

'Good thinking,' he said gravely, standing up to go to the bar. 'Back in a minute.'

Nat looked after him, glad that she would have some company. There were a few of Cutting It's regular groupies there but she hadn't wanted to join them. She had a feeling that if all went according to plan tonight,

Ken and Cutting It would be parting company.

'Have I missed anything?' Luke was back already with the drinks and pulled his stool closer to hers.

'No,' she said, suddenly conscious of his extraordinary good looks. 'So what brings you here? I would have thought you'd have a lot more important places to be.'

He frowned. 'Why would you think that?'

'Ah, come on now, you're one of Dub's movers and shakers,' she teased.

'No, I just tag along, most of the time. I'm a lot happier having a quiet pint in good company.'

He smiled at her and Nat felt her cheeks reddening.

A group at the top of the room started a slow hand-clap and Nat turned to look at them. There were a few heckles and she saw Leila peer nervously from behind the curtain. 'I'd better go and see what's up,' she said to Luke and, leaving her drink, she made her way back-stage. 'What's happening?' she asked Ken, who was pacing back and forth.

'The lads won't play.'

Leila rolled her eyes. 'They're not happy doing all of Jackson's songs; they want to do some of their own.'

'But they agreed,' Nat protested.

'Yeah, well, they changed their mind,' Ken told her.

'Then you'll just have to go it alone,' Nat told him.

Ken stopped and looked at her. 'What?'

'You've an audience out there and they are getting pretty restless. If you want to be a serious player in this business, then you have to be a professional and, as the saying goes, no matter what happens, the show must go on.'

Leila beamed at her, delighted. 'She's right, Jackson. You've got your wonderful voice, you've got your guitar, you don't need anything else.'

'But the lads—'

'Could have made the most of this opportunity, but didn't,' Leila said firmly. 'You did your best for them, Jackson, now you've got to do what's best for you.'

'And your fans,' Nat added. 'The room is packed.'

Ken looked at her and then nodded. 'Okay then, let's do it.'

Leila hugged him and then turned to the compère. 'He's going on.'

'Oh yeah? So what's his name?'

'Jackson,' Leila said.

'No.' Ken pulled himself up to his full height and looked straight ahead. 'It's Ken Jackson.'

Nat hurried back to her seat as the compère came on stage to announce Ken.

'What's happening?' Luke enquired.

'The band don't want to play Ken's music so he's going to go it alone.' Nat sat on her hands to stop them from shaking. The compère was telling the audience that there had been a slight change in tonight's show. Nat looked round nervously when there was some booing, but when it was announced that Ken Jackson of Cutting It would be performing solo, a cheer went up.

'Come on, Ken, you can do it,' she breathed as she watched him walk on stage. There was a reasonable round of applause and a couple of whistles. Ken nodded his thanks and then launched into his first song, a ballad he had written shortly after Nat met him and one she loved. His voice soared and Nat looked around at the crowd. All eyes were on Ken. She nudged the man at her side. 'What do you think?' she whispered.

Luke nodded. 'He's really good.'

'He is, isn't he?'

At the end of the first song there was a moment of silence as the last note died away and then the audience burst into a round of applause and cheering. Ken looked up, surprised, and then, grinning delightedly he launched into a faster number that had everyone clapping along and tapping their feet.

'Now all we need is Tom Durrane,' Nat said, looking at the door. 'It would be great if he saw the way this crowd is reacting. If he doesn't come, Ken will be devastated.'

'I wouldn't say so, not after a session like this. It's obvious from the reaction of the audience that he's on to a winner as a solo act.'

'You're right,' Nat agreed. 'It's only a matter of time before he's discovered now. He's better than a lot of the acts on television these days.'

'Most of them – hey!' Beer sloshed down on to his jeans as Nat clutched his arm excitedly.

'Oh, sorry, Luke – but look! It's him!'

A small, stout man in a leather jacket was standing at

the back of the room, another younger man whispermg in his ear.

Ken was on to his third number now and obviously enjoying himself. It was another ballad and the crowd were completely silent.

Nat watched as Leila, who'd been standing near the exit, joined Tom Durrane. They shook hands. Nat hoped Ken wouldn't notice them, fearing it might distract him and break the mood. But Ken, eyes closed, was in his own world and singing his heart out. When he finished it took him a moment to open them and acknowledge the roars of the crowd, some of them on their feet. Nat jumped up and down, shouting and clapping. 'Oh, I wish I could whistle,' she said. 'Can you whistle Luke?'

He obliged and she giggled. 'Oh, this is wonderful, isn't it?'

'Yes, but don't look now—'

Nat followed his gaze and her smile froze as she saw Durrane making his way to the door.

'Shit! How can he be going? He's only been here a few minutes. My God, that's disgraceful.'

'His loss,' he said, patting her arm. 'There'll be others.'

Nat didn't hear him, she was making her way through the crowd towards Leila. 'What the hell's going on? Why has he left?'

'He's on his way to another gig.'

'But that's not fair, he didn't give Ken a chance.'

Leila smiled. 'Don't worry, Nat, he saw and heard all

he needed to. We have a meeting at his offices at ten o'clock tomorrow morning.'

Nat let out a shriek and hugged her.

'Shush, your boyfriend's trying to sing,' Leila laughed.

'Oh, my God, I can't believe it.'

'You didn't think I could do it, did you?'

Nat looked sheepish. 'Sorry, I thought you just fancied him.'

'Oh I do, but I'm more interested in his talent.'

The two girls exchanged smiles. 'I wish he'd take a break,' Nat breathed. 'I can't wait to tell him.'

'Let him sing – he's enjoying himself. Now, I'm going to get some bubbly. By the way, who's the hunk?' Leila nodded over to where Luke was sitting.

Nat felt her cheeks grow hot. 'Oh, just a friend.'

'Will you introduce me?' Leila asked, not taking her eyes off him.

'If you like,' Nat said, 'but I don't think he's in the market for a woman at the moment.'

Leila laughed. 'That's never been a problem before.'

Chapter 21

Alastair walked across the beach in Banford and was about to head back to the car but felt himself drawn yet again to the little cottage at the end of the lane. The For Sale sign was still up and he was surprised at the relief he felt when he saw it. It could be really special and he made up his mind that he would get Miriam down here and convince her it would be a perfect retreat from the city. He could even live here during the summer and she could come down at the weekends. With all the travelling she was doing lately he didn't see that much of her anyway and when she was home she was usually closeted in her office, working.

Miriam had always been a workaholic, but in the past she'd been fun too. These days there wasn't much fun. Alastair couldn't remember the last time they'd had friends over to dinner or gone to a party. When he'd commented on it, Miriam had just said it was the lull before Christmas festivities started, and that in a couple of weeks his head would be spinning with all the socializing. Alastair saw the truth in this, but there hadn't been the usual twinkle in her eyes although Miram usually lived for these events. Maybe she was just too busy or tired for fun, perhaps it was the menopause – he didn't ask as he didn't really know about such things and wasn't sure he wanted to. Maybe he should ask Grace what she thought, if he ever saw her. She seemed to be as busy and elusive as Miriam, and any time he'd suggested they get together she'd made an excuse. And that's exactly what it had sounded like – an excuse.

It made him feel sad and a little embarrassed, as he'd always assumed she enjoyed his company as much as he enjoyed hers. Perhaps he was wrong and she had just been kind and he was, in fact, making a nuisance of himself.

He leaned against the cottage gate and stared out to sea. If there was one thing he was sure of, Grace would absolutely adore it here. He wondered idly what way she would redecorate the cottage. She would undoubtedly rip out the bathroom and kitchen, but what style would she go for? In the cty, he knew, she favoured a clean, contemporary look, but out here that would seem inappropriate. Alastair felt it was the kind of place where you left your wellies by the door to go in and sit by a roaring fire, a real one. He was tired of the cold, formal lines of his own stylish home and hankered after something more homely.

Old age, he grinned to himself as he reluctantly made his way back to the car. Maybe he should buy himself a pipe and some slippers. He laughed out loud, imagining

Miriam's horror if he turned into such a boring old fart. She'd be out the door in seconds, looking for a younger model. Alastair was always astounded at her energy; he was active but she was positively hyper. Sometimes he wished she'd slow down and enjoy life a bit more. He never had the kind of lazy lunches with Miriam that he had with Grace. God, he missed her, probably a lot more than was decent, given that they were both married to other people. It was probably just because she was so easy to be with and they enjoyed the same things. Miriam was wild, exciting and unpredictable. Grace was calm, serene and reliable.

Why, he asked himself as he guided his car down the windy roads leading back to the motorway, was he comparing the two women? It wasn't as if he had a choice, and his energies would be better channelled into his garden, a much safer occupation and a lot more fitting at his age.

While Alastair was making his way home, Miriam was going through her wardrobe trying to decide what to wear to the fashion show next Tuesday. She was rather nervous about it as it would be the first function that she and Grace had attended together since their split, and she was worried about Grace's ability to carry it off. She was especially nervous about Alastair being there as he usually gravitated towards Grace, saying she was the only woman who didn't waffle on about fashion as if it was a religion.

Miriam closed her eyes briefly, wondering how she would explain it if Luke didn't turn up. Alastair wasn't stupid, he'd already commented on the fact that her brother hadn't been around. Miriam told him they'd had words about Bridget, a completely credible reason, but they'd never ever argued for more than a couple of days before this and she knew Alastair was suspicious. Knowing her husband, he'd probably been in touch with Luke, trying to play peacemaker, and the fact that Luke still hadn't called was testament to how annoyed he was with her. Alastair's suspicions would be raised even further if Luke didn't show up at the fashion show but Miriam was hoping that Bridget, being the selfish bitch that she was, would badger him into going. Then she would have to spend the evening worrying if Grace or Luke were going to spill the beans or just give the game away by ignoring her point blank. Whatever happened, it was going to be a tough evening and Miriam needed to dress up to the nines to give herself the courage to get through it.

She had narrowed her choice down to three outfits when the doorbell went. She ignored it at first and tutted impatiently when it rang again.

'All right, all right, I'm coming!' she yelled as she ran downstairs and threw open the door. 'Luke!' Her expression changed from anger to delight. 'Come in, come in. Oh, it's so good to see you. Alastair isn't here so we can have a nice chat and I'll tell you anything you want to know and—'

'I'm only here because Grace asked me to come,' he said, cutting in on her nervous diatribe.

'Of course, why else?' Miriam's mouth twisted into a sardonic smile.

'Don't start,' he warned. 'You just don't seem to realize how lucky you are to have got away with this.'

'I haven't gotten away with anything. I've handed over my half of the business, what more do you want – blood?'

He shook his head. 'I just wish I could understand how you could do it. How you could betray your own friend?'

'Oh, please, enough,' Miriam groaned. 'You are so bloody naïve, Luke. I'm a businesswoman and she's not my friend, she's my *partner* – or was.'

'She was your friend too, even if you weren't hers,' he shot back.

Miriam saw that if she didn't say what he wanted to hear he'd be out the door and she probably wouldn't see him again. 'You're right, I have behaved badly but I am paying for it, Luke, I promise you. It's hurt me financially, but more than that,' she added quickly as he rolled his eyes, 'it's put a huge strain on my marriage – and look at what it's done to us. It's broken my heart not having you around, and Alastair keeps asking where you and Grace are.'

'Which is why I'll be at the fashion show next Tuesday.'

'Oh Luke, that's wonderful. Thank you.'

'But don't go dragging me around the room introducing me to everyone.'

'I won't.'

'In fact, don't even talk to me.'

'Oh, Luke . . .'

'You know what I mean. Just don't push it, okay?'

She nodded, smiling. 'Thanks, I appreciate this.'

'I'm doing it for Grace and Alastair.'

'Of course,' she said through gritted teeth. 'I suppose Bridget will be coming?'

He grinned. 'You tell me – she's your employee, isn't she?'

'Only because she's your girlfriend.'

'Not any more.'

'What?' Miriam stared at him.

'You've been had. Bridget and I broke up weeks ago.'

'But Grace—'

'Gave you a taste of your own medicine. Tell me, how does it feel being on the receiving end?'

Miriam glared at him. 'If Bridget doesn't work out she'll be out the door.'

He shrugged. 'Then I'll have to tell Alastair everything.'

Miriam scowled. 'It's really over?'

'Yes, it is. Happy now?'

'She wasn't good enough for you.'

Luke raised an eyebrow. 'I don't think you're in a position to judge anyone, do you? I've got to go. I'll see you on Tuesday. Oh, and by the way.'

'Yes?'

'Dad's fine, thanks for asking.'

Bridget almost forgot about Miriam's date in the Clarence, she was so thrown by seeing Luke and Grace together. She didn't know what to make of it. It seemed incredible that Luke would be attracted to Grace, she was *so* not his type. But what other explanation could there possibly be for Grace lying to her? Her first inclination had been to barge straight in and ask Grace what the hell was going on, but something had made her hold back, something her mother used to say about keeping your powder dry. For the moment she decided to concentrate on getting more dirt on Miriam, and she hoped to do that in the Clarence.

She took her time applying her make-up even though there was a good chance she would end up hiding behind pillars all evening. If he had resent the messages and Miriam turned up, she would try to get a photo of them together on her mobile phone. If she didn't, and Bridget was able to figure out who the boyfriend was, she might strike up a conversation with him and find out what she could. She'd decided to wear a black trouser-suit. It was an outfit she usually reserved for funerals, but teamed with a coffee-coloured satin camisole, it looked both sexy and sophisticated. A chunky gold choke and bracelet and very high black sandals completed the effect. She didn't own a briefcase so she decided instead to bring a large suede shoulder bag and carry a file under her arm. The fact that there was just a magazine inside the file was immaterial: it would create the image she wanted.

She got her mobile, checked the battery was charged and then went out to the car. She was just starting the engine when there was a knock on the window.

'Hi, Bridget.'

'Luke!'

'Is this a bad time?'

Bridget checked her watch. It was almost five and it would take about forty minutes to get into town. 'No, it's okay.' She got out of the car. 'Come inside.'

Luke followed her into the hall and then stood there awkwardly shifting from one foot to the other.

'How are you?' Bridget asked.

'Fine. Look, Grace said I should talk to you.'

'Did she?'

'Yes. She said we needed to tie up loose ends.'

'Before you move on?' Bridget said tightly. The two-faced bitch.

'Now obviously isn't a good time. Do you want to meet for a drink before the fashion show on Tuesday?'

'Is there any point?'

Luke looked baffled. 'You're the one who's been pestering me to meet up, Bridget.'

'Yeah, okay, then.'

'I'll pick you up about seven.'

The fashion show started at eight so he obviously didn't think there was much to say. 'Fine. Luke?'

He turned back. 'Yes?'
'Were you at Grace's today when I phoned?'
He looked at her for a moment and then nodded.
'And you told her to get rid of me?'
'Look, Bridget—'
'Bye, Luke.'

On the drive into town Bridget tried to figure out what to do next. Luke certainly wasn't interested in getting back with her. He hadn't even reacted to her outfit and she'd made sure to stand close enough to ensure that he got a good eyeful of cleavage. But it was equally obvious that he wasn't interested in Grace, and that was something. Losing Luke was one thing, losing him to an older woman was unthinkable.

When she walked into the Octogon Bar, Bridget made her way to a small table in a corner and sat down. As she'd walked through the room she had covertly studied the other occupants. There were only five men and two women; Miriarn wasn't among them. Three of the men and the two women were together, and it looked like they'd been there for a while. The other two men were sitting separately at the bar, one reading a newspaper, the other talking on a mobile phone. The newspaper man was in his late forties, Bridget figured, and the phone man was probably a few years older. Either of them were possible candidates.

A waiter came over and she ordered a mineral water.

She didn't know how long she was going to be here and she needed to keep a clear head. She opened her file, careful to keep it at an angle so no one could see the contents, and pretended to study it while at the same time craning to hear the man who was on the phone. Sadly, the group of men and women were getting rowdier and she couldn't make out any discernible accent. It would narrow things down if she could hear Miriam's mystery man speak. She turned her attention to the newspaper man, who was drinking a pint of Guinness and reading the *Irish Times*. She doubted Miriam would have anything to do with a man who drank pints but then, who knew? He was dressed in a sober though well-cut suit but his tie was quite boring and probably Polyester, another no-no in Miriam's book. The phone man, who had now finished his call and seemed to be texting, was wearing a tweed suit with a lemon shirt and a paisley tie that was obviously silk. Bridget's pulse quickened – it had to be him.

Phone Man was quite good-looking in a rather obvious way. He didn't have Luke's more natural, rugged features. His hair was neatly cut, in an old-fashioned style, but his skin was amazingly clear and tanned, and his teeth – he was sharing a joke with the waiter now – were even and white. The biggest giveaway was the shoes, however – highly polished black loafers. Miriam always judged men by their shoes and Bridget was sure she'd found her man.

Now all she had to do was sit tight and see what

happened, although the dilemma was how long to wait before moving in. She was in luck as a few minutes later, the group left and she heard the waiter asking Phone Man if he wanted to reserve a table for dinner. The man shook his head and said he hated eating alone and might just have a snack at the bar. Bridget immediately drained her glass and went up to the bar to get a refill. She stood near to him but not too near, and smiled at the waiter as he approached to take her order. 'I'll have a glass of dry white wine, please, and is there any chance of getting something to eat?'

'Certainly, madam. You could have a light snack here or I could reserve a table for you in our dining room.'

'Oh no, I hate eating alone. Something here would be fine.' She sat up on a barstool and set the file down in, front of her.

'Hotels are very boring places when you're alone, aren't they?' Phone Man said.

Bingo! Bridget smiled briefly. 'They are.' He had an English accent. That was another box ticked. It had to be him.

'I love to eat out but it's just not the same when there's no one to talk to.'

'Your wine, madam, and I'll fetch you a menu.'

'Thank you.' Bridget took a sip of her drink and then pretended to check the messages on her phone. As she listened, she scribbled notes and numbers on the file and tried to look businesslike. She put the phone down when the waiter returned with the menus, one for her and one for Phone Man. She studied it carefully, opening her jacket at the same time and turning slightly sideways so that her camisole was on view. In less than a minute he was over.

'Nigel Prince,' he said, holding out a hand.

After a moment, Bridget took it briefly. 'Bri—' Shit, she couldn't use her real name. 'Breda Dunne.'

'Nice to meet you, Breda. Now, please don't take this the wrong way, but as we both hate eating alone and we both want to eat, what do you say we keep each other company?'

Bridget, never one to miss an opportunity, gave a sad smile. 'Nice idea, Nigel, but I'm afraid nothing here really takes my fancy.' She tossed the menu back on to the bar.

'Well, we don't have to eat here. We could go into the restaurant.'

'I'm afraid my expense account doesn't run to the main restaurant.'

'Then you must be my guest.'

'Oh, I'm sorry, that wasn't a hint.' Bridget stared at him in horror.

'Of course, I know that – but really, you would be doing me a favour. It would be a pleasure to have such lovely company.'

God, he was a right sleaze, Bridget thought, and if he was Miriam's lover he didn't appear to be the faithul sort. From the way he was eyeing her up, he was definitely after more than a dinner companion, but Bridget would play along until she'd got the information she needed. Apart from which, she hadn't been in a decent restaurant since Luke left. 'I'd be happy to join you,' she said graciously.

'Excellent.' He turned to the waiter who'd been watching the floor show with a knowing smile. 'Could you organize a table for two in your restaurant, please?'

'Certainly sir. Would you like to go straight in?'

'After we've finished our drinks?' He looked at Bridget.

She nodded. 'Yes. I don't want to have too late a night, I have a presentation in the morning.'

The waiter nodded and left.

'So, what do you do?' Nigel asked.

Shit, shit, shit, why had she said that? She had nothing prepared and she could hardly tell him she was in the fashion industry. She decided to use the only other profession she knew something about. 'Terribly boring, I'm afraid. I work for a plumbing contractors. We're touting for a new, very big account based here in the city centre.'

'That's an unusual occupation for a woman, or is that very sexist of me?'

'It certainly is. Anyway, I'm a saleswoman and selling is selling, regardless of the product.'

'Very true. I'm in the opposite game myself. I'm a buyer for a large chain of boutiques in the UK.'

'So what brings you to Dublin?'

'We have three Irish suppliers and I come over three or four times a year to check out their new designs.'

'Sounds a lot more fun than plumbing,' she laughed.

'Well,' he eyed her appreciatively, 'you'd be very at home in the fashion industry. You obviously have an eye for good clothes.'

'Thank you'

The waiter returned with their menus and Nigel ordered some wine.

'And some water for me too, please,' Bridger said, remembering she was driving. 'So, Nigel, where are you from?'

'Originally from Plymouth, but now I live in a place called Gravesend – that's on the east coast, south of London.'

'And is there a Mrs Prince and little Princes?' she murmured.

He smiled. 'There are.'

'Good, I'm glad you didn't lie.'

'How would you know?' he countered.

She grinned. 'Married men are usually better dressed and better co-ordinated than single ones. It would have been more difficult with you though, you being in the fashion industry.'

'Or I could have been gay.'

Her eyes held his. 'No, definitely not.'

The waiter came to take them to their table and Nigel chose the seat next to her. She was going to have fun getting away from this one, Bridget realized. 'Tell me, do you know any of our boutiques here in Dublin? I go to a wonderful one in Rathgar, it's called Lady M's.'

'I know it,' he said smoothly. 'They have some nice stuff.'

'Miriam Cooper, she's the owner, is quite a celebrity here. Do you know her?'

'Yes, we've bumped into each other a few times,' he said as the waiter returned with their wine. 'Now Breda, try this, I think it's a bit special.'

Bridget sniffed and sipped the way she'd seen Miriam and Alastair do. 'Lovely,' she pronounced.

'Excellent!' Nigel beamed. 'I think you'll find it will go very well with the duck or the beef.'

Bridget, who'd actually been planning to have the lobster, decided not to push her luck. 'Yes, the duck sounds good. So you know Miriam?'

'We've bumped into each other,' he repeated, keeping his eyes on the menu.

I'll bet you have, Bridget thought, and tried changing tack. 'Apparently, she has a bit of an eye for the men.'

'Oh?' He still didn't look up.

'Yes, although I suppose you can't blame her. She's married to an older man, a retired schoolteacher – he probably bores her to tears.' This was a very misleading description of the handsome, charming man Bridget knew but she somehow doubted Nigel had ever met him.

'You seem to know a lot about her,' he remarked, finally raising his eyes to hers.

'Like I said, she's a bit of a celebrity here and always in the gossip columns.' She slipped off her jacket and put it on the back of her chair. 'I'm a sucker for gossip,' she admitted, leaning closer to him, her bare arm brushing his jacket.

'Well, you never know, I might be able to give you some,' he whispered in her ear. 'And some gossip too!'

Bridget threw back her head and laughed. 'You are awful!'

'So tell me, Breda, is there a Mr Dunne?'

Bridget looked blank and then realized he was asking if she was married. 'No. I've just broken up with my partner, actually.'

'Oh, I'm sorry.'

She shrugged. 'It was time to move on.' God, she should be an actress, all this came very naturally to her.

'He was crazy to let you go.'

'You think?'

'Absolutely! You're beautiful, witty, and obviously intelligent.'

'Oh, please go on, you're doing wonders for my ego,' Bridget laughed.

'And you're very sexy,' he murmured, his lips close to her ear.

Bridget turned to face him, her lips just inches from his. Maybe it was because Luke had left, maybe it was seeing him with Grace – Bridget wasn't sure what the reason was – but right now she was beginning to feel very turned on. The restaurant, the wine and the attentions of this attractive man were quite a heady combination.

There was a discreet cough beside them. 'Sir, madam, are you ready to order?'

'I'm ready.' Nigel kept his eyes on Bridget's. 'Are you?'

Chapter 22

Grace was dressing for the fashion show and feeling very nervous about the evening ahead. She hadn't seen Alastair since she'd discovered Miriam's treachery, and she was afraid he knew her too well to believe it was just because she was busy. At least Luke would be there and he'd rescue her if necessary. To Grace's amazement, Bridget would also be there. Luke had phoned earlier and admitted he'd told Miriam that he and Bridget had separated weeks ago.

'I just couldn't resist it, Grace. I wanted her to know that you had pulled a fast one on her.'

'That's all very well, Luke, but it will probably cost Bridget her job and then you won't be so happy. Bridget has been in much better form since she started work and she's stopped obsessing about you.'

'If Miriam even thinks about firing Bridget I'll threaten to tell Alastair everything. That will keep her in line.'

'Aren't you fed up with all of this, Luke? I know I am. I'm not sure I can carry on.'

'You have to,' he'd said quietly. 'Now stop worrying about Tuesday. I'll be there to hold your hand, I promise.'

Grace stepped into the long chocolate skirt and matching sleeveless silk embroidered top and added long earrings, an intricate necklace and a bracelet made with beads the colour of topaz. The shades suited her colouring but the overall effect was slightly bohemian so she decided to catch her hair back in a knot to make it more formal.

Michael walked in as she was stepping into the brown suede shoes. 'You should wear your hair down,' he told her.

Grace's eyes met his in the mirror. 'Do you think so? I thought it made me look like a gypsy.'

'You look lovely.'

She smiled at him, surprised at the compliment. They'd hardly exchanged a polite word in the last couple of weeks. 'Okay then,' she said, and took out the grips holding her hair in place.

'Much better,' he said, touching it gently.

'Michael—'

'Look, Grace—'

They both broke off and laughed.

'Sorry,' Grace said. 'I know I haven't been easy to live with.'

'I'm sorry too,' he said, taking her in his arms. 'Why don't we get out of this place as soon as the show is over and grab a late supper somewhere quiet, just the two of us?'

'I'd like that.'

He smiled. 'So, what will I wear?' He turned to his wardrobe.

'Your dark-grey suit?' she suggested.

'Okay then. I'll just go and have a quick shave. Will you pick out a shirt and tie for me?'

'You're useless,' Grace laughed.

'I know, but you're so much better at that sort of thing.'

Feeling happier, Grace selected a black shirt and a grey tie.

'Oh, my Chris Tarrant look,' he remarked when he returned.

'You look much better than him.'

'I should hope so – he's a lot older than me. I think he might even be older than Alastair.'

Grace said nothing. She would never put 'Alastair' and 'old' in the same sentence. He was a vibrant man, and to her he seemed ageless.

'Where are my silver cufflinks?' he asked, breaking in on her thoughts.

'In your drawer, where they always are.'

'No, they're not.'

'They must be. It's either that or you've left them in the last shirt you wore them in.'

'Then they'd have gone in the wash.'

'Rosa would never have put them in the washing-machine. I'm sure they must be here somewhere.'

'She probably took them.'

Grace stared at him. 'Michael, Rosa would never do that, what a terrible thing to say.'

'You're so bloody trusting, Grace. When are you going to realize that not everyone is as honest as you?'

'Rosa is,' Grace muttered, pulling her wrap from the wardrobe. 'I'll see you downstairs.'

'But what about my cufflinks?' he called after her.

'Wear the gold ones.'

By the time they got to the fashion show Grace was ready to scream as Michael kept up a monologue about the missing cufflinks and his suspicion that Rosa had something to do with it.

'Oh, for Christ's sake will you forget the fucking cufflinks?' she finally exploded as they parked outside the hotel.

'There's no need for that kind of language,' Michael said critically, following her inside. 'Now I see where Nat gets it from.'

Grace paused in the doorway of the ballroom and took off her wrap. 'I tell you what, Michael, why don't you put our coats in the cloakroom and then go and get yourself a large drink?'

Taking her wrap he glared at her and turned on his heel.

'Hello, Grace.'

She whirled around to see Alastair standing there, resplendent in a dark-green jacket. 'Alastair, don't you look marvellous!'

He bent to kiss her cheek and then stood back to look her up and down. 'Not even close to how marvellous you look, my dear. What a stunning outfit, and such a welcome change from all this black. What is it about these fashion gurus and black?' he added *sotto voce*.

Grace giggled. 'I think the idea is that they look scary and sophisticated.'

'Well, they got the first one right. Most of them scare the hell out of me! Now, where's Michael?'

'I sent him to the bar. He's in a strop because his cufflinks are missing and he's convinced Rosa took them.'

Alastair stared. 'Rosa would never do that.'

'Oh, he knows that. He's just annoyed that he's misplaced them and he has to blame someone.'

'Grace, hi, you look lovely.'

Grace froze as Miriam joined them, a bright, false smile pinned to her lips. She was wearing a black tuxedo with her hair slicked back, and the effect was rather severe and unflattering.

'Hi, Miriam.' Grace forced a smile. 'How are things going?'

'Okay. Nothing to report so far, just the usual gathering of bods.'

'Right.'

'Let me get you a drink, Grace. White wine?'

'Thanks, Alastair, that would be lovely.'

'Luke isn't here yet,' Miriam said when he had gone.

'Oh?' Grace watched the room.

'He told me, you know, about him and Bridget breaking up.'

'Did he?'

'That was very clever of you, Grace, using our situation like that.'

Grace shot her a brief look of intense dislike. 'I've had a good teacher.'

'It won't last, of course,' Miriam continued. 'Bridget is a disaster and Annabel will want to get rid of her probably within days.'

Grace smiled. 'Do you think so?'

'I know it.'

'Funny, as they seem to get along so well.' Grace nodded towards the door where Annabel and Bridget stood chatting amicably.

Miriam's eyes narrowed. 'If she puts a foot wrong—'

'Excuse me, Miriam, but I'd much rather talk to someone else.'

'But you can't go, what will Alastair think?'

'That you've sent me off to tout for business, that's what you usually do. Now I'm going to do my damnedest to have a normal evening, so stay out of my way, okay?' And leaving the other woman staring after her, Grace crossed the room to say hello to Bridget.

Bridget saw Grace approaching and swallowed hard. She hadn't told Grace that she had seen her and Luke together and found her friend out in a deliberate lie. She forced herself to return Grace's hug and pasted a smile on her face. 'Grace, you look well.'

'Stunning,' Annabel agreed. 'That's a beautiful top.'

'Thank you.'

'It makes us all look very boring in our black.'

Bridget's smile disappeared. She knew she looked very sexy in her short, black dress. 'Black is almost a uniform in this industry, it shows you belong.'

'Quite right,' Grace agreed, laughing, 'and I don't.'

'So why are you here?' Bridget said before she could stop herself.

Grace didn't seem to notice her tone. 'Oh, you know, Miriam likes to use these events to get more business for Graceful Living. I must say, there's quite a crowd tonight. Maybe we should go to our seats.'

'I'm just waiting for Luke,' Bridget replied, watching Grace closely. 'He's gone to get me a drink.'

Grace's eyes widened and she smiled kindly. 'Really? Oh, that's wonderful, Bridget. Are you two—'

'We're just having a drink, Grace,' Luke said, appearing at her side. 'Can I get you something?'

'No, that's okay, Alastair's gone to get me one.' Grace looked around but couldn't see him anywhere.

'Where's Michael?' Luke asked.

'Probably at the bar.'

'Is everything okay?' he murmured.

'Sure.' Grace nodded. 'Fine.'

'Ladies and gentlemen, if you will take your seats please, the show will commence shortly.'

'I'd better go and find Michael,' Grace said. 'See you all later.'

'In a few minutes, actually,' Annabel called. 'All our seats are together.'

'Lovely.' Grace melted into the crowd.

'Grace, there you are! I've been looking everywhere for you.' Alastair came towards her, a large glass of wine in his hand, and Grace took it gratefully.

'Have you seen Michael?' she asked.

He shook his head. 'No, but it's absolutely chaotic up there. Why don't we take our seats. I'm sure he'll make his way over to us.'

'Okay, then.' Grace didn't really care whether he did or not, but at the same time, it would be easier if he was there. The less time she had alone with Alastair, the better.

Their seats were in the first and second rows to the right of the catwalk. Miriam was already there and she jumped up when she saw them approach. 'Alastair, over here! I've kept a seat next to me.'

'Oh, let Bridget take it,' he said as he spied Bridget in the second row behind a very tall young man. 'She's much more interested in this stuff than I am.'

'Thanks, Alastair.' Bridget blew him a kiss and quickly moved around to sit beside Miriam and Annabel.

'No problem, my dear.'

Grace found herself sitting with Alastair to her left and Luke the far side of him. The seat beside her remained vacant as there was no sign of Michael. Luke was chatting to Alastair and as Grace listened to them talk, she wondered how he could carry on as if nothing had changed. She was a nervous wreck and the show hadn't even started yet.

'Where have you been?' she asked crossly as her husband finally appeared and sat down beside her.

'At the bar. Hello, Alastair, Luke.'

Bridget turned around and smiled. 'Hi, Michael, we were wondering where you'd got to.'

Michael reddened. 'Bit of a queue at the bar. Hello, Miriam.'

Miriam smiled and probably Grace was the only one who saw the strain in her eyes. 'Hello, Michael, lovely to see you.'

'And you.'

Grace couldn't resist exchanging a smirk with Luke. If Miriam kept up this polite façade all night she'd blow a gasket.

Bridget, who was still turned in her seat, caught the exchange between Grace and Luke and frowned. Those two were way too cosy for her liking. Grace was supposed to be her friend although she seemed to have forgotten the fact. Her drink with Luke had been disappointing and a bit humiliating. He had been almost nice to her while at the same time making it clear that they had no future together.

'Who says I wanted you back?' she'd snapped.

He sighed. 'You did, on several text and phone messages.'

'Well, I've changed my mind.'

'Good, I'm glad to hear it. Now, you should know that Miriam knows we've split up but I don't want you to worry about your job. I've told her she's not to take this out on you.'

'That's very big of you,' Bridget had said, 'but I can handle your sister.'

Luke had shaken his head. 'I wouldn't be so sure.'

Bridget's eyes narrowed. 'What's that supposed to mean?'

'Nothing.'

'Have you two had a row?'

'I said it's nothing.'

And that had been that. Bridget couldn't get another word out of him. She felt angry with him and was more determined than ever to show Grace, him and his bitch of a sister that she didn't need any of them. She stared at the catwalk in front of her as the lights went down, but as the willowy models strutted down towards her, all she could think about was getting even.

Chapter 23

Nat was cleaning up after a sick child, thinking that it was a fitting end to a really bad day. How Dad would laugh if he could see her now. Her tears plopped on to the cleaned floor and she sat back on her knees to wipe her face on her arm.

'Are you okay, Nat?' Jan stood over her, a worried look on her face.

Nat jumped and knocked the bucket of water over. 'Oh, shit! Sorry, Jan.'

'It was my fault,' Jan said, fetching the mop. 'I didn't mean to make you jump.'

Between them, they finished cleaning the floor and then left the bucket, mop and dirty cloths outside the back door. 'Vi, our cleaner, will take care of that later.'

'She won't be too pleased.'

Jan laughed. 'She's got six kids of her own – believe me, she's well used to it. Now, there are only three children left and Jill's looking after them, so why don't you and I have a cup of tea? I'll put on the kettle and you get the mugs and biscuits, and then you can tell me why you were crying.'

'I wasn't.'

'You were.'

Nat sighed. 'It's Ken.'

'Have you two had a row?'

Nat laughed sadly. 'I haven't seen him for long enough to have a row.'

'Is stardom blinding him?' Jan asked as she popped two teabags into the mugs and poured boiling water on top of them. Nat had told her all about Ken being discovered.

'No, but he always seems to be in a meeting or a sound studio or going shopping with Leila.'

Jan raised an eyebrow. 'Ah.'

'Yes. Ah.' Nat took a sip of her tea. 'It's hard to compete, you know? She's beautiful, clever, funny and she's got a really cool job.'

'Minding kids is pretty cool.'

Nat made a face. 'You know what I mean.'

'I do.'

'And she's able to do something that I can't.'

'What's that?'

'Make his dreams come true.'

'I'm sure you're part of his dreams too,' Jan said.

'I'm not. At the moment he doesn't seem to even notice I'm alive.'

'You just have post-exam blues.'

Nat laughed. 'Surely I should have post-exam euphoria.'

'No, you've been studying hard these last few weeks and now, suddenly, you're at a loose end and the man that you'd like to spend all that free time with is otherwise engaged.'

'That's about the size of it.'

'You need to be patient with him.'

'You're right.' Nat drained her mug and stood up. 'I'll go home, glam myself up to the nines and maybe he'll remember I'm his girlfriend.'

'So where are you going tonight?'

'He's doing a gig on his own again and he's trying out some new songs.'

'And you'll be in the front row, clapping your little hands off?'

Nat beamed. 'I certainly will.'

Only he still didn't seem to notice. It didn't help that good old Leila was there again and that when Ken took a break she was counselling him on his diction or the way he should hold the mike. Decidedly fed up, Nat went for a smoke. She was disappointed to find herself alone on the porch; she had got used to meeting Luke and having a good moan. God, that's probably why he wasn't here – she'd scared him off. So here she was, in her silky red bodice, tight black jeans, suede knee-high boots and tons of make-up and no one to appreciate it.

'Hello there.'

She looked up and there he was, and she felt ridiculously happy to see him. 'Hey.'

He was staring at her appreciatively. 'Wow, you look amazing.'

'Thanks.'

'Going somewhere special?'

She shook her head. 'No, just my exams are over and I'm having a private celebration.'

'Isn't Ken joining you?'

Nat looked glum. 'Ken doesn't even know I'm alive.'

'I'm sure that's not true. He's probably just a bit—'

'Distracted – yes, I know.'

'Anyway, congratulations. How do you feel you did?'

Nat shrugged. 'I don't know and I've decided not to think about it.'

'Good strategy. Is Ken playing tonight?'

'Yeah, he's just about to start his last set.'

'So do you want to go back in?'

Nat hesitated, then said 'I don't think so, no. Tonight I'm going to suit myself.'

He chuckled. 'In that case, I insist you let me get you a drink. I don't believe in anyone celebrating alone.'

Nat smiled. 'Okay, then.'

'How about champagne in slightly more salubrious surroundings?'

Nat looked around the dimly lit restaurant, recognizing some well-known faces.

'Thank you so much, I'm having a lovely time.' She

took a sip of her wine. 'I've only ever been here once before with Mum and Dad.'

'Once Ken hits the big time you'll be hanging out in places like this all the time.'

'I don't know about that.' Nat had texted Ken to let him know she was leaving and had received back the rather disappointing reply: OK C U LATR

'Don't you think he's going to make it?'

'Oh, I do – I'm just not sure I'll be around to see it happen.'

'How do you feel about that?'

She looked at him from under her lashes. 'I'm not sure.'

He held her gaze. 'Can I offer you some advice, Natasha?'

She loved the way he said her name. She loved that he refused to use the diminutive.

'Natasha?'

'Oh, sorry – yes, go ahead.'

'You can do better.'

'What do you mean?'

'You can do better than Ken Jackson. He doesn't deserve you.'

Nat felt a warm glow spread through her.

'Have I gone too far?' he asked.

She shook her head. 'You think I should dump him?'

He shrugged. 'You're a beautiful and clever young woman, and I just feel he doesn't begin to appreciate that. Tell me, did he ask you how you got on at your exams?'

She bent her head 'Well, no—'

'Has he asked you lately how your job is going?'

She shook her head.

'Has he told you how beautiful you look tonight?'

She raised her eyes to his. 'No.'

'Then he's an idiot and you're better off without him.'

'And should I go for someone more like you?' she teased.

He laughed. 'God, no, I'm a total loser – ask Bridget.'

'She didn't deserve you,' Nat said staunchly.

He chuckled. 'Have you been talking to my sister?'

'So,' Nat smiled at him, emboldened by the champagne, 'as we've got so much in common, maybe you and I should get together.'

Luke burst out laughing. 'God, I could just see your dad's face if you brought *me* home.'

'Hey, it wouldn't matter who I brought home, Dad wouldn't be happy. Nothing I do or say makes him happy. You could say he's only happy when he's unhappy.'

Luke glanced at his watch. 'I'd better get you home or your mum won't be too pleased either.

Nat scowled. 'I'm not a child, Luke, I'm a woman.'

Luke smiled. 'Sure you are.'

'Don't patronize me,' she said angrily.

Luke looked at her in surprise. 'Natasha, darling, I'm not. What's wrong? What have I said?'

'Nothing,' she muttered. 'Just take me home.'

*

They drove home in silence, Nat staring out of the passenger window the whole time. Luke pulled up at the end of her road. 'Look, Natasha—'

'Thanks for dinner, Luke.' Nat hopped out and walked quickly away. She didn't slow her pace until she heard him drive off, then she ground to a halt, covered her eyes and groaned. What a fool she'd made of herself. Although he had led her on, she reasoned, all those compliments, the expensive dinner, the champagne . . . what was she supposed to think?

She let herself quietly into the house, praying she could get up the stairs without meeting either of her parents. She was in no mood for an inquisition from her dad, and if her mum was nice to her she'd just burst into tears and blurt out the whole sorry story. As she tiptoed up the stairs, she could hear the sound of a football match on the television in the lounge. Upstairs, her parents' bedroom door was closed. She hesitated outside, but then went on to her own room and closed the door. She was just taking off her jacket when her phone beeped and she pulled it out to read the text message. It was from Ken.

SLEEP WELL. I'LL CALL U 2MORO. X

She climbed into bed feeling tired and confused. He would go and complicate things by being nice to her now. Hearing her father's footsteps on the stairs, she closed her eyes and buried her head under the covers. Seconds later there was a light tap on her door and he looked in.

'Nat?'

She said nothing, forcing herself to breathe steadily.

'Good night, God bless,' he whispered and left, closing the door quietly behind him.

Nat opened her eyes and sniffed. God, even Dad was being nice – this was all too much. Glad of the effects of the champagne, she closed her eyes again and went to sleep. In her dreams Leila and Bridget danced around laughing and looking gorgeous while she sat in a corner feeling miserable. Every time she tried to join in, she found her legs wouldn't work, and when she called out for help, no one could hear her. She woke up feeling exhausted and relieved that it was Saturday and she didn't have to be anywhere. Pushing her embarrassing behaviour of the previous night firmly to the back of her mind, she buried her head under the covers and went back to sleep.

Grace stretched and yawned as she stepped into her slippers. Michael had left early this morning to go fishing and she was looking forward to a long, leisurely breakfast with no arguments. She heard the newspaper thump on to the mat in the hall and went out on to the landing, pulling her dressing-gown tight around her against the morning chill. Nat's door was closed and Grace moved quietly so as not to disturb her. She'd been working so hard lately, the girl deserved a nice rest. When she eventually surfaced Grace would make her French toast or pancakes, whatever she fancied, and maybe later the two of them could go shopping together. It had been ages since they'd had a girly day out.

With all that had happened lately, Grace was feeling quite vulnerable and in need of some time with her daughter. Nat made her feel useful and loved. Things had got worse with Michael since their silly squabble before the fashion show. They hadn't gone for their planned dinner afterwards, they were barely talking by that stage, and now they had reached a point where they maintained a polite, but cold front, avoiding each other at all costs.

It made Grace unutterably sad. She had never expected to end up actually disliking Michael. She had loved him when she married him, and she still remembered the wonderful times they'd had together, the day Natasha was born being without doubt the best. Actually, Grace thought as she made a large pot of coffee, all the best times included Natasha – and perhaps that was significant.

Grace was at a loss as to what to do next. She was still coming to grips with running Graceful Living alone and though she hated to admit it, she now realized how much of a load Miriam had carried. That in no way excused her behaviour, of course, Grace reminded herself as she made some toast. She had behaved in an unforgivable manner and that was the end of it. But no Miriam also meant no Alastair, and that was hard. Seeing him on Tuesday night had reminded her how much she enjoyed his company, and when he'd told her about the little cottage by the sea that he'd fallen in love with, she longed to visit it with him. He had suggested a trip to it and the garden centre, but Grace didn't trust herself to be alone with him. She had given her word to Miriam that she wouldn't tell him what had happened, and she would stand by that. If she didn't, it would make her as bad as her partner. *Ex*-partner, she corrected herself as she carried her breakfast to the table and poured herself a large mug of coffee. Determined that her breakfast wasn't going to be spoiled by thoughts of Miriam, Grace propped up the paper in front of her and concentrated on that instead.

Chapter 24

Alastair was determined to pin Miriam down and talk to her tonight. He wanted that cottage and he was going to get it; he just needed the money. Alastair had never bothered too much with savings over the years. He had only himself to worry about, he'd had a dependable job, he'd paid his pension and insurance premiums and his needs were simple. Miriam, however, was loaded. It hadn't bothered him one way or the other that she had bought their house and their cars. These things were as unimportant to him as they were important to her, and he knew that was one of the main factors in her accepting his marriage proposal.

Now, for the first time though, he was going to ask her to part with some cash. He had no qualms about doing so as it was to buy something for them both. The cottage was a good investment and there would come a day when even Miriam would have to retire and then she would welcome the peace and beauty of Banford.

He had booked a table in the Red Bank restaurant in Skerries; he knew she'd love that, but first he'd take her to see the cottage. He whistled as he headed out to his car, confident that she'd agree. The biggest problem would be dragging her away from work in the middle of the afternoon, but he'd checked with Annabel that she was at the shop and he'd told the manager to do everything she could to keep her there. The rest was up to him.

'Annabel, these camisoles aren't priced correctly.' Miriam scanned the rail, her brow furrowed. 'They're twenty Euro cheaper than they should be. '

'It wasn't my fault, Bridget did it,' Annabel said defensively. Although her relationship with Bridget had improved dramatically, she was fed up with the girl's laziness and lack of attention to detail, and she certainly wasn't going to take the blame for her.

'Have we sold any?'

Annabel counted the camisoles. 'One.'

'Shit. Re-label them now, for God's sake. Where is Bridget?'

'On her coffee-break in the back.'

Miriam marched down through the shop and into the small kitchen where Bridget was flicking through a glossy mag and smoking a cigarette. 'Put that out. You know you're not allowed to smoke in here.'

Bridget looked up at her and took a long drag on her cigarette. 'Ask nicely' she said insolently.

Miriam fumed. 'Don't push your luck, lady. Do you realize you priced that rail of camisoles twenty Euros cheaper than they should have been? One has already been sold and that money is coming out of your salary.'

'That won't leave much,' Bridget retorted.

'Now look here, Bridget, you are on borrowed time as it is.'

'Oh, I don't think so.'

'If you think my brother can save you, you're wrong.'

'I don't need Luke any more,' Bridget retorted, stubbing out the cigarette in her saucer. 'I've got something much better than that. I've met an old friend of yours – a very close friend.'

'What are you talking about?' Miriam snapped but the confident look in the girl's eye made her feel uneasy.

'Well, let's say I can understand why you spend so much time in London.'

Miriam turned away. 'You've got five minutes then I want you back out front.'

'Nigel Prince. It's a lovely name, isn't it?'

Miriam turned back and stared at her. 'What do you want?'

Bridget laughed. 'I can understand the attraction. He's cute – very sexy, too.'

'You've met him?' Miriam said, gripping the back of a chair to steady herself.

'You could say that,' Bridget said with a dirty laugh. 'I'm sorry to tell you he's not the faithful sort, but then you already knew that. Tell me, what do you make of his tattoo? I think it's quite nice, but it must have hurt getting one in such a sensitive place, don't you think?'

'What is it you're after?'

'Just job security, Miriam. I'm not greedy, although a raise would be nice, what with Christmas coming up.'

'I wouldn't bank on that, or the job.'

Bridget stared past Miriam, who whirled around, horrified to see Alastair standing behind her.

'Alastair.' She stretched out her hand to him, but he pushed it away, his expression hard. 'I had planned to take you out for the afternoon and then to dinner in a beautiful restaurant,' he said, almost conversationally.

'Great, I'll just get my coat—'

'But I've changed my mind,' he said, turned on his heel and strode back down the shop past a bewildered Annabel.

'Is everything all right?' she asked as Miriam hurried after him, her face twisted with anguish.

'Which way did he go, Annabel? You must have seen!'

'Er . . . left, I think,' the woman dithered, but Miriam was already gone. 'What happened?' Annabel asked as Bridget joined her.

'He heard something he wasn't supposed to,' Bridget muttered. So much for her ace in the hole; now she was completely screwed. 'I'm going home.'

'But you can't,' Annabel protested. 'It's only three o'clock. Miriam will fire you for sure.'

'I think she's about to do that anyway.'

Miriam ran up and down the streets looking for Alastair, also watching out for the distinctive red Rolls Royce she'd bought him for his sixtieth birthday, but there was no sign of either. At a loss what to do, she called her brother. Luke was cool, but when he heard the distress in her voice he softened.

'I've no idea where he is,' she told him. 'What will I do?'

'Call his mobile?'

'Of course I tried that. There's no answer, but then it's probably sitting at home on the kitchen table – he's always forgetting it. Either that or he just won't talk to me.'

'What were you arguing about?'

'That's not important.'

'Was he very upset?'

'Yes,' Miriam sobbed, 'and angry.'

'Look, calm down, he's probably just gone home.'

'Yes, maybe you're right.' Miriam started to breathe easier. Of course Luke was right, he'd gone home.

'Do you want me to come and get you?'

'No, I have my car.'

'You don't sound in any condition to drive. I'll pick you up.'

But when they got to the house, there was no sign of Alastair or his car. 'Think, where else would he go?' Luke asked his agitated sister.

'I don't know. Maybe our local wine bar, possibly the pub, but if he'd gone there he'd have dropped his car off first.'

'I'll call Grace.'

Miriam frowned. 'Why would you call her?'

'Maybe he went to see her. They are friends, aren't they?'

'Not so much any more.'

Luke shrugged. ' It can't hurt to call. Why don't you have a look around and see if his mobile phone is here or not.' When he was alone, he quickly dialled Grace. 'Hey, Grace, it's Luke.'

'Luke, hi.'

'You haven't seen Alastair, have you?'

'No, why?'

Luke lowered his voice. 'He and Miriam have had a row – a big one by all accounts.'

'Oh.'

'I think it must be about you. That's why I thought he might have gone to see you.'

'No – no, he hasn't. Poor Alastair.'

'Indeed. I don't suppose you've any ideas of where he might go?'

'There's the pub we go to down the road . . . either that or that little place up in north Dublin – what's it called, Banford. He seems to be nuts about the place.'

'Look, Grace, I can't leave Miriam, she's in a right state. Would you check out that pub and see if he's there? If not, call me back and I'll take her up to Banford.'

'I'll go straight away,' Grace promised, and rang off.

He was sitting at the end of the bar nursing a brandy

when she walked in, and from the slump of his shoulders, Grace guessed it wasn't his first.

'Alastair?' She climbed on to the stool beside him.

He looked up. 'Grace. Well, well, well, I take it this isn't a coincidence?'

She shook her head. 'Luke called me. Miriam's worried about you.' She reached into her bag for her mobile. 'I'll just phone and let them know you're okay. '

Alastair put out a hand to stop her. 'Let them wait.'

'Are you okay?'

He laughed softly. 'Am I okay? Good question. Can I get back to you on it?' He turned to face her and she could see that already his eyes were slightly bloodshot. 'How long have you known?'

'A couple of months,' she admitted.

I knew it – I knew you were behaving strangely with me. I thought it was something I'd said or done.'

'No, of course not. I'm sorry I've been so distant, Alastair, but I just didn't know how to handle the situation.'

'You know, if I'm really honest, I'd have to say I guessed she was up to something.'

Grace froze. 'You did?'

He nodded. 'You can't live with someone and not notice these things, no matter how much you may want to.'

'But why didn't you say something?'

'I'm not much of a man, am I, burying my head in the sand?'

She stared at him. 'I can't quite believe it.'

'Yeah, well, believe it, it's true,' he said bitterly. 'Anyway, where are my manners? What will you have to drink, my dear?'

Grace shook her head and stood up. 'I'm not staying.'

'But Grace—'

'Goodbye, Alastair,' she whispered and walked out of the pub, oblivious of the tears spilling down her cheeks. How could he have just stood by and done nothing while Miriam stole from her? How could he have spent so much time with her and not warned her? Obviously he didn't care about her as much as she'd imagined. She had thought she could never feel as hurt as she had when she found out about Miriam's betrayal. She was wrong.

Grace drove around for hours before finally making her way home. When she walked in to the kitchen, both Michael and Nat were sitting at the table eating one of Rosa's beef stews.

'Hi Mum. Have some of this, it's lovely.'

'I'm not hungry.' Grace automatically went to fill the kettle.

'Already eaten, I suppose,' Michael grunted. 'Or are we expected to believe that you were working till this hour?'

'Dad.' Nat gave him a look.

Grace said nothing but instead spooned three spoonfuls of coffee into a mug.

'Mum, look what you are doing!' Nat laughed.

Grace stared at the spoon in her hand. 'Sorry.'

Michael put down his knife and fork as he noticed, for the first time, how pale and distraught his wife looked. 'What's wrong?'

Grace opened her mouth to say everything was fine and then decided not to bother. The cat was out of the bag now so they might as well know the truth.

'Mum?'

Grace emptied her coffee down the sink and instead poured herself a large whiskey. She carried it to the table and sat down. 'I found out something.' She thought of Alastair's face as he told her he knew, and swallowed hard. 'Miriam's been stealing from me.'

'What?'

'Miriam, she's been stealing from Graceful Living for years.'

'Oh, Mum.' Nat reached over to squeeze her hand.

'The devious, conniving bitch – I never trusted her,' was Michael's predictable response. He stood up and went in search of the phone. 'Have you called the police? She won't get away with this. By the time I'm finished with her she won't be able to stay in this town.'

'It's all sortcd,' Grace told him, not looking up.

'So you've talked to the police? What did they say?'

'I decided not to involve them.'

'What? Are you mad?'

'It would have taken too long and I didn't want it all coming out in the papers – that wouldn't do anyone any good. I thought it would best if I sorted it myself.'

'And exactly how did you do that?' he asked, his voice heavy with sarcasm.

'Miriam has signed over her half of the business to me.'

Michael just stared as Nat whooped. 'Well done, Mum, that's fantastic!'

Grace managed a wan smile for her daughter. As she'd talked, she'd realized she couldn't possibly tell Michael the real reason for not going to the police. He wouldn't understand.

'I suppose that's not so bad,' he was saying now. 'Still it's a shame that she's got away with it.'

'She hasn't. Luke is furious with her and Alastair too.'

Michael frowned. 'So exactly when did all of this come to light?'

'A few weeks ago,' Grace said without thinking.

'What?'

Nat was looking at her too, now. 'Mum?'

'Miriam and I agreed to keep it between ourselves in the short term.'

'But Luke knew and Alastair knew.'

'Luke found out, and Alastair . . . well, he just found out today.'

'So now you tell me. Now that the rest of the world knows, tell good old Michael.'

'Please, Michael, it wasn't like that.'

'No? So how was it?' he snapped.

'I had promised Miriam I would keep quiet. It was part of the deal.'

He threw his hands up in the air and strode over to the counter. 'Oh, well then, you promised Miriam, that's all right then. To hell with your husband of twenty-five years, your loyalties are with the woman who screwed you.'

'Dad, stop.'

He flung off Nat's hand. 'Don't you bloody start. God, you're as bad as each other.'

Nat stared. 'What the hell have I done?'

'You creep in at night, keeping your secrets, going out of your way to avoid me. Oh yes, I know you do,' he said as her eyes slid away from his. 'God forbid you let your father into your life.'

'You're not interested in my life,' she protested, 'unless I live it the way you want me to.'

'Please, stop.' Grace looked on in alarm as father and daughter stared each other down.

'You're a spoiled little bitch,' Michael said, unstoppable now. 'It's very easy for you to live your silly little life when you've got me to fall back on.'

'Michael!' Grace stood up.

'It's okay, Mum,' Nat said, her voice shaking, her face pale. 'He's right.'

'Of course he isn't!'

'He won't realize that I'm serious until I stand on my own two feet,' Nat continued, 'so that's what I'll do.' She turned on her heel.

'Where are you going?' Grace called after her.

'To pack.'

Grace looked at her husband in disgust. 'And you wonder why we don't come to you when we're in trouble,' she spat before hurrying after her daughter.

Chapter 25

Nat hadn't figured out exactly what she was going to do next when she was flinging clothes into a case. Her mother had stood looking at her, begging her not to go, but Nat had made up her mind. She was fed up with her dad's jibes and sarky comments, and she was damned if she was going to stay another night under his roof.

'But where will you go?' Grace had protested.

'To a friend.'

'What friend? Nat, please, tell me. I won't get a wink of sleep until I know you're safe.'

Nat gave her mother a quick hug. 'I'll phone you.' And she'd left before Grace could talk her out of it. Michael had stayed in the kitchen while all this was going on and Nat had considered putting her head round the door to issue a parting shot, but as she could-n't think of anything sufficiently witty or cutting, she decided to say nothing at all.

It was only when she was on the bus to Ken's flat that she remembered he was in London. His flat would be deserted and she didn't have a key. 'Shit!' she exclaimed earning a dirty look from the elderly woman next to her. What the hell would she do now? She had no girlfriends that she could really turn to, having lost touch with them when Ken came on the scene. The bus was just rolling up Ken's road when she remembered that Hazel in the flat below had a key. All she had to do was pray that the girl was home. Nat lugged her backpack down the bus and staggered off, glad that the stop was so near Ken's flat. 'Yes!' she breathed, quickening her step when she saw the light on in Hazel's bedroom.

She lost heart, however, after she'd rapped on Hazel's door three times and there was no sign of the occupant. She must have gone out and forgotten to turn off the light, she decided, giving one last knock, just in case.

'What the fuck do you want?' Hazel flung open the door, a towel clung to her naked form.

'Oh, sorry to disturb you, Hazel, I just wanted the key to Ken's flat.'

Hazel looked past her. 'Where is he?'

'Oh, he's in London. It's for me, I'm staying for a few days.'

'He didn't mention anything to me.'

'Well, no, he doesn't know.'

'Then you don't get the key.'

'No, you don't understand, he won't mind.'

'Look, love, for all I know, you guys have had a row and you're here to torch the place.'

'No, no, we haven't.'

'I need to hear that from him.' Hazel started to close the door.

'No, wait!' Nat pulled out her phone and dialled Ken's number.

'Wait, I'll get him.' But all she could get was the answer machine.

Hazel smiled thinly. 'Seeya.'

'Oh, but Hazel, I've nowhere to go,' Nat protested, but the girl had already shut the door firmly in her face. 'Great, thanks. Thanks for nothing.' Turning away from the door, she wondered what to do next. She decided to go to the pub and have a beer. She could keep trying Ken's number and hopefully get this all sorted. If she couldn't get hold of him tonight, she'd have to find a B & B which would clear her out until payday, three days away.

Instead of going to the pub on the corner, Nat made her way to the one where Ken performed and, yes, where she might bump into Luke.

She ordered a Sprite and nursed it as she tried to figure out what to do next.

'Hi.'

She looked up to see Luke standing over her and felt her cheeks grow hot. 'Hi.'

'Can I join you?' He sat down on the stool next to her.

'Looks like you already have,' she said, trying to sound cool.

'Listen, about Friday night . . .' he started awkwardly.

She groaned. 'Please don't remind me. I can't believe I made such a total fool of myself.'

'You didn't,' he said softly.

'I did.'

'It was just the champagne – it has a funny effect on some people.'

Nat shot him a grateful smile. 'That must be it.'

'So we're okay, yeah?'

'Sure.'

'So how come you're here? There's no music on tonight, is there?'

She shook her head. 'I've left home.'

Luke signalled to the barman and ordered a pint. 'Want another one of them?'

Nat wrinkled her nose and shook her head.

'Something stronger?'

'Okay, a bottle of beer please.'

So what happened?' he asked after they had their drinks.

'I had a row with Dad. He was giving out about me living at home so I left.'

'Michael wanted you to leave?' Luke looked incredulous.

'Probably not, but he was making the point that I could afford to make mistakes in my life, and in my career, because he was always there for me to fall back on.'

'I suppose technically that's true. Sorry,' he added when he saw her expression.

'If I was training to be a lawyer or a doctor he'd be only too happy to support me,' she said bitterly.

'Well, for what it's worth I really admire you for

standing up to him. You must really care about what you do, to put up with such flak. Those kids are lucky to have you.'

'I'm the lucky one,' Nat confided. 'I absolutely love them all and they're a lot easier to deal with than adults.'

'Now that I *can* believe.'

Nat studied him for a second. 'Mum told us what happened.'

'Oh?'

'Theres no need to be cagey, she told us all about what Miriam did.'

'How did your dad take it?'

'He went ballistic. Honestly, you'd think it was Mum's fault, not Miriam's, and when I told him to take it easy, he turned on me.'

'It must have been a shock for him.'

'How's Alastair taking it?'

He shrugged. 'He stormed off when he found out and we haven't seen him since. Miriam proceeded to get completely plastered so I waited until she passed out and then I went looking for him but I've had no luck. Your mum was going to check out a couple of places but she didn't call me back so I assume she had no luck either.'

'She never mentioned it so I suppose not. What a mess. Miriam has a lot to answer for.'

'Yes.'

She looked at him. 'I'm not having a go at you – it's not your fault she's your sister.'

He smiled. 'Kind of you to say so.'

'Like they say, you can pick your friends but you can't pick your family.'

'No.'

'You're sticking by her, despite it all though.'

'Somebody has to. I'm the only one left. I don't know how she's going to cope if Alastair doesn't come round.'

'She'll cope,' Nat said, her voice hard.

'She's not always as tough as she seems, especially where Alastair is concerned.'

Nat's phone rang and she glanced at the display. 'It's Mum. Hi, Mum. Yeah, look it's fine, I've got it all sorted. Just a friend's okay? I'll phone you tomorrow, I promise. Okay then, night night.' Nat rung off. 'She's worried about where I'm spending the night.'

'Where are you spending the night?'

Nat looked away. 'I'm not sure yet, I'm waiting for a call.'

'From Ken?'

She nodded. 'He's away and I can't get into the flat until he calls his neighbour and tells her I'm not an axe murderer and she can give me the key.'

'You can stay at my place, if you like. I'm not suggesting—' he added hastily.

Nat laughed. 'Oh, I know. You made that quite clear on Friday.'

'I hope I didn't offend you, Natasha. It's just you're like a niece to me.'

Nat winced. 'Oh, please.'

He grinned. 'Anyway, are you coming home with me or not?'

'When you ask so nicely, how can I refuse?'

Grace couldn't relax. She was worried about Nat, she couldn't bear to be around Michael, and she most certainly couldn't sleep. Not knowing where she was going, she left the house, got into her car and drove aimlessly through the city streets. She kept going over and over her brief conversation with Alastair, trying to find some way to excuse him. The only answer she could come up with was that he loved Miriam so much he turned a blind eye to anything she did that he didn't agree with, including betraying Grace. Her eyes filled up, blurring her vision, and she quickly blinked back the tears. Running someone down or wrapping herself around a tree was no way to solve this sorry mess. The temperature gauge on her dashboard told her it was only two degrees outside and she hoped fervently that Nat really did have somewhere safe and warm to stay.

She realized she was in Sandymount, quite near Luke's flat, when she remembered she was supposed to have phoned him if she found Alastair, but that had all gone right out of her head. He was probably wondering what was going on, might even be worried as she'd had her phone switched off. Knowing that he would still be with Miriam, she decided to drop a note through his door. She turned into his road, found a parking spot and, pulling a piece of paper out of the glovebox she scribbled a quick note.

Hi Luke,

Sorry I didn't call. I found Alastair in the pub and it seems he'd already guessed what was going on. You'll understand I didn't hang around after that. I'll call you in a few days, I need a bit of space right now.

Love Grace

Climbing out of the car she walked down the road, pausing when she saw his van parked across the road from his flat. So he was home. That could mean Miriam was with him. As she stood trying to figure out what to do next, the door of the van opened and Luke jumped out.

'Come on,' he said, going around to the passenger side and opening the door. 'Let's get you to bed.'

And Grace watched in horror as her daughter stepped out, giggling, and they crossed the road to the flat, hand in hand.

Scrunching the note up in her fingers she quickly followed them, placing her foot in the door just as Luke went to close it.

'Grace!'

'You look surprised, Luke. Sorry if it's inconvenient, my turning up like this just in time to stop you screwing my daughter.'

'Mum!' Nat stared at her, her face going red with embarrassment. 'Don't be so ridiculous.'

'Calm down, Grace,' Luke told her, putting a hand on her shoulder.

Grace flung him off. 'You're as bad as Miriam – no, you're worse. At least she only screwed me.'

'Mum! ' Nat said again. ' Stop it, you're making a fool of yourself.'

'So what are you doing here?' Grace flung back.

'I'd nowhere to go. Luke just offered to put me up for the night.'

'Oh, what? You bumped into him in the street, did you?'

'Well, no . . .'

'You've been seeing her, haven't you?' Grace turned furious eyes on Luke.

'Not in the way you mean,' he said quietly.

'All the time you've been holding my hand, all the time I've been crying on your shoulder you've been seeing her as well.'

Nat's eyes widened. 'You've been seeing my mum?'

'No!' Luke ran a weary hand through his hair. 'It's not like that.'

'You're sick,' Nat spat out, picking up her rucksack and heading for the door.

'Where are you going?'

'She's coming with me,' Grace told him, 'and I don't want you anywhere near either of us ever again.'

'But Grace, I –' Luke called after them, but mother and daughter were almost running to the car and within seconds were speeding off down the road – 'haven't done anything wrong.'

*

Grace drove in silence for a while until finally she found the courage to say the words. 'Did you and Luke—'

'No, I told you! Did you?'

'No!' Grace shot a reproachful look at her daughter. 'I would never do that to your father.'

'So what's going on? It's a bit weird, you two seeing each other, considering what Miriam did.'

'Luke found out almost immediately what Miriam had done. He was very kind to me, helped me get back on my feet, and he was there when I needed someone to talk to.'

'He's a nice guy.'

Grace snorted. 'I used to think so. How long have you been seeing him?'

'I haven't been seeing him at all, Mum. We bumped into each other a few times and he took me to Chez Nous once.'

'What?' Grace screeched as her daughter mentioned the famous Michelin-star restaurant.

'He just did it to cheer me up. Ken was messing me about.'

'Ken?'

'Ken Jackson, he's my boyfriend.'

Grace swerved into the car park of the next pub they came to. 'I think we need to talk.'

Chapter 26

Nat and Grace had just finished their second drink when Ken rang. To Nat's relief he was qulte happy for her to move in and said he'd call Hazel immediately. Grace wasn't entirely pleased about the arrangement but as Ken was going to be away for another three weeks she decided not to argue. There had been enough upheaval for one night and they were both exhausted.

'We should phone Luke,' Nat said as Grace pulled up outside Ken's flat. 'I think we owe him an apology, don't you?'

Grace frowned. Though Nat and Luke's relationship had been totally innocent, she still didn't like the way he'd behaved. It seemed underhand and reminded her that he was related to Miriam. Still, she didn't want to upset Nat so she said, 'I'll call him in a couple of days, darling. It's been the most horrible day and I really can't deal with any more tonight.'

Nat nodded her understanding. 'What are you going to do, Mum?'

'Just get on with it, I suppose.'

'Why don't you go away for a few days?'

'I couldn't.'

'You said you were between jobs,' Nat pointed out, 'and now you've got John to keep an eye on things, what's stopping you?'

Grace thought about it. She did feel exhausted and upset, and her argument with Michael had left her feeling out of kilter. Some space would be nice and she knew exactly where she'd find it.

'Mum?' Nat broke in on her thoughts. 'Will you think about it?'

Grace reached over to hug her daughter. 'Maybe I will.'

Nat smiled. 'Great.'

'You take care of yourself, okay?' Grace rummaged in her bag and shoved some money into Nat's hand. 'And don't forget to eat.'

'I won't.'

'And, Nat? Please think about going to see your dad.'

'No chance.'

'Please. He loves you, he really does, and he just wants what's best for you. I know sometimes he has a lousy way of showing it, but it's true. You are the most important person in his life.'

Nat looked closely at her mother. 'I thought you were that.'

Grace shook her head sadly. 'Not any more.'

It didn't take long for Grace to organize a flight, and as soon as she'd finalized her plans she had a meeting with

John to talk him through any issues that might arise
while she was away.

'Email me if there are any problems,' she said finally.
'I'll check my mail every night. And be sure to lock the
place and put the alarm on when you are leaving.'

'I'll take care of everything. You just go and have a
good time.'

Grace smiled weakly. As far as her accountant was
concerned, she was going to Paris for a week of shopping
and pampering with her girlfriend. If only it were that
simple.

When she had told Michael she was going to stay with
Joy, he'd barely acknowledged her. She'd thought about
trying to talk to him, to explain everything, but she
didn't know if she could and she doubted it would make
any difference. The house felt weird without Nat, and
Grace was looking forward to escaping it for even a short
time.

When she'd called her friend, Joy had asked no questions but told her she was welcome to stay as long as she
wanted. Grace had been hugely touched and grateful
that she had at least one friend she could still rely on.

She had refused to speak to Luke since that night in
his flat, deciding he could wait until she got back from
France. She still found it odd that he had been seeing so
much of both mother and daughter, and yet not
mentioned it to either of them. As for Alastair, she'd
heard nothing from him, and as Luke was her only source

of information, she had no idea what was happening between him and Miriam. Still, she thought, she was better off in ignorance as she felt that any further confrontations or revelations would destroy her completely.

As the plane began its descent into Charles De Gaulle airport, Grace could already feel the tension start to leave her body. Joy had warned her that she was working all hours, and apart from sharing the occasional meal and a glass of wine, Grace would be left to her own devices. Joy ran a very successful little antique shop on the Rue St Paul that specialized in jewellery and porcelain, and with Christmas just weeks away, she was run off her feet. Grace assured her that company was the last thing she needed and Joy, being the good friend she was, laughed and told her she was coming to the right place. Grace looked forward to roaming the streets of Paris, revisiting all her favourite places and then spending her evenings with her friend in her beautiful little apartment in St Germain.

It was early afternoon when Grace arrived and Joy was still at work, but she had left a key with her neighbour. As Grace let herself into the sumptuous flat that looked more like an art gallery than a home, she felt a peace descend on her in this haven of beauty. When she'd unpacked her few clothes, she went into the stark white bathroom, turned on the taps of the ornate roll-top bath and poured expensive oil into the water. Then she lit all the candles that Joy had positioned on every surface and went into the kitchen to fetch herself a large glass of extremely good and deliciously cold Sauvignon Blanc. Shedding her clothes in a heap on the bathroom floor, she stepped into the foam and groaned with pleasure as she lowered herself into the water.

When Joy came home two hours later, Grace was dressed in a simple black polo-neck and jeans, and her hair hung damply around her shoulders.

'Welcome,' she said, enveloping Grace in a warm hug. 'You look tired and thin.'

Grace hugged her tightly. 'I'm okay.'

Joy pushed her away and looked her in the eye. 'Sure you are. Now, I thought we would have dinner in the little bistro at the end of the road. It's nothing fancy but it's quiet, it's near and the chicken is wonderful.'

'That sounds perfect, but would you not prefer to stay in? You must be very tired after such a long day.'

'I never stay in,' Joy assured her. 'Just let me change and we'll be on our way.'

Over some excellent soup and then juicy roast chicken, Joy filled Grace in on her life both professional and personal and Grace listened, laughed and thanked God for a friend who understood her so well. As they walked back to the flat arm-in-arm, Grace told her very briefly what had happened with Miriam. Though Joy uttered a few angry expletives in perfect French, she commented no further, just asking Grace how she would like to spend the next few days.

'Doing very little,' Grace told her. 'I think I'd just like to wander around the shops and galleries and get lost in something that has absolutely nothing to do with me personally.'

'There's nowhere like Paris to escape' Joy said with affection. The city had been her adopted home now for almost eighteen years and she never tired of it. She had moved here after falling in love with a Frenchman whom she'd met on a brief holiday in the South of France twenty years ago. He was married with young children and she'd resisted his advances for almost two years before finally agreeing to move to Paris and become his mistress.

Grace had been horrified and tried to talk her out of it. She liked Didier Feroux a lot and understood why Joy was so attracted to him, but such a relationship could only end in disaster. But her friend had made up her mind and so Grace had just prepared herself to pick up the pieces when Didier tired of her or his wife found out and put an end to her husband's philandering. But it hadn't happened. Joy and Didier were closer than ever, and now that his children were grown and had families of their own, he talked of leaving his wife and setting up home with Joy.

'Can you imagine anything worse?' Joy had said. 'My lovely home littered with dirty socks, my bathroom with shavers and my closet crammed with his business suits and loafers?' She shuddered. 'He must get *that* idea right out of his head or I'll have to give him his marching orders.'

'Wouldn't you like to share your life with Didier?' Grace said when they were back in the flat, sitting on the floor in front of the fire, two large cognacs in their hands.

'I already do,' Joy explained, 'but sharing my apartment is another matter entirely. You know me, Grace. I like to have at least two cups of coffee in the morning before I'm ready to talk. I like to hog the bathroom and use all the hot water. I like to sleep when I want to sleep and not feel that I have to be glamorous twenty-four hours a day. I'm too old to change now.'

'I feel bad now about coming to stay,' Grace apologized.

'Oh no, no, no.' Joy reached out a hand to her friend. 'You are my guest, my beloved friend, you are always welcome. Besides,' she grinned, 'you're not a man.'

'No, and I promise my inclinations are still very much heterosexual in nature.'

Joy looked at her from under her dark fringe, her large hazel eyes curious. 'And is Michael still the one?'

Grace stared into her glass. 'I'm not sure how to answer that.'

'You already have.'

'I love him still, of course I do. We've shared a life, a home, a child – we have a history together.'

'But?'

Grace sighed. 'We don't talk any more. We row – a

lot – over silly things mostly. It's got worse lately though. He's so nasty to Natasha and I just can't cope with that.'

Joy frowned. 'Is this still about the teaching?'

Grace nodded.

'My God, she's in her second year of college, doesn't the man know when to give up?'

'Apparently not.'

'But it is not just about Natasha,' Joy remarked, with her usual insight. 'She is not the only one coming between you, is she?'

Grace didn't meet her friend's eyes. 'There's my work, and now he is furious that I didn't tell him about the embezzlement immediately.'

'Why didn't you?' Joy said softly.

'Because I knew how he'd react. I knew he'd sneer at me for being taken in so easily, and that he'd try to take over and tell me what I should do.'

'That doesn't sound like the Michael I knew,' Joy commented. 'Yes, I could see him telling you how foolish you'd been and all of that, but in the end he'd stand by you and support you, surely?'

'He's changed.' Grace shrugged. '*I've* changed.'

'There's another man,' Joy said simply.

'No! '

'Yes.' Joy watched her steadily and eventually Grace shrugged. 'Anyone I know?'

'It's not important and it's not a runner but yes, there has been someone who's been on my mind a lot. It would never have come to anything, it couldn't have but somehow . . .' Grace said quietly, 'I found myself comparing him to Michael all the time.'

'And this man came out on top.' Joy's lips twitched. 'If you know what I mean.'

Grace's face clouded over. 'Yes, until recently when I discovered he wasn't the knight in shining armour I thought he was.'

'They all have feet of clay, and until you accept that you will never be happy with any man.'

'It doesn't matter any more,' Grace assured her. 'I'm concentrating all my love and attention on my daughter from now on, and the rest of the world can go to hell.'

Joy rose to her feet. 'I think you have come to Paris just in time, my dear friend. Now I must get some sleep – I have an early start.'

Grace glanced at her watch and was shocked to see it was nearly midnight. 'Oh, I'm so sorry, Joy, I didn't realize it was so late.'

'Don't be silly, I've enjoyed our evening – it's been a long time since we had a good chat. It's just not the same on the phone. Now, would you like some hot chocolate or milk to take to bed with you?'

Grace shook her head as she stood up. 'No, I'll just finish my drink.'

Joy kissed her on both cheeks. 'I hope you have a peaceful night. I will creep out in the morning so as not to wake you, but please, just make yourself at home. Meet me at the shop tomorrow evening and we shall have dinner in the most wonderful Japanese restaurant in Paris.'

Grace frowned. 'What about Didier?'

Joy shrugged in a very Gallic manner. 'Didier can wait. This time is for you and me.'

They said goodnight and Grace went into the small guest room and sat down by the window. She sipped the last of her cognac as she listened to her friend moving around in the next room, and thanked God that she had this special place as a bolthole. If she couldn't get her emotions under control in this wonderful environment, then there was no hope for her. Tomorrow, she decided, she would look for a very special Christmas present for Nat. It was the only present she had to buy, she realized sadly. She had already got Michael new waders, not very romantic but that's what he'd wanted. She had organized her parents' present months ago and it was the same as it had been every year; a trip to Alberta, Canada, to see her aunt, her mother's sister. Marian had emigrated almost fifty years ago now, after meeting and falling in love with a Canadian policeman who was on vacation in Waterford. The sisters rarely saw each other over the next twenty years as airfares were a lot pricier then and they were both busy raising their families. Once Grace started to earn some real money though, she'd bought air-tickets for her parents and they'd enjoyed themselves so much she'd done it every year since.

Having no other family, the only other gifts Grace ever bought were for Miriam, Alastair, Luke, Bridget and, of course, Rosa. She already had a beautiful wrap for her housekeeper, a health spa gift token for Bridget, and as for the other three – well, the days of exchanging presents with them seemed to be at an end. Tears welled in her eyes as she thought of the special gift she'd planned for Alastair.

She had toured several garden centres looking for something special for his planned orchard, and finally ordered a lemon tree that he would be able to keep in the large porch in winter and then plant in the garden during the warmer months.

But Grace couldn't give it to him now; in fact, she couldn't imagine even talking to Alastair again after what he'd done. He and Miriam had probably made up by now and were once more sharing a drink, or a bed, Grace long forgotten. She rested her head against the windowframe and large silent tears rolled down her cheeks, splashing into her drink unheeded.

The next day, she got up soon after Joy left, made some coffee and toast and set out on her shopping expedition. It was colder here than it was in Dublin but the sky was blue, and as Grace emerged from the apartment block, she held her face up to the winter sun and closed her eyes. Feeling better than she had in days, she headed for the beautiful Au Bon Marché on Rue de Sèvres, a large department store that was a haven of fashion and chic.

Less than an hour later she was heading for the checkout clutching a soft, caramel-coloured Dior leather jacket that she knew would look fabulous on her daughter. It was ferociously expensive but so what? Who else had she to spend her money on?

After it had been carefully wrapped and paid for, Grace made her way to the famous flea-market Les Puces de Saint Ouen where she spent hours wandering through small shops that sold everything from old furniture to designer clothes to old postcards. After Grace had found a beautiful antique gold necklace with almost translucent orange and red stones that would look stunning on Joy, she took a break at a small café and ate some cheese and bread with a warming bowl of soup. Her eyes filled up as she watched a young couple kiss and cuddle in a corner, marvelling over a pregnancy test stick, and she remembered how happy she and Michael had been when they found out that Nat was on the way. It was hard now to believe they had ever been that close.

Tearing her eyes away from the couple, Grace abandoned her lunch and headed for the Left Bank where she wandered in the chilly afternoon breeze, soaking up the atmosphere and allowing Paris to draw her into its warm embrace and cushion her from the harsh realities that awaited her back in Dublin. When the afternoon had melted into dusk, Grace went back to the flat to offload her shopping and get ready for her evening out with Joy. Though she loved her friend and enjoyed her company, she couldn't help wishing that she could just go to bed and pull the covers over her head. If she did that though, she was afraid she might never get up again.

Chapter 27

With both Miriam and Grace away, Luke decided to check on Alastair and see how he was doing. He was no wiser as to what had actually happened between him and Miriam as his sister had given him the run-around for days and then buggered off to Italy, supposedly on business. He had tried a number of times to contact Alastair but either his brother-in-law was out a lot or just not answering the phone. Luke decided to pay a visit and was pleasantly surprised when he pulled into the driveway to see that Alastair was working in the front garden. 'You look busy,' he said, getting out of the van.

Alastair shrugged, grim-faced. 'Just doing a bit of tidying up, the garden was full of leaves.'

'So, how are you doing?'

Alastair looked at him as he pulled off his thick gardening gloves. 'You knew all along, didn't you?'

'No, of course not.'

'But you knew before me.' Alastair turned from him and led the way around the back to the kitchen door.

'Yes, shortly after Grace,' he admitted.

Alastair kicked off his boots and stepped into the house, crossing the kitchen to put on the kettle. 'I can understand *you* not saying something – she's your sister after all – but Grace . . .' He shook his head and stared out of the kitchen window, his eyes sad.

She was only doing what she thought was best. Miriam knew how upset you'd be if you found out and asked Grace to say nothing. It wasn't easy for her, Alastair, she was devastated, as you can imagine. You were the only reason she didn't go to the police.'

Alastair sat down heavily and stared at him. 'The police? Why on earth would she go to them?'

It was Luke's turn to stare and Alastair gestured to the chair opposite, his eyes steely. 'I think you'd better tell me everything, Luke – and I mean *everything*.'

Miriam had been in Milan for a week and returned home feeling apprehensive and wondering what awaited her. Up until her departure she and Alastair had co-existed in cold silence. Any attempt she made to apologize or explain was greeted with a stony look and Alastair would exit the room. Luke had called several times asking her what was going on but she remained vague and brief, afraid that if he knew her latest sin he would wash his hands of her completely. He obviously hadn't been talking to Bridget, for that little cow would have taken great delight in telling him all about Nigel.

Miriam had uncharacteristically kept a very low profile during her trip abroad, refusing invites to drinks or dinner and eating alone in her room. Bridget's revelations and Alastair's subsequent reaction had shaken her and she was feeling out of control, a sensation she was unaccustomed to and one she didn't like. She had tried to get hold of Nigel to find out exactly what had happened between him and Bridget, but he wasn't returning her calls or texts and that in itself was damning.

In the taxi home from the airport, Miriam touched up her make-up with shaking fingers and rehearsed her speech. She was going to make Alastair listen this time and throw herself on his mercy. He was a kind, fair man and he would forgive her, he had to. Miriam pulled out 40 Euro and threw it at the driver as he pulled up outside the house. 'Keep the change.'

As she climbed out of the car she noticed Luke's van on the side of the road. With a sense of foreboding she walked towards the house, stopping short when the front door opened and Luke and Alastair emerged together. Luke saw her first, and in his eyes she could see both anger and pity. She looked at Alastair and gasped at the expression of utter contempt on his face. He turned back to Luke. 'Could you give me a few minutes, Luke?'

'No problem,' Luke said, walking past his sister to the van.

Miriam approached Alastair, smiling nervously. 'Hi.' As she reached the doorway she saw the small case at his feet. 'Where are you going?'

'I'm moving out. Your brother has very kindly offered me a bed for a few days till I get myself sorted.'

'But Alastair, this is ridiculous, you don't have to leave.'

'If I stay another day, I may well put my hands around your bloody neck and strangle you.'

Miriam was more shocked by Alastair's language than his threat. 'But—'

'There is nothing you can say that will fix this,' he said through gritted teeth. 'I could have forgiven you for being unfaithful, I had guessed as much, but embezzlement – thieving from Grace, our friend? Dear God, Miriam, are you completely without morals?'

'Who told you?' she said, swaying slightly and putting her hand out to grab the door frame.

'What difference does it make?'

'I can explain.'

'No, Miriam, even you can't explain this one.' Alastair bent to pick up the case and brushed past her.

'Alastair,' she begged, grabbing his sleeve. He looked down at her hand and then brushed it from his arm as if it were dirt. 'There is nothing you can say or do to make this better, Miriam. We're finished.'

'But Alastair!' she wailed as he strode out to the van.

'Let's get out of here, Luke,' she heard him mutter and with a last reproachful look, Luke drove off, Alastair sitting straight-backed by his side.

Miriam stood staring after them. She knew she should probably go inside but putting one foot in front of the other required an effort that she seemed incapable of making.

*

As they drove the short distance to his flat, Luke shot his brother-in-law a sideways glance. 'Are you okay?'

Alastair nodded. 'Did you know? About Miriam's affair?'

'No, no, I didn't.'

'So when I said I'd guessed something was going on, you thought I was talking about Graceful Living?'

'Well, yes.'

'And so must Grace,' Alastair groaned.

'What?'

'She came to look for me, that night. I'd had one too many but I remember saying to her exactly what I said to you – that I'd guessed. She must have thought that I was talking about the embezzlement.'

Luke nodded. 'That's exactly what she thought. You see, we'd heard that there had been a terrible row at the shop so we just assumed . . .'

Alastair closed his eyes briefly. 'What must she think of me? I must go and see her, I must explain.'

'You'll have to wait, I'm afraid. She went to stay with a friend in Paris. I think it all got a bit too much for her.'

'The poor girl.'

Luke glanced at the older man's miserable expression. 'We need a drink,' he announced. 'Let's drop your stuff off and go round to my local.'

They were on their fourth pint when Luke turned to Alastair, his expression confused. 'I don't understand one thing, Alastair. You seem more upset by what Miriam did to Grace than by her affair.'

The older man shrugged. 'I always suspected she saw other men.'

'If I thought Bridget had been messing around I'd have killed her, or him or probably both.'

Alastair smiled. 'I'm way too old for such dramatics and anyway, when I married Miriam I knew exactly what to expect.'

Luke blinked. 'Are you saying you had an open marriage?'

'Oh, we didn't discuss it in detail but we agreed that we were both too old to change our ways and that we would make allowances for each other.'

'I'm not sure I could live like that.'

'It's better than living alone.'

'So what now? Will you go back to her just because you don't want to be alone?'

'No, she's gone too far.'

They sat in silence for a moment and then Luke slapped Alastair on the back. 'Hey, we could find a bigger flat and set up home together.'

Alastair laughed. 'You don't want me hanging around, cramping your style.'

'You won't be, I'm finished with women.' Alastair shook his head, laughing, and Luke grinned. 'Well, for the moment anyway. Seriously though, you're welcome to stay as long as you like.'

'Thanks, Luke, I appreciate that, but it would put you in a terrible position.'

'Don't worry about that,' Luke assured him. 'You may

be Miriam's husband but you're also, I hope, my friend.'

Alastair nodded solemnly. 'Well, thanks, then, I appreciate it but it shouldn't be for long. I have plans.'

'Oh?'

'I'm going to buy a house.'

'With what?' Luke spluttered on his pint.

'With the money from the Rolls.'

'You sold your car?'

'I did,' Alastair grinned. 'Couldn't wait to get rid of the bloody thing, to be honest.'

'But when?'

'I went straight to the dealer after I found out about Miriam's fling. It was just the excuse I needed to get rid of the monstrosity.'

Luke roared with laughter. 'Most people would kill for a car like that.'

'One car is much the same as the next, as far as I'm concerned.'

'So you're going to buy a house.'

'Already have, really – just got some loose ends to tie up and it's mine.'

'So you were going to leave Miriam anyway?'

Alastair shook his head. No, I'd planned it as a weekend getaway, but now it will be my permanent home.'

'So where is this house then?'

Alastair sighed. 'In a beautiful little spot in north county Dublin called Banford.'

Chapter 28

Natasha was sitting on the floor helping some three year olds put a wooden puzzle together when Jan put her head around the door. 'You have a visitor.'

'Who is it?'

'Your dad. Go on, I'll take over here.'

Reluctantly, Nat got to her feet and went outside. Michael stood in the small reception area looking out of place and uncomfortable. 'Dad.'

'Hello, love.'

'Is there something wrong? Is Mum okay?'

'I haven't heard anything from your mum so I assume she's okay.'

'So what is it?' Nat said impatiently. 'I'm busy.'

'So I see.' Michael smiled as a chain of toddlers made their way out to the bathroom to wash their hands before lunch. 'Look, I just wanted to say I'm sorry. I shouldn't have lost my temper. I want you to come home.'

'I don't think so.'

'It's where you belong.'

Nat waved a hand around her. 'This is where I belong, Dad, want a tour?'

'I have a meeting,' he said, backing towards the door. 'I'll see you at home, okay?'

Nat shook her head. 'No.'

He stopped, a look of irritation crossing his face. 'I've apologized Natasha, what more do you want?'

'It would take too long to explain, Dad, and like you said, you have a meeting.'

'I don't understand you.'

'No, you don't,' she said and went back to her class.

Her father's visit played on her mind all day and when she let herself into Ken's flat she was still feeling disturbed and slightly depressed. She couldn't wait for her mother to get home from Paris. Though she'd only been gone a week, Nat missed her and was worried about her. They talked on the phone daily but it wasn't the same and they hadn't discussed at all what Grace would do on her return.

Nat was so preoccupied she didn't notice the bag in the hall or the jacket thrown carelessly over the back of the sofa. She had just sat down to take off her boots when a noise in the bathroom alerted her to the fact that she was not alone. Looking around for something she could use as a weapon, she grabbed a heavy glass ashtray and edged towards the door. She heard footsteps and had raised it over her head when Ken came out, completely naked, drying his hair with a towel. 'Nat, you're here!'

'Oh Ken, you scared the wits out of me!'

He took the ashtray from her hands and put it back down on the coffee-table. 'What kind of a welcome home is that?' he joked and pulled her into his arms. 'I'm so glad you're here,' he murmured into her hair.

'I can tell,' Nat laughed as he pressed himself against her.

'You've got way too many clothes on,' he said, starting to open her belt.

'I have, haven't I?' Nat pulled at her shirt. They should talk, they had a lot to talk about but ... His mouth came down on hers and she closed her eyes, thinking there'd be plenty of time for that later.

There *was* a lot of talk later but it was all one-sided and Nat watched mesmerized as Ken waxed lyrical about his new life.

'It's so competitive, Nat. You only get one chance and you have to take it. Tom's great though, I'm so lucky to have him.'

'He's lucky to have you too. If you start to make big money—'

'When,' he interrupted.

Nat grinned. 'When you start to make big money, he'll get his cut.'

'I don't begrudge him a penny. I'd never stand a chance without him. People listen to him, Nat, he's known in all the record companies and you can see they respect him.'

'That's good.'

'He thinks I have to be very careful what I do next, who I sign with.'

Nat's eyes widened. 'There's a choice?'

'Yes,' he said excitedly. 'Tom's convinced them I'm the next big act and they're actually fighting over me.'

'You'd want to get some legal advice before you sign anything. You want to make sure you can write your own material and not get forced into just doing cover versions.'

'Leila takes care of all that,' Ken said with a dismissive wave of his hand.

'She's an agent, not a solicitor,' Nat pointed out.

'She knows what she's doing, Nat, stop fussing. You sound like my dad.'

'What do your folks think about all this? They must be proud of you.'

Ken snorted. 'Dad thinks I'm being taken for a ride and Mam just keeps crying about me leaving the country.'

Nat sat up in the bed. 'You're leaving Ireland?'

'Tom says I have to if I want a chance at the big time,' Ken explained. 'London is where it's at. It's not enough to get a record contract – I need to be accessible for interviews, be seen at functions, that sort of thing. Being visible is everything, he says.'

'But it's only a fifty-minute flight away,' she said faintly.

'Getting a black cab is easier than catching a plane.' He reached out a hand and cupped her breast. 'Hey don't look so sad.'

'It's just a bit of a shock. '

'Would you miss me?' he asked, bending his head to kiss her nipple.

'I might,' she said, trying not to respond to his caress.

He lifted his head and looked into her eyes. 'Then come with me, Nat. Think of the fun we'd have in London.'

'But what about my job?'

'They have kids in England too. What do you say?'

Nat looked at the excitement in his eyes and was tempted. She had never seen him so vital or passionate before, and he'd never shown such love for her as he had this afternoon. But he hadn't actually said the words either. He'd asked her to come with him because they'd have some 'fun'

'Nat?' He was looking at her, his fingers combing her hair back from her face.

She pulled away from him and reached for her bra. 'I don't know, Ken.'

'What?'

'You can't expect an answer just like that,' she said, laughing nervously as she dressed. 'It's a big decision.'

'Oh, for God's sake, Nat, I'm offering you a once-in-a-lifetime opportunity.'

'To be a hanger-on?'

'To have some fun. To live a little. God, you've turned into such a stick-in-the-mud, you know that?'

'Sounds like you'd be better off without me,' she muttered.

'Where are you going?' he asked as she finished dressing and walked to the door.

Nat paused. It was hard to make a grand exit now that she lived here. 'To make some coffee – want some?'

Ken dropped the subject of her coming to London with him and spent most of the rest of the evening with his headphones on, working on a song. Nat, who was pretending to read, watched him covertly, marvelling at the change in him. He was much more confident and outgoing, and she'd seen little evidence of his habitual moodiness. There was an air of tension and excitement about him and even the way he'd made love to her had been more frenetic and passionate. She wondered if he was on drugs, but thought that he was basically just high on happiness and excitement, and who could blame him? But she still wasn't too sure where she fitted in. If he'd asked her to go with him a few weeks ago she'd probably have jumped at the chance, but she had changed and she knew she had Luke to thank for that.

Now she valued herself more and was less willing to put Ken's interests before her own. And though he had asked her to go, he still hadn't mentioned any sort of commitment and hadn't given a second thought to what she would be giving up to be with him. He knew nothing of her life outside of the time she spent with him, and she doubted he cared. Surprisingly the realization didn't hurt and Nat knew she would be able to wave him off and wish him well without any misgivings. It left her with the minor issue of being homeless, however, and while Ken made his music she tried to figure out where to go next.

It was almost ten when Ken suggested they go to the pub. There was a band playing he wanted to check out and Nat happily agreed. It was a distraction she needed, and hopefully would be too noisy to allow any sort of normal conversation. Walking through the main lounge, she spotted Alastair and Luke at the end of the bar, looking rather the worse for wear. 'You go on,' she told Ken. 'I need to have a quick word.'

Ken frowned when he spotted Luke. 'Him again. Who's the other guy?'

'A good friend of my parents,' Nat told him. 'I'll just say a quick hello, okay?'

Ken went on into the back room and Nat winced at the loud, raucous sound that emerged as he opened the door. Winding her way through the tables she leaned up against the bar beside Alastair. 'Hi.'

Alastair struggled to turn around and tried to focus. 'Grace?'

'It's Nat,' she laughed, thinking he must be really pissed.

'Hi, Natasha.' Luke waved and gave her a lopsided grin. 'What will you have?'

'Just a glass of lager, please.'

'Have you heard from your mother?' Alastair asked as Luke called the barman.

'Yes, we talk every day.'

He seemed to sober up instantly. 'How is she?'

'Okay, considering,' she said carefully. She liked Alastair and she knew her mother did too, but he was still married to Miriam.

Luke handed Nat her drink. 'Give her our best, Natasha, will you?'

She nodded.

'When will she be home?' Alastair asked.

'I'm not sure – a couple of days, I think.'

'I really need to talk to her,' Alastair slurred. 'Will you tell her something for me, Nat?'

She nodded. 'Sure.'

Alastair looked at her intently. 'Tell her I didn't know.'

'Didn't know what?'

'She'll know what I mean. You won't forget, will you, Nat? It's very important.'

'I won't forget,' she assured him, shooting Luke a confused look.

Alastair patted her hand. 'You're a good girl.'

'How's your dad doing?' Luke asked.

Nat made a face. 'He came to see me today to ask me to come home.'

'That's great.'

'I said no.'

'Don't be too hasty, my dear,' Alastair counselled. 'No one will ever love you the way your parents do.'

Nat rolled her eyes and Luke laughed. 'I think you'd better shut up, Alastair. Natasha is an adult now and I'm sure she knows what she's doing.'

'Don't mind me, my dear.' Alastair bowed slightly. 'I always dole out unwanted and unnecessary advice when I've had one too many.'

'That's okay, I know you're right. Deep down, very deep down, Dad loves me but he has to learn that just because he's older doesn't necessarily mean he knows best.'

'I can't argue with that,' Alastair said with a sigh. 'Age hasn't stopped me making one mistake after another.'

'Likewise,' Luke acknowledged.

'Still, they say it's never too late,' Alastair continued.

'I'm sure you and Miriam will get back together,' Nat said kindly.

Alastair put his glass down and looked her in the eye. 'That will never happen, Nat, I assure you.' He stood up slightly unsteadily. 'Now I think I'd better go home before I make a spectacle of myself.'

Luke stood up too. 'Sure.'

'Oh no, you stay,' Alastair protested.

Luke laughed. 'You live with me now, remember?'

'But we can't leave the lovely Natasha to drink alone.'

'That's okay, I'm here with someone.' Nat stood up too.

'Goodnight then, my dear.' Alastair kissed her cheek. 'You won't forget to give your mum that message, will you?'

'I won't.'

Chapter 29

Bridget stretched a hand out of bed and picked up the two magazines from the floor. She'd read them from cover to cover several times but she couldn't afford to buy new ones. It had been three weeks since she walked out of Lady M's and she was broke. She had half-heartedly gone through the Vacancies columns in the paper, but the thought of another boring dead-end job held no attraction. She'd have to sign on the dole to keep her going and go through the motions of seeking employment, but Bridget knew that what she really needed was a man – a rich one. Any hope of getting Luke back was gone. By now he'd have heard of her dismal attempt to blackmail his precious sister and it was strange that he hadn't been round to read her the riot act. She was almost disappointed, as Luke in a temper would brighten up her dull and boring days.

Tossing aside the magazines, she reached for a cigarette – her last, she noted with a frown, and lit it, staring out at the rain slamming against the window. Life really sucked at the moment, and the only thing she had to look forward to was a date with Nigel, if you could call it a date. Miriam's lover had turned out to be a lot more tight-fisted than he'd first appeared, and had twice suggested a nice quiet night in. Well, Bridget knew exactly what that meant – sex without the dinner – and that definitely wasn't on.

Tonight Nigel had agreed to take her out, but it was to a small Italian bistro, a glorified pizza joint and not Bridget's idea of a restaurant. Still, it was a night out and she would get fed. At the moment she was living on yoghurt, cornflakes and soup, and though it was doing wonders for her weight she didn't like living hand to mouth like this. She thought of returning to her little black book in order to find a new benefactor, but as all of the entrants knew either Miriam or Grace – Grace! Of course! How could she have been so stupid? Grace would get her back into circulation again and, in the meantime, Bridget knew, her friend would be happy to help her out financially. Bridget's lips curled into a satisfied smile. There was always a way out if you looked hard enough, and this time Grace was it. After the way she'd behaved with Luke – well, it was the least she could do.

She finished her cigarette and went for a shower. Afterwards she massaged in the last of her expensive moisturiser and put on the cream silk bra and pants that she'd bought at cost price from Lady M's. Getting cheap designer clothes was something she was certainly going to miss about her old job. Still, if she found the right man, she wouldn't have to worry about that. She frowned when the doorbell rang. Nigel wasn't due for at least an hour. It rang again and she pulled on her silk robe and went out to the door. 'Who is it?' she called.

'It's me.'

Bridget opened the door a fraction and saw Luke standing there, his beautiful eyes flashing angrily. 'Hello, darling, I've been expecting you,' she said and opened the door wider. Stepping back, she allowed her robe to fall open.

'You are one sick bitch,' he said, standing over her, his voice trembling.

Bridget's eyes widened. 'Why, what's wrong?'

'Don't try that innocent shit on me – I know what you've been up to. Alastair told me all about your attempts to blackmail Miriam. I didn't think even *you* could sink that low.'

Bridget sank on to the sofa and yawned. 'It was hardly blackmail. I just told her to stop threatening to sack me or I'd have to tell Alastair about Nigel. It's not my fault that he overheard. It's such a shame, really – it would definitely have worked.'

Luke clenched his fists at his side. 'And so you've destroyed their marriage.'

Bridget put a finger to her chin and frowned. 'No, I'm pretty sure it was your sister who did that. Look – I think you're exaggerating and Alastair will forgive her. She'll need to be a bit more discreet in future, of course.'

'It's over, Alastair's moved out.'

'Good for him. It's about time he stopped letting her walk all over him.'

'They were happy together, Bridget, and you've ruined that.'

'And you'd never do anything to mess up anyone's marriage, would you, Luke?'

He frowned. 'No, no, I wouldn't.'

'Oh, really? I wonder what Michael would have to say if he knew how much time you spend with his wife?'

Luke grabbed her by the arm and dragged her up to face him. 'Don't even think of stirring it, Bridget. I can understand, at a stretch, why you might want to hurt Miriam, but Grace has done nothing to hurt you – quite the reverse, in fact. I've been seeing so much of her because she was pestering me to sort things out with you, and it was thanks to her that you got that job in the first place.'

'God, why don't you canonize her and have done with it?'

Luke flung her away from him in disgust. 'I can't believe I ever thought I loved you.'

'You did and you still do,' Bridget told him. 'I can do things to you that no other woman ever could.'

Luke looked at her coldly. 'That's sex, Bridget, not love. And you made sure I paid for it.'

'You bastard! How dare you talk to me like that?'

'You're a tart, Bridget, and you're a horrible, nasty piece of work too. I'm just sorry it took me so long to realize it. Now, if you have any decency left in you, you will leave me, my family and Grace and her family alone.'

'Who are you to talk for Grace? She's *my* friend.'

He laughed. 'I doubt it. not after what you've done. You've blown it now. You're on your own.'

'That suits me just fine,' she called after him as he headed for the door. 'I don't need you, I don't need any of you.'

He turned and smiled. 'Then we're all happy, aren't we?'

Bridget ran to the door as he walked away and slammed it as hard as she could. She'd show him, she'd show all of them that she didn't need them or anyone else. She would have the last laugh. They were a bunch of losers and she was better off without them all.

By the time Nigel arrived she'd pulled herself together, had applied her make-up and donned a rather sober black dress.

Nigel frowned when she opened the door. 'Who died?' he joked.

'Me,' she muttered, turning her head so his kiss landed on her cheek. 'Let's go.'

He pulled her back into his arms. 'What's the rush? I thought we could work up an appetite first.'

She pushed him off her and stared hard into his face. 'What exactly do you take me for?'

'Bridget, come on, what's your problem?'

'I don't have one, other than you told me you were

taking me to dinner and now you just want to take me to bed.'

'Of course I want to buy you dinner,' Nigel said, pulling her close again. 'It's not my fault you're so irresistible and have this effect on me.' He rubbed himself against her. 'I can hardly go into a restaurant like this now, can I?'

Bridget smiled slowly and reached down to pull at his belt. 'I suppose not.'

'Have you seen Miriam?' she asked when they were sitting in the small, empty bistro waiting for their starters.

'No, I thought it better to keep a low profile for a while.'

'What do you care? You said you didn't want to see her any more.'

'Yes, but I don't want to get on her wrong side. It's not good for business and Miriam's not the sort to take prisoners.'

'She can't have a go at you without it reflecting on herself.'

'Maybe, maybe not. She's not a woman I would ever underestimate, and you shouldn't either.'

Bridget shrugged. 'I don't work for her now and I don't date her brother. There's nothing she can do to me.'

'Well, it's thanks to her you're sitting here and not in Chez Nous or L'Ecrivain. If she were to see us out together she might decide to tell my wife, and I really don't need that.'

Bridget scowled. That damn woman was messing up her life even now. 'Surely you must have something on her?'

Nigel laughed. 'No, darling, you took care of that.'

'What about on the business end of things?' Bridget persisted like a dog with a bone. 'I'm sure she can't be straight up.'

Nigel shrugged. 'No idea, and I don't want to know. Now can we please forget Miriam Cooper and concentrate on something more pleasant?'

Bridget was about to argue the point further when the door opened and Nat walked in with a man. 'Great, that's all I need.'

'Who is it?' Nigel asked, looking nervously at the couple.

'No one you need worry about,' Bridget murmured, plastering on her smile as Nat spotted her and waved.

'Bridget, hi, how's it going?'

Bridget stood to hug her. 'Fine, darling, and you?' She shot Ken a curious glance. He'd gone straight to their table and his head was now buried in the menu. 'I didn't know you had a boyfriend. He's very nice.'

Nat peeped at Nigel from under her fringe. 'Likewise.'

Bridget laughed. 'How's your mum? I haven't seen her in a while. Tell her I'll drop over in a day or two.'

'She's in Paris with Joy at the moment.'

'Oh, I didn't know she had any holidays planned.'

Nat grimaced. 'She didn't, but with all that's been going on over the last few weeks, and the added pressure of running the business alone, she needed the break.'

Bridget's ears pricked up immediately 'The poor thing. We'll definitely have to plan a night out when she returns.'

Nat smiled. 'I think she'd like that.'

'Tell me, have you seen Miriam at all?'

Nat shook her head vehemently. 'God, no, she wouldn't dare show her face after all that's happened.'

'I suppose not.'

Nat glanced over at Ken who was looking pointedly at his watch. 'I'd better go. Nice to see you, Bridget.'

'You too, darling and don't do anything I wouldn't do!'

'She knows Miriam?' Nigel hissed.

'Relax, she doesn't know anything about you two.'

'What was all that about anyway? Isn't Grace her partner in the interior-design business?'

Bridget smirked. 'Was, by the sound of it.'

'But why? They hardly parted company over me and Miriam.'

'I don't know, Nigel, but I assure you I'm going to find out.'

Chapter 30

Grace walked back into her premises with a heavy heart and a sore head. On her last night in Paris, Didier had taken her and Joy to a very chic club where she drank too much champagne and enjoyed being anonymous. She had a reasonable understanding of French and could manage some stilted conversation, but last night she'd pretended total ignorance and sat back to enjoy the peace of being in a crowd but being apart from it at the same time. Joy, who as usual had read her mood correctly, told Didier to let her be and he had done so but made sure that her glass was always full.

Going straight to the tiny kitchen, Grace put on the kettle and rummaged in her bag for some painkillers. She was just making the coffee when John walked in.

'Hi, Grace, welcome home. Did you have a good time?'

She gestured at the tablets. 'You could say that.'

He laughed. 'Oh dear. So now's not a good time to tell you that your appointment book is full for this week.'

'Not really,' Grace groaned. 'Want a cup?

'I'd love one.'

'Any problems while I was away?'

John took off his coat and hung it carefully on the peg by the door. 'None at all.'

'Any messages for me?' she asked lightly as she handed him his coffee.

'There's a list on your desk.'

Grace smiled gratefully. 'Well, I'd better get stuck in. Are any of those appointments for today?'

'No, I thought you'd like a day to settle back in.'

'Bless you.' Grace took her mug and went through to her office. After she'd gulped down the tablets and switched on her laptop, she put on her reading glasses and studied the neat page of notes that John had left for her. Both Miriam and Luke had left messages asking her to contact them, but there was nothing from Alastair.

Turning her attention to her laptop, she checked her emails but there was nothing urgent so before she started work, she decided to phone her daughter. They hadn't talked in a few days because Grace had dropped her phone on the marble tiles of Joy's bathroom and it had been dead as the proverbial dodo since. If she phoned now, she should just catch Nat before she started work.

'Mum! Where have you been?'

'Sorry, darling, my phone is broken.'

'You could have used Joy's,' Nat said reproachfully,

sounding more like the mother than the daughter.

'Sorry but as I was coming home anyway . . .'

'You're home?'

'Sitting at my desk as we speak. Any chance we could meet up for lunch?'

'Yeah, that would be great.'

'Everything okay? Have you talked to Dad?'

'Listen, Mum, I have to go. I'll fill you in on everything at lunchtime.'

'Okay, then, I'll pick you up at one, okay?'

'Fine, see you then.'

Before Grace lost her nerve she called Michael. She had come direct from the airport to the office but she would have to talk to him sooner or later, if only to find out where she was sleeping tonight.

'Hello?'

'Michael, it's me.'

'Oh? To what do I owe the honour?'

Grace bit back a smart retort. 'I'm home.'

'No, actually, *I'm* home and you're definitely not here.'

'I meant I'm back in Dublin.'

'And what has that got to do with me?'

'Michael, this isn't helping. Why are you being like this?'

'Look, Grace, lately neither you nor your daughter have felt the need to tell me anything or include me in your lives—'

'That's not true!'

'So let's leave it like that, shall we?'

Grace digested his words for a moment. There was silence at the other end of the phone. This wasn't like her husband, not at all. He always ranted and raved, and she didn't know how to deal with this new cold, uncaring approach. 'Michael, we need to talk.'

'Why?'

'Look, Michael, what do you hope to achieve by being like this?'

'Nothing, Grace. But I don't think talking is going to help much at this stage, do you?'

She felt the tears form in her eyes at the defeatist note in his voice. 'Please.'

He sighed. 'What time will you be home?'

Grace waded doggedly through John's list and was feeling slightly better at the end of it, when she had secured two jobs that had been sourced post-Miriam. Michael's intimation that the success of the business was down to Miriam had rankled and shaken her confidence, but now she felt she might actually be able to go it alone. With a promise to John that she would be back by two-thirty, Grace left to meet her daughter.

At the school, Nat ran out to meet her and Grace caught her breath at the fresh, natural beauty that was her daughter. 'You look great,' she said, hugging her.

'I've had a mad morning,' Nat laughed. 'We were playing with water and it got a bit messy, to say the least.'

Grace took in her daughter's damp, crumpled clothes. 'Do you want to go home and change?'

'No, let's go to the pub down the road and we'll sit by the fire. I'll soon dry off.'

'And how are things with Ken?' Grace made an effort to keep her voice light. She had taken an instant dislike to the boy, based purely on what Nat had told her about him, but she wouldn't let her daughter know that.

'Okay.'

Grace noted the change in her voice and suppressed a triumphant grin. Maybe she wouldn't have to learn to like Ken, after all.

'Is he still in London?'

Nat shook her head. 'No, he got back a couple of days ago.'

Grace swallowed this information and tried hard not to imagine her young daughter in bed, naked with this man.

'You won't believe who I saw the other night with a new man,' Nat went on.

'Who?'

'Bridget.'

Grace snapped back to the present. 'Bridget, with a guy? Where?'

'In a pizzeria. He was a lot older than her but quite good-looking.'

'What was his name?'

'Dunno, she didn't introduce us. Anyway, she was

saying she'd come and see you but I told her you were in France recovering from all the madness.'

Grace closed her eyes. 'What exactly did you say, Nat?'

Nat shrugged. 'Just that you were having a tough time running the business on your own and you needed a break.'

'Oh, my God.'

'What?'

'Bridget didn't know anything about what happened.'

Nat looked crestfallen. 'Sorry, Mum, I just assured she knew. She's your friend, isn't she?'

'I'm not too sure who my friends are, any more.'

'Look, she doesn't know any of the details and it's not like she's the competition or anything.'

'I suppose.'

'And speaking of Bridget, I saw Luke last night.'

Grace's head snapped up.

'Before you have a go at me, we just bumped into each other and I was with Ken.'

'Oh.'

'He was with Alastair – they were both in a right state.'

'Alastair?' Grace frowned. 'Where was this?'

'The pub we always go to, Luke's local. Alastair has moved in with him.'

Grace struggled to keep her attention on her driving. 'You're kidding!'

Nat shook her head. 'No – oh, and Alastair asked me to give you a message.'

Grace felt her pulse quicken. 'What was that?'

'He said he didn't know.' Nat shrugged. 'Sorry, that's it, but he said you'd understand.'

Grace digested the words and then started to smile slowly.

'What?' Nat shot her mother a curious look. 'You're smiling.'

'Am I? Oh, look there's a parking spot. I hope they have some nice soup on the menu, I'm freezing.'

After they'd found a comfy sofa near the fire and ordered soup and sandwiches, Grace had to steel herself not to question her daughter about every detail of her meeting with Alastair. How did he look, how did he seem, what nuances had he used when he'd said those words. She couldn't say any of this to Nat though, it would sound very strange. Instead she moved to a subject closer to home. 'Have you talked to Dad?

'Not since he came to the school.'

'That was a big step for him, Nat. He's never found it easy to say he's sorry.'

'He doesn't know how to say sorry,' Nat retorted. 'He starts off okay and then within seconds he climbs back on that high horse of his. I don't know how you've put up with him all these years.'

'I'm no angel either,' Grace said quietly.

'Have you talked to him?' Nat asked.

'Briefly.'

'So are you going to go home?'

'Well, of course. Where else would I go?'

'Mum, you don't have to put on an act for me. I'm not a kid any more.'

'I don't know what you mean.'

'Fine, if that's the way you want to play it.'

Grace looked across at this mature young woman whom she had always considered her little girl, someone to be protected and sheltered from the harsh realities of life.

Nat looked up and held her gaze. 'I'm here if you need me.'

Grace said softly, 'I'll remember that.'

Their food arrived and they tucked into it, switching to less emotive topics. Grace filled Nat in on her time in Paris and the colourful life that Joy led, and Nat talked about the school and the exciting opportunities that were opening up for Ken.

'I had no idea he was doing so well,' Grace marvelled. 'You'll have girls hanging around the door looking for autographs soon.'

Nat groaned. 'His ego will be the size of a small planet if that happens. As it is, his agent Leila, is always telling him how wonderful he is and he laps up every word.'

Grace laughed. 'I suppose anyone would. It must be exciting. Do you think he has the strength to handle it?'

Nat considered the question. 'He's quite sensible really and he's adamant he's only going to perform his own songs, but I'm not sure if he'll stick to his principles when they start throwing lorryloads of money at him.'

'Where do you fit into the picture?' Grace asked as she cut her sandwich in half.

'I'm not sure I do.'

Grace looked at her. 'How do you feel about that?'

'I'm okay now.'

'What about your living arrangements?'

'What about yours?' Nat shot back with a grin.

Grace sighed. 'Can I get back to you on that?'

She dropped Nat back at school and hugged her tightly. 'It was so good to see you.'

Nat looked into her eyes, her expression grave. 'Whatever happens, Mum, it's okay with me.'

Grace sniffed. 'Where on earth did I get you from?'

Nat laughed and ran inside and Grace drove back to the office. Her afternoon was not as productive as her morning had been, her mind wandering between Michael and Alastair. She successfully fought the urge to ring Alastair's mobile but she couldn't stop thinking about his message. It had made her heart soar and she'd felt as if the sun had come out at the end of a very grey and stormy day. That feeling alone filled her with guilt over Michael, although she hadn't actually done anything to feel guilty about. Then again, she hadn't been given the opportunity. She chastised herself for her silly girlish thoughts. She was chasing rainbows when she should be channelling her energies into sorting out her marriage.

Michael was a good man and he had never let her down, not when it really mattered, and although he didn't always show it, she knew he adored Natasha. They were too alike, of course, that was the problem. Both so sure that their way was the right way and there was no room for deviations of any sort. Grace wondered why this trait in her daughter made her feel proud but in her husband merely irritated her. The honeymoon was truly over and the things she'd loved about him when they'd first met now drove her crazy. She didn't remember when everything had changed but it seemed to have been a gradual process that she hadn't noticed until it was too late. Just as carpet faded or paint flaked, so their marriage had gone through its share of wear and tear. And though Grace's job was all about bringing houses back to life, she had no idea how to do that to her marriage and no real inclination to try.

Though Grace would gladly have worked late she knew that today of all days she needed to get home on time. So promptly at five she switched off her computer, set the answering machine and the alarm, and locked up. As she drove home she wondered what Michael would do or say. Was he going to continue with the cold sarcasm or would he have reverted to form and shout and rail at her stupidity and selfishness? She would take whatever he threw at her, feeling she deserved it, but if he said one word about Nat . . . She forced herself to take some slow deep breaths. Getting worked up before she even got there wouldn't help.

When she pulled into the driveway she sat in the car for a moment in an effort to prepare for what lay ahead. She knew in her heart that what happened in the next few minutes would affect the rest of her life. For Natasha's sake she had to make sure there was a positive outcome. She had to avoid antagonizing Michael and try not to interrupt or contradict him outright. If she handled him carefully, explained things in a rational manner, surely as two mature adults they could work things out? She wasn't expecting roses and champagne, but perhaps they could patch up their differences, stick the relationship back together and muddle on. She knew plenty of other couples who did just that.

Suddenly she was overwhelmed with sadness and was tempted to reverse back out of the driveway, but she looked up to see Michael standing in the doorway watching her. With a shaky smile she got out of the car and walked towards him and for the first time in years found herself praying.

'I made some tea.' Michael gestured at the pot and two mugs on the table.

'Great.' Grace nodded her thanks. 'I'm dying for a cup.' She poured some for both of them, added milk and sat down. Michael took the seat opposite. Neither of them touched their tea. 'Thanks for agreeing to this.'

He shrugged and looked slightly bored.

Grace tensed. He wasn't going to make this easy. 'I was wrong not to tell you what happened, but—'

'There's always a "but", isn't there, Grace? Never a straightforward apology.'

'It's just a manner of speaking, Michael. I *am* sorry – very sorry. It was a terrible situation and I didn't know what I was doing half the time. I couldn't believe what she'd done. I kept checking the books, the invoices, convinced that I'd find proof that I'd imagined it all.'

'I told you she wasn't to be trusted.'

'Oh Michael, does it matter? Does this have to come down to "I told you so"?' She struggled to contain her temper, frustrated that within minutes of walking through the door they were bickering again. 'We have to talk properly, seriously. We have to stop this silly squabbling or we don't stand a chance.'

'We should have talked years ago.'

Grace stared at him. 'Are you saying it's too late?'

Michael rubbed his eyes wearily. 'You just don't see it, do you, Grace? You were faced with one of the biggest crises of your life and you didn't turn to me. What does that say about us?'

Grace didn't have an answer.

'You didn't trust me, you didn't believe I could help, you acted as if I didn't exist, as if you were a single woman.'

'I knew you would take over, you would tell me what to do, and you'd preach to me and tell me what a fool I'd been.'

'Well, haven't you?'

Grace threw up her hands in frustration. 'You see?

You have absolutely no faith in me and you always treat me like some gormless fool. I have a successful business and now, because of the way I handled things *on my own*, that business belongs to me outright.'

Michael shrugged. 'So you don't need me any more.'

'Stop putting words in my mouth,' she hissed.

He stood up and walked to the door.

'Where are you going? Don't walk out now, we have to sort this out.'

He paused in the doorway. 'There's nothing *to* sort out. You've already made yourself perfectly clear.'

'Why is it that just because I'm capable of dealing with problems alone it's some sort of insult to you?'

He watched her steadily. 'Because most couples discuss things, most couples take decisions together and most couples appreciate each other's support.'

'You're not interested in doing anything *together*, you just want everyone to dance to your tune,' she retorted.

He held up his hands. 'Like I said, it's sorted.'

'And what about Natasha?'

'This has nothing to do with her.'

'Then why did you turn on her when you were angry with me?'

'That wasn't fair,' he admitted, 'but it might bring her to her senses.'

Grace shook her head. 'I keep telling her that you love her but I'm beginning to wonder.'

'I care about her more than anything else in the world,' he said, his face contorted in pain. 'If I didn't, I'd be happy to sit back and let her make a mess of her life.'

'She's happy, Michael – isn't that the most important thing?'

He looked away. 'I wouldn't know.'

Grace stood up and went to him. 'Aren't you happy?'

He looked at her, his eyes desolate. 'I've never felt lonelier in my life.'

Grace reached out to him but he pushed her hand away.

She stood staring at him. 'What do we do?'

'I'm going away for a few days.'

'Where?'

'Just fishing. When I come back, I think we should talk to Nat and decide what we're going to do next.'

'What are you saying?'

He sighed. 'Grace, our marriage is over. You don't love me and I don't love you. It's time to move on.'

'You don't love me?' She stared at him, her voice barely a whisper.

He looked uncomfortable and wouldn't meet her eye. 'I do, but not like I used to. And for once, Grace, be honest, because I know you don't love me.'

'You're wrong, I do, but,' she looked up at him, her eyes sad, 'not the way I used to.'

He smiled faintly. 'Honesty at last.'

'What will we tell Natasha?'

'The truth.'

Grace sighed. 'I suppose we should sell the house—'

Michael dismissed her with a wave of his hand. 'I

can't get into any of that tonight. We'll talk about it when I get back. Goodbye, Grace.'

For the first time Grace noticed his bag and fishing gear waiting in the hall and she watched as he bent to pick it up, carried it to the door and walked out without looking back. 'Goodbye, Michael.'

Chapter 31

Miriam jumped as she heard junk mail thump into the hall. The house was so quiet without Alastair, the slightest thing made her start. She didn't understand it. She'd lived alone for years before her marriage and it had never bothered her. Now the solitude she used to enjoy was closing in on her and she hated it. The invitations were stacking up on the hall table but she'd no interest in going anywhere now Alastair wasn't with her or waiting for her when she came home. There was a hole in her life and it couldn't be filled with a quick fling. In fact, she'd totally lost interest in other men and sex. The excitement had been in the fact that it was forbidden, and now that she had no one to deceive, it had lost its appeal.

Luke was right, she must be a truly horrible person; it was hard to believe they shared any genes at all. She laughed softly and emptied the wine bottle into her glass. Reaching for her cigarettes she cursed when she realized the pack was empty. It was nearly ten o'clock at night, she was in her pyjamas, had no make-up on, and the nearest shop was at the filling station, a ten-minute walk away. She was sorely tempted to drive, but as she'd lost count of the number of drinks she'd had and was feeling slightly dizzy, she decided against it. Instead she wrapped herself in a full-length black wool coat, pulled a scarf over her head and went out into the night.

She had just reached the shop when she realized she'd forgotten her bag, but scrabbling in her pocket she pulled out enough change to buy ten cigarettes. It would keep her going till morning.

Inside, she asked for the cigarettes and handed over the money, oblivious to the curious glances she was getting from the cashier. As she hurried back to the house, she pulled out a cigarette and then remembered that her lighter was on the kitchen table. 'Damn.' She shuffled on, anxious to get back into the warmth of the house. As she walked into the driveway she reached into her pocket for the key only to find she'd forgotten that, too. 'No, no!' she wailed. 'It must be here!' But it wasn't and she knew it was exactly where she'd left it – on the hall table with her purse and her phone.

Hurrying around the side of the house, she tried the handle of the back door but of course it was locked. She was about to put a rock through the back window when she remembered that Alastair kept a spare key hidden outside for just such emergencies. If only she could remember where. She was on her hands and knees rummaging in a flowerpot when a figure loomed over her.

'What the hell are you doing?'

Miriam screamed and lashed out as the man pulled her to her feet.

'Stop! It's me – Luke! Will you shut up before someone calls the guards.'

'What the hell are you doing creeping around at this hour of the night? You scared the shit out of me,' she said, distraught and not a little drunk.

'You can talk,' he said, eyeing her wet slippers and the muddied hem of her pyjamas.

'I locked myself out,' she said unnecessarily.

'I worked that one out, but what you were doing outside in that get-up is another matter.'

'I ran out of cigarettes . . .'

'Save it,' he said, as her teeth started to chatter. 'You go out and sit in the van and stay there until I figure out how we can get in.'

'There's a key here somewhere,' she said vaguely.

'You go on, I'll find it.' When she'd shuffled off he rang home and when Alastair answered he asked him about the key.

'It's hidden under the white stone on the edge of the flowerbed nearest the door – why?'

'I'll explain later,' Luke said and rang off. Ten minutes later, brother and sister were in the kitchen and he was making a large pot of coffee.

'To hell with the coffee,' Miriam said, going to the drinks cupboard. 'I'm having a whiskey. Want one?'

Luke shook his head. 'I'd say you've had enough.'

'I'd say you should mind your own business.'

'I come here and find you patently pissed, scrabbling around in the garden in your pyjamas, and you tell me to mind my own business?' He slammed cupboard doors and banged two mugs down on the counter. Miriam winced. Luke poured the coffee and brought it to the table. 'Drink some.'

'I don't want it.'

'Drink the bloody coffee, you silly cow, or you're going to have a major hangover in the morning.'

Miriam glared at him. 'What the hell do you care? What the hell does anybody care?'

'Cut the dramatics,' he muttered. 'You've always got me and Dad.'

'My beloved dad? Huh, as if *he* ever cared.'

'For crying out loud, what did Dad ever do to you?'

'You know damn well what he did,' she said, her face twisted with bitterness.

Luke sighed. 'Miriam, that was over thirty years ago – and surely, meeting Alastair made up for all that?'

She stared at him, wild-eyed. 'I found Alastair when I was forty-one! I spent all my adult years until then alone when I should have had a husband and family.'

'I didn't know he meant that much to you. What was his name again?'

'Alan,' Miriam murmured.

'Why didn't you run away with him?'

'Dad went to see his parents and warned them to keep him away or he'd call the guards in. I was only seventeen, technically still a minor and he was nineteen. His dad packed him off to work on his brother's farm in Offaly and I never saw him again.'

'Why didn't you go looking for him when you got older?'

Her eyes filled with tears. 'When he didn't come back for me after I turned eighteen, I assumed he had found someone else. But he hadn't. I met his mother in town a few years later and she told me he'd gone to Australia. She said that when I didn't answer any of his letters he was devastated and decided to make a completely new life for himself as far away from Ireland as possible.'

Luke frowned. 'Why didn't you answer the letters?'

'Because I never got them. Dad destroyed every one.'

'No, he wouldn't do that.'

She nodded. 'He did – he admitted it to me himself.'

'But why? Was it because of me?'

Miriam shook her head. 'No, no, it was nothing to do with you. It was because of Mum.'

'Now I'm totally confused. Mum died long before Alan came along.'

'Mum was a very religious woman, did you know that?'

'Well, yes, I suppose. Dad always said that I had to say my prayers and go to Mass, or Mum would be crying in Heaven. He said that she could see everything I did. It gave me nightmares, to be honest.'

'She used to go to Mass every day and during Lent she only ate one meal a day.' Miriam added, 'I don't know why she didn't become a nun.'

'I still don't understand what this has to do with Alan.'

'He was a Protestant.'

'Oh.' Luke nodded in understanding.

'Dad said Mum would turn in her grave if she knew, and that if I had loved her at all, I wouldn't have anything more to do with him.'

'That's terrible. I had no idea. Why didn't you tell me?'

Miriam shrugged. 'By the time I found out, you were a teenager dealing with your own problems and I didn't want to come between you and Dad. You were always so close.'

Luke looked at her and smiled. 'You're not the hard-nosed bitch you pretend to be, are you?'

Miriam smiled but her eyes were bright with tears. 'Don't you believe it.'

'Would you have liked kids?'

Miriam nodded. 'Oh, yes. You were the only thing that kept me going when Alan left. You were just seven and so affectionate and funny. I couldn't wait to get married and have lots of babies but I could never find anyone like Alan.'

'Until Alastair. Why didn't you try for a baby with him?'

'Oh, it was too late.'

'Why? You were only forty-one.'

Miriam shrugged.

'Did you and Alastair discuss it?'

She laughed, but her eyes were sad. 'It never even occurred to him that I would be interested in children. He only knew me as a workaholic.'

Luke poured more coffee into his mug. He emptied her untouched one down the sink and poured her a fresh cup. 'Please have some.'

Miriam watched him. 'How come you haven't given up on me, Luke?'

'You know I never would.'

'I thought this time you had. I thought I'd lost you.'

'You came close, very close. To hurt two people who care as much about you as Grace and Alastair, well that just seems downright bad.'

Miriam stubbed out her cigarette with a shaky hand. 'Or stupid.'

'No.' He looked at her, his face pale. 'I'm sorry, Miriam.'

'For what?'

'For what Dad did. It was very wrong.'

'They were different times,' she said wearily.

'But you haven't forgiven him, have you?'

'What difference does it make now? I'm tired, Luke. Go home.'

He shook his head. 'I think I'll stay here tonight.'

'I don't need babysitting. Go and look after your lodger.'

'But Miriam—'

'Stop worrying, Luke. I've had a rough time, I've had too much to drink, but I'll bounce back. You know me, I always do. Now please, I need some sleep.'

'Are you sure you don't want me to stay?'

'Quite sure. Go home and tell Alastair that I'm doing just fine without him.'

'That's hardly going to help you patch things up.'

Miriam looked surprised. 'Oh Luke, we'll never patch this one up.'

'You don't know that.'

She patted his arm. 'Oh, I do.'

Chapter 32

It took all of Grace's courage to finally pick up the phone and even then, she could only bring herself to text. CAN I BUY U LUNCH? USUAL PLACE? 1? GRACE

She waited and waited but there was no reply and she decided that she must have misinterpreted the message. But at twenty to one her phone beeped and his answer came through.

SORRY. JUST GOT YOUR MESSAGE. C U THERE

Grace tidied her hair, freshened her make-up and looked at the woman in the mirror with the sparkling eyes and inner smile. 'Stop it,' she chided herself. 'He's your friend, that's all.'

She walked into the pub at exactly five to one. She knew the woman was always supposed to be late but she'd never been one to play games. She couldn't wait to see him and she didn't mind him knowing that. She wandered around the busy pub, finally settling herself at a table in a small snug. She was tucked away from the main pub but she knew he'd find her.

'Can I get you something?' A girl smiled down at her.

'No, I'm waiting for someone.'

'I'll leave a menu with you then.'

Grace nodded her thanks and pretended to read it, but the card shook in her hand and the print swam before her eyes.

'Hello.'

She looked up to see Alastair standing over her, his smile warm and tender.

'Hello.' She stood up, not taking her eyes off his, and when he opened his arms, she fell into them. The tears came then and Alastair settled her back on the small sofa, shoved his immaculate handkerchief in her hand and waited for her to stop.

'I'm sorry, Grace, I'm so sorry.'

Grace dried her eyes and blew her nose. 'Why are *you* sorry, Alastair? You haven't done anything.'

'For the misunderstanding. I realize how it must have upset you.'

I should have known better.' Grace dabbed her eyes and smiled as the waitress approached for the third time and did another prompt U-turn.

'Yes, you should,' Alastair said sternly. 'If I'd had an inkling of what she was up to, you know I would have put a stop to it. In fact, I wouldn't have been as kind as you – I would have called the police.'

Grace shook her head. 'You wouldn't.'

'I would,' he said stoutly. 'She's broken the law and she shouldn't get away with it.'

'But she hasn't. Her greatest fear was that she would lose you, and now she has.'

His face hardened. 'If she knew how I'd feel and she cared that much about it, she would never have conned you in the first place.'

'It's as if she can't help herself.'

'I find it hard to believe sometimes that she and Luke are related,' Alastair said, putting up a hand to attract the waitress. 'He's such a good man.'

Grace didn't comment but when Alastair suggested a bottle of wine she nodded and smiled, just happy to be with him again.

'So how are you?' he asked, taking her hand when they were alone again.

Grace watched him stroking it and felt she would like to sit like this for ever. 'I'm okay,' she said, and felt the tears bubble up again.

'Oh, Grace.' He squeezed her hand. 'What you've been through . . . And instead of helping you I just made things worse. Michael must be furious with me and Miriam.'

'With Miriam and with *me*,' Grace corrected. 'He hasn't mentioned you.'

'Why is he angry with you?' Alastair asked, confused.

'He's hurt that I never told him.'

'I'm not sure I understand that myself. Luke filled me in on what happened, but I'm still not clear on why you did keep it all a secret.'

'You don't know?' Grace felt her face redden.

He shook his head.

'It was all for you, Alastair,' she whispered.

He was about to reply as the waitress returned with their wine. 'Would you like to order some food?'

'Not right now, my dear, we'll give you a call when we've decided.' Alastair smiled kindly at her before turning back to Grace. 'I don't understand.'

'Miriam knew how furious you would be if you found out about the embezzlement. She said your marriage would be over and she begged me not to go public. In return, she signed over her half of the business to me.'

Alastair nodded. 'I see, but surely you knew that if you went to the police, you could have got all that and more. Didn't you want to see her named and shamed?'

Grace bent her head over her glass. 'Yes, but I couldn't bear to see you hurt. It was her crime, not yours, and I thought you'd be devastated if you knew the truth. You love her so much.'

Alastair stared at her hard. 'Did you tell Michael?'

'What?'

'Did you tell Michael that I was the reason you didn't go to the police?'

Grace shook her head, not looking at him.

'What did you tell him?'

'I said I didn't want us all dragged through the mud, that it would be bad for the business and it was easier all round to sort it out quietly.'

'Very plausible.' He nodded and took a sip of wine. 'And do you think he swallowed it?'

Grace frowned, not entirely sure where this was leading. 'I was just doing what I thought was best.'

'For me?'

'Yes, for you,' she said, louder than she intended. A couple of women at a table nearby turned to look at her.

'And it might have worked,' he said contemplatively. 'We might have all gone on as normal for years.'

'Yes.'

'If it hadn't been for Luke spilling the beans, Miriam and I would still be together and Michael need never have known anything about it.'

'Well, yes, I suppose so.'

Alastair lifted his glass. 'To Luke.'

Grace stared at him. 'What do you mean?'

He smiled at her. 'Don't you see, he's done us all a favour? He's shown me that Miriam was never the woman I thought she was, and also how far you are willing to go to protect me. I don't want to make a total fool of myself here, Grace, but I think that maybe you care more about me than I ever realized – maybe more than *you* even realized.' He put his finger under her chin and lifted her face so that he could look into her eyes. 'Is that true?'

She stared back at him, taking in the flecks of green in his blue eyes, the straight nose, the strong chin and the lips that always seemed to be smiling at her.

'Grace?' he whispered.

'You're talking in riddles, Alastair, and I don't have the answers.'

'I'm sorry,' he said quietly, 'but for the first time in weeks I feel that there might be a light at the end of the tunnel.'

'It could just be an oncoming train,' she teased.

He chuckled. 'I think the express has been and gone, don't you?'

'Maybe we should order.' Grace looked around frantically for the waitress.

He patted her hand. 'It's okay, Grace, I won't interrogate you any further. Suffice to say that I'm glad, very glad that we're friends again.'

She smiled. 'Me too.'

'Let me tell you about my house instead.'

'Your house?'

'Remember the little cottage I told you about?'

'In Banford – yes, of course.'

His eyes twinkled. 'I bought it.'

'No!'

He nodded. 'Yes. I sold that monstrosity of a car and bought this beautiful little house.'

Grace threw back her head and laughed. 'That's brilliant!'

'You think so? Everyone else seems to think I've gone completely mad.'

'No, that car never suited you. It was an old man's car.'

'And I'm an old man.'

'You are not, and you know it. Stop fishing for compliments. Now tell me, when do you move in?'

'In a couple of weeks; the place is being rewired as we speak and then new windows are going in.'

'I can't wait to see it.'

'I can't wait for you to see it. I badly need your advice – the whole place needs decorating and the garden is a shambles.'

'The garden is your problem,' Grace laughed, 'but I'll be happy to help with the decorating.'

'I'm so looking forward to it,' he confided, beaming. 'I can't wait to wake up there in the morning. To walk along the beach every day and cook fresh fish for supper.'

Grace listened to him talk excitedly and wondered for the first time if he was still in shock and this was some kind of rebound effect to Miriam's betrayal. 'Are you running away, Alastair?' she said, cutting through his chatter.

'Absolutely. Away from the noise, the traffic, the fast-food restaurants. I'm going to be free.'

'I meant, are you running away from your marriage?'

'I have no marriage,' he retorted, picking up the menu. 'Oh look, Irish stew – it's ages since I've had that. Rosa is a wonderful cook but there's nothing like some plain, comfort food like your mother used to make.'

With a heavy heart, Grace listened to him thinking he was just too happy and light-hearted; it didn't make any sense.

'So what will you have, Grace?'

'I'm not hungry.'

'Drinking on an empty stomach isn't such a good idea, I'll have to carry you home.'

Grace didn't laugh. 'When you first saw this cottage, you thought it would make a wonderful refuge for you and Miriam, didn't you?'

'Well, yes.'

'That could still happen.'

'Excuse me?' He stared at her.

'I think you're giving in too easily. You told me, remember, what a change she made to your life.'

'But that was before I knew—'

'She conned me, Alastair, not you.'

'It doesn't matter, it was unforgivable.'

'You said that when you married, you agreed to accept each other's differences,' she persisted.

'Stealing is hardly that,' he protested.

'You could get past this, Alastair. Don't be so quick to throw it all away. You love her and, whatever her faults, she still loves you, I'm sure of that.' Grace stood up. 'Sorry about lunch.'

'But Grace—'

'I'm sorry,' she repeated, and walked out of the pub.

Chapter 33

Nat crept out of the bedroom so as not to disturb Ken. She had no idea what time he'd got home; she had waited up for him until midnight but had then fallen into bed exhausted. He had been putting in very long hours recording in a studio in town, and though he was worn out, Nat had never seen him so happy. She was delighted that things were working out so well for him, but she still didn't see a place for her in his new life. Ken had brought up the subject a couple of times but she had managed to wriggle out of giving him an answer.

She finished dressing in the bathroom and then realized she'd left her watch by the bed. Tiptoeing back into the bedroom, she froze when his hand snaked out and grabbed her.

'Ken, you scared the life out of me!'

'Give me a kiss,' he mumbled, pulling her down beside him.

She gave him a long lingering kiss and then extricated

herself. 'I have to go to work. How did the recording go?'

Immediately he was awake. 'It was so cool, Nat, it came together for me like never before. I kept stopping and rewriting – know I drove the producer crazy – but the result is the best song I've ever written.'

Nat hugged him hard. 'I am so proud of you.'

'But you're not coming with me.'

'I'm sorry, Ken,' she said, and she meant it. 'I have thought about it, but my life is here.'

He nodded. 'I never really thought you'd come. You've always known exactly what you wanted and where you were going, and I was never a part of that.'

Nat looked at him in surprise. 'You never wanted to be!'

He grinned. 'Now, why do you say that?'

'You didn't want to talk about the future, especially our future, and you think commitment is a dirty word. You just want to have fun.' She drew quote marks in the air and rolled her eyes.

He laughed. 'You've got me well sussed.'

'I have.'

He stroked her hand. 'Did you want more?'

'I thought I did.'

'And then you fell for that old guy.'

'Luke?' Nat laughed. 'No, he's not in the picture – no one is.'

'Including me?' He pulled a face.

'Don't worry. Now you're an up-and-coming rock star, the women will be queuing up to date you.'

'How will I cope?' he chuckled.

'So what happens now?' she asked softly.

'Now I find somewhere to live in London and find a lodger for this place.'

Nat's eyes widened. 'You own this flat?'

'My dad does. Mam made him buy it for me when he threw me out, and as property is always a good investment, he agreed.'

'Very nice.'

He made a face. 'Not really. I always felt dependent on him even though I'd made the grand gesture of leaving home. Now for the first time, I'll be able to pay my own way. So how do you fancy becoming my lodger?'

'You're kidding?'

'No. Dad would prefer to have a tenant he knew than to take in strangers who might wreck the place.'

'I couldn't possibly afford it.'

'You could if you got a flatmate. In fact, the second bedroom is big enough for two beds, so you could split the rent three ways.'

Nat chewed on her lip. 'Can I think about it?'

'Sure. I'm not going to be leaving for a few weeks, so there's no rush.'

Nat kissed him. 'Thank you.'

'Thank *you*,' he said, looking into her eyes. 'I would never have got this break if you hadn't pushed me. I'll always be grateful for that.'

Nat smiled. 'Then I'll expect front-row tickets at all your concerts.'

'And backstage passes,' he promised. 'Now why don't you get back in here and let me make you late for work?'

Grace was finding it very hard to work at the moment and she found herself making mistakes too. Only this morning she'd measured a bathroom in square yards instead of square metres and so hadn't ordered enough tiles. She'd had to apologize to the customer and absorb the cost of the extra tiles, and it was sheer luck that she'd been able to get more of the rather unusual Italian porcelain. The fact that Alastair had kept calling for days after their aborted lunch hadn't helped, but it was worse when he stopped calling. Also, Luke had been trying to talk to her and she'd refused to take his calls. She still felt angry with him, and in her current state she didn't feel up to a confrontation.

It was only three in the afternoon when Grace pulled into the driveway, her head hammering. Rosa was busy hoovering the hall when she walked in and immediately the younger woman turned off the vacuum cleaner and smiled at her employer.

'Grace, how are you? You're home early.'

'Hi, Rosa. Not so good, I'm afraid. I keep getting these God-awful headaches.'

Rosa shot her a knowing look. 'Michael has gone?'

Grace smiled nervously. 'Fishing.'

Rosa raised a perfectly arched eyebrow. 'Really?'

Grace walked past her into the kitchen. 'I think

I'll have a cup of tea – want one?'

'I'll hoover the lounge and then I'll join you.'

Grace had just set the pot on the table when the housekeeper walked in. 'You've lost weight,' Grace remarked, admiring Rosa's figure.

Rosa beamed and patted her flat tummy. 'I've been going to WeightWatchers and have lost nearly a stone.'

'Well, you look marvellous.'

'Good, because I have a new man to keep happy.'

Grace's eyes widened. Rosa had been widowed for five years and despite being beautiful, fun and only thirty-five, Grace had never known her to date a man since. 'That's wonderful! What's he like?'

Rosa stared dreamily into the distance. 'Tall, dark and very, very handsome.'

'Is he Italian?'

The young woman shook her head, her dark eyes gleaming. 'No, he is an Irishman.'

'I thought you didn't like Irishmen?'

'I like this one,' Rosa sighed. 'He is very romantic.'

'You'll have to introduce me.'

Rosa watched as Grace swallowed two painkillers with her tea. 'I think you could do with a little romance yourself.'

Grace made a face. 'I'm an old married woman, remember?'

'Not for much longer.'

Grace lowered her cup. 'Did Michael say something?'

Rosa shrugged. 'He's here, I'm here, we talk.'

Grace stared. 'I see.'

'Some things aren't meant to be.'

'I tried,' Grace said, almost in a whisper.

Rosa nodded. 'You did, but Michael is the kind of man who likes to stay home and likes his wife to stay home with him.'

'That's not what I want.'

'No, *he's* not *who* you want,' Rosa corrected.

Grace felt her cheeks redden. 'He's not your new boyfriend, is he?'

Rosa threw back her head and roared with laughter. 'No, oh, you are so funny!'

Grace sighed. 'I wish I felt it.'

'There is someone else,' Rosa asked gently, but it was more of a statement.

'Not really,' Grace lied.

'Give it time,' Rosa advised. 'Time is important. Now, I must go.' She stood up and went to the sink to wash her cup. 'I have to go to Miriam's.'

'But you don't usually go on Tuesdays.'

'At the moment I drop in most days. The place is a tip since Alastair left and Miriam, she's not too well.'

Grace frowned. 'What do you mean?'

Rosa raised an imaginary glass to her mouth. 'She is a bit depressed.'

'I didn't know,' Grace murmured.

'You two don't talk any more.' Again it was a statement.

'Not really, no. We're both so busy.'

'Sure.'

'Rosa, you don't understand—'

Rosa smiled kindly. 'I understand more than you think. She is not a very nice person. Alastair, however, he is a lovely man and he deserves better. But still, she needs looking after.' She shrugged. 'I hope that is all right with you.'

Grace nodded. 'Of course. Does Luke know?'

'Oh yes, and she is lucky to have him – he is a good brother. Now I go.' Rosa blew her a kiss as she walked down the hall. 'There's lasagne for dinner. Just one portion, the rest is in the freezer.'

'Bye, Rosa.'

Grace stared after her and wondered exactly how Rosa knew so much about everything. When she'd referred to Miriam not being a good person, Grace didn't know if she meant the affair or the fraud, but somehow it wouldn't surprise her if she knew about both. The fact that quiet, reserved Michael seemed to have confided in her took her completely by surprise. As far as Grace was concerned, Rosa came to her home twice a week to cook and clean, but it seemed she'd been doing a lot more than that. Grace was grateful that Michael had someone to talk to, but – and she had to laugh – Rosa, the woman he'd accused of nicking his cufflinks? Who'd have thought? Rosa Di Paola, Grace decided, was wasted as a housekeeper and could make a fortune as a counsellor.

*

Rosa had only been gone an hour when the doorbell rang. Grace dragged herself off the sofa where she'd curled up in the hope of getting rid of her headache, and went out to the door. When she opened it, Luke was standing there.

'Hello, Grace.'

'Luke.'

'I know you don't want to see me, but there are things I have to tell you.'

'It's okay, I've seen Alastair.'

Luke shook his head. 'It's not just that.'

Grace sighed wearily. 'You'd better come in.'

'How are you?' he asked when they were seated in the living room.

'Fine. Look, I'd offer you a drink but I was just on my way out.'

'I won't keep you. I just needed to talk to you about Bridget.'

'Bridget?' Grace frowned.

'Do you know how Alastair found out about Miriam's affair?'

Grace shook her head.

'Bridget found out about it and was going to use the information to blackmail Miriam.'

'I don't believe it,' Grace scoffed. 'Miriam's making it up.'

'It wasn't Miriam who told me. Alastair walked in on them and heard everything. That was the day they had the row in the shop, and we assumed it was over you.'

'I know that now, but I didn't know Bridget was involved. Alastair never said a word.'

Luke studied her. 'I didn't realise you'd seen Alastair.'

'Briefly,' she replied without looking at him.

He stood up. 'Well, I just wanted to warn you about Bridget.'

'Nat saw her the other night, with a guy.'

'Probably Nigel.'

'Nigel?'

'The man Miriam was seeing. Bridget has sort of taken him over.'

Grace pulled a weary hand through her hair. 'This is like one of those ridiculous soap operas. I just don't know what to expect next.'

'I'm sure everything will settle down now.'

Grace groaned as she remembered what Nat had told her.

'What is it?'

'Nat told Bridget that I was running the business alone now. She assumed, because we're friends, that I would have told Bridget everything.'

'Oh no, that's all we need!'

'She doesn't know any of the details, just that Miriam is no longer my partner.'

'And she won't stop ferreting until she finds out why,' Luke said grimly. 'I'd better go and warn her off.'

'If you do that, she'll know she's on to something.'

Luke stood up and paced the room. 'You're probably

right, but I feel I should do something. Miriam can't take much more.'

'She should have thought of that before.'

Luke held up his hands. 'I know that, Grace, you know I do, but I'm worried about her.'

Grace watched him as he sat down again and cupped his face in his hands. 'Rosa says she's drinking.'

He nodded.

'Well, she always liked a drink. I wouldn't worry too much about that.'

'She's letting herself go. When I went over there yesterday, she was wearing a tracksuit, can you imagine? Miriam Cooper in a tracksuit and she had no make-up on.'

Grace stared. The only time she'd seen Miriam without make-up was in the beauty salon, and she was usually dressed in sharply cut business suits seven days a week. 'Have you told Alastair?' she said at last.

'He walks away if I even mention her name.'

'You have to make him listen,' Grace urged.

Luke shot her a quizzical look. 'Why do you care, after all that Miriam's done to you?'

'I don't care.'

'Oh please, Grace, we've known each other too long for games.'

'I don't know you,' Grace hissed. 'I don't know you at all.'

Luke held her gaze. 'Nothing happened with Natasha – how many times do I have to tell you that? If you don't believe me, don't you at least believe your own daughter?'

'You were playing with her and you could have really hurt her. You took her to Chez Nous, for God's sake, you bought her champagne, you swept the girl off her feet. What kind of message did you think you were sending?'

'It was a bad idea, I see that now,' he admitted, 'but I swear to you that I was just trying to make her feel better. Natasha is like a niece to me.'

Grace scowled. 'You take nieces to McDonald's, not Michelin-star restaurants.'

'I was wrong, what more can I say?'

Grace looked into the beautiful blue eyes, so sincere and open. 'I don't know what or who to believe any more.'

Luke came over and took her hands in his. 'You can trust me. I'm your friend, yours and Natasha's, and I always will be. If you want me to keep away from her, I will.'

Grace shook her head, her eyes filling with tears. 'No, she's probably going to need you. Michael and I are splitting up.' Luke gathered her into his arms and she let the tears flow, wishing it was Alastair who was holding her.

'Hey, it's okay, it will all be fine, you'll see.'

Grace pulled a tissue from her sleeve to dab at her eyes. 'You don't seem surprised.'

'The only surprise is that you two have stayed together this long.'

Grace stared at him. 'Why would you say that?'

He shrugged. 'Sorry, Michael's a nice man but I never

had much in common with him and I didn't think you did either.' He stood up. 'Now, I'll go. I just wanted to warn you about Bridget. And whatever happens, Grace, I'll always be your friend, do you believe that?'

She nodded slowly.

'Good. I'll see myself out.'

Chapter 34

Bridget's mind had been working overtime since Nat had let slip that wonderful little nugget of information. She had to find out what was going on between Miriam and Grace, but she didn't know who to talk to – or, more importantly – who would talk to her. Her only real contact was Annabel, but she'd probably been warned not to talk to Bridget again. There was Grace's new accountant, what was his name? John. He'd answered the phone a couple of times when she'd called Grace, so he knew they were friends. Bridget ran upstairs, pulled her sexiest outfit out of the wardrobe and went to take a shower. It was time to pay a visit to Graceful Living.

When she got to Blackrock she parked around the corner from the premises and walked up and down the road looking for Grace's jeep. When she was satisfied it wasn't there, she went to the door and rang the bell.

'Hello?'

'John?'

'Yes.'

'Hi, it's Bridget here.'

'Oh hello, come on in.'

Bridget adjusted her skirt, fixed a wide-open smile to her lips and pushed open the door.

'Nice to meet you at last.' John stood in the office doorway, beaming at her, his cheeks red.

'And lovely to meet you, John.'

'I'm afraid Grace isn't here today.'

Bridget's face dropped. 'She isn't? But we arranged to have lunch together.'

'Oh, I am sorry, she must have forgotten. Shall I phone her?' He turned back to his desk.

'Oh no,' Bridget said hurriedly, 'don't do that. She would be so upset that she'd let me down and I think she has enough on her plate at the moment, don't you?'

'That's very kind of you.'

'But I wouldn't say no to a coffee.' Bridget sat down on the other side of his desk and allowed her skirt to ride up an inch. 'If it wouldn't be too much trouble.'

'I was just going to have one myself.' John bustled off to the little kitchen. 'You're welcome to share my egg sandwiches, if you're hungry.'

Bridget winced. 'Oh no, I wouldn't dream of it. I'll just have my coffee and be on my way and let you get back to work. Tell me, John, do you like it here?'

'Very much,' he told her, pouring boiling water into two mugs. 'Grace is a lovely lady.'

'She is, and I can't tell you how much better we all feel, knowing you're here to look after her interests.'

'Well, that's very nice of you to say so.' He carried the coffee over to the desk and sat down facing her. 'I assure you no money will go missing while John Crowe is around.'

Bridget bit her lip to stop herself smiling. 'That's good to know. Have you met Miriam at all, John?'

The older man scowled. 'She's been in a couple of times, but I promise you I never leave her alone for a minute.'

'You're a wise man,' Bridget nodded solemnly, 'and a busy one. I won't take up any more of your time.' She stood up and walked to the door.

'But you haven't finished your coffee,' he said, hurrying after her.

'Too much caffeine is bad for the skin' she told him, and kissed him on both cheeks. 'Goodbye, John. Thank you so much, for everything.'

Miriam was in the lounge when Luke's van pulled into the driveway. She swallowed hard and gripped the arm of the chair to steady herself. He'd called yesterday to warn her but she still found it hard to believe it was actually happening. He'd suggested it might be easier if she went out but she had to see him, just one last time. Luke swung down from the van and moments later she heard the passenger door bang and watched as Alastair walked around the van and stood looking up at the house. She went out into the hall to open the door and then found that she couldn't move. He rang the doorbell and when she still didn't answer he put his key in the door and opened it, stopping in his tracks when he saw her standing there.

'Miriam.' He nodded, his eyes expressionless.

'Hello, Alastair.'

'If it's a bad time we can come back,' he started.

'No, that's okay.'

Luke stepped into the hall and looked from one to the other. 'Do you want me to wait in the van?'

Miriam looked at her husband.

'No, let's get started,' Alastair said, and moved past her to go into his study.

'I'll leave you to it,' Miriam said, walking by her brother.

He caught her arm. 'If you want I'll come with you.'

'No, I've got business to attend to,' she told him, and taking her bag and car keys, walked out the door.

Alastair came to join him as she drove away. 'Are you sure you don't want me to use a removal company?' he asked.

Luke shook his head as he watched his sister drive away. 'No, let's get it over with.'

Miriam was sitting in a car park in Sandymount, staring out to sea, when her mobile phone rang. Looking down, she saw the caller was Nigel. She ignored it but a moment later a message came through. NEED 2 TALK. HEARD OF AN OPP U MIGHT BE INTERESTED IN

Despite her sadness, Miriam felt the old adrenalin

rush that only making money gave her. She picked up the phone and called him.

Nigel was laughing when he picked up. 'Glad to see you haven't changed.'

'I was wondering when you'd crawl out from under your rock,' she drawled.

'Now, Miriam, be nice,' he chided her. I have a deal you might be interested in.'

'Spit it out then.'

'Meet me at the Four Seasons in an hour.'

Miriam hung up. The hotel was less than five minutes away, so that gave her enough time. She quickly dialled a number. 'Sally, it's Miriam Cooper. Can you fit me in for a wash and blow dry in five minutes?'

When she walked into the hotel bar, Nigel came to meet her and kissed her cheek. 'Miriam, you look wonderful.'

'Save it, Nigel,' she told him. 'I don't have long.'

He smiled, unperturbed by her sharp tone. 'Gin and tonic?' he asked.

She shook her head. 'Just mineral water.'

He raised an eyebrow but without another word went to the bar and returned moments later with her drink and a large whiskey for himself. 'Cheers.'

Miriam looked around. 'I hope your new girlfriend isn't joining us.'

'Not today,' he said smoothly.

'You're going to regret getting mixed up with that one – she's poison.'

'Well, thank you for the warning but I think I can handle her.'

'Don't say I didn't warn you,' Miriam said with a shrug. 'Now, what did you want to talk to me about, Nigel? Some of us have work to do.'

'Do you remember Paul Charleston?'

'Small dark man, owns a chain of boutiques in Scotland?'

'That's the one.'

'What about him?'

'He's selling up.'

Miriam's eyes narrowed. 'I thought he was about to expand. What went wrong?'

'He has a bit of a problem with the gee-gees and his bookmaker wants paying – or else.'

'Or else what?'

'Or else he'll spend the rest of his days in a wheelchair – if he's lucky.'

'You're having me on.'

Nigel shook his head. 'These guys don't mess around. If you can't pay in money then you pay with your limbs or your life – depending on how much you owe, of course. Paul owes a lot.'

'So what's this got to do with me?'

'He wants a very quick sale, no questions asked, and I thought you might be ready for a change of scene.'

Miriam digested this. 'How many shops are there?'

'Seven. One in Edinburgh, two in Glasgow and one each in Inverness, Aberdeen, Perth and Ayr.'

Miriam's eyes widened. 'Turnover?'

Nigel opened the briefcase at his feet and pulled out a file. 'Very healthy. You'll find everything you need to know in there.'

Miriam clutched the file in her hands. 'But I wouldn't be able to come up with the money quickly.'

'It's a bargain, Miriam, and you could always sell up here.'

'Sell Lady M's?' She stared at him, but all she was really seeing was Alastair removing all his belongings from their house.

'Think about it.' Nigel drained his glass, picked up his briefcase and stood up. 'But don't take too long.'

'What's in this for you, Nigel?'

He grinned. 'Five per cent.'

Miriam sat for a long time after he left, going through the file. It included the audited accounts for the last three years and they looked very healthy, a lot better than Lady M's. Picking up her phone, Miriam arranged a meeting with her accountant for first thing the next morning and with her head reeling with figures, drove back into Donnybrook and walked into an estate agent's office.

'Is that it?' Luke asked, wiping the sweat from his brow.

Alastair leaned back against the van and stared up at the house. 'I think so.'

'Any regrets?'

Alastair smiled sadly. 'Many.'

Luke stared out across the garden. 'I wonder where she's got to.'

'She will be okay,' Alastair told him. 'I promise you.'

Luke nodded and went back inside to set the alarm.

'I'm sorry this is all landing on your shoulders, Luke,' Alastair said, as they drove away, 'and I can't tell you how much I appreciate you taking me in.'

'That's okay. I know you'd do the same for me.'

'Absolutely. There's a room in my house for you whenever you fancy some fresh sea air.'

Luke grinned. 'I might take you up on that.'

'Although it would be best if you waited until I buy a bed, and a sofa – oh, and a table.'

Luke laughed. 'I think you have some shopping to do.'

'I'm hopeless at that sort of thing.'

'You need a woman.'

Alastair rolled his eyes. 'I don't think so.'

'I know someone who could help,' Luke said gently.

Alastair shot him a wary look. 'I don't know about that . . .'

'Trust me, Alastair, it will be fine.'

Chapter 35

Grace was on her hands and knees staining floorboards in a Victorian terraced house in Bray when Michael phoned to say he was on his way back. 'What time will you get here?' she asked, smiling her thanks at the carpenter who was holding the phone for her.

'About six. I thought Nat could come over for dinner.'

'Er, dinner?'

'I'll bring pizza,' Michael told her.

'Great, see you at six.' Grace turned to the carpenter. 'Would you mind dialling my daughter's number, Jack?'

He grinned. 'It'll cost more.'

'I'll bring chocolate biscuits tomorrow.'

'You're on.'

'Nat? Hi, it's Mum. Dad's coming home today. Can you come over for dinner about six? I know it's short notice but we need to talk. Yes, that's right. Great, I'll see you then. Bye, sweetheart. Okay, Jack, whatever happens, throw me out of here by five-thirty.'

'We'll never be finished by then.'

'We'll have to be.'

It was nearly seven when Grace finally got home. She had called ahead to tell Michael about the traffic accident that was holding her up, but she was still a bundle of nerves when she finally climbed out of her car and walked into the house. Michael and Nat were sitting at the table in silence. 'Hi.'

'Hi, Mum,' Nat muttered. 'I hope you're not hungry, Dad got anchovies on the pizza.'

Grace looked from her daughter to her grim-faced husband. 'Well, we can pick them off, I suppose.'

'I don't want any.'

Grace took off her coat and slid into the seat beside her. 'I'm not that hungry myself. How was the fishing trip?' she asked Michael.

'There wasn't one,' he said, pouring her a glass of wine.

Grace met his eyes for the first time. 'But you said—'

'I didn't go fishing, I went to Dubai for a job interview.'

Nat stared wide-eyed at her father. 'I never knew you were interested in working abroad.'

Michael smiled slightly. 'There's a lot of things you don't know about your boring old dad.'

'So what happened?' Grace asked. He frowned. 'At the interview, Michael?'

'Oh yes, I got it. The job, that is, I got the job. It's initially a two-year contract.'

'Congratulations. How long have you been planning this?' Grace asked quietly.

Michael didn't look at her. 'I've been thinking about it for a while but I only sent in the application a couple of weeks ago.'

'After I told you about Miriam.'

'That's not why I did it.'

'Then why didn't you tell me?'

Michael raised an eyebrow. 'Isn't keeping secrets what this family's all about?'

'Oh Dad,' Nat groaned. 'If you're doing this just to get back at us—'

'I'm doing this for me,' he interrupted. 'I think it's time I put *my* life first for a change. I've spent my married life trying to do what was right for us as a family and got no thanks for it.'

Nat rolled her eyes. 'Oh, please—'

Grace held up her hand. 'Your dad's right. Nat. He's always taken care of us and now he's entitled to do something for himself. You above anyone should know how important it is to be in a job you enjoy. ' Grace looked at Michael. 'Will you enjoy it? Are you sure this is what you want?'

He seemed taken aback by her support. 'I don t know really, but it will be a nice change and I'll certainly enjoy the weather.'

'So what happens at the end of two years?' Nat asked. 'Will you come back to work in Dublin?'

Michael met his daughter's eyes. 'Probably not.'

Nat looked from him to Grace. 'So this is it?'

Neither of them answered.

Nat stood up and shrugged into her jacket.

'Don't go,' Grace begged. 'We have things to talk about.'

Nat shook her head, her eyes bright with tears. 'No, you two have things to talk about.' And she walked out of the room.

Grace stood up to follow her.

'Leave her, she's right. This is between us.'

Grace sat down again and the couple remained in silence for a few minutes.

Michael refilled their glasses. 'Are you annoyed with me?' he asked.

She shook her head. Not really. But you're angry with me.'

'No, not any more, just sad.'

She looked at him, her eyes brimming with tears. 'You're the one that's leaving.'

'Only because you would never have had the courage to go,' he said softly. 'But you left in here,' he pointed at his heart, 'a long time ago.'

'When do you leave?' she asked.

'For Dubai? In two weeks.

Grace stared at him, shocked. 'But what about Christmas?'

He laughed. 'You think I should stay so we can play Happy Families? Please, Grace, give me a break. As it is, Nat probably wouldn't even want to spend it with me.'

'I'm sure you're wrong,' Grace started.

'Are you? I've made up my mind, Grace, and I need to do it quickly.' He looked straight into her eyes. 'There's nothing for me here now, is there?'

Grace steeled herself to hold his gaze. 'Things may be tough between you and Nat at the moment, but she loves you, Michael.'

He nodded and cleared his throat. 'We need to discuss, some economic details. I jotted down a few things on the flight home.' He pulled a small notepad out of his jacket pocket. 'We should get everything transferred into your name. Now the house—'

'I want to sell it,' Grace said.

'There's really no need, and when I'm gone I'm sure Nat would move back in.'

'No, I want to sell,' Grace repeated. 'We might have had our problems, Michael, but this has always been an equal partnership and you're entitled to your fair share.'

'Okay, but you don't have to rush into anything. I won't need the money; the job comes with a car and an apartment.'

'Still, it's what I want to do.'

He shrugged. 'Fine.' He went through several pages of notes about bank accounts and contact numbers, and when her car needed servicing, but although Grace kept her eyes on him and nodded from time to time, she wasn't hearing any of it. Was this how a marriage ended? Did it come down to where the spare car keys were kept and how to fix the dodgy tap in the utility room? Was that how you brought an end to a twenty-four-year relationship?

Michael went to bed early. 'I have a very busy week ahead; there are a lot of jobs that have to be finished before I leave. I'll use the spare room.'

Grace just nodded. After he had gone upstairs, she sat alone at the table for a while and then grabbing her coat, bag and keys she ran out of the house.

'Grace!' Bridget looked slightly wary when she found her friend on the doorstep, tearful and dishevelled.

'I'm sorry for just turning up like this, Bridget, but I needed to talk to someone.'

'Sure, come on in.' Bridget led her into the kitchen, poured a large gin and tonic and shoved it in her hand. 'What's happened?'

Grace took a long drink and sat down. 'My marriage is over.'

Bridget sank into the chair opposite, her eyes out on stalks. 'Oh my God, why?'

Grace laughed, but there were tears rolling down her cheeks. 'I'm not sure.'

'Was it Michael? God, he hasn't had an affair, has he?'

'No, nothing like that, but it was his decision.'

'And he didn't tell you why?'

'He said he had to leave because I would never have the courage to.' Grace looked up at her. 'He was right.'

'Oh Grace, I know it's sad, but it's probably for the best.'

Grace frowned and then looked long and hard at Bridget. 'Luke said you were trying to blackmail Miriam.'

Bridget groaned. 'That bloody man won't be happy until he's convinced everyone I'm the Princess of Darkness! I was winding Miriam up, Grace. She was giving me a hard time, as usual, and I thought I'd have a little fun. It was just unfortunate that Alastair happened to walk in at the wrong moment.' Her expression sobered. 'I was sorry about that, I've always liked Alastair. Still, I've probably done him a favour. He's better off without that hard-hearted cow.' She shot Grace a look from under her lashes. 'You're not her biggest fan at the moment either, are you?'

'What do you mean?' Grace said faintly, wiping her eyes on her sleeve.

'I'm not dumb, Grace. You two have obviously split up and that night at the fashion show you could have cut the atmosphere with a knife. What did she do, come on to Michael?'

Grace smiled despite herself. 'No, nothing like that.'

Bridget pouted. 'Don't tell me, if you don't want to. I know you don't trust me.'

'Of course I do,' Grace reached out to the only friend she had left. 'She stole some money from Graceful Living.'

Bridget looked suitably shocked. 'No way.'

Grace nodded.

'But I don't understand. Why isn't she in prison or something?'

'She agreed to hand over her share of the business if I said nothing.'

Bridget let out a low whistle. 'Grace Mulcahy, you're some businesswoman.'

'Not really,' Grace said bitterly. 'I just didn't want to admit to Michael and the rest of the world that I'd been so stupid.'

'Michael doesn't know?'

Grace sighed. 'He does now.'

'So that's why he's leaving.'

Grace shook her head. 'Not really, but I suppose it was the catalyst.'

Bridget frowned. 'Does Nat know? Only I met her the other night and she seemed in great form.'

'Michael told us tonight that he's taking a job in Dubai and he never suggested I go with him, so I imagine she got the message. I'll go and see her tomorrow though, and explain everything.'

'Isn't she living at home?'

'No, she and Michael had a row and she moved out.'

'So where's she staying?'

Grace met Bridget's eyes. 'With her boyfriend.'

'Does Michael know?'

'That she's living with Ken? God, no! She said she was moving in with a friend and in his innocence he just assumed it was a girl from college.'

'Daddies hate to admit that their little girls grow up,' Bridget said, filling up their glasses.

'Oh, I can't drink any more, I have to drive,' Grace protested. 'I was probably over the limit, driving over here.'

Bridget put an arm around her and kissed her cheek. 'You're not going anywhere tonight, Grace,' she said firmly. 'You were there when I needed you and now it's my turn.'

Bridget tiptoed into the spare room the next morning to check that Grace was still asleep and then went back into the kitchen. Going to the drawer she pulled out the business card she'd been given the previous week and dialled the number on the bottom of it. 'Hi, can you put me through to Jaz Corcoran, please.' Bridget frowned. 'She's not in yet? Well, let me talk to someone else who works on the gossip column then. I've got some information that they want to hear.'

Chapter 36

It was eleven and Miriam was still in her towelling robe, but only because she hadn't had time to wash and dress. She'd started work in the study and had filled three bin-bags of documents for shredding, two bags of rubbish and two boxes of papers that would come with her. She was just sorting through a file of user instruction booklets when she heard a key in the door and realized it was Rosa. 'Shit.' She walked to the door and peered out. 'Rosa.'

'Hello, Miriam.' The housekeeper smiled kindly. 'How are you today?'

'Fine,' Miriam said shortly. 'Now I want you to give the bedrooms a good clear-out today – they need freshening up.'

Rosa frowned. 'But it's Friday. Fridays I do the weekly shop and make the food for the weekend.'

'I'll be out all weekend so I don't need food. Just do the bedrooms, please,' and she closed the door in Rosa's face.

An hour later there was a knock on the door. 'What is

it?' Miriam called, engrossed in some share certificates she'd forgotten she had.

'I've brought you some coffee.'

'Leave it there, I'll get it in a minute.'

'Are you okay, Miriam?'

'Fine, fine. Have you done those bedrooms yet?'

'Two are done.'

'Then you'd better make a start on the others.'

She heard Rosa go back upstairs and went to rescue her coffee. Miriam never could figure out why, but Rosa's coffee always tasted better than anyone else's. She returned to her desk and looked at the list in front of her. There was still a lot to be done, but she was limited to what she could do with Rosa's eagle eyes on her. She decided to start work on her own bedroom. She'd tell Rosa she was having a lie-down – that would keep her away for a while.

When she went upstairs she poked her head into the second bedroom and sniffed with appreciation at the scent of fresh clean bedlinen. Rosa came out of the en-suite and smiled.

'Can I do anything for you?'

'No, thank you. I've a bit of a headache so I'm going to lie down. Please don't disturb me.'

'Of course not. I hope you feel better soon.'

Miriam's lips twisted into a bitter smile. 'You're probably the only one who does.'

She had cleared out her dressing room and filled three suitcases by the time she heard Rosa leave. Feeling exhausted but exhilarated, she went to shower and dress. She had a meeting with the bank at four and then she needed to go to the Mercedes garage and see about her car. The phone rang while she was in the shower and went to the answering machine.

'Miriam, it's me, Luke – are you there? Please, pick up.' He waited for a moment and then, 'Okay, give me a call when you get this.'

Miriam stepped out of the shower and walked back into the bedroom. She saw the flashing light on her phone and ignored it, knowing it would be Luke again. Quickly drying her hair, she applied her make-up carefully, added a splash of Chanel No. 19 and then put on her simple but elegant black Joseph suit. Slipping on a pair of high Prada suede shoes, she took her matching bag and went downstairs. Collecting her briefcase and phone, she opened the door to leave and then stopped. Setting down her briefcase again, she walked back to the drinks cupboard in the lounge, poured herself a large measure of vodka and swallowed it down in one gulp. Two deep breaths later, Miriam went back outside, collected her briefcase and left, popping a mint into her mouth as she drove down the road.

Luke sat at the bar nursing a pint and wondering where Miriam was and what kind of a state she was in. He'd phoned three times today and she hadn't returned one of his calls. He could go over and bang the door down again but she was a grown woman and he couldn't babysit her for ever. If she wanted to drink herself into oblivion then that was her choice. She wasn't his problem, he told himself, he had his own life to live. However, he was slightly taken aback at Alastair's rather indifferent reaction to Miriam's behaviour.

'You really don't have anything to worry about,' he'd told Luke. 'Miriam will always look out for Miriam.'

Luke had thought it was an uncharacteristically harsh remark but then Miriam had treated Alastair very badly so he could hardly blame the man. He was taking it all harder than he let on, Luke figured, as after his initial enthusiasm on moving into the cottage he'd done virtually nothing with it since. Any time Luke had been up to visit, he'd found Alastair wandering aimlessly along the beach or pottering about the garden, and he'd wondered if it had been wise of Alastair to move so far away from his friends.

'You look like you have the weight of the world on your shoulders.'

Luke whipped his head around and smiled when he saw Nat standing over him. 'Not quite the whole world. Are you stopping for a drink or just passing through?' He nodded towards the back room.

'Passing through, but I'll have a quick drink with you.' She climbed up on the stool beside him. 'Alastair not with you tonight?'

Luke called the barman and asked for a lager for Nat before answering. 'He's moved into his new house. I quite miss having him about, actually.'

'How does Miriam feel about that?'

Luke scrunched up his face. 'Who knows how Miriam feels about anything? I certainly don't. So where's lover boy tonight?'

'With his public in there. We're having a goodbye party – he's moving to London next week.'

Luke's eyes narrowed. 'Oh, I'm sorry.'

'Don't be. He did ask me to go but I said no.'

He grinned. 'Good for you.'

'Aren't you going to ask me why I didn't go?'

'Okay then,' he said, playing along. 'Why didn't you go?'

She looked at him solemnly. 'I couldn't bear to leave you.' Luke choked on his drink and she burst out laughing. 'Sorry, I couldn't resist it.'

Luke scowled at her. 'Thanks very much.'

'No, thank *you*,' she said, suddenly serious. 'You made me sit back and see him as he really is, and though I know he cares for me, he doesn't love me. And I don't really love him either.'

'Well, I'm delighted it's worked out for you. I'm fed up hearing about broken hearts.'

Nat's face clouded over. 'Speaking of which, have you heard Mum and Dad have split up?'

'Yes, I did. I'm sorry.'

Nat shrugged. 'They've been having problems for a while but the whole business with Miriam seemed to be the last straw. Dad just couldn't believe that Mum didn't tell him what was going on.'

Luke shook his head sadly. 'My sister has an awful lot to answer for.'

'Oh, I don't know, it might be the making of both of them. Dad's going off to work in Dubai for a couple of years, can you believe it? The man that never went further than Cork on his holidays!'

'You seem very cool about the whole thing,' he remarked.

'I am,' she agreed, 'although it was a shock. But they haven't been happy together for a while now so I suppose things can only get better. I mean, Dad would never have done anything this wild if he'd stayed with Mum. You know, he's asked me to go out and visit him?'

'And will you?'

'I'm not sure. It's hard to storm out after an argument when you're in a strange country!'

He grinned. 'Good point.'

'Luke, can I ask you a personal question?' Nat leaned her chin on her hand and looked very serious.

'I suppose so.'

'Aren't you ever going to date again?'

Luke threw back his head and laughed. 'Well, Miss Nosey, funny you should say that because I'm actually meeting my new girlfriend here tonight.'

Nat's eyes widened. 'Really?'

Luke's smile broadened as the door opened. 'In fact, here she comes right now.'

Nat whirled around to look and did a double-take when she saw who it was. 'I don't believe this.'

'Hello, Natasha, this is a nice surprise.'

Nat stood up and hugged the older woman. 'Hi, Rosa,

you kept this one quiet, didn't you?' She looked from one to the other.

'Can you blame us?' Luke said.

Rosa rolled her eyes. 'Miriam won't be happy.'

'Does Mum know?' Nat asked.

'No, you're the first,' Luke told her.

'Do you want me to keep it a secret?'

Luke slipped an arm around Rosa and pulled her against him. 'I don't know, Rosa, what do you think? Are you ready to face the world?'

She looked up at him, her eyes warm. 'Oh, I think so.'

Nat smirked. 'Bridget is not going to be impressed. No offence, Rosa, but her fella running off with the housekeeper – she'll be furious.'

Luke laughed. 'That's a bonus. I also get to sample Rosa's wonderful cooking on a regular basis and it does-n't cost me a penny.'

Rosa looked at him in mock outrage. 'So that's all you're after.'

'No, I assure you I'm after a lot more,' he murmured.

'Oh, that's it, I'm off'

'No, no, no, Nat, don't leave,' Rosa begged, laughing.

'I have to, really. My boyfriend's having a party in the back room and he'll be wondering where I am.'

'Have a good evening, then,' Rosa said.

'Bye, Natasha, take care.'

'Bye you two.'

'She's a nice girl,' Rosa said, taking Nat's seat.

'Yeah. Glass of wine?'

'Please.' She waited while he ordered the drink. 'Have you talked to your sister?' she asked when he'd turned his attention back to her.

'No, I've been trying to get hold of her all day.'

'I'm worried about her,' Rosa said. 'She's behaving very oddly. Today, when I got there at eleven, she was still in her dressing-gown and she locked herself in the study and wouldn't come out.'

'Drinking,' Luke said glumly.

'I don't know for sure. She told me to springclean the bedrooms, but when I said I had the shopping and the cooking to do, she said that she'd be out all weekend and wouldn't need food.'

'Oh God, what am I going to do?'

'It gets worse, I'm afraid. She came upstairs after a couple of hours and said she had a headache and was going to lie down and I wasn't to disturb her.'

'How did she seem?'

Rosa frowned. 'Okay, but in all the time I've worked for her I've never known her to go to bed in the middle of the day. Even if she was feeling ill, she'd still be on the phone or the computer. It's just so unlike her.'

'Alastair leaving seems to have floored her. What should I do?'

Rosa touched his cheek and smiled sympathetically at him. 'You're a good man and a great brother, just be there for her.'

'I'm fed up of other people's problems.' He turned his

head to kiss her fingers. 'I just want to concentrate on you.'

'I think I would like that.'

'Now that my lodger has left I have an empty flat not far from here.'

She raised an eyebrow. 'Does it need cleaning?'

'I don't think so,' Luke said playfully, 'but then my standards aren't quite as high as yours. I changed the sheets today, though.'

'Really?'

'And there's a bottle of wine in the fridge.'

'Italian?' she asked.

'Of course.'

'Then what are we waiting for?'

Chapter 37

Alastair pulled another huge weed from the so-called flowerbed and threw it on the growing pile at his side. Sitting back on his heels, he wiped the sweat from his brow and looked around him. Yet again, he had been drawn to the garden today, even though there was a mountain of work to be done in the house. He didn't like to think why he was avoiding the work, but instead concentrated on the garden where he felt comfortable and distracted.

'Who's winning?' a cheerful voice called from across the fence.

Alastair looked up and smiled at the man. 'Definitely not me. Alastair Summers,' he said, standing up and going over to the man, pulling off his gloves and stretching out his hand.

'Alf O'Leary.' The man shook it. 'Welcome to Banford.'

'Thank you.'

'I live across the way,' he nodded at a pretty dormer bungalow across the road, 'with my wife, Teresa. Are you married?'

'Separated.'

'Oh, I'm sorry.'

Alastair grinned. 'Don't be, I'm not.'

The other man chuckled. 'In that case, congratulations. You must come over for dinner some night. Teresa loves entertaining. When she finds out you're on your own she'll be on your doorstep day and night with pies and cakes.'

'Sounds like the perfect neighbour.'

'Aye, but watch out if she wants to introduce you to any of her friends. She's a terror for matchmaking.'

'Now that I don't need.' Alastair shuddered.

Alf winked at him. 'I'll keep her on a short leash.'

'What are you saying about me, Alf O'Leary?' A small pretty woman with snow-white hair appeared at Alf's side.

'Teresa, meet Alastair Summers.'

'Welcome to Banford, Alastair,' she smiled at him. 'I hope you'll be very happy here.'

He waved a hand at the view before them. 'How could I not be?'

'It is lovely,' Teresa said, 'and though it's a small community, it's a friendly one. You can be alone if you want and you can have company if you want – it's that kind of place.'

'Sounds perfect.'

'Is there a Mrs Summers?'

'What did I tell you?' Alf shook his head.

'What?' Teresa looked at her husband.

'Come on, Teresa, let's leave this man to his work. Drop over sometime, Alastair.'

'I will,' he promised. 'Nice to meet you both.'

Alastair chuckled as Alf led Teresa away before she could ask any more questions. He could just imagine the short shrift Miriam would have given the poor woman if she'd been here. Miriam didn't like nosiness and she would have been disdainful of the older couple and their friendly overtures. In all the time they'd lived in the house in Donnybrook, they'd only ever been on nodding terms with their neighbours. Perhaps that was one of the reasons Alastair had felt no regret at leaving his old home, or perhaps it had just never really suited him in the first place. He liked the idea of passing the time of day with the residents of the little village, and he looked forward to being on first-name terms with the postman and the grocer, the butcher, the baker, the candlestick-maker. He smiled as he went back to his weeding. He was definitely showing his age.

Grace regretted staying over at Bridget's as soon as she woke and her head started to throb. She couldn't remember much about the previous night but she was fairly sure she had spilled her guts to her friend. Bridget had been kind and provided a firm shoulder to cry on and Grace felt vaguely annoyed at the way Luke had vilified her. She wondered now if it had been a deliberate attempt to come between the two friends, and promised herself she'd have it out with him the next time she saw him.

She went out to the bathroom, splashed water in her face and brushed her teeth with her finger. When she'd dressed she went through to the kitchen where she found a note propped up on the table. Grace smiled affectionately when she read it.

Hi, Grace,

Sorry to run out on you but I had a date with the Social Welfare man. Help yourself to breakfast (lunch.) and I'll see you later.

X

Grace picked up the pen and scribbled a note back saying she had to go, thanking her friend for her kindness and promising to call the next day. As she drove to work it occurred to her that Michael hadn't even called to check on her and see if she was okay, but then he mightn't even have realized she'd gone out last night and assumed she'd just left for work early. She sighed. It would be strange not to have Michael questioning her movements and criticizing her working hours. She would only have to answer to herself from now on, and could work round the clock if she wanted without anyone worrying or caring. The thought brought tears to her eyes and she swallowed them back with annoyance. Michael's controlling nature had driven her mad for years, and now that she was going to be free of it, she still wasn't happy!

Today she decided that she would distract herself with practicalities and make a few calls to estate agents to arrange valuations of the house. She hadn't given any thought to where she was going to live and she didn't have time to go house-hunting at the moment, but she could surf the internet tonight and see if there was anything suitable on the market. She favoured the idea of somewhere small with a second bedroom that she fervently hoped Nat would use. It amazed her how much she was missing her daughter, considering how little they'd seen of each other when she had been at home. But simple little things like buying her favourite biscuits or making sure that there was always a supply of her preferred shampoo or conditioner in the bathroom press had made Grace feel useful, and she longed to cosset her daughter.

Of course, Nat might well still decide to go to London with Ken – in which case Grace would be devastated, but she promised herself she wouldn't show it. Nat was entitled to live her own life, and all her mother could do was keep the home fires burning in case things went wrong.

Grace arrived into the office to find Lily sewing curtains and matching duvet covers for the house in Bray. 'They look beautiful,' she praised them. 'Do you think you'll finish them today?'

Lily glanced at the clock. ' Should do.'

'Great, I really appreciate you coming in today. Once I hang these on Monday, we'll be finished with the job.'

'Don't bet on it. Jack was on to say that the owner isn't happy with the built-in cupboard. She thinks it clashes with the paintwork.'

Grace groaned. 'The cupboard is white oak and the walls are painted a pale yellow – how on earth can they clash?'

Lily chuckled. 'Now remember, Grace, the customer is always right.'

'Except when they're wrong,' she retorted. 'I'll be glad when this job is finished – it's been a right pain.'

'Will you have any work for me next week?' Lily asked hopefully.

Grace frowned. 'It's two weeks before Christmas. I would have thought you'd have enough on your plate.'

'Yeah, but I could do with the money. Tommy is making his confirmation in February and I've already spent a fortune on Christmas, what with the food and clothes.'

'Well, the good news is there'll be a little bonus in your pay-packet this week. It's been a good month and there are already two jobs lined up for January.'

Lily's face lit up. 'Oh, that's great, Grace, thanks.'

'I think you've earned it.'

'What are you doing for Christmas?' Lily asked.

'Er, not sure yet. You?'

'We're going to my mother's so I'm planning to do as little as possible and let someone else play mediator with the twins.'

Grace laughed. Lily always had a funny story to tell

about her eight-year-old boys, and though she'd shake her head in despair at their antics, she was obviously very proud of them.

'What did they ask Santa for?' she asked.

Lily rolled her eyes. 'A Playstation, so you can imagine the ructions over whose turn it is.'

'I don't think it matters what they get, really. Kids just love Christmas, don't they? Now I'd better go out to Bray and see if I can sort this woman out before Jack gives her a black eye. See you later.'

Grace was in the car on her way out to Bray when the phone rang. She thanked God she'd invested in a hands-free kit as she seemed to get more calls in the car than anywhere else.

'Grace, it's Miriam.'

'What do you want?'

'We need to talk.'

'I'm listening.'

'Not on the phone and not at the office. Where are you now?'

'On my way to a job in Bray.'

'How long will you be?'

'I can't say for sure, but a couple of hours anyway, and then I have to go back to the office.'

'Believe me, this is more important. Meet me in the Royal Hotel at six.'

'I can't guarantee I'll be there by then.'

'I'll wait,' Miriam said and rang off.

Now what on earth was that all about, Grace wondered. If it was to do with the business, Miriam would have come to the office, and if not, what else did they have to talk about? She wondered if it was about Alastair, but couldn't think what – unless he had said something. Grace shook her head. He had nothing to say.

She hadn't given Alastair much thought in the last twenty-four hours, what with Michael's bombshell and her subsequent drinking session with Bridget, but now he was back on her mind, those beautiful eyes twinkling at her, warm and affectionate. She wondered how she'd manage to conceal her feelings if Miriam told her that she and her husband were reconciled. Her hands tightened on the wheel. She would be devastated – and yet she felt that it was probably what Alastair wanted. And if she really cared for him, shouldn't she just be happy for him?

Turning into the driveway, Grace's thoughts were interrupted by the sight of her carpenter and customer in heated discussion on the doorstep. Grace stepped out of the car and went to mediate, thinking, with a quiet chuckle, that it wasn't unlike Lily sorting out her twins.

Chapter 38

Miriam was sitting in a quiet corner of the lounge talking on the phone, when Grace walked in.

'There must be something we can do, Gareth – they can't get away with this.' She listened for a moment. 'Do what you can,' she finally barked and rang off. 'Do you want a drink?' she asked Grace.

'Just mineral water,' Grace replied, wondering why Miriam was talking to her lawyer.

Miriam clicked her fingers at a waiter. 'Two mineral waters.'

Grace raised an eyebrow. 'On the wagon?'

'You haven't a clue what's going on, have you?' Miriam hissed and then pressed her lips tightly together while the waiter served their drinks.

Grace noted for the first time the rings under Miriam's eyes and the pallor of her cheeks.

'*Ireland Weekly* is running a story about us tomorrow.'

'Us?'

'They know everything. Can you explain that?'

'No, of course I can't. It must be a mistake.'

'Jaz Corcoran, that ditzy gossip columnist, rang me and asked me to comment.'

'What did you say?' Grace asked.

'Nothing, of course, but you can bet she'd been on to everyone we know and got all sorts of crap from them.'

'But no one knows,' Grace reasoned.

Miriam's eyes narrowed. 'Are you sure about that? What about Nat, Michael—'

'Alastair, Luke,' Grace retorted.

'They wouldn't and you know it.'

'I do, and you should know that neither would Michael or Natasha.'

'Someone did. Who else is there?'

'I've no idea.' Grace stood to leave.

'Where the hell do you think you are going?'

'This is hardly my problem.'

Miriam's laugh was harsh. 'God, you can be very obtuse sometimes. Do you really think you're going to get off scot-free?'

Grace sank back in her chair. 'What do you mean? Why would they have a go at me when I'm the injured party?'

'It's a story, dear – they don't give a damn who's innocent and who's guilty, they just want to fill column inches. They'll print anything they can find – on you, on your family, on your marriage breakdown.'

'How did you know?'

'Jaz Corcoran told me. It's true, then'

Grace put her head in her hands. 'I don't believe this.'

'When did you and Michael split?'

'We only really decided yesterday.'

'Then it should be easy to figure out who told the press. It's either Michael . . .'

Grace shook her head.

'. . . or someone he told.'

'He wouldn't,' Grace started – but then how did she know? She'd never have thought he would confide in Rosa.

'Or someone *you* told.'

Grace put a hand to her mouth. 'Oh, no.'

'Who?'

Grace turned tortured eyes on Miriam. 'Bridget.'

'You stupid cow!' Miriam slapped her hand down hard on the table. 'What were you thinking of? Don't you know that little bitch would never miss an opportunity to take a pot-shot at me?'

'But not at me,' Grace whispered.

'Stop kidding yourself, will you! Bridget would betray her own mother if it meant making a few quid.'

'She would have got paid?'

'Of course.'

'I can't believe it – she was so kind to me last night.'

'Listened to all your problems, did she?' said Miriam sarcastically. 'Poured you another drink, told you to tell Aunty Bridget everything? I can't believe you could be so stupid! Didn't Luke tell you what she did to me?'

'Yes, but I thought he was exaggerating.'

'He wasn't.' Miriam glared at her.

'What do we do now?' Grace asked. 'What does your lawyer say?'

'That we can't stop it and can only sue them if they get any of the facts wrong.'

Grace felt a flicker of compassion for the other woman. 'I'm sorry, Miriam, you know I would never have done this intentionally. How will it affect Lady M's?'

'I have no idea. Can we agree at least that neither of us will talk to the press until we've seen this article and agreed the way forward?'

Grace nodded. 'Have you warned Luke and Alastair?'

'I've told Luke, he'll tell Alastair, and I've left it up to him whether to tell Dad.'

'Oh God, I hadn't even thought about the rest of the family, Grace murmured. 'The phone's going to be hopping tomorrow.'

'Well, for God's sake, warn all of them to say nothing if they're approached by any journalists.'

Grace nodded.

'I'll call you tomorrow but we won't be able to do anything until Monday. Meet me at Gareth's office at eight-thirty.'

'Okay, and Miriam,' Grace said, but Miriam was already marching towards the door, her heels clicking angrily on the tiled floor. 'I'm sorry.'

Alone, Grace sat back in her chair and thought about what to do next. The first thing was to warn Michael and

Nat. She could just imagine her husband's horror when she told him about this. He'd be high-tailing it to Dubai on the first flight he could get, and Grace didn't blame him. She couldn't believe that Bridget would do such a thing, but there was no doubt that she was the only possible suspect. Deciding there was no point putting off the inevitable, she picked up the phone and rang home. Michael answered on the first ring and she took a deep breath.

'It's me.'

'Ah, I was wondering when you'd surface.'

'What do you mean?' she said warily.

'You're in great demand today, mainly by the press.'

'Oh God.'

'Didn't you get my messages? I left several on your phone.'

'Sorry – I never checked, it's been a hectic day. You didn't talk to them, did you?'

'What do you take me for?'

'Sorry, sorry. Look, I'm on my way – I'll be there in twenty minutes. Will you call Nat and ask her to come over.'

'She's already here.'

'Right, great, see you soon.' Grace hurried out of the hotel and back to the car. As she drove home she wondered for the first time how Nat would react to the news that her life might be splashed across the papers. Grace didn't see why it should be, or what possible interest it would be to the general public, but she had told Bridget some things about Nat so it was entirely possible.

Oh shit! she swerved as she remembered that she'd told Bridget how Nat was living with her boyfriend. If that came out, Michael would be furious and there would be another blazing row, ending with Nat storming out. Grace felt close to tears at the thought of another traumatic, emotional evening. When was it all going to end?

Nat opened the door and came to meet her, a sympathetic smile on her lips. 'Hi, Mum.'

Grace hugged her gratefully. 'I think you might be hitting me rather than hugging me when you hear what I have to tell you.'

Nat's smile faltered. 'Why, what's it got to do with me?'

'Let's go inside and sit down with Dad.'

Michael was sitting reading the newspaper when they came in. Taking off his glasses he looked up at her and shook his head. '*Ireland Weekly*, the thrill of it all.'

'Don't,' she said, flopping into a chair. 'It's really not funny.'

'Presumably it's Miriam they're after.'

'Yes, I suppose so, but they'll probably give background details about us too.'

Nat shrugged. 'So? All they know about us is that you were her partner, she cheated on you and now she's not your partner any more. Big deal.'

Grace closed her eyes. 'It's a bit more complicated than that.'

'How complicated?' Michael's voice was dangerously soft.

'I was upset last night after our talk and I couldn't sleep so I went out.'

'Where?' Nat asked.

'To Bridget's. I told her everything – about the fraud, about you and me splitting up and,' she turned her gaze on her daughter, 'about you moving out.'

Michael stared at her. 'Are you saying it was Bridget that went to the newspaper?'

'She's the only one who knew you were going to Dubai, unless you told someone,' Grace said.

He shook his head.

'But she's your friend – how could she betray you like that?' Nat was shocked.

Grace shrugged. 'She was probably out to get Miriam and Luke.'

'She was probably out to get money,' Michael retorted.

'That' s what Miriam said, but I think it' s a combination of the two.'

'What a cow,' Natasha fumed. 'What a disgusting thing to do.'

The phone rang and Michael went to answer it. 'Say nothing to anyone,' Grace warned.

Michael shot her a withering look. 'That's good, coming from you.'

When he'd left the room, Grace turned to her daughter. 'I told Bridget you were living with Ken.'

'Oh, great. Did you tell her who he is?'

'I only know him as Ken.'

'But did you tell her he was a singer?'

Grace nodded slowly. 'I think so.'

'Oh, Mum,' Nat groaned.

'I'm sorry, darling. Maybe it would be better if you told your father about Ken tonight. You don't want him to read it in a tabloid.'

'But they mightn't print it.'

'They might.'

Nat sighed. 'Oh okay, I'll tell him, but if he starts sounding off, I'm out of here.'

Grace smile. 'You'll be out of here anyway, won't you? Listen, whatever you do, don't talk to anyone about the article. Miriam and I are seeing her solicitor first thing on Monday morning.'

Michael walked back into the room. 'That was Luke. Apparently a journalist tried to get into the nursing home to interview his dad.'

'That's despicable!' Grace gasped. 'He didn't get to see him, did he?'

'She – and no, the receptionist on duty was immediately suspicious as Luke is the only one who ever visits.'

'Miriam never visits her own father?' Nat asked.

Grace shrugged. 'They've never been close.'

'Still, he's her father.'

'Does that mean you'll feed me grapes when I'm on the scrap heap?' Michael asked, his lips twitching.

Nat gulped. 'That depends. If you start treating me

like an adult I might take you out in your wheelchair for the odd romp.'

'I'll do my best,' he promised, smiling.

'Okay then, let's see if you're serious.' She shot her mother a nervous look. 'When I moved out, I moved into my boyfriend's place.'

'I know.'

'How?' Nat stared at him.

'I followed you home from college the next day.'

'You did what!' she exploded.

'Look, I didn't mind you moving out, but I wanted to make sure that you had somewhere safe to go.'

Grace looked at her daughter. 'You can't blame him for that, can you?'

'I suppose not.'

'So would you like to tell me a bit about him, or do I have to wait and read it in the newspaper,' Michael prompted.

Nat took a deep breath. 'His name is Ken Jackson and he's not my boyfriend any more. He's moving to London next week.'

'And you're not going with him.' Grace said, her heart soaring.

'No, I'm going to stay and finish college here,' Nat said firmly.

'And where will you live?' Michael asked.

'Ken wants to keep the flat and he's asked me if I'd like to lease it.'

'But why not come back and live with me?' Grace asked.

'I was going to say the same to you,' Nat replied. 'There are two bedrooms, it's in a nice neighbourhood and not far from the office.'

Grace frowned. 'I hadn't thought about renting.'

'It might be as well in the short-term.' Michael agreed.

'I suppose so, but once the house is sold I would like to buy a place of my own.'

'No problem. I'm sure I'll find another flatmate easily enough.'

'Wouldn't you move with me?' Grace asked, crestfallen.

'Let's see how it goes, Mum, okay?' Nat stood up. 'I'd better go and warn Ken about this article. I'll call you tomorrow.' She bent to kiss her mother and Michael walked her to the door.

'Can I give you a lift?' he offered.

'That's okay, Dad, but thanks for the offer. Bye.'

'Bye, darling, take care.'

Chapter 39

Grace slept badly that night and staggered out of bed early to get to the newsagent. When she got downstairs, however, Michael was already sitting at the table with several copies of the tabloid in front of him. She sat down beside him and studied his face. 'Well?'

He sighed. 'It's pretty much what we expected.'

Grace grabbed a copy and pulled it towards her.

'Page twenty-eight,' he told her.

She leafed through the paper until she found the page and then gasped at the large picture of Miriam with a banner headline saying BOUTIQUE OWNER DEFRAUDS HER OWN PARTNER. There was a smaller picture of Grace taken at the launch of Graceful Living, and one of Alastair at his sixtieth birthday party standing beside the Rolls Royce. 'At least they've left you guys out of it.'

'No, we're in too. Take your time and read it,' he said gently. 'I'll make some tea.'

'Coffee for me, please. I think I'm going to need it.'

By the time Michael set a large pot of coffee and two mugs on the table she'd read the article through twice.

'What do you think?' he asked, sitting down beside her.

'I feel sorry for Alastair, for Luke, for poor Mr Cooper – although let's hope he never finds out about this – and, you'll think I'm mad, but I even feel a little bit sorry for Miriam.'

'Yes, you are mad. How can you feel sorry for someone who's treated you so badly?'

Grace threw the paper down and poured the coffee. 'She's paid for it now though, hasn't she? How will Lady M's survive this? How can she continue to do business in a little country like this? Her name will be mud.'

'I don't believe that at all. For God's sake, there are politicians who've done a lot worse and they've gone on to stand for election again and done better than before.'

'I suppose. Can the police bring any case against her?'

'Not unless you ask them to – you're the one who has been wronged. However, other companies that have done business with her may call for an investigation into her financial affairs.'

'I suppose if she cheated me, then she probably cheated others too.'

'You can bet on it.'

'I don't like the piece about Luke – it makes it sound as if he were in on it.'

'You've got to remember that Bridget is the source. He was always going to come off badly.'

'Maybe I should talk to the press and set them straight.'

'No, don't do that. Say nothing. It will soon blow over and I doubt very much if it would bother Luke.'

'It's tough on Alastair too. There he is, trying to start a new life in Banford, and now everyone will know about him.'

'Alastair is well able to take care of himself, Grace, don't you worry about that. So what happens now?'

'We meet Miriam's solicitor in the morning to see if there's anything that can be done.'

'Closing the stable door after the horse has bolted?'

Grace shrugged. 'No idea, but given it's my fault that the tabloids got hold of it, I have to do what I can to make it right.'

Michael stood and picked up his jacket.

'Where are you off to?'

'I'm going into town to do some shopping.' He grinned. 'My current wardrobe doesn't really suit Dubai temperatures. See you later.' Going into the hall, Michael opened the door and then cursing, banged it closed again.

'What's wrong?' Grace asked when he came back into the kitchen.

'We're surrounded,' he told her.

'What?'

'There are journalists and photographers everywhere.' The doorbell and knocker went as he spoke.

'Mr Mulcahy, have you anything to say?'

Michael opened the door a fraction. 'Yes, the name is Hughes and if you don't get off my property, I'll call the police.' He closed the door in the journalist's face.

Grace went into the lounge and peeked out from behind the curtain. Immediately a flurry of flashbulbs went off in her face. 'Dear God.'

Michael joined her. 'Can you imagine what it's like outside Miriam's house?'

'I'd better call her.'

'Call the mobile. If she has any sense, she won't be answering the house phone.'

Grace went to the phone and dialled. 'Miriam? Hi, it's me. Are you okay?'

'Sure.'

'The reporters and journalists must be knee-deep around your door.'

'No idea, I'm in a hotel. Gareth warned me that they'd be around.'

'Huh, thanks for telling me.'

'Hey, what are *you* worrying about? They're not out for your blood. You haven't talked to them, have you?'

'No, of course not. Are they badgering Luke too?'

'He's gone to stay with Alastair. Thankfully you didn't spill the new address so they should be safe.'

Grace ignored the jibe. 'I heard they tried to get to your dad.'

'Sick bastards would stop at nothing to get a story.'

'Did Luke talk to him?'

'I don't know. Look, Grace, I need to go, I'm expecting Gareth to call.'

'Do you still want to meet at his office in the morning?'

'I'm not sure. If you don't hear from me, I'll see you there, okay?'

'Fine, bye.' Grace hung up.

'Well?' Michael walked back into the room.

'She's staying at a hotel, her solicitor had warned her that the press would be hounding her.'

'Nice of her to tell us,' he grumbled.

'I think that's her way of getting back at me for telling Bridget. I suppose I can't blame her.'

'Dear God, Grace, the woman has treated you abominably and still you make excuses for her.'

'Please don't start, Michael, this is hard enough.'

'Fine, fine, I'm going out anyway.'

'But what about them?'

'So they take my picture, so what?'

'What about me?'

'Why don't you go and stay with Nat for a couple of days?' She stared at him blankly and he sighed. 'Go and get dressed and we'll leave together.'

'Thanks, Michael,' she said, and sped up the stairs to her room. When she returned ten minutes later, he burst out laughing. 'What?'

Michael looked from the headscarf, to the long raincoat, to the dark glasses in her hand. 'You look ridiculous.'

'But I don't want them to recognize me,' she argued.

'Not only will they recognize you, you'll be plastered all over the paper again tomorrow if you go out dressed like that.'

Grace turned on her heel and went back upstairs.

'And don't take all day,' Michael called after her. 'I've got things to do.'

'So you said,' Grace muttered, pulling off her scarf and coat and turning back to her wardrobe. If she was going to be splashed all over the papers, she decided, she wanted to look good, so she pulled out a well-cut tweed coat, very high black patent shoes, and then she sat down at her dressing-table and brushed her hair till it shone and applied a dark red lipstick. Clipping on gold hoop ear-rings, she put on the coat and shoes and appraised herself in the mirror. She looked good and as a result felt more confident. She would walk out of this house with her head held high, and to hell with all of them.

Michael was waiting in the hall and he did a double-take as she walked down the stairs.

'Will I do?' she asked, as she paused on the bottom step.

'You look wonderful,' he murmured and turned away, but not before she saw the sadness in his eyes.

'Michael—' she started.

'Come on, let's make a run for it.'

'I'm right behind you,' Grace said, and took a deep breath as he opened the door.

She called Nat en route into town and they arranged to meet for lunch. Thankfully no press had turned up at Ken's flat but Grace didn't want to take any chances. For all she knew, some of them could have followed her.

When she walked into the busy bistro, Nat waved from a table at the back of the room and Grace threaded her way through the tables.

'Mum, you look great,' Nat said as they hugged.

'I was originally wearing my "no comment" costume, but your dad thought I looked ridiculous so I decided to go to the other extreme. I've nothing to be ashamed of, after all.' She smiled at the waiter who came to take her coat, revealing the simple black dress beneath, and then sat down across from her daughter. 'So what did Ken have to say to our little drama?'

Nat grinned. 'I think he was disappointed that he didn't get a mention. Leila has it drilled into him that any publicity is good publicity.'

Grace shivered. 'I can't say I agree. Those people hanging around outside the house this morning were like a pack of hungry wolves. Would you like some wine?'

'Go on then.'

Grace caught the waiter's eye and ordered a bottle of Chablis.

'Did you hear from Miriam?' Nat asked. 'She must be pretty devastated – they really trashed her.'

'I talked to her briefly and she sounded fine.'

'Is she going to sue?'

'I don't know yet, but I'm not sure she can, since it was all true.'

'Yes, but somehow they made it seem even more sordid. Did you talk to Bridget yet?'

Grace scowled. 'I was going to call her but she probably has the phone bugged.'

'Luke will take care of her, don't you worry. Miriam might be a cow but he'd protect her no matter what and you too, for that matter.'

Grace nodded.

'Are you two okay again?' Nat asked.

'Yes, although I owe him an apology. I didn't believe him when he told me that Bridget had tried to blackmail Miriam, I thought he was deliberately trying to turn me against Bridget.'

'You know he'd never do that, Mum, he's your friend. And though I admit that I had a bit of a crush on him, it was completely one-sided.' Nat grinned. 'Which reminds me, he has a new girlfriend.'

Grace's eye widened. 'How do you know?'

'I met her in the pub the night of Ken's going-away party. It's someone you know,' Nat teased.

'Tell me,' Grace demanded.

'It's Rosa.'

'Rosa? Our Rosa?'

Nat nodded. 'You should see them together, they're crazy about each other.'

'Well, who'd have thought it?' Grace breathed. 'I didn't even know they knew each other that well.'

'Luke's been round at Miriam's a lot more lately, and when he's working, Rosa's been keeping an eye on her for him.'

'Of course, she told me that, although I don't know

why he's worried about Miriam. When I saw her yesterday she was her usual bad-tempered self.' Grace smiled slowly. 'Does she know about Luke and Rosa?'

'Can you imagine?' Nat giggled suddenly. 'First Bridget and now the hired help – she'll be apoplectic.'

Grace laughed. 'Then that's the icing on the cake.' The waiter returned with their wine and Grace tasted it. 'That's lovely, thank you.'

'How's Dad?' Nat asked when they were alone again.

Grace ran her eye down the menu. 'Surprisingly relaxed, and he handled the reporters like a pro.'

'I think he's quite looking forward to going to Dubai.'

'Or glad to be getting away from me,' Grace joked.

'Are you okay about that, Mum?'

'A little shell-shocked,' Grace admitted, 'but I'll survive.'

'It is what you wanted, isn't it?' Nat persisted.

'Why do you say that?'

'Well, it's obvious that you're not happy.'

'How long have you thought that?'

'I don't know, weeks, months. You hardly talk to each other any more, let alone spend time together.'

'I'm sorry,' Grace whispered, tears catching the back of her throat.

'Why are you apologizing to me?'

'You've been caught in the middle. No wonder you left home.'

'You know that's not why I left.'

'I'm still sorry. I feel a failure as a wife and a mother.'

'Oh please, Mum, give me a break,' Nat said, rather impatiently. 'If you want to torture yourself go ahead – but leave me out of it. If you and Dad are going to be happier apart, then I'm pleased for you.'

'I think you are more mature than your mum and dad put together,' Grace marvelled.

'It comes from working with kids,' Nat laughed. 'You have to use basic commonsense.'

'Ah well, you know what they say about common-sense, don't you?'

'It's not that common,' they said in unison.

'Let's order some food,' Nat said. 'I'm starving.'

'Gosh, so am I. I just realized I forgot to have breakfast.'

'You should have the bangers and mash, they're lovely.'

'Bangers and mash is a bit basic for a place like this, isn't it?'

'It's not the kind of bangers and mash you have at home,' Nat explained. 'More of a posh version.'

'In that case I'll have the posh fish and chips.' Grace closed the menu with a snap and beckoned the waiter over. They quickly gave their order and asked for some bread too.

'Aren't you sad at all?' Grace asked. 'About Ken going I mean?'

'A little, but in a way it's like the end of an episode in my life and the beginning of a new one, and I'm kind of gearing up for the new one.'

'You are such a little philosopher. I don't know where you get that from – certainly not me or your dad.'

'Grandad is quite laidback.'

'My dad? Yes, I suppose he is really. It must be like one of these genes that skip a generation.' She sighed. 'I wish it hadn't.'

'Take up yoga or hill-walking, Mum,' Nat told her, diving on the bread that the waiter had set down between them. 'Or move to Banford with Alastair.'

Grace choked on her roll and reached for her water glass.

'You okay?' Nat clapped her on the back.

'Yes,' she gasped. 'It must have gone down the wrong way.'

Nat smirked. 'Right.'

'What's that supposed to mean?'

'Nothing, sorry.'

'I'm fed up with all your innuendos, Nat. I have never been unfaithful to your father.'

Nat's mouth fell open. 'Mum, I never said you had.'

'No, you just hint. You're always making funny comments and remarks about Alastair, and I don't like it.'

'I'm sorry.'

'Yeah sure.'

'Mum!' Nat looked truly distressed now.

Grace suddenly realized she was blowing things out of proportion. 'I'm sorry, darling. It's been a difficult time and I'm a bit touchy.'

Nat looked at her worriedly. 'Please move in with me,

Mum. I hate the idea of you living alone.'

'I'm absolutely fine,' Grace said with more conviction than she felt, 'but I'd love to move in with you.'

Nat's face lit up. 'That's brilliant. Ken's leaving on Tuesday and his dad is getting all his gear moved out on Thursday so why don't you move in on Friday?'

'Don't you want to come home for Christmas?'

Nat shook her head. 'It wouldn't be the same without Dad. I think it's best if we celebrate Christmas at the flat.'

'Then that's what we'll do.' Grace smiled but the tears weren't far away. Her phone beeped and she picked it up to read the text that had just come through. MEETING AT 8.30 CANCELLED. I'LL CALL U 2 MORROW

'It's Miriam,' she said. 'We're not meeting at the solicitor tomorrow.'

'So she mustn't have a case.'

'Good. Maybe we can put it all behind us now.'

'You might be able to, but she won't. What do you think she'll do?'

Grace shook her head. 'I've no idea and I don't really care.'

Chapter 40

Miriam finished packing just as the doorbell rang three times. She hurried to let her solicitor in.

'All this cloak and dagger stuff, I feel like James Bond,' Gareth joked. 'I thought I was going to have to fight my way to the door through a barrage of reporters.'

'I left the house earlier in full view and then sneaked back in through the garden, so hopefully they're wandering around the city looking for me. Have you brought all the papers?' Miriam led him into the study.

'All here,' he said, setting his briefcase on the desk and opening it. 'Sign where I've marked.' He slid the first documents across to her.

Miriam took a pen and signed with a flourish. 'Now, have you put together the letter to Grace?'

'Yes, although I'm not sure I agree—'

'I don't pay you to agree with me. Let me see it.' She quickly read through the letter, made a few corrections and handed it back to him. 'Make sure that it's put into her hand today.'

Gareth inclined his head. 'What about the house?'

'You'll have to take care of the sale and then lodge the money in my sterling account.'

'And Alastair? What about him?'

Miriam glanced at him over the top of her reading glasses. 'What about him?'

'He would be entitled to half.'

'He won't want it. Anything else?'

'Bridget Crosby?'

'Ah yes, Bridget.' Miriam took off her glasses and smiled coldly. 'I want you to give her this.' She reached into her desk and handed a cheque over to Gareth.

Gareth stared at her. 'Half a million Euros? I don't understand.'

'You give her that if she signs a retraction and apology, which you will draw up. I want to read it first, though.'

'Is it really worth spending that much money just for an apology?'

'It will completely discredit her and that is worth any money.' Miriam stood up. 'Now, if there's nothing else, I have a plane to catch.'

Michael suggested that Grace take the day off and let things die down, and she readily agreed. Though she was the innocent party, she still found the attention unnerving. Even in the restaurant yesterday she and Nat had become aware of stares and whispers. She had phoned her parents, telling them to ignore the article and saying that she would fill them in on the facts when they came to Dublin after Christmas. She also warned them that they might get calls from reporters, looking for comments. It was unlikely, of course, it was already yesterday's news, but Grace wasn't taking any chances.

She peered out of the window from time to time but the press had obviously found some other poor sod to pester and the road was deserted. Michael returned home at lunch-time and after a sandwich immediately excused himself. 'I have just two more reports to write and then I am officially closing Michael Hughes Quantity Surveyors Ltd.'

Grace smiled. 'Congratulations, I suppose.'

'Yes, I think so.' He paused. 'Look, Grace, I just wanted to say that it wasn't all you.'

'What do you mean?'

'Our marriage breaking down. I know it came out as if I blamed you for it all, but that's not the case. I was just as much to blame.'

'Thank you.'

He nodded and smiled, looking slightly awkward. 'Right, I'd better go and finish those reports.'

Left to herself, Grace sipped her tea and stared out at the garden. She should be happy that this separation was all so civilized, but somehow it seemed to trivialize their marriage. The doorbell rang and Grace went to answer it.

'Ms Grace Mulcahy?'

Grace's eyes widened at the large man in her porch. 'I've no comment,' she said, closing the door.

He stuck his foot in to stop it and smiled at her.

'Neither do I.' He handed her an envelope. 'This is for you. Have a nice day.'

'Who was that?' Michael asked from the top of the stairs.

'I don't know.' Grace opened the envelope and pulled out a single sheet of paper.

'What is it?' Michael asked as her face clouded with confusion.

'The bloody cow!'

'Grace?'

'It's from Miriam's solicitor. She's suing me for breach of contract.'

'You're kidding?' He came down to join her.

Grace handed him the letter. 'And to think I felt sorry for her.'

Bridget was painting her toenails when someone started banging on her door. She ignored it, just as she had been ignoring the phone and door all weekend. Jaz had suggested she go away for a few days but there was no way Bridget was going to miss this. She'd gone out early this morning and bought the newspapers and switched on the radio and the television to see if there was any reaction to the story, but it got little or no mention.

Jaz had said as much. 'As crimes go, this is fairly minor. It takes a lot to shock the public these days.' The banging on her door started again, then there was silence, and then she heard a key the door. She smiled slowly as Luke stormed into the room. 'Hello, Luke, what brings you here?'

'You little bitch.' He glared down at her, clenching his hands as if to prevent himself hitting her.

'Nice to see you too.'

'Was it the money?'

She didn't bother pretending she didn't understand. 'Partly, but mainly it was the opportunity to destroy your sister that I couldn't pass up.'

'What did she ever do to deserve this? And what about me? Don't you feel anything for me after all our time together?'

Bridget snorted. 'Are you kidding? If I hurt you, it was a bonus!' Her eyes turned cold. 'No one walks out on Bridget Crosby. As for Miriam, she's always treated me like dirt.'

'So how do you explain betraying Grace?'

'She should thank me for bringing all this into the open. Think of the sympathy she'll get.'

'So why mention the fact that her marriage has broken up?' Luke demanded.

Bridget waved a hand in the air. 'Oh, the tabloids like all the background information and they said it would make readers feel sorrier for Grace.'

'So if you did it out of the goodness of your heart you've probably called her and talked to her about it.'

Bridget concentrated on her toes. 'Haven't had a chance.'

'Well, I wouldn't bother. I hope you got lots of money

for that story, Bridget, because you're going to need it to buy new friends.'

'I'll do fine on my own,' she retorted. 'Now please get out of my house.'

As Luke stormed out he nearly knocked a man over in the driveway. 'Sorry,' he muttered and kept going, thinking vaguely that the man looked familiar.

'Ms Crosby?' Gareth knocked on the open door.

'Who are you?' Bridget poked her head around the kitchen door.

'My name is Gareth O'Connell, I'm a solicitor acting on behalf of Ms Miriam Cooper.'

'I have nothing to say to you.'

He smiled grimly. 'Maybe not, but I think you might be interested in what *I* have to say to *you*.'

Annabel Riordan was putting change in the till when a man walked into the shop. 'I'll be right with you,' she trilled, flashing him a smile.

He nodded curtly and walked around the shop, stopping occasionally to examine the merchandise.

'Is it something particular you're looking for?' Annabel said finally, bustling down the shop.

'Annabel Riordan?' he enquired.

'Yes, that's right.' She looked at him, surprised. 'Do I know you?'

'No, madam, I work for the owner of this shop.'

'For Miriam?'

'No, for Mr John Litton. As of last Friday he owns the Lady M chain.'

Annabel opened and closed her mouth like a goldfish.

'This is for you.' He handed her an envelope.

'What's this?' she asked faintly.

'It's self-explanatory,' he assured her. 'Now I need your keys.'

'My keys?' she repeated.

'For the shop.'

'I'm not sure—'

'Why don't you read the letter?' he suggested and walked over to lean against the desk.

Annabel tore open the letter and pulled out several pages. 'Oh no,' she gasped as she finished the first page and quickly scanned the attachments. 'You can't do this.'

'Nothing to do with me, Mrs Riordan, I'm just following orders. Now, may I have the keys please?' He glanced at his watch. 'I can give you thirty minutes to get your things together.'

As Annabel tearfully gathered her belongings together, so did the managers of the Cork and Galway offices. Each tried to reach Miriam on her mobile but there was just a recorded message saying it was out of service.

'She's gone,' Jean, the manager of the Galway office, said to Annabel later on the phone. 'All that stuff in the papers must have been true and she's done a runner. How could she do this to us after all these years?'

'Because she's a selfish old bitch,' Annabel sniffed.

'She could have sold the business to someone who'd keep Lady M's up and running, but no, she had to sell to a hairdresser.'

'Money is all she cares about,' Jean agreed. 'Even our redundancy settlements are minuscule.'

'You'll get another job, no problem, Jean,' Annabel assured the other woman.

'And you will too, Annabel. We're probably better off out of it and in a few months we'll laugh over this.'

'Of course we will.' Annabel reached for another tissue.

Chapter 41

Luke entered the hallway of Brook Lane Nursing Home, raising his hand in greeting to the receptionist. 'Hi, Maria, how are you?'

'Fine, thanks, Luke.'

Taking the stairs two at a time to the second floor, he breezed through the double doors and strode down the corridor to his father's suite. He knocked once on the door and stuck his head in. 'Only me,' he started, pulling up short when he saw his sister sitting by the bedside. 'Miriam!'

'Hi.'

He smiled warmly. 'I'm glad you came. Hey, Dad, isn't it great to see Miriam?'

Thomas Cooper's eyes never flickered as he stared straight ahead.

'You never told me he was like this,' Miriam murmured.

'He has good days and bad, don't you, Dad?' Luke kept his voice loud and bright. 'Some days he's not in the mood for conversation, but then we all have days like

that, don't we? The football is on soon, Dad, will I turn
on the television?' No answer came and Luke reached
for the remote and switched on the sports channel. 'It's
Chelsea and Leeds, should be a good match.'

'Can we talk?' Miriam mouthed.

'I'll just bring Miriam down for a cuppa, Dad. We'll be
back in a few minutes.'

When they were outside, Miriam slumped against the
wall. 'Why didn't you tell me?'

Luke shrugged. 'What was the point?'

'How long has he been like this?'

'A couple of months.'

'Can he not communicate at all?'

'Sometimes he says things, but they don't usually
make much sense. Sometimes he laughs and,' Luke
gazed off into the distance, 'sometimes he cries.'

Miriam shuddered. 'I never want to end up like that.'

'If you did you wouldn't know anything about it, but
I'm sure you'll go on forever,' Like told her, not unkindly.
'No disease would dare to take you on.'

Miriam smiled reluctantly.

'How are you?' he asked softly.

'Okay.'

'That was some slating you got in the paper yesterday.'

'And I suppose you think deservedly so.'

He held up his hands. 'I said my piece a long time
ago. As far as I'm concerned, it's history.'

'What did Alastair say?'

'Nothing,' Luke said looking away.

'Liar.' Miriam smiled sadly. 'It's okay, I don't want to know anyway.'

'So why did you come?'

She looked at him. 'I came to say goodbye.'

'Oh? Where are you off to this time?'

'Edinburgh.'

'Very nice.'

'For good.'

'What?' Luke looked at her, confused.

'I've sold the business and I've bought a chain of shops in Scotland. I'm flying out in four hours and I won't be back.'

Luke walked away from her down the corridor and then back again. 'Are you sure this is what you want?'

'There are seven shops with a much better turnover than Lady M's. It's the kind of set-up I've always dreamed of.'

'And that's all that matters?'

She looked into his eyes. 'It's all I have.'

'What about the house?'

'I've put it up for sale. Now, I really must go.'

'Say goodbye to Dad first.'

'You say goodbye for me. He doesn't even know who I am.' She gave him a quick hug and turned to leave.

'Miriam?' Luke called after her as she strode down the corridor.

She turned.

'Take care.'

Blowing him a kiss, Miriam went through the double doors and out of his life.

It wasn't until he got back in the van and switched his mobile on that he found out about the legacy his sister had left behind. First there was the anguished message from Annabel, apologizing for calling him but looking for some kind of explanation as to why they were out of work with no notice or explanation; she was sure there must be some mistake. Luke grimaced as he drove back towards the city. The second message was from Nat, asking him where his bloody sister was and what the hell did she think she was playing at, screwing her mother yet again. The third message was from his boss, asking what the hell was going on that some bloody reporter kept calling, asking for him. The last message was a clipped, formal request from Grace asking him to call. Swinging off the motorway, he decided to go straight to her house first.

Grace opened the door as soon as he got out of the van.

'I just got your message – what's wrong?'

She led him inside and handed him the letter without uttering a word.

'Oh God, Grace, I'm so sorry,' he said when he'd read it.

'You didn't know?'

'Of course I didn't.' He looked hurt.

'Sorry.'

'I'm sure your solicitor will be able to fight this. Miriam is probably just giving you a rap on the knuckles for talking to Bridget.'

'Hasn't she done enough to me?' Grace murmured, almost to herself.

'You're not the only one,' he told her. 'She's sold the shops and all the staff are out of work as of today.'

Grace's eyes widened. 'Oh, my God, that's terrible. But surely the new owner will keep them on?'

'The new owner is a hairdresser.'

'Your sister isn't going to be able to walk the streets of this city any more after this,' Grace said angrily.

'She's not going to.' Luke looked at his watch. 'Right now, she's on her way to the airport. She's moving to Scotland.'

Grace went to the cabinet, pulled out a bottle of whiskey and poured them both a drink.

'She must have been planning this for ages,' she said, sinking into a chair.

'Your guess is as good as mine, Grace, she never told me a thing. The first I knew about her selling up was today. I went to the nursing home to see Dad and she was there before me.'

'She went to see him?' Grace's eyes widened.

'To say goodbye.'

'How did he take that?'

Luke smiled sadly. 'He didn't even know who she was. It's probably just as well. If he knew about all the things she'd done, he'd be devastated.'

'I'm sorry, Luke. I'm so caught up in what she's done to me I keep forgetting how all of this is affecting you. And I also owe you an apology about Bridget. I didn't believe you when you told me about the blackmailing; I thought you were just trying to come between us. You have been a true friend to me when everyone else let me down, and yet you're the only one I doubted. Can you forgive me?'

He smiled. 'Of course I can. It hasn't exactly been the easiest of times to think straight.' He shot a questioning look upwards at the loud thump on the ceiling.

'Michael's packing,' she explained. 'He leaves for Dubai in a few days. I'm going to move in with Nat.'

'That's good, I'm glad you won't be alone.'

'And you won't be either, will you, Luke?' she grinned, remembering the news about Rosa.

He chuckled. 'Ah, you've heard then.'

'Yes, and I'm delighted for both of you.'

'She's a wonderful girl. I've no idea what she sees in me, or how she's going to feel about having Miriam as a sister-in-law.'

Grace gasped. 'You're getting married?'

Luke groaned and hit the heel of his hand against his forehead. 'Oh shit, I wasn't supposed to say that.'

'Your secret's safe with me,' Grace promised, smiling excitedly. 'Oh, this is a wonderful end to a really lousy day.' She started to laugh out loud. 'Does Miriam know?'

'She doesn't even know we're dating.'

'Probably just as well. She'd have done her best to break you up.'

Luke sighed. 'True.'

'How's Alastair?' she asked, trying to keep her voice light. 'Does he know that Miriam's gone?'

'I doubt it, but I don't think he'll be interested one way or the other.'

'But what about the article? Surely his neighbours must have seen it?'

Luke shrugged. 'I really don't know, Grace, he never said. He's become quite subdued – or maybe that's just with me because I'm Miriam's brother.' He frowned, obviously bothered by the thought.

'She has never come between you and never will,' Grace said with conviction. 'You know Alastair better than that, Luke.'

'Yes, I suppose you're right.' He drained his glass and stood up. 'I'd better go. You're only the first of many calls I need to make tonight. I tell you, Grace, I'm a plumber but I've never shovelled as much shit as I have in the last few months – and it's all thanks to my beloved sister.'

When he got home, Rosa stood up and walked straight into his arms. 'Have you seen Miriam today?'

'Yes, for the last time for a while. She's gone to live in Scotland.'

Rosa hugged him to her. 'I was so worried. I went to the house today and all her things were gone but her phone was on the kitchen table. I was afraid she'd done something silly.'

'No, just something cruel. She left the phone because

half the city is trying to get hold of her and none of them are happy.'

'At least she is safe.'

Luke buried his face in her hair. 'I love you.'

'*Ti amo,*' she murmured, pressing her body closer so that they touched from head to toe. After a moment she pulled her head back so she could look up into his face. 'There have been a lot of messages for you.'

'And I got a load of calls on my mobile. I called into Grace on the way here, she's in a right state.'

'Why?'

'Miriam's suing her for breach of contract.'

Rosa's eyes were round. 'No!'

'Yes. Oh, by the way, she knows about us and she's very happy about that.'

'We knew Nat would tell her.'

'Yes, but I'm afraid I let it slip that we were getting married.'

Rosa shrugged. 'No matter. Once we tell my parents after Christmas we can tell everyone.'

'She's promised not to say anything.'

'And she won't.'

Luke bent his head and kissed her. 'I want to take the phone off the hook and take you to bed.'

'You have things to do,' she soothed, 'and I will still be here when you're finished. I am making you some ravioli for dinner, it will give you strength.'

He nodded as he went to get the phone. 'I have so much to tell you.'

She went through to the kitchen, poured him some wine and carried it back to him. 'You can tell me everything over dinner.' She dropped a kiss on his forehead. 'For now, do what you have to do.'

Luke called Annabel Riordan first. He'd known this woman for at least twelve years, he knew all about her children and her husband who suffered badly with asthma and had had to give up work. He knew that losing this job was going to cost the Riordan family some hardship and there was nothing he could do. Annabel knew that Luke had no part in the business but was desperate enough to call him to see if he could intercede with Miriam and at least secure a better redundancy.

'I talked to her today, Annabel, but although she told me she'd sold the shops, she never mentioned the rest. She's left the country but I'm sure she will be in touch at some stage and I will do my best to help you.' Getting the home numbers of Jean and Maura, the managers of the Galway and Cork offices, Luke said goodbye to Annabel with a promise to call as soon as he had more news.

He contacted the two women, making them the same promise, but with his sister's phone sitting right here in front of him, he knew that it was hopeless. Miriam wouldn't be in touch, at least not until all the fuss died down. He could call that pompous solicitor of hers, of course, but he didn't expect much help from that corner. It seemed that Miriam had put all of her affairs in order in a very selfish way and now she was gone. He wondered, if he hadn't bumped into her at the nursing home, would she even have bothered to say goodbye?

He phoned Nat next to tell her he'd seen Grace.

'How is she? Can you sort it out? Surely you can talk sense into that crazy sister of yours.'

Again, Luke explained that Miriam was gone and for the moment, she wasn't contactable. 'But I'm sure your mother's solicitor will find a way around it. Miriam was probably just doing it to wind Grace up.'

'Well, she succeeded,' Nat muttered. 'She was really upset, Luke. Talk about kicking her when she's down.'

'She did break the agreement when she talked to Bridget,' Luke pointed out.

'Yes – another supposed friend who went and sold her story to a tabloid. Can't you imagine how that makes her feel?'

'Yes, I can, Natasha, but there's not much I can do, I'm afraid.'

'And I suppose she has something on Alastair too,' Nat mused.

Luke grinned. 'I've just had a wonderful idea.'

'Oh, yeah?'

'I need to talk to Rosa about it first, I'll call you back later. Bye, Natasha.'

Before he joined Rosa for dinner, Luke made one more call to the nursing home to check his father hadn't had any adverse reactions to Miriam's visit. The night porter put him through to the nurse on duty.

'Hi, Fiona, how is he?'

'Sleeping peacefully,' she assured him

'My sister, Miriam, visited him today. He hasn't mentioned her, has he?'

'No.'

'Okay, Fiona, thanks. I'll check in with you in the morning, but you have my number . . .'

'I'll call you if I need you,' she assured him.

Luke hung up and went into the kitchen. 'That smells wonderful,' he said, coming up behind Rosa and snaking his hands around her waist.

'Sit down, it's ready,' she said, pushing him gently out of her way. He topped up their wine glasses and then sat and watched as she served the steaming pasta. 'Did you get to talk to everyone you needed to?'

He shook his head. 'There are a couple of Lady M suppliers that I need to call but I only have their work numbers so it will have to wait till morning.'

'You could turn on that thing,' Rosa nodded towards Miriam's phone, 'but you might regret it.'

'I already tried but she's got it password protected.'

'I got such a fright when I went into the house.' Rosa shuddered. 'After the drinking and the way she was shutting herself off from everyone, I feared the worst.'

'While she planned her getaway.' Luke shook his head in disgust. 'Alastair was right, she is a completely self-sufficient woman and it's a waste of time and energy worrying about her. Which,' he wagged his fork at her, 'reminds me of an idea I had.'

'Yes?'

'How would you feel about inviting Grace, Natasha and Alastair for Christmas?'

Rosa smiled. 'It's a nice idea, but I'm not sure Alastair and Grace would agree.'

'You don't think they'd want to be with us?'

'No, I don't think they'll want to be with each other.'

'But why not?' Luke said, puzzled. 'They've always been good friends.'

'I tell you what, why don't we invite them all but not tell them who else is coming?' Rosa suggested.

Luke shrugged. 'Whatever, but I don't see the need for the secrecy.'

Rosa laughed. 'Just humour me.'

'Okay then, you call Grace and I'll call Alastair. ' He smiled at her. 'Are you sure you don't mind? It's our first Christmas together, after all.'

She shook her head. 'The more the merrier. Anyway, when they've all gone home, I'll still have you – but what about your father?'

'He can't be moved. I'll go and see him in the morning before the guests come.'

'Can I come with you?'

'I would love you to come with me,' he said tenderly.

Rosa kissed him 'Then it looks as if Christmas is organized.'

Chapter 42

Luke tried phoning Alastair a number of times to invite him for Christmas but didn't get an answer and Alastair hadn't bothered with an answering service. The first chance he got, Luke drove up there, slightly worried, but he relaxed at the sight of Alastair and another man in the front garden inspecting a small dinghy.

'Ahoy, Captain,' he said, jumping down from the van and walking over to them.

'Luke, how are you?' Alastair stood up and shook his hand warmly. 'Alf, this is Luke, my brother-in-law.'

Alf shot him a wary look and Alastair laughed. 'It's okay, he's a friend.'

Alf immediately stretched out a hand. 'Then I'm pleased to meet you.'

'I didn't know you were into boats, Alastair,' Luke said, crouching down to examine the craft.

'I'm not, it's Alf's.'

'I haven't sailed in years,' the man told Luke, 'but Alastair said he fancied having a go so I said I'd take him out when the weather warms up a bit. I think it needs a few coats of varnish first though.'

'I'd give the engine an overhaul too, if I were you.'

Alf looked at him. 'Do you know anything about engines?'

Alastair laughed. 'Careful, Luke, or you'll get roped in.'

'I wouldn't mind at all, but it will have to be another day. I just came up for a quick word, Alastair.'

Alf looked at his watch. 'I'd better get this back in the garage and go in for my lunch or the cattle will get it.' He nodded to Luke. 'Nice to meet you.'

'He seems okay,' Luke said as they wandered into the house. ' Sorry to interrupt you.'

'Oh, that's okay, we were just passing the time of day. Fancy a cup of tea or coffee?'

'Coffee, please.' Luke looked around as Alastair busied himself in the kitchen. 'You've really been working hard on this place, haven't you?' he called as he went from room to room, looking in vain for any sign of renovation. He went back to the kitchen as Alastair poured water into the mugs. 'Are you sorry you bought this house?'

Alastair shook his head. 'No.'

'You don't seem very convinced.'

Alastair sighed. 'I always imagined Grace would help me do this place up.'

'I'm sure she'd be delighted to.'

'No, not now,' the older man said.

'Why, what's happened? Have you had a row? Please tell me you haven't fallen out over Miriam.'

'Not directly.' Alastair frowned in concentration.

'Why don't you just ask her? You're a bit long in the tooth to hang around just wondering.'

'Thanks for your honesty.'

'You know Grace – she would do anything to help you and you've been friends for so long.'

'Indeed.'

And suddenly Luke understood. 'You wanted to be more than friends and she knocked you back, that's it, isn't it?'

'In a nutshell,' Alastair admitted his expression miserable. 'Are you shocked?'

'If I'm honest, you and Grace seem a lot more compatible than you and Miriam ever were,' Luke replied. 'But Grace doesn't feel the same way?'

'I thought she did but I was completely wrong.'

Luke thought about their plan for Christmas and figured he'd better come up with Plan B.

'Excuse me a sec, will you, Alastair – I just have to nip out to the van.' As soon as he was in the privacy of his cab, he phoned Rosa and told her what Alastair had said. 'So I thought either we shouldn't invite Alastair for Christmas or not invite Grace and Natasha.'

'Invite Alastair,' she told him. 'I'll take care of everything.'

'Okay then, see you later.' He went back inside. 'Sorry about that, just needed to call the boss.'

'Do you have to go?'

'No, I'm all right for a little while.' Luke sat down and stretched his long legs in front of him.

'Listen, Rosa and I were wondering if you'd spend Christmas with us.'

Alastair chuckled. 'Ah, so you really *were* phoning the boss! There's no need to feel sorry for me, Luke, I'll be perfectly fine on my own. You and Rosa need some time alone together.'

'It's not going to happen,' Luke assured him. 'As far as Rosa is concerned, Christmas is a time for family and friends and she won't be happy unless she has a houseful.'

Alastair smiled sadly. 'She's a wonderful girl, I'm so happy you two got together. I always thought it a shame that she hadn't married again and had a family. Can't you just see her with a large brood of children?'

Luke laughed. 'I don't know about a large brood, but one or two would be nice.'

Alastair clapped him on the back. 'That's wonderful, Luke, no more than you deserve. I never understood how you and Bridget lasted so long. She didn't exactly seem the maternal type.'

'She wasn't, but I did what most blokes do. I closed my eyes and believed it would all work out in the end.'

'And it has!' Alastair said.

Luke laughed. 'Yes, I suppose it has. It's just a bit sad that when I'm finally ready to start a family of my own, neither Miriam nor Dad will be around to see it.'

'Your father's not doing well?'

'Sometimes I think he'd be better off dead,' Luke confessed, then: 'Isn't that a terrible thing to say?'

'Not at all. You feel that way because you love him. I'm so glad Miriam went to see him.'

'I don't think she was,' Luke said bitterly. 'She couldn't get out of that room fast enough.'

'It must have been a shock for her. The last time she saw him, he was well able to talk.'

Luke frowned in surprise. 'When was that?'

'Oh, about a year ago.'

'She never told me.'

'He didn't either,' Alastair pointed out, 'and there was nothing wrong with his mind then. Miriam likes everyone to think she's hard, but it wasn't always true.'

'Dad treated her very badly when she was young, did she tell you?'

'About Alan? Yes, she told me.'

'Maybe if he'd handled things better she wouldn't have turned into such a selfish person. I can't believe she treated her staff so badly. Absolutely no notice and the minimum redundancy payment.'

'I don't believe it!' Alastair stared at him, shocked.

'I'm sorry – I thought you knew. It was on the news and in all the papers yesterday.'

'I don't really bother with either these days. I can't believe it.'

'For the first time I wish I was rich and could afford to give them something.'

Alastair pondered. 'Maybe there's something I could do?'

'I don't see how – you're as penniless as I am.'

'But Miriam and I are still married.'

'I don't follow you.' Luke eyed him curiously.

'Well, maybe I have some rights to Miriam's millions. I'll have a word with an old barrister pal of mine and see what he thinks.'

Luke stood up. 'I'd better get going. You never answered my question: will you join us for Christmas?'

Alastair smiled. 'I'd be delighted.'

Luke was just climbing into his van when the phone rang.

'Hello Grace, how are you?'

Alastair immediately turned away.

'What? You're kidding! But that makes no sense. Okay – well, call me if you find out anything.' He rang off and shook his head a look of total confusion on his face.

'What is it?' Alastair asked. 'Is there something wrong?'

Luke looked up at him. 'Bridget has just printed a retraction and an apology too. She says the story was fabricated and she did it because Miriam had fired her when she caught her stealing from the till.'

Alastair looked dumbfounded. 'But the story was completely true, Miriam never said anything about Bridget stealing!'

'No, and that's one thing she wouldn't have kept to herself.'

'It's very strange. What does Grace think?'

'That Bridget's conscience is troubling her and she's trying to make amends.'

Alastair looked sceptical. 'A Road To Damascus sort of thing? I find that hard to believe.'

'Me too. Anyway, Grace is going over there now and she's promised to call me later. I'll let you know what happens, or at least I will if you answer your phone.'

Alastair smiled. 'I'll be in all evening. Goodbye, Luke, safe home.'

Chapter 43

Grace had been sitting at the kitchen table leafing through the newspaper when Joy had called. She had been thrilled to hear from her friend, especially when Joy told her that she would be home for a visit after Christmas.

'That's good,' Grace said happily, 'because I have so much to tell you it would cost a small fortune in phone calls.'

'And you think I'm going to wait until January after a comment like that?' Joy said. 'Tell me everything.'

'Where to begin,' Grace mused. But as concisely as she could, she told Joy of the developments over the last few weeks. She was halfway through telling her about Miriam leaving Ireland when Joy's doorbell went.

'Hang on a sec, I'll have to answer that.'

As Grace waited, she scanned the paper in front of her, coming up short at the small box with the black border at the bottom of the page headed APOLOGY. As she read, her eyes got wider and wider. 'My God, what on earth is going on?'

'Sorry?' Joy said at the other end of the phone.

'Me too, Joy, but I'm going to have to call you back – something's come up.'

Grace hung up before Joy could reply and dialled Bridget's number but got the engaged tone. She tried the mobile, ditto. Quickly she phoned Luke to tell him the news and then she grabbed her coat. She had to take Michael to the airport later but she had enough time to check up on Bridget. Whatever had led her to do this? Grace imagined that the girl was feeling pretty down at the moment, and though she knew her family would think she was mad, Grace had to give her a second chance.

Bridget had always been the sort to act first and think later, and the money would have been hard for her to resist at such a low point in her life. If she had actually handed it back and not just that but taken the blame for everything, how could Grace do anything but forgive her?'

Grace guided her car through the afternoon traffic to Bridget's flat, wondering what she'd find when she got there. She sincerely hoped the place wouldn't be littered with reporters – after all, this was rather a strange turn of events, but when she got to the flat, all was quiet. Going to the door she rapped on the knocker and rang the doorbell. 'Bridget, it's me, Grace.' Through the glass she saw a figure coming towards her and moments later, Bridget opened the door, smiling broadly.

'Grace, this is a surprise!'

'Hi.' Grace was momentarily wrong-footed by Bridget's good humour.

'Come on in, you'll have to excuse the mess.'

Grace followed her into the bedroom where Bridget was folding clothes and packing them into two expensive suitcases.

Grace's eyes widened at the pile of designer shoes in their special covers waiting to be packed. Maybe Bridget had been on the fiddle, after all. She certainly couldn't afford this lot.

'I didn't nick it all, if that's what you're thinking,' Bridget laughed. 'It's all mine. I've been shopping solidly for two days and it's been heaven.'

Grace sank onto the edge of the bed. 'I don't understand. I came over here to forgive you, to say thank you for the apology in the paper. I thought it meant you'd had a change of heart.'

'Seen the error of my ways, you mean?' Bridget snorted. 'God, you are *so* gullible. No wonder Miriam conned you – it must have been like taking candy from a baby.'

Grace flinched. 'Why do you hate me? What have I done? I thought we were friends.'

Bridget continued her packing, impervious to the stricken look on Grace's face. 'Oh, please, don't be so sensitive, it's nothing personal.'

'You tell all the details of my private life to a reporter for money and you tell me not to take it personally?'

'I did you a favour – I outed Miriam Cooper.'

'And then you retracted your statement and said it was all fabricated,' Grace retorted.

Bridget shrugged. 'Ah yes, sorry about that but she made me an offer I couldn't refuse.'

Grace sat for a moment trying to absorb what Bridget was saying. 'Do you mean Miriam paid you to change your story?'

'Generously.' Bridget flashed a brilliant smile. 'So all's well that ends well.'

'I beg your pardon?'

'Miriam's gone for good, you own Graceful Living, and I'm rich. Perfect.'

'What about all the hurt you've caused? Thanks to you, Miriam sold her business and all her staff are out of a job.'

'Hey, don't lay that one at my door. No one can sell and buy a business overnight. She must have been planning that for weeks.'

Grace's eyes narrowed. 'What do you know about it?'

'Let's say I know a little bird who knows Miriam rather well.'

'The man she was having the affair with,' Grace said, almost to herself. 'Are you seeing him?'

'I was.' Bridget wrinkled her nose. 'But he's outgrown his usefulness.'

'Oh, you've found a new victim to live off?' Grace spat.

'Not yet, but that's the plan.'

Bridget's calm in the face of her anger made Grace want to scratch her eyes out.

'I've decided to move to the South of France,' Bridget continued, 'and find someone who can keep me in the manner to which I'd like to become accustomed.'

'I hope you find someone as sick and twisted as you are. I hope you fall in love with him and I hope he breaks your heart.'

Bridget pouted. 'Now that's not very nice, is it?'

'I'm glad this has happened,' Grace said, on a roll now, 'all of it – every bloody, nasty, shitty minute of it. If it means you are out of our lives for ever, then it's all worth it.'

'Grace, please, you're hurting my feelings.'

'You're a cow and I never want to see you again.'

'Oh, you'll see me again,' Bridget promised her, 'if not in person then in the social columns, pictured at all the big parties and mixing with all the right people.'

'You are a sad and unbelievably shallow person and I thank God that Luke didn't go back to you.'

'I never wanted him back,' Bridget said scornfully. 'He was always a loser.'

'Well, I'm delighted to tell you that the loser is now in a wonderful new relationship and he's very happy.'

Bridget looked thrown for a moment. ' Who is it – one of the little tarts from work?'

'No, it's Rosa,' Grace said, desperate to hurt her. Bridget stared at her wide-eyed for a moment and then threw back her head and laughed. 'He's ended up with

Mrs Mop? Oh, that's hilarious. Thanks for that, Grace, you've made my day.'

Grace turned on her heel and walked out of the flat, but Bridget's laughter followed her and she almost ran to the car to escape it.

When she arrived at the house to collect Michael he was striding up and down the hall, his face red. 'What time do you call this? We should have left nearly an hour ago. If I miss this flight there isn't another one for forty-eight hours?'

'I'll get you there on time,' she said through gritted teeth. 'Just put your stuff in the car and let's go. We have to collect Nat on the way.'

''We don't have time to do that now,' he ranted, carrying the cases out and heaving them into the boot.

Grace stared at him. 'Are you saying you'd leave the country without saying goodbye to your daughter? God only knows when you'll see her again.'

'I can phone her to say goodbye! Now can we please go?'

Grace turned to face him, trembling with anger. 'No, we bloody can't. We either collect Nat on the way or you can phone a taxi, it's your choice.'

'It's too late for me to call a taxi now.' He sighed in frustration. 'Okay, okay, let's go get her. Who cares if I miss my flight?'

'You won't,' Grace promised, pulling out before he'd even closed his door. 'Even if I have to jump every light to do it.'

'There's no need for that,' he said hastily.

She shot him a vicious look. 'Oh yes, there is.'

Twenty minutes later she pulled up outside Ken's flat and Nat ran down the stairs. 'Hey guys, you're running a bit late.'

'Are we?' Grace said brightly. 'I hadn't noticed.'

Michael shot her a bewildered look and shook his head.

'So, Dad, are you all set?'

He turned to his daughter and smiled briefly. 'Yeah, I think so.'

'Well, I've a bit of good news for you before you go,' she said, grinning from ear to ear. 'I got my exam results and I passed with flying colours.'

Grace beamed at her daughter in the rearview mirror. 'That's fantastic, darling, I'm so proud of you. Isn't it great, Michael?' she added when he said nothing.

'Yeah, great.'

Nat made a face. 'There's no need to sound so thrilled.'

'It just confirms what I've always thought, that if you'd gone for a real degree you'd have sailed through.'

'Michael!'

'Thanks, Dad.' Nat visibly shrank in her seat and stared out of the window.

Grace put her foot on the accelerator and prayed that they would get to the airport on time because if they didn't, she was going to kill this man.

'You know, it's not too late to change, Natasha,' Michael said, ignoring his wife's growl.

'You, Dad, are evidence to the contrary.'

They travelled the rest of the way in silence and as they drove into the airport, Michael was already pulling out his tickets and passport. 'Drop me at Departures,' he commanded. 'There's no time for you to park and come in with me.'

'Oh, what a pity,' Grace said, her voice dripping with sarcasm. She pulled into a spot outside the entrance to the departure area and he hopped out. Nat and Grace followed and watched as he pulled his cases from the boot.

'Don't just stand there, Nat, get a trolley,' he snapped.

Nat wandered over to the trolley bay and when she returned, Michael flung his cases on to it.

'Right, time to go.' He gave Nat a quick, awkward hug and kissed her head. 'Take care, darling.'

'Bye, Dad.'

He turned to Grace and looked at her, obviously at a loss what to do. Grace took the decision out of his hands and kissed his cheek. 'Safe journey, Michael, take care of yourself.'

He smiled. 'You too. And Grace?'

'Yes?'

'I hope things work out okay for you – really I do.'

Grace reached up to hug him. 'I wish the same for you,' she said quietly.

'Bye then.' He smiled from one to the other and then quickly walked away.

Grace slipped an arm around Nat's shoulders as they watched him leave. 'Are you okay?'

Nat nodded. 'Yeah.'

'Then let's go.'

As they drove back to the Southside of the city, Grace told Natasha an edited version of her encounter with Bridget.

'I can't believe she's turned into such a money-grabbing cow,' Nat marvelled, 'and as for Miriam, there seems to be no limit to what she's capable of.'

'I can't figure out why she paid Bridget off,' Grace said. 'I mean, she was leaving the country anyway, so what difference did it make?'

Nat shrugged. 'Perhaps she plans to come back some day and didn't want a stain on her record.'

'Like a printed apology would make a difference,' Grace said dryly. 'Mud sticks, Nat, especially in this town. No, I think she was trying to destroy Bridget.'

'By writing her a very large cheque? How much did she give her?'

'I've no idea, but judging from the amount of designer clothes, shoes and the firstclass plane ticket to Nice, I'd say quite a lot. Anyway, my theory is, she was punishing her by making sure everyone knew she was a liar.'

'Which she wasn't,' Nat pointed out.' At least not on this occasion.'

'Hear me out. I reckon Miriam wanted to publicly shame her, ensuring she wouldn't be able to move in the sort of circles that are so important to her, and also, force her to leave the country.'

But Miriam, was leaving the country herself, so why would she care if Bridget stayed or left?'

Grace thought about this before answering. 'Maybe she did it for Luke.'

'There's no way he'd ever have got back with her, especially now he's got Rosa.'

'But Miriam doesn't know about Rosa,' Grace pointed out. 'Anyway, that's not what I meant. Maybe she did it so Luke and her father wouldn't have to feel ashamed of her.'

Nat wrinkled her nose. 'That theory suggests Miriam actually cares about other people and we know that's not the case.'

'You're wrong,' Grace said slowly. 'She adores Luke and I believe, in her own way, she loved Alastair.'

'Yes, but her own way meant cheating on him.'

'Whyever she did it, maybe it's for the best. I hate the fact that Bridget has come out of this so well, but at the same time I'm thrilled she's leaving the country. If I was seeing her around town on a regular basis it would do terrible things to my blood pressure and it would only be a matter of time before I gave her a good slap.'

'Mum!' Nat laughed. 'I never thought you were the violent type.'

'After my experiences over the last few months, I think I'd be capable of anything.'

Nat patted her knee. 'Are you going to miss Dad?'

Grace put her head on one side. 'You know what? I really don't think so.'

They looked at each other and giggled guiltily. 'Let's go home and pack,' Grace suggested.

Chapter 44

'Mum, are you ready?' Nat called as she slipped into her new leather jacket and admired her reflection in the mirror over the fireplace.

'Coming.' Grace was putting in her earrings as she walked into the room.

'Thanks for this, Mum, I really love it.'

Grace smiled. 'It looks beautiful on you. And thanks for my scarf, it's lovely.'

'Sorry, that's all I could afford.'

'When you're qualified and running your own school you'll be able to buy me everything my heart desires.'

Nat looked at her with a determined expression. 'I will do it, Mum – run my own school.'

Grace nodded solemnly. 'I don't doubt it, darling.'

'We'd better get going. Rosa said two o'clock, didn't she?'

Grace sighed. 'Yes.'

'Oh, come on, Mum, get in the Christmas spirit.'

'I'm sorry, I'm finding it a bit hard,' Grace admitted. 'Everything is just so different from last year.'

'You don't like the flat, do you?'

'It's okay,' Grace said half-heartedly. 'It's just it doesn't feel much like home.'

'I'm sure you could decorate it if you want. I doubt that Ken's dad would mind.'

'He seemed like a nice man.'

'I'm not sure Ken would agree,' Nat grinned. 'Now come on, let's go.'

'Have you got the presents?'

Her daughter picked up a large bag. 'Right here.'

'Oh, I forgot the champagne.' Grace hurried back to the fridge, took out the chilled bottle and slipped it into a pretty wine bag. 'Okay.' She fixed a smile on her face as she went out to join her daughter. 'I'm ready.'

'Merry Christmas!' Luke opened the door and hugged first the mother and then the daughter.

'Don't you two look great?'

'I wish I could say the same for you,' Nat retorted, looking from the Santa hat on his head to the reindeer slippers on his feet.

Luke batted his eyelashes. 'You've no idea, darling, this is the latest look on the catwalks.'

'Something smells wonderful,' Grace said as he led them into the living room.

'Yes, I've been slaving over a hot stove all morning,' he replied.

'I hope not,' Grace laughed, 'or I'm going home.'

Rosa bustled in, her face flushed from the heat of the kitchen. 'Hello, hello, Happy Christmas,' she said, embracing them both. 'Come into the kitchen and have a drink. We're making cocktails.'

Nat's eyes lit up. 'Cool!'

'Strictly non-alcoholic for me,' Grace said, handing over the champagne.

'Oh, how lovely, we can have this with the pudding.'

'I didn't know Italians ate plum pudding,' Nat remarked.

'They don't,' Rosa agreed, 'but as I'm the only Italian, this is going to be an entirely Irish meal.'

'Oh' Nat said, looking somewhat disappointed.

'Rosa's version of an Irish meal,' Luke added, 'which isn't quite the same thing.'

'Oh, good.' Nat rubbed her hands together.

Luke looked at Rosa. 'So let's go and get those cocktails.'

'Yes, indeed.' She smiled nervously and led the way through to the kitchen.

'I've made Hong Kong Gin Fizz,' Alastair said, 'without the grenadine but I think you'll like it.' He looked up and the smile on his face froze. 'Grace!'

'Hello, Alastair, Merry Christmas' Grace shot a suspicious look at Rosa. 'What a nice surprise.'

'For me too,' he murmured, coming over to kiss her cheek. 'Hello, Natasha, darling, don't you look beautiful?'

Nat hugged him warmly. 'Hi, Alastair, good to see you.'

'So,' he clapped his hands together, eyes twinkling, 'who's going to try my concoction?'

'Not for the cook,' Rosa told him. 'I need a clear head.'

'I'll try it,' Luke told him, 'although I don't want to keel over before dinner.'

'It's not too strong, I decided to wean you in gently.'

'And no drinking on an empty stomach,' Rosa said, setting down a tray of seafood nibbles interspersed with slices of lemon, lime and soda bread.

'I see what you mean about the Rosa version,' Grace said, flashing a grin at Luke. 'Oh Rosa, I'm going to miss your cooking.'

'You don't have to,' she replied. 'Just because you've moved to a smaller place doesn't mean you're not going to eat. I can cook you a few meals every month, freeze them in single portions and you can take them out as you need them.'

Nat's eyes lit up. 'Wow, that would be great. The thing I've missed most about home is your cooking.'

'Thanks a bunch,' Grace complained.

'Trust me, Mum,' Nat told her. 'You'd feel the very same way.'

'You've spoiled us, Rosa,' Grace said simply.

'Anyone can cook,' Rosa said modestly. 'A good store cupboard is the secret. If you keep a few canned and dried foods in the cupboard, you'll always be able to throw something together.'

'I never bothered cooking when I was on my own,' Luke said, sipping his cocktail. 'It was such a relief not to have to go to restaurants all the time with Bridget, I quite enjoyed eating ready meals and baked beans for a change.'

'It's not a healthy way for a grown man to live,' Rosa chided, patting his stomach. 'I plan to fatten you up.'

'Feel free,' he told her. 'This is very nice, Alastair, very nice indeed.'

'Are you sure I can't tempt you to try one, Grace?'

'Go on, Grace,' Luke said. 'You won't be going home for ages yet.'

'No, really, I'd prefer to have a glass of wine with my meal.'

'Then I will make you the best non-alcoholic cocktail I know. Miriam never believed it was non-alcoholic, it tasted so good.'

There was a short, awkward silence and Alastair bent his head over the drinks.

'Look, everyone,' Luke said, holding up his hands, 'let's not pussyfoot around each other here. It's been a lousy few months, particularly for Grace and Alastair—'

'It hasn't exactly been fun for you either,' Grace interjected.

'No, it hasn't,' he agreed, 'but today I am a very happy man and if it took that set of circumstances to get me here, then so be it.'

Alastair nodded. 'Well said.'

Luke smiled at him and raised his glass. 'Let's drink a toast to survival and to us, the survivors.'

'And to Rosa,' Grace reminded him. 'A very welcome addition to the group.'

'Amen to that,' Alastair beamed at them. 'And I'd like to say that it is a pleasure to be with you all today and I appreciate enormously the support you have given me over this rather difficult time.'

'That goes for me too,' Grace said, her eyes bright with tears. 'I couldn't have made it without you.'

'Nat hugged her mother and then held up her cocktail. 'To us!'

'To friendship,' Grace said.

'To the future,' Luke said, looking down into Rosa's eyes.

After a dinner of venison in a redcurrant and wine sauce, with roasted vegetables and fluffy baked potatoes, they sat around chatting and laughing at Nat's stories about the children in her class. 'You just never know what they're going to do next and they come out with the funniest things.'

'I think I'd like to work with children,' Rosa remarked.

'You would be great with them,' Nat said enthusiastically. 'You need patience, and lots of it.'

'Rosa's very patient,' Luke said, stroking the inside of his girlfriend's wrist.

Rosa smiled. 'But I enjoy my cooking too.'

Grace winked at her daughter. 'What you need, Rosa, is a family.'

'Grace is right,' Luke said, and Rosa laughed.

Nat's eyes widened. 'Have you two got something to tell us?'

Rosa nudged Luke. 'Oh, go on, I know you're dying to tell them.'

Luke smiled at her and then turned to the others. 'Which bit should I tell them? That we're getting married next month in Florence or that we've just found out you're pregnant?'

The small room exploded with shrieks of delight from Nat and Grace and there was a moment of chaos as they moved around each other to hug and kiss.

'And before anyone asks, no, this is not a shotgun wedding,' Luke laughed. 'I asked Rosa to be my wife before she got pregnant!'

Rosa slipped her hand into his. 'He proposed on our third date. I told him he was crazy!'

'But you said yes in the end.'

'And now you're going to have a baby, ' Grace sighed.

'It's too early to even talk about it.' Rosa crossed herself.

'Everything will be fine,' Luke assured her, 'and now I think I'll open that champagne.'

Nat followed him out to the kitchen. 'I'm very happy for you, I really am.'

'Thanks, Natasha,' he said, as he reached up to get the champagne flutes. 'I hope we can rely on you for babysitting duties.'

'Anytime,' Nat promised.

*

As Luke poured the champagne, Rosa served the pudding.

'I've no idea where I'm going to put this,' Grace said, looking down at her plate.

'You don't have to eat it if you don't want to,' Rosa told her.

'Ah, but that's the problem,' Grace grinned. 'I want to.'

'My dear Rosa,' Alastair said after tasting it, 'you cook a wonderful Irish Christmas dinner.'

'I don't think I'll ever enjoy turkey again,' Nat agreed. 'This has been a lovely day.'

'It's not over yet,' Rosa said. 'We have to play charades or Scrabble or something.'

Nat groaned. 'Couldn't we just watch some TV? *Shrek* is on.'

'Excellent,' Luke agreed.

'I think I'll go for a walk,' Grace said as she finished her dessert and took a sip of champagne.

'I'd offer to join you but I think I need to have a little nap,' Rosa said, her eyelids drooping.

'You go ahead,' Luke told her. 'I'll clean up. Alastair, why don't you go with Grace?'

Grace stood up quickly. 'There's no need, I'll be fine on my own.'

'But I'd like to,' he said quietly.

'Nat, are you sure you won't come?' Grace shot her daughter a desperate look.

'No, I'm too full. I'll help Luke clean up.'

'I'll get the coats,' Alastair said.

Luke smiled at Grace. 'See you later.'

Feeling uncomfortable and inexplicably sad, Grace stepped out into the sharp evening air and took a shaky breath.

'Wonderful news,' Alastair said as they walked in the direction of the park, 'about Luke and Rosa.'

'Yes, wonderful.'

'I'm delighted for Luke. He's had a rough time, what with Miriam and his father. Now he'll have a family of his very own.'

'Yes,' Grace said, rooting in her pocket for a handkerchief.

Alastair sighed. 'It's a lovely time of year to find out you're going to be a parent, I imagine.'

'Are you sorry you didn't have children?'

'Oh yes, of course, but,' he shrugged, 'it wasn't to be and there's no point in dwelling on it.'

Grace paused to pick up a leaf and she smoothed it between her hands as they walked on. 'I didn't want to come here today but I'm glad I did.'

'I felt the same,' he admitted.

'So much has changed and I feel very unsettled. All that I thought was solid and dependable in my life has disintegrated and I'm not sure what the future holds. It's quite frightening.'

Alastair looked down at her tenderly. 'It will get better, Grace, give it time.'

She nodded. 'Yes, of course it will, and at least Nat and I are back together.'

'Yes. It's good that you have each other.'

'And you have your lovely new house.'

'Yes. You really must come and see it,' Alastair said enthusiastically. 'There's a lovely little pub a few miles from Banford. We could have lunch there – it would be just like the good old days.'

Grace looked at him, slightly puzzled. 'There's no going back to those days, Alastair – you must realize that.'

'No,' he said with a small, pained smile. 'Of course there isn't.'

Chapter 45

Grace was sitting cross-legged in the middle of the living-room sewing cushion covers when the buzzer for the front door went. Struggling to her feet she cursed as she pricked her finger reaching for the button. 'Hello?' she said and shoved her finger in her mouth. The last thing she needed was blood on the oyster-pink silk.

'Grace? It's Luke.'

'Hey, come on up.' She opened the door and stood waiting for him as he took the stairs two at a time. 'You don't look too bad for an old married man,' she joked as she went up on her toes to hug him. 'When did you get back?'

'This morning, and Rosa's been in bed ever since.'

Grace's eyes filled with concern. 'Why, what's wrong?'

He laughed. 'Absolutely nothing. She just can't keep her eyes open.'

Grace nodded, relieved. 'It's just a stage she's going through. She'll be fine in a few weeks.'

'I hope so, because she's determined to go back to work.' He sounded exasperated.

'Of course, I'd forgotten about the new job. What are the hours like?'

'Great. They're an elderly couple and they just want her to come in every day from ten till three. She'll do the cleaning, get them some lunch, clean up and then she's finished. It's the perfect job – or it would be if she wasn't pregnant. I know she's not sick, Grace, and that lots of women have to do it, but I hate the thought of her heaving vacuum cleaners about or cleaning windows.'

'Why not see how it goes?' Grace suggested sympathetically. 'Right now she's healthy, isn't she?'

'Except for the tiredness, she is absolutely blooming,' Luke said.

'Then you just have to let her get on with it.'

'I suppose. Anyway, tell me, what's been happening here?'

Grace smiled. 'Nat's found herself a new man.'

'Really? Not another rock star, I hope?'

'You sound like a father already,' Grace teased. 'No, he's a teacher, actually. They met at a seminar just after Christmas.'

'Have you met him?'

'Yes. He's very sweet and seems absolutely potty about her.'

'Good, she deserves a bit of pampering. So does the fact that she's dating make you feel a bit of a spare?' Luke enquired.

'You could say that,' Grace agreed. 'I try to give them time together, it's not as though they can afford to go out much, but the sad fact is, I don't have anywhere to go.' She was joking but her eyes were sad.

'Well, we're back so you can come round to us.'

Grace put a finger to her chin. 'Courting couple, newlyweds, courting couple, newlyweds – ooh, it's a tough one.'

Luke laughed. 'But Rosa's asleep all of the time so you'd be doing me a favour. Anyway, what about Alastair? Don't you go and see him?'

Grace picked up her sewing and studied the stitching. 'No, I've been pretty busy.'

'Are you saying you haven't seen him since Christmas?'

'No, why would I?'

'Oh, Grace.'

'What?'

'You two should be together.'

Grace's head snapped up and she stared at him. 'Don't be ridiculous.'

'What's ridiculous about it?'

'He's Miriam's husband, your brother-in-law.'

'Soon to be ex-husband,' he corrected.

Grace's eyes narrowed. 'So she's filed for divorce?'

'No—'

'It doesn't matter, Luke, I'm not interested. I've just broken up with my husband and I am not looking for a new partner, especially one as damaged as Alastair.'

Luke shook his head. 'Oh, Grace.'

'Please don't start all that again.'

'Just let me tell you one thing – just one thing,' he said hurriedly as she put her hands over her ears, 'and then I'll go away and leave you alone.'

Letting her hands drop into her lap, she looked at him. 'Go on, then.'

'He's selling the house.'

'What? Why? He loves it up there.'

'He loves you more,' Luke said gently. 'He can't stand not seeing you, and even if you never agree to be with him,' he stopped as he tried to remember the exact words, 'he'd rather be able to live where he might occasionally glimpse you in the street than live with no hope of seeing you at all.'

Grace sat staring into space, stunned into silence.

'I'll go now. Take care, Grace.'

'Here you are, Mrs Tierney.' Alastair handed over the money and piled his groceries into a bag.

'Thanks very much, Mr Summers. Are you off fishing today?'

'No, I'll probably just do a bit of gardening before the rain comes.'

'Aye, it's coming all right,' she told him. 'My back's acting up and that's always a sure sign. Bye-bye now.'

'Goodbye, Mrs Tierney.' Alastair walked out on to the street and back through the village towards his house. He hated the idea of leaving this peaceful place. The estate agent was coming to do an evaluation tomorrow but as Alastair had done so little to the house, he didn't hold out much hope of making a profit. Not that it mattered – he didn't need money. His solicitor had forced Miriam into giving him half the proceeds of the house, and after handing over half of that to Miriam's ex-employees, the other half sat in the bank, untouched. He'd wanted to just give it away but his solicitor had pointed out that he wasn't getting any younger and at some stage he might need it for nursing care. Charming, Alastair had thought, but seeing the logic of the man's argument had reconsidered.

He turned from the lane into his driveway and walked up to his house, cheered by the sight of the snowdrops starting to flower along each side of the path. It wouldn't be long before the daffodils came out but he probably wouldn't be here to see them. He stopped short at the sight of a large plant pot in his porch. Frowning, he moved closer and pulled out his reading glasses so he could study the tag hanging from the tree. 'Dwarf Meyer Lemon Tree,' he murmured and sniffed appreciatively at the small white fragrant blossoms and tiny fruit. He searched among the leaves for a card but there was none, and no hint as to where this beautiful plant had come from.

Standing up again, Alastair looked around, his eyes lighting on a lone figure at the other end of the beach. Even at this distance he recognized the figure, her hair glinting in the winter sunshine and his heart skipped a beat.

*

'I love it, thank you,' he said softly, catching up with her as she neared the pier.

She turned to him with a shy smile. 'I wanted to find you something special.'

'You did.'

They walked on in silence for a moment. 'Luke says you're thinking of selling up,' she said finally.

'Yes.'

She waved a hand around at the breathtaking scenery. 'I don't know how you can bear to leave.'

'Because I can't bear to stay,' he said, simply.

'Have you heard from Miriam?' She kept her eyes on the fishing boats bobbing in the bay.

'No, all of our communications are through our solicitors.'

'I'm sorry.'

'I'm not.'

She stopped and turned. 'You loved Miriam.' Her eyes searched his face.

He shook his head. 'No, I thought I did. It was only when the real thing came along that I found that out.'

Grace started to walk back down the beach.

'Grace?'

'I don't know, Alastair, I just don't know.'

'It's okay, Grace,' he said, catching up with her. 'I'm not looking for decisions or answers, I'm just glad you're here. Come and see the house. Please?'

She sighed. 'All right then.'

Alastair smiled happily and led her towards the house as the first drops of rain started to fall.

As they walked from room to room and Alastair told her how he'd imagined each one, Grace's eyes filled up. By the time they reached the main bedroom, the tears were rolling silently down her cheeks and she moved to the window to stare out at the sheets of rain rolling in across the bay.

Alastair turned her to face him and wiped the tears gently with his thumbs. 'Why are you crying?'

She looked at him through her tears. 'Because I wish it could be different.'

'It could.'

'I'm afraid.'

He smiled tenderly into her eyes. 'Don't be. I love you and I'd like to spend the rest of my days making you happy.'

Grace cried harder.

'I obviously have a lot of work to do,' he said with a sigh, and she started to laugh through her tears. 'Grace, more than anything I would love to share my life with you, but if that's not what you want, then at least let me be your very good friend. I can't live without you in my life.'

She smiled faintly. 'Have you never heard that actions speak louder than words?'

Needing no further encouragement, Alastair bent his head to hers and kissed her lightly on the lips. Pulling away, he looked at her and then taking her face between his hands, he kissed her again, and again and again. When he finally pulled away, Grace's eyes were still closed. 'Grace?' he whispered.

Her eyes opened and she looked at him. 'Please don't sell the house.'

'Only if you agree to help me renovate it.'

'I will, but you have to let me choose the colours.'

He smiled. 'I can live with that.'

'Some nice warm colours for the living area, I think,' she said. 'And white for the kitchen.'

'Sounds good.'

'And this room should be pale yellow.' She raised her eyes to his. 'I like waking up in a yellow room.'